I0741528

SHADOW LIFE

JASON MATHER

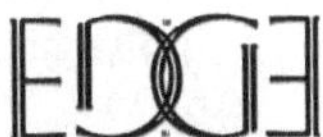

EDGE SCIENCE FICTION AND FANTASY PUBLISHING
An Imprint of HADES PUBLICATIONS, INC.
CALGARY

Shadow Life

Copyright © 2017 by Jason Mather

This is a work of fiction. Names, characters, places, and incidents are the products of the author's imagination or are used fictitiously and are not to be construed as real. Any resemblance to actual events, locales, organizations, or persons, living or dead, is entirely coincidental.

EDGE SCIENCE FICTION AND FANTASY PUBLISHING
An Imprint of HADES PUBLICATIONS, INC.
P.O. Box 1714, Calgary, Alberta, T2P 2L7, Canada

The EDGE Team:
Producer: Brian Hades
Acquisitions Editor: Ella Beaumont
Edited by: Michelle Heumann
Cover Design: Ella Beaumont
Cover Art Elements: tasosk, Kheng Ho Toh
Book Design: Mark Steele
Publicist: Janice Shoults
Copywriter:Myles McDonough

ISBN: 978-1-77053-165-9

EDGE Science Fiction and Fantasy Publishing and Hades Publications, Inc. acknowledges the ongoing support of the Alberta Foundation for the Arts and the Canada Council for the Arts for our publishing programme.

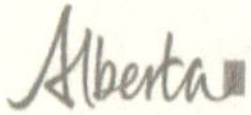 

Library and Archives Canada Cataloguing in Publication
CIP Data on file with the National Library of Canada
ISBN: 978-1-77053-165-9
(e-Book ISBN: 978-1-77053-160-4)

FIRST EDITION
(20180130)
Printed in USA
www.edgewebsite.com

Publisher's Note:

Thank you for purchasing this book. It began as an idea, was shaped by the creativity of its talented author, and was subsequently molded into the book you have before you by a team of editors and designers.

Like all EDGE books, this book is the result of the creative talents of a dedicated team of individuals who all believe that books (whether in print or pixels) have the magical ability to take you on an adventure to new and wondrous places powered by the author's imagination.

As EDGE's publisher, I hope that you enjoy this book. It is a part of our ongoing quest to discover talented authors and to make their creative writing available to you.

We also hope that you will share your discovery and enjoyment of this novel on social media through Facebook, Twitter, Goodreads, Pinterest, etc., and by posting your opinions and/or reviews on Amazon and other review sites and blogs. By doing so, others will be able to share your discovery and passion for this book.

Brian Hades, publisher

PROLOGUE

The dead woman was crying.

Rain poured through a hole in the roof, the bleak sky beyond the shattered timbers indistinguishable from the dirty, peeling white ceiling, ready to come crashing down. A chandelier hung improbably underneath, its filthy sconces filled to overflowing, its once ornate iron rusted and shabby, providing a makeshift sluice for the rain to wander down, pooling underneath the shallow arches at its bottom, combining and impregnating one another with grime from metal and sky, falling heavily onto the charnel house below.

She sat nearly upright in a chair that had once been some kind of plush red fabric, head cocked slightly, hair cascading over the hole in her neck. Water fell from the chandelier above, landing in her hair, making its way slowly down her face, pooling in the crevices of her glazed eyes, dripping down pale cheeks, curving up under her chin, down neck and torso, mixing with the slowing blood flow, some soaked up by the low-cut top, some making its way down the curve of one naked breast, torn from its covering.

Rarely can one cry for one's own death. He certainly couldn't. Couldn't cry, couldn't yell, couldn't move, couldn't feel anything beyond face and lips. Probably a blessing. Whatever had hit him had not left much worth feeling. Something had torn its way through this room, a tornado of whirling metal and flying shrapnel, before exiting through the roof. Had the other two escaped? Unlikely.

It was not how he'd imagined dying.

He was not afraid to die, merely angry that it was right here, right now. It was his reputation he grieved for, here among these dead lowlifes. Chiding himself for pointless vanity, he tried to shut his eyes. Let death take him. They wouldn't move.

She was smirking at him, privy to his thoughts and the great cosmic joke that had brought them both here.

Five hundred. That's what he'd been offered. A man on a corner waved it and the package under his nose. Five hundred to walk the package three blocks and up two flights of stairs. Five hundred that would pay to get him outside the city limits and onto a monorail headed home. Five hundred he desperately needed. Five hundred that now sat, wasted, in his jacket, currently piled on the floor by the dead woman's impractical stilettos.

Her smirk taunted him. *Smirk all you want, lady, you're just as dead as me, even more so at the moment, sitting there obscenely exposed to a perfect stranger, lacking even the propriety to cover up that bloody tit of yours.*

She'd met him at the door with a slightly raised eyebrow and a frown, before melting back into the dark apartment, which did not yet have its meager skylight. Two men had frisked him, both in identical suits and overcoats. She'd handed him the money without a word, gingerly taken the box from him, and had turned to leave when … something … had ended it all. A mere breath or two. Three dead crooks and one dying idiot.

A keening sound was coming from a direction he couldn't identify. Maybe sirens. Maybe it was his oxygen-starved brain. The light coming through the skylight flickered slightly, though the possibility of it just being his eyes finally giving out was more likely.

There were worse ways to go, he guessed, and worse final sights, though he'd never been a breast man.

CHAPTER 1

He opened his eyes, startled. The bland normalcy that greeted him approached the surreal. He was propped up in a small bed with a deep mahogany footboard. The headboard was likely of the same material, but, as he was currently unable to move his head, he would make no assumptions. A window made up the whole wall to his left, the view dominated by immense vertical farms. Great glass spires filled with the machinery of the new agriculture, enough to feed the population of millions, with food left over for trade with other city-states. Bridges seemingly made of crystal connected them together every dozen floors, landing pads sticking out like misshapen ears.

Beige walls. Beige floors. Beige curtains. Beige sheets. About the only thing in the room that wasn't beige was a small viewscreen showing a stream of numbers and graphs that could have been anything from stock market figures to vital stats.

A hospital then, the assumption based on a dawning realization that he had somehow survived. He wasn't counting out dying just yet, though, mostly because of what he could, and couldn't, feel. He could feel his feet and hands, move his fingers and toes, though only just. His stomach felt slightly hungry, his lungs breathed easily, heart pumping calmly, any elevation due to the strangeness of his current environment. More importantly, and critically, other than a slightly dry mouth and some mild discomfort from some kind of restraints on his hands, feet, and head, he felt no pain. Last he knew his guts had been spread around a small, empty apartment, blood covering ancient blue shag. If he was really still alive, and he still couldn't quite assure himself of that, then he was thoroughly confused … and pissed off.

He pulled weakly on the restraints. It did no good, but it didn't matter. He'd never been able to handle any sort of restraint, physical or mental. When he pulled hard enough he noticed the viewscreen numbers started to scroll faster and turn slightly red; even harder and a speaker set in the ceiling began to beep softly. How fast could he get them to scroll? Could he get the beep any louder? Pulling against all the restraints simultaneously produced the most satisfying results. He balled up his abdomen and legs, pulled as strongly as his weakened state would allow. He had no illusions about breaking the restraints; he just hoped he was annoying somebody.

The door opened and a man entered. He didn't appear to be a doctor. No white coat or green scrubs, just a tweed suit and loafers.

"Those restraints are designed to stop psychiatric inmates in the midst of a psychotic episode, pulling on them like that is just going to bruise your limbs." He turned and tapped the screen, causing it to go black and the beeping to stop.

His snappy retort was stopped by a coughing fit.

"Really, Hans, pulling on your restraints to get my attention was unnecessary. There's a call button right underneath your right hand."

Hans did not try to respond this time. This man had the advantage of knowledge and freedom over him, and Hans would not participate in this glib charade.

"There is a water tube just to the left of your mouth. I'm going to release your head. Don't drink too quickly, as your digestive track is not accustomed to food and water yet." The man tapped the screen again and Hans could move his head. He found the water tube and sucked mightily on it. After three large gulps, his stomach revolted and sent most of it back up over the sheets covering him, and, in his partially prone position, nearly drowning him. He lay coughing and staring petulantly at the ceiling.

The man laughed heartily.

"If you're trying to kill yourself, I can bring a morphine pump or something equally efficient. There's no need to drown yourself."

Hans' choked epithet elicited another laugh. The man sat in an unseen chair by the headboard.

"I was told you were a bit strong-willed, and I know you're confused by your current situation. I'm here to answer your questions. My name is Doctor Laud."

"Where...?"

"You are currently on the fifty-sixth floor of Denver General. The hospice wing, though you are no longer dying, as you may have discovered. Before you ask, you are not a prisoner. Those restraints are there to keep you from rolling over and suffocating yourself. You've been in medical stasis while we repaired your injuries."

"How long?" Hans was stupidly pleased that he had managed to choke out two words back to back without coughing.

"Fourteen months."

Hans' eyes widened.

"I have seen very few people recover from the injuries you sustained. We had to replace nearly forty percent of your internal workings. New heart. New lungs. Two new kidneys. Twelve feet of small intestine. One third of your liver. A completely new pancreas. It takes quite a while to grow these things, and you being conscious would have been a hell of numb paralysis while the machines kept you alive."

Hans kept silent at this news, suppressing anger by staring out the window. The sun sat low behind the buildings. He didn't know which way the window faced and the buildings obscured possible mountains, so he did not know whether this meant morning or evening. He'd lost over a year, and did not expect to assimilate this knowledge well or quickly. More importantly, the system had ignored his express wishes. His medical file spelled out explicitly that he was not to be revived or rebuilt.

"The decision to keep you alive was not mine," Laud predicted his thoughts. "You were nearly killed under highly suspicious circumstances in which you were the only survivor. This is all the information to which I was privy. I imagine others will want to talk to you."

Hans rolled his eyes. The doctor chuckled again.

"That is for later, however, and entirely up to me. I am your doctor, not your jailor. Let's get those restraints off."

Laud walked over to the screen again, tapped it. Hans' hands and feet were free. He began weakly checking that everything was in place. Doctor Laud laughed.

"Never fails. I've been rebuilding people for forty years. Women always check the face first. Men go straight for the jewels."

Hans moved his hands quickly to his sides. Doctor Laud turned and continued.

"We have managed to rebuild almost forty percent of your body to optimum efficiency, with a minimum of scarring. All your organs are essentially your own, making the possibility of rejection infinitesimal, but brand-new. Based on the state of your old lungs, you might consider ending what was obviously a heavy smoking habit."

"I was greatly looking forward to destroying another set."

"Well, I'll see you again soon then." The doctor's smile showed no sign of sarcasm, though he may have winked, it was hard to tell. Hans had no physical craving for a cigarette, though whether that was because of medical meddling or from being nearly dead for fourteen months was hard to say. He planned to get a pack as soon as possible anyway.

"Did I also get the penis enlargement?"

"Your penis sustained almost no damage, and should function normally. Seeing as how you never had any work done previously, I assumed you'd want to retain the familiar." Another possible wink.

"So, I'm as good as new, maybe better. Does that mean I can get the hell out of here?"

"There are a couple of things currently preventing your exit. The first is that, while they should be in working order, it will be a few days yet before your muscles are able to support and transport your weight. It's a side effect of the stasis we had you under."

"And the other's your bill?"

"Your rehabilitation has already been paid for."

"Who?"

The doctor shrugged. "All I know is that your bill has been handled. Also, certain agencies that have power over our funding would prefer you stay here until they can talk to you."

Hans huffed and laid his head back.

"However, because I am your doctor, I have full discrepancy over when that may be."

"Great."

"You are not a prisoner."

"Of course not, I'm just not allowed to leave."

"At the moment you would not be able to leave anyway."

"Is that door guarded?"

"Which door?"

Hans just stared.

"Yes, there is currently a man monitoring your room."

"What kind of ID is he carrying?"

Another shrug. "He hasn't shown me any."

"Don't you think you should have asked?"

"If he was not authorized to be here the central computer would have let us know."

"Another soul with complete trust in his machines."

"I take it you don't trust computers."

"You can't trust something that has no reciprocity."

"True enough, though computers do have something that makes them very trustworthy."

"What's that?"

"A distinct lack of humanity."

— «» —

Hans desperately had to take a piss. He'd been informed that, though somewhat un-natural feeling, the bed was designed to absorb any waste products, whisk them away, and disinfect. But he was damned if he was going to lay there and piss his bed like a child. Modern medical convenience would have to take a back seat to his dignity.

He could see a door about four feet to his left, in the wall behind his head. He hoped it led to the bathroom, because, after the effort it would probably take to get there, he was going to piss on whatever was inside. His arms were working at about half efficiency, and he still had very little feeling in his legs. Laud had informed him that it would be another forty-eight to seventy-two hours before it all came back, but Hans was planning on beating the timeline and getting out of this pit as quickly as possible.

For now, he'd start with demanding his essential male right to pee standing up.

Step one. He'd have to either climb over the bed railings or lower them. The only controls he knew of were at the viewscreen across the room. A quick search of the side and headboards revealed no obvious way to lower the railing. Climbing it was.

Hans was surprised by the effort that it took to even turn on his left side. The sheet covering him bunched under his abdomen, applying extra pressure to his bladder. The urgency increased greatly. It was a near thing, but he continued to hold.

A little shifting and pulling got the sheet out from under him. A quick yank and he was uncovered, mostly. He had nothing on underneath. He was about to drag himself naked across the floor. What was that about dignity?

After a little manipulation, Hans managed to swing his right arm over the rail and get a grip on the lower bar from outside. His plan was to pull himself over and … well, he actually hadn't thought any farther than that. He guessed if he could get past the tipping point gravity would handle the rest.

A quick initial pull did little. Half strength was being generous. He pulled harder. It felt like his whole lower half was just a pile of wet socks. Stronger pulling, still no luck. Hans tried to rock back on his left shoulder a little to gain momentum. That helped a little.

The urgency in his bladder was peaking. It was now a race between his own strength and the inevitable. Hans tightened his fingers into a death grip on the bar and leaned back for one more try. With a grunt, he threw himself at the bar and pulled as hard as he could manage.

Three things happened simultaneously.

He pulled his body on top of the railing, far enough that he pitched over the other side of the bed and landed askew on the tile flooring beneath. Pain shot through his left wrist as it twisted underneath him. The door to the hall opened and a cross-looking nurse came in. She began yelling at him when she saw him topple over the side. Then the inevitable won. As the urgency faded, Hans hoped that the floor had the same disinfectant abilities as the sheets.

— «» —

The nurse brought in what looked like a small, articulated forklift to help him back into bed. Its arms were padded and warm. When the nurse, whose nametag alternated between the name "Toni" and an animated hologram of a smiling bear, finally got him situated and covered, she began checking him for injuries. He winced when she manipulated his wrist.

"What were you doing, Hans?"

"I was trying to take a piss."

"The bed is perfectly capable…"

"Yes, I know, the bed is designed to whisk away all piss and shit and wipe my little tushie for me, but that's hardly dignified now, is it? Have you guys starting selling these things to the masses of useless trolls out there yet? They could just intake and excrete without ever leaving the comfort of bed. Why ever do anything else again?"

"But, Hans, you've been…" she stammered.

"Yes, I know. I've been destroyed and rebuilt. I'm fucking Lazarus, or maybe just a broken scooter. Well, I didn't ask you to rebuild me, did I? In fact, I believe my file said specifically to *not* rebuild. You'll excuse me if I don't seem grateful for having my wishes tacitly ignored. And don't call me Hans. "

The silence that greeted his outburst was the first moment of genuine pleasure Hans had felt since awakening. He could tell from the sour look on her face it wasn't going to last, though.

"And what, exactly, should I call you, if not your name?"

"You can call me Mr. Ricker, or patient number whatever, or bastard."

He could see she was tempted by the last suggestion.

"Well, Mr. Ricker, I'll have Doctor Laud in shortly to see what we can do about that wrist. In the meantime…"

She walked to the console and tapped on the screen a few times. The restraints returned to his head and feet.

— «» —

Hans had three visitors that night.

The first made himself known through a sharp pain in Hans' hurting wrist, yanking Hans out of an uncomfortable doze.

"*Ow*! Shit!"

"Sorry," Laud pushed at the sore spot again, watching Hans' eyes as he did so. Hans refused to give him another sign of pain. "I don't think it's broken. Try not to do anything strenuous with it for a few days and it should be fine."

The windows had tinted themselves black. A soft glow came from light strips running along the seams of roof and wall. Hans stared at Laud with what he hoped was menace, but it had little effect.

"Is there anything else you'd like to do to me while I'm here and helpless. Poke my eyes? Smack me in the nuts?"

"No, I think the wrist will be enough."

Laud set Hans' aching wrist down, but continued to stand quietly at the side of the bed.

"Somethin' on your mind, Doc?"

Laud's mouth opened, then shut. He took a deep breath, let it out slowly, eyes turning to the windows. Eventually his body followed, walking over to the wall and tapping a recess in the corner to make the windows transparent. A jumpcraft flew past outside, transporting some VIP from rooftop to rooftop.

"Who do you think runs this hospital, Mr. Ricker?"

"The computers. They run everything here."

"Where is here? This hospital?"

"This hospital. This city-state. This country, whatever's left of it."

Laud nodded, but did not turn around.

"You don't live in the city, do you?"

"Not when I can help it."

"I thought not. "

Hans wanted to turn and relieve a crick in his neck, but Laud had not released his restraints.

"You may be correct about the computers running the country, even the city-state, but I must correct a misperception on your part as to who runs this hospital."

"Is this where you give me the 'I alpha, you beta' talk?"

"Oh no, Mr. Ricker, I assure you, I do not run this hospital. Neither do the administrators, nor the board of directors, nor even the computer systems."

"If you're going to start getting religious on me, I'd really rather…"

Laud's laugh cut him off. "No, Mr. Ricker, no god either."

Hans waited.

"The nurses run this hospital, Mr. Ricker. They feed and clothe and wash and dispose. They provide comfort where needed. They handle nearly every necessity that keeps a place like this running. One will not get far abusing their good will, doctor or patient."

"So, this is about Toni?"

"Maybe you can explain to me, Mr. Ricker, why, when I arrived for my evening rounds, I found Ms. Juarez sitting at her desk with running makeup and red-rimmed eyes."

"If she's gonna cry about something like that, maybe she's not cut out for this."

"I can assure you that her credentials and skills are as good as they come, or she wouldn't be working on this floor."

"Has she had an emotional evaluation?"

"To prove what? That she has compassion? That she cares about her patients? That she is a human being? That her feelings can be hurt?"

"Sure."

For the first time during his lecture, Laud turned and looked at Hans.

"I have been doing this work for a long time, Mr. Ricker. I have dealt with many difficult patients and bull-headed mules like yourself, most of them my superiors. But no amount of training will prepare you for your first experiences with the reality of this work. Ms. Juarez is somewhat new here, her first posting after university. Actually, her tenure here is almost exactly the same length as yours. When you arrived, we almost lost you. Although our capabilities for sustaining and repairing of the human body are highly advanced, they are not infallible, and they are not routine. Miss Juarez has been taking care of you from the time you were merely a head and partial torso hooked into the maximum amount of life-sustaining architecture this institute has to offer. She has participated in every surgery, monitored every threat to your existence. Over this last year she has nursed you back from the brink of death. I know you didn't ask for or want that, but that has nothing to do with her. Because this was her first case, she has become a bit more emotionally attached than we would wish, but that is a usual part of the training experience."

"So... what? She's in love with me?"

"Hardly. But she has taken it upon herself to make your well-being personal. No matter how little you care for your own life, Mr. Ricker, you owe most of it to her training, her work ethic, and her caring."

Laud walked back over to the side of the bed.

"I do not think you are a bad person, merely difficult. But you would do well to think on these things before you wield that blunt weapon between your nose and chin at a kind-hearted woman to whom you owe your life."

Laud exited the room quickly. He did not undo Hans' restraints.

— 《》 —

Hans' second visitor was the last person he wanted to see after the scathing rebuke that Doctor Laud had given him. Toni arrived with his dinner, at this point still mostly a pungent broth and various other liquids. Hans had been promised that he would receive some solid food very shortly.

The nurse had obviously fixed and reapplied her makeup. She gave him a strained smile and asked if he needed any help.

"What's Toni short for?" Hans' voice cracked on the last word, which did not help his attempt to sound relaxed.

"Antonia."

"Can I call you Antonia?"

"Ms. Juarez will do."

He probably deserved that.

"I guess it'd be best if I continued to go by bastard. Unless you'd prefer 'son of a bitch' or 'bull-headed idiot'."

"Is there anything I can do for you, Mr. Ricker?" Not even a hint of a smile. Hans was too weak and confused to maintain his stubborn ego any longer. He did something extremely rare.

"You could accept my apology."

She cocked her head and pursed her lips together.

"I thought I was dead. Instead I'm in the last place I'd want to be. I am helpless, I am dependent, I am scared, and I hate every single second of it. I've lost fourteen months of my life, all because I was an idiot."

"Hans..." so maybe they were back to first names, "you don't have to tell me any of this."

He tried to wave her interjection away, but instead whacked his wrist on the bed railing. Charm and intimacy were both impossible when grimacing in pain. When it faded it a bit she was still standing by his bed. Hans tried to clear his throat and coughed dryly. Toni picked up a plastic cup with a straw and held it to his lips. The restrained angle of his head caused some of the liquid to go down his cheek. She wiped it efficiently with a hand towel from the tray.

"None of this..." he coughed a little more, "none of this has anything to do with you. All you've done is nurse an ungrateful man back from the brink of death. A man who will, based on prior knowledge of himself, continue to be sullen and difficult. So, I would ask that, on this rare occasion when he admits to being the ass he is, you would simply accept his apology before the last of his dignity is whisked away by the magical sheets. I owe you my life. It's not worth it, believe me."

"Every life is important, Hans."

"I knew you'd say that."

"You don't believe me?"

"Let's just agree to disagree, with the understanding that I know the world needs more people like you and less like me."

She took a pause, considering her options. "You can call me Antonia if you wish, though only my mother calls me that. My friends call me Toni."

"Antonia it is. I don't like the name Toni."

She actually smiled at this, "Are we back to being difficult already?"

"It's what I do."

"Well then, Hans, do you need any help eating?"

"No, thank you, Antonia, though if you could release my head so I won't dribble on myself I would appreciate it."

"I think you've dribbled enough for one day." She started for the door, but paused near the entryway.

She undid his restraints before she left.

— «» —

Visitor number three almost had to be a hallucination, appearing as he did in a cloud of smoke. Hans had finally managed some genuine sleep, the recovering strength in his body allowing him to turn on one side. It was a glorious change in routine. He had been dreaming about a good cigarette, so initially wasn't surprised to smell the smoke. It was only when his eyes began to water that he came to enough awareness to see the man sitting next to the bed. Black pants, black turtleneck, leather jacket, a cigarette sticking improbably out of the side of his mouth.

"I'm pretty sure you can't smoke in here."

"Places like this got air filtering systems out the ass, I doubt it's going to be noticed."

"I'm noticing. Can't you see I'm a very sick man?"

"I figured the smoke would bring you around. A bit of heaven for a dying man."

Hans did not disagree. "You got one I can borrow, or are you going to bogart the whole pack?"

Leather Jacket held out a black case to Hans as he tried unsuccessfully to sit up. Eventually the man went around to the console and tapped something that raised the back of the bed into a sitting position.

"You got a light?"

Jacket placed the cigarette to Hans' lips and held the lighter against it. Hans inhaled deeply, forgetting that his new lungs had never had the pleasure. He coughed violently, room spinning. The speaker in the ceiling began to beep, but no one came to answer it.

After he was mostly sure he wasn't going to pass out, Hans took another puff. This one went a little better. He'd have himself back to a couple of packs a day in no time. It was the first time since awakening that he felt human.

"Good?"

"Very."

They sat and smoked. Hans had always been of the opinion that truly comfortable silence could only be enjoyed by fellow addicts. Eventually his curiosity peaked.

"You watching the door?"

"Yeah."

Another pause as they both puffed away. Hans finished his and Jacket offered him another.

"What's with the getup? You trying to look civilian?"

"Sure."

"And you picked this? Or is there a standard military dog uniform I don't know about?"

"I like dogs, they're loyal."

"And stupid."

"Used to have an uncle with an old mutt. He trained it to get him beer from the fridge, was always claiming that he had nearly trained it to make him a sandwich. That was a great dog."

Hans stared at him.

"Not sure I really believed him about the sandwich, though."

Hans couldn't help laughing at that one.

"Why'd she send you, Gino?"

"The commander wanted you protected."

"I understand that, but why you specifically? I'm sure there're plenty of stooges she could have sent."

"Grit doesn't hire any stooges."

"We have a different definition of the word stooge."

Gino sat back and considered Hans. "You think I'm a stooge, Hans?"

"You said that, not me."

"You insinuated…"

"No, I believe you inferred."

"I don't follow."

It was good to finally have someone inferior to joust with.

"Forget it. Last I heard you were two spots from the top."

"Only one now."

"One huh? Truly your career as a boot-licker is reaching new heights. You her personal secretary now?"

Gino shrugged off the insult. "In charge of the commander's personal protection and proper designation of responsibility to lower ranks."

"Was that what it said on the job description?"

"Yeah, right underneath the heading 'head cook and bottle washer'."

Or maybe not so inferior.

"So, you're right up next to her now huh? I'll bet you enjoy that."

Gino bit down on his cigarette.

"If you're trying to infer that I slept my way to the top, there's a hell of a lot of perps with holes in 'em that may beg to differ."

"Truly the gun is the ultimate tool of promotion."

"I'm not going to have philosophical argument about the proper application of force."

"Surely not. But are you going to deny that you've got the hots for her?"

Gino's glare made Hans think he may have actually gone too far with that one.

"Fraternization between officers and subordinates is strictly forbidden."

"Duty before booty, huh?"

Gino snickered, lightening the tone between them.

"I am here as a personal favor to the commander. She ill-advisedly considers you a high-value property."

"When you care enough to send the very best."

"Yeah."

"So…" every puff of the cigarette was making him feel more civilized.

"So...?"

"Are you here to interrogate me?"

"Nah, I just thought you might want a cigarette."

"It's good to see someone familiar, even if it is you."

"Grit wants to talk to you herself."

"Her Highness is coming all the way down here to see me? Impressive."

"She wants to know what the hell happened."

"I'm not sure what help I'll be. I'm not sure myself."

"And she's worried about you."

Hans sniffed.

"Don't be that way Hans. Grit is a hard-ass, we all know that."

"You more than most."

"But... she's been worried sick ever since we found you laying on the floor in two pieces."

"We... you guys found me?"

"One of our squads."

"Why the hell were you there?"

"That's not really information I can give you right now."

"Of course not."

"Anyway, she's been monitoring your progress. "

"I imagine there are quite a few administrators in this place that already hate hearing her name."

"Yeah, well, she gets things done."

"So, she paid for all this."

"Dunno."

"Don't know or can't say?"

"What's the difference?"

Hans finished his second cigarette. Gino didn't offer another.

"Is Grit worried somebody might be coming after me?"

"Grit understands the concept of underestimating the danger."

"Well, I'm glad it's you, Gino."

"Just for the next few days, then you'll have one of my stooges."

"I don't expect to be here for more than a couple days."

"We'll see."

Hans frowned, "Yeah… we will."

"Hans…?"

"What?"

"I know this is probably wasted effort, but don't be an idiot, all right?"

"Never have been."

"Besides falling out of bed and pissing on the floor, you mean."

"Could you piss the bed? Even if it cleaned up after you."

"I've spent days laying in a hole shitting in a diaper."

"I'd rather not know anything about what you and the commander get up to in your private time."

"Yeah, anyway, just listen to the doctor, ok?"

"We'll see."

Gino stubbed out his cigarette on the sole of his boot and slipped their used butts inside his jacket pocket.

"I'll dispose of these."

"When's she coming to see me, Gino?"

"Next couple of days."

"I'll put on my happy face."

— «» —

The next day was a long series of firsts. First standing piss, first good BM, first shower. The room in the corner turned out to be a multifunction economy bathroom the size of large shower stall, crammed with nearly every bathroom-related item. A shower-head in the ceiling sprayed water throughout the whole room. Hans had always liked these. They were cozy and he'd always enjoyed being able to take shit and shower at the same time. It saved time and toilet paper.

He had been able to waddle over to the bathroom with the help of the day nurse, a well-muscled older woman. He'd been a little uncomfortable with her help in showering, but she'd just bulled her way in, telling him that she'd washed his willy a thousand times and wasn't about to get all coy now. He'd pretty much exhausted himself getting to the room and doing his other business, and submitted as meekly as possible to the vigorous and thorough scrubbing before she stepped out to turn on the water and let him rinse.

"Don't drown on me in there, we just got you back."

Hans liked her, and not just because she was the first woman he'd been intimate with in years.

After getting him back into bed she brought him his first solid food. A plate of slightly mushy vegetables, some broth with a little tofu in it, and some kind of synthetic meat, which Hans chose not to eat. He never could stomach the lab-grown crap. It was good to actually chew his food.

Despite warnings to the contrary, Hans was so happy to have solid food that he ate way too fast, thus resulting in his first really good heave since waking. He had limited ability to turn himself and mostly covered the sheets. The day nurse sprayed something liquid and green on the sheets to help break it down and Hans got to watch as the sheets quickly absorbed the spew and began to wick the stains down toward the foot of the bed. The whole process took a couple of minutes. When it was done Hans took the sheets off, too creeped out to have them touching his skin.

Hans called his mother. The day nurse (he felt a little odd not knowing her name, but she wasn't wearing a nametag and Hans had promptly forgotten the first and only time she'd told him) brought him a portable with which he could access e-books, watch television and movies, or make phone calls. Hans' mom picked up on the third ring, sounding slightly distracted. The viewscreen had the capacity for video calls, but his mom, like himself, had never really seen the point. "I don't want to have to make myself presentable just to talk on the phone," she'd often told him. "Besides, I take a lot of my calls in the toilet."

When she realized it was him, Hans could almost hear her focus.

"They'd told me you were going to be coming around soon. I'm glad you're ok."

"Yeah, they say I'm gonna be able start right into destroying a completely new body."

"Hans... I..." Hans had a frightened moment when he thought she was going to say something inappropriately personal, but she backpedaled. "What happened, Hans? What were you doing?"

"Trying to get home."

"You sure took the scenic route."

"Wasn't that scenic."

"They wouldn't tell me exactly where they found you or why."

"Not really surprising."

"No. I suppose you won't either."

"It's not really important. I made a stupid decision and these people picked up the pieces."

"Are you coming home?"

"When they let me."

"So, you're a prisoner."

"They explained it to me a bit differently."

"They would."

"Yeah. I've been told I can leave as soon as I answer a few questions." This wasn't exactly a lie.

"Well, don't make any more stupid decisions. A year is a long time to worry if your son is gonna live or not, Hans. Your little decision probably cost me a decade."

"I'm not planning on any more stupidity."

She snuffed at him for that. "Have you talked to your sister?"

"Not yet. I imagine I'll probably see her in the near future."

"You call her. She's been worried as sick as me."

"I will, Mom."

"OK. Gonna get off the phone now, Hans. You take care and call me tomorrow. Don't pull any of your shit on those nurses and doctors. "

"I won't."

Hans' mother was not a particularly long-winded.

Hans dozed off and on most of the day, still regaining his strength. Lunch came and he took his time eating it, less because of his fear of throwing up and more because he did not want to see the sheets do their creepy voodoo dance again. He tried to watch the little viewscreen they gave him, but he'd never really been into TV and the only movies he watched were too old to be on the movie lists. He did manage to find an old Raymond Chandler book in the vast library. He was about a quarter into it when Gino peeked his head in.

"Commander's on her way in."

"Now?"

"About thirty minutes."

— «» —

The commander arrived exactly thirty minutes later, resplendent in the type of suit that only military people thought represented civilian wear, a black skirt suit with too much shoulder and not enough leg.

Hans raised his eyebrows.

"Dressing up for me? What's the occasion?"

"Not for you. Formal function tonight."

"Well, I'm sure you'll have every eye in the room."

She ignored him and took the chair next to his bed, trying desperately to simulate an air of relaxation.

"Thank you for hurrying out here so quickly, Grit."

She just stared out the window.

"Jesus, Hans. What the hell were you doing there?"

"It's nice to see you, too."

"Do you have any idea what it was like to walk into that room and see my own brother laying on the floor?"

"I might have preferred it to where I was."

Her next comment was cut short by her internal communicator. Hans could tell by her expression she was listening to something he couldn't hear. She sub-vocalized something and turned back to him.

"Seriously, Hans, how did you get there?"

"I needed the money."

"You needed the money? And so you decided to walk into an exchange between two major criminal organizations?"

"News to me. A man offered me five hundred to carry a box up to a room in an abandoned building."

"And you didn't think that was suspicious?"

"I was desperate. I had no money and was trying to get home."

"I would have given you the money. I didn't even know you were in the city. Has Jackson been screwing around with your tag again?"

"I don't need your money."

"No, but you needed money from some random stranger handing you a package."

"Safer bet."

"Fuck you, Hans."

The door opened and Antonia came in carrying his dinner. It looked like a repeat of lunch.

"Put it there," Grit ordered, pointing at the foot of the bed. Antonia seemed not to hear, and came around the opposite side to place the tray in front of Hans.

"Old girlfriend?"

"Antonia, meet my sister, Greta."

Antonia smiled at her. "Hans and Greta?"

Grit just glared.

"My mother has a strange sense of humor," Hans said.

"I'll bet."

Greta tried her best to smile. Her face had never been quite able to pull it off. "Could you leave us alone for awhile, Antonia?"

"Toni."

"Hmmm?"

"Call me Toni. Only my mom calls me Antonia."

"Your mother and Hans."

Toni shrugged.

"Look, Toni, I really need to talk to my brother alone, so, if you don't have any other duties…"

"The doctor would really rather you don't upset him."

"The only person upset here right now is me at having my orders questioned."

"Heaven forbid. I'll be outside if you need anything, Hans."

Hans piped in before his sister, "Thank you, Antonia, I'll let you know."

Antonia beat a slow retreat.

Grit stared at him, "Already flirting with the nurses, Hans?"

"Don't follow."

"Antonia?"

"I didn't like Toni."

"Neither do I."

"Anyway, this isn't some kind of cheap porn. Antonia's been nursing me since I came here, she's sort of adopted me."

"So now you're a lost puppy. Seems about right "

"Did you have anything else you wanted to know?"

"Yes, how...." That distracted look came over her face again as she received another internal communiqué. Hans hated talking to people with those damn things installed. Grit grimaced and stood up.

"Damn it. I have to go, Hans. Crisis in the works."

"There always is."

She took a moment to lean over and air-kiss his cheek. "I'm glad you're OK, Hans. I'll be back soon."

"Yep."

Grit exited quickly, on her way to save the free world.

— «» —

She motioned to Gino without stopping. He fell in beside her.

"Who's on the door?"

"Carlton's on his way down."

Sensing their proximity, the elevator opened immediately. Grit had put it on a security override when she arrived.

"Floor, please," the elevator said.

"Roof."

"Yes, Commander."

The doors shut. Grit did not want to discuss the situation until they were back on board the jumpcraft. Gino would not break the silence until she did.

The doors opened onto the rooftop security check. Grit barreled through, heading out the doors to the insectile vehicle on the pad. A burly black man passed them, heading down to replace Gino.

"Nothing happens to him, Carlton," It was not a question. "I want him healthy and uninjured. So, I can kill him."

"Yes, ma'am, no one kills him but you." The scarred face smiled, sort of.

The jumpcraft's jets were still running. Grit had told the pilot to keep them powered up while she was inside.

She and Gino climbed up through the hole in its belly and strapped themselves in.

"Go." The pilot responded instantly to her command, thrusting the engines to full, causing the craft to plummet off the side for a moment before it caught its balance.

"Do we need to send you back to training, Juan? Or get you a smaller vehicle?"

"Just trying to keep you entertained, Commander," They both knew he was the best around, or he wouldn't be her chauffer. She turned to face Gino across the aisle.

"You heard?" she asked him.

"Yep."

"Do you know where we're going, Juan?"

"Yes, ma'am. ETA eight minutes."

Grit was nervous. There had been no sign of the package since it disappeared from the scene of Hans' injury. Her intelligence team had been working overtime trying to figure out a way to track its signature, to no avail. And yet, thirty-six hours after Hans woke up, suddenly it came up on the radar. She did not trust either the signal or the situation, but did not have any other options.

"What do you think, Gino?"

"I'd prefer the skirt a little shorter." He smirked.

"I'd prefer trousers, but neither of us got our choice tonight."

"This situation seems very convenient and very hinky. I don't think we should go in there by ourselves. "

"I have a light strike team on the way."

"Always prepared."

They didn't talk the rest of the way.

The area where the signal was emanating from was one of the mostly abandoned neighborhoods left from when the city dwellers had migrated to the super skyscrapers near the center of Denver. The outlying areas were in severe disrepair, despite efforts to save some of them for historical reasons. Many of the areas had already been significantly reclaimed by wild flora and fauna. Denver University had been one of the first in the nation to start up a college dedicated to studying the wild reclamation of these areas. Grit's primary concern with them was their state as a nearly ideal place to conceal, transport, and trade a vast quantity of illegal contraband.

"Strike team nearing location," her comm informed her.

"Form a perimeter and wait for my arrival."

"Gotcha."

Grit took a lot of flak from other high brass for her soldiers' use of what they saw as "overly familiar" chatter, some of the comments gender-specific. They couldn't do much about it, however, as her results had spoken for her troops many times. Whether they agreed with it or not, her method of forming them into a family made them a stronger fighting group. She viewed their protests as yet another reason why so many positions of power were female-dominated nowadays. She expected that at some point they would take a good look around and realize what century they were living in.

"ETA three minutes, Commander."

"Thanks, Juan."

Her comm chirped at her again.

"Grit, we have a problem."

"What?"

"The signal just disappeared."

She looked at Gino, her concern mirrored in his eyes.

"Evacuate everyone immediately. I want you out of there in two minutes."

"You think it's a trap?" Gino asked.

"Probably, but not for us." She cursed under her breath. "Juan, turn around and head back to the hospital, quickly. You still on the line, Lieutenant?"

"Yes, ma'am."

"Take your team and meet me at Denver General. I think this is a setup to get us away from Hans. When you get there, I want you to enter at ground level and run a sweep and contain."

"I'm not sure I have the manpower for that."

"I'm sorry, there's no one else. I know you'll do the best you can with what you have, and we don't have time to scramble any more forces. I need your skill here, Lieutenant; someone may be trying to kill my brother."

"We'll handle it, Grit, no one gets through."

"Thank you."

The engine noise increased as Juan ran the engines up to max.

— «» —

He'd been waiting twelve months for this opportunity, quietly biding his time on the janitorial staff. He could afford to be patient, as he was being paid an exorbitant amount. The command had come in while he was taking his coffee break in the cafeteria, just two words over his comm.

"We're go."

He stood up and exited the cafeteria as quickly as he could without drawing any suspicion from the monitoring system. Anyone running or hurrying unnecessarily would be instantly flagged down by the security scanners. It was inevitable that eventually the system would detect what was going on, but he needed it to be as late into the process as possible.

The doors to the elevator opened quickly when summoned. This late in the evening there would not be much traffic in them.

"Floor, please."

"Fifty-six."

"You are not authorized for that floor."

"Check again, I'll think you'll find differently."

There was a lengthy pause, then a short crackle from the speaker. The elevator began to rise, though the voice did not return.

He checked the pistol hidden in the small of his back, certain the elevator override had also shut down the scanners and cameras. It was tiny, made from plastics, and it only held four bullets. One use only, as four shots was the max it could handle before it melted too much to be useful. One for the bodyguard, one for the target, two for unforeseen circumstances.

The doors opened onto the hospice ward.

— «» —

The signal brought it to instant awareness, checking systems and finding no problems.

Attention: target compromised. Ascertain and neutralize danger. Please confirm.

It sent a quick confirmation signal and then burrowed in to the security scanners. An elevator had been blacked out and the system could not confirm its location. It took little effort to find the hijacking signal. One person on board, elevated heart rate, elevated breathing. Currently at floor thirty-six, heading toward the target.

It stretched its limbs, loosening them from the exterior wall that it had been attached to. The target's room was directly below its current position. It clambered down to window level and waited.

— «» —

The doors opened directly onto the nurse's station. He had prepared his best approximation of a smile for this eventuality. There was a pretty Latina woman behind the desk. She did not seem to believe his smile.

"This floor is limited access. I'm not sure…"

He put a bullet in her head. This had to go quickly and smoothly, and he didn't have time to sweet talk her. She went down quietly.

"I'm here," he said into his comm.

"Target in room fifty-six sixteen."

He had familiarized himself with the layout of the floors in his time here, and knew the basic whereabouts of the room even though he'd never been on this floor. Two lefts and a right from the nurse's station, probably guarded, probably military, though he was counting on the guard being only lightly armed and armored so as not to scare the hospital staff. Their mistake.

— «» —

It heard the bullet leave the gun and make its way through a human head, could tell these things from the changes in sound and frequency. It heard footsteps heading toward the target's room. One of its limbs cut a hole in the window big enough to allow its spherical body to enter, holding the circle of glass behind it and quietly pulling it into the room. The target continued to sleep.

— «» —

It was a close thing. He hadn't expected the guard to be quite so prepared or aggressive. His first inkling was having a high caliber bullet ricochet off the liquid armor wrapped around his upper torso. He knew he continued to breathe only because he was considerably taller than average, as the guard had obviously taken aim for a head shot.

Before the guard got another round off he put a bullet between his eyes.

— «» —

It could hear the guard fall outside the door, could hear his pulse and breathing go crazy before stopping altogether. It quietly crossed the room to the door, crouching and waiting, sensors registering that the target was probably awake.

— «» —

Hans held his breath. His first awareness of something abnormal came when he was woken by sounds from outside the building. Cars on the street below, jumpcraft whining in the air, distant wind and thunder. For a moment he thought that maybe he'd left the viewscreen on, but then realized he could smell the outside also, and feel a small breeze coming in.

A muffled crack came from outside his door, then another. The doors in this place were mostly soundproof, and his alarms bells began to go off. He'd just decided to make his way to the bathroom when everything took a turn for the bizarre.

Something about the size of a medium dog scuttled across the shadows on the floor. It was holding what appeared to be a piece of the strengthened window in one articulated limb, while the other three moved it over by the door. Hans was too stunned to propel himself off the bed.

He wouldn't have made it anyway, as just then the door opened.

— «» —

His first thought after the door opened was to wonder why the lights were off. Had the target left already? Her schedule had said half an hour. Had someone tipped her off? His second thought was to switch to plan B. If all else failed, kill the brother. There was no time for a third thought.

— «» —

When the door opened, it took in everything it needed to know in a microsecond. Dead guard. Unknown unauthorized stranger. Weapon in hand. It drew back the tendril with the glass and threw the piece of window at high speed, jumping after it a split second later.

— «» —

Hans had a brief glimpse of a man in the doorway, saw what looked like an oddly shaped gun, and then the creature on the floor pounced. The glass in its grip was immediately airborne, shearing off the gunman's hand at the wrist. The creature leaped and landed on the assassin's head as he was still falling, and the only sound the man made was a soft grunt as he hit the floor.

Seconds passed, and Hans hoped the creature had exited the room. Then the scuttling began again. Hans curled up on his bed, certain it was what had gotten him before, knowing that there was nothing he could do to fight it off.

But it detoured toward the window, climbing up wall and glass with ease, exiting through the hole it had made.

— «» —

Once back outside, it sent one more message.

Threat neutralized. Target safe.

CHAPTER 2

The creature left silence in its wake. Ear-straining, bowel-churning silence. Enough strength had returned to his legs that Hans was able to maneuver himself over the railings and stand beside the bed, using it for support.

The dead man lay sprawled in the open doorway. The circular glass jutted, unbroken, from the viewscreen. The strange gun lay close by, displaced hand still wrapped around it. Hans considered picking it up, but squashed the idea. He had no expertise with guns. Probably end up shooting himself. Besides, severed body parts made him squeamish. So did dead bodies.

Afraid to draw attention to himself, he did not call for help, but he couldn't stay in here, either.

Hans let go of the bed and hobbled to the wall, left leg dragging a bit more than his right. He was sick and tired of feeling helpless and disabled, but any attempt to get more speed out of his legs would result in him toppling over, so he fought his own nature and moved carefully.

He followed the wall around to the door, passing the creature's handiwork. The dead man's eyes were missing, now just two bloody holes. The creature had stabbed him with its appendages. Scrambled brains. Efficient. Sickening.

Another dead man lay in the hallway, facing away from Hans and spilling blood onto the floor. One of Grit's soldiers, wearing the same pseudo-civilian outfit they all wore when they were unsuccessfully trying to blend in. Hans did not recognize him, had never met many beyond Gino and a couple of other officers.

Belatedly he realized that he was completely naked. There was a robe hanging by the bathroom, but Hans' urge to exit overrode his decency. He doubted he was the first naked man to go wandering around the halls of this place, and he couldn't spend another second in this room.

Getting around the body in the doorway was a near thing. He almost tripped trying to step over the sprawling legs, but images of falling onto the corpse steeled his resolve. Once in the hallway he turned to his right, the other way blocked by two hundred pounds of dead soldier. He could hear a phone ringing down the hall and headed toward it. No one was in the hallway, out of fear or because of the late hour, he didn't know. The emptiness did little to relieve his nerves.

Hans put one hand on the left wall and struggled toward the T-junction a few dozen feet in front of him. His legs were already tiring, but he was determined to find someone, anyone. The urge to yell was tickling the back of his throat, but his fear throttled it. There was not much he could do if there was anyone else on this floor who wanted him dead, but he wasn't going to make it any easier.

At the junction, he turned left. The phone continued to ring. Why hadn't anyone answered it yet? Where the hell was the nursing staff? Where the hell was Doctor Laud? *Somebody answer the goddamn phone!* He almost yelled then, but regained what little composure he had and followed the nearly identical hall to the next junction, taking a right this time because he could see an exit sign hanging from the ceiling. He was shivering, both from the AC and the adrenaline. If anyone found him in this state they were going to be both shocked and unimpressed.

The sign at the junction led him to another right and he could see the nurse's station. The volume of the ringing increased and he realized what he had taken for a phone was actually some kind of alarm. The nurse must have triggered it. "Patient lockdown" was flashing above the desk. That explained the empty hallways. Everyone had been locked in. Everyone who didn't have a dead man lying in their doorway.

The trip down the final hallway took all the energy he had left, the red light and ringing goading him along. When he finally reached the desk he desperately needed to sit down, so he scooted his way around the edge to the chair on the other side.

Until he tripped over Antonia.

He landed with a thud right next to her, his hands lame attempt to catch him leaving them covered in her blood. Her eyes were open and glazed, a neat hole in her forehead, mouth agape.

Hans did yell then, though not much noise came out.

— «» —

Grit was out of the jumpcraft before it had finished landing, decorum damned by her half roll in the mid-length skirt. Gino followed, eyes aware. He had recommended they wait for the strike team to be in position before entering, but Grit wasn't having any of it. It was reckless of her, but he knew, despite their differences and arguments, she would do anything to protect her brother.

The elevator opened immediately.

"Emergency security override, military use only."

"Emergency override already in effect, floor please."

Grit gave Gino a confused look. As far as she knew the two of them were the only people on premises capable of a full military lockdown. The building must be compromised, but Grit had never encountered anyone capable of cracking a government building.

No extra words of caution were necessary between them. The elevator descended.

Hans was huddled, naked and shivering, in the hallway in front of the nurse's station. She could see blood on his hands and face. Grit moved to him. A glance at Gino and he was stalking off down the corridor.

"Hans?" She could see no obvious wounds.

"Help her," his voice was monotone.

"Are you hurt?"

"Never mind me, help her, goddamn it!"

The nurse from earlier was lying on the floor, shot through the head.

"What happened, Hans?"

He raised his head to look at her.

"You want something from me, you get on the fucking comm right now and get someone up here to help her."

"I don't think anyone can help her at this point."

"They saved me, they can save her."

"Carlton's dead, Grit," Gino chirped into her comm.

"Shit."

"There's another body in here, don't recognize him."

"Bring me something to cover Hans."

"Sure."

Grit turned back to her brother. "Can you walk?"

"Find Laud."

"Christ, Hans, I don't know where he is."

Hans put his head back down and would not talk to her.

"Gino."

"Yeah?"

"Can the viewscreen in there locate Doctor Laud?"

"It probably could if there wasn't a piece of the window sticking out of it."

"What?"

"There's a hole in the window in here. The missing piece is buried in the viewscreen. Looks like it took our stranger's hand off on the way."

"So, he was killed by a piece of window shrapnel?"

"It doesn't look like shrapnel, it's perfectly circular. Also, whatever killed him lobotomized him."

Too many unknown variables were at work here. What the hell was going on? Hans made a noise and fell over on his side.

"Hans, we have to…"

"I'm not going anywhere till you get Laud in here to help her." Hans was beyond sense. She wasn't talking him out of here. She wasn't sure where she would put him, anyway. She took off her suit jacket and balled it up under his head so at least he wasn't laying his damn fool head on the tile floor.

"Gino, what's your threat assessment?"

"It looks to me like the threat has already been eliminated."

"I'm going to call off the lockdown and try to locate Laud. Any concerns?"

"None worth mentioning."

Grit stood and moved over to the nurse's console.

"End lockdown, authorization Greta Ricker."

The alarm beeping stopped.

"Locate Doctor Laud."

The screen showed his location to be in his office on this floor, though almost immediately the signal began moving in her direction.

"Commander, this is Lieutenant Kinsley. We are in position to move forward with a sweep and contain."

"Hold position for now, Lieutenant, the situation has changed a bit."

"Where do you want me?"

"Cover the ground entrances and wait for my next order."

"Roger. How's your brother?"

"Alive. Thank you."

Gino rounded the corner into view carrying a robe for Hans. Doctor Laud was right behind him. As the doctor neared and saw Hans, he moved to crouch beside him. "Is he hurt?" the doctor asked Grit.

"The blood isn't his, it's the nurse's."

Laud noticed Antonia for the first time. His reaction was quick and professional. He moved immediately to the nurse's station and began talking into the microphone. Two nurses, freed from wherever the lockdown had trapped them, came around the corner within moments, wheeling one of the motorized lifters.

"Take her to the stasis unit, and get her settled as quickly as possible," Laud instructed. They went about their business efficiently, though the shock on their faces was evident. "Who did this?"

"We don't know, but it was most likely a man who is already lying dead in Hans' room."

"Did you stop him?"

"No."

Laud looked like he had more questions, but kept them to himself. Grit turned to help Gino wrestle Hans, now unconscious, into the robe. The nurses wheeled Antonia off down the corridor.

"Can you save her?" Grit asked the doctor.

"I don't know, but I'm going to try. We need to get Hans bedded down."

"Do you have any other open rooms?"

"There's always a few on this floor, that's why I'm allowed to keep some of my patients here. "

"Show me where." Grit bent down and lifted Hans bodily off the floor.

"Have you ever thought about being a nurse?"

"Couldn't. Too squeamish and I don't handle stress well."

— «» —

When Hans came around, he was confused. The room looked exactly the same, same windows, same screen, same poor decoration, same bed.

A figure in nurse's scrubs stood by the window across the room, the view outside different from what he had grown accustomed to. Mountains in the distance.

"Antonia?" Hans' voice was hoarse and groggy.

"She's in stasis."

Memory returned with anger. Hans struggled against the restraints.

"Hang on, Hans, I activated them because you were thrashing around a bit and the doctor said I shouldn't wake you," Hans recognized Grit's voice now. She moved to the controls. The restraints retracted. The lights came on. Hans could see her clearly now, absurdly wearing a shoulder holster over the top of the purple scrubs.

"You finally decide to get a real job?"

"My suit was ruined. This is what was available."

"So, you're my guard now? I'm flattered."

"Gino's on the door. I've got two men on the roof and two more in the lobby."

"Again, I'm flattered."

"You've become an important commodity."

"Commodity, huh?"

"Cut it, Hans, I don't need your bullshit right now." Her eyes glazed slightly as she listened to something on her comm. "I need to know what happened."

"And here I thought you were standing guard out of a sense of love and familial duty."

No one could glare like Grit.

"Could you get me a glass of water?"

"There's a drinking tube next to your head."

"I'm not a fucking hamster."

Grit rolled her eyes and spoke softly into her comm. "One water coming right up, Your Highness."

They faced each other, silence multiplying. Hans broke first.

"How'd I get back here?"

"I carried you."

"Oh." He wasn't quite expecting that answer. "Did you bathe and clothe and tuck me in, too?"

"Actually, yes." Hans hadn't expected that, either. He was rapidly losing ground. Gino came in with his water.

"Denver's finest at my beck and call. Could you bring me a fluffed pillow and one of those little mints?"

Gino grasped Hans' hand and placed the glass in it, only letting go when he was sure Hans wouldn't drop it. He exited quickly.

"It must have been awkward for you," Hans continued.

"It's not the first time I've given you a bath."

"First time in thirty years."

"Not much different really. Some of you is bigger than I remember. Some of you isn't."

"I've always had undersized toes. Hurts my balance some." He drank his water. Grit walked over to the bed and took it from him when he was done, catching his hand in her free one.

"Hans. I'm… glad you're OK. When I came out of that elevator and saw you on the floor with blood all over you, I thought I'd really lost you this time." Hans was taken aback, spluttering for something to diffuse this sudden intimacy. "I know we don't get along well most of the time, and that we disagree about most things, but you're my brother and that should count for something. I've been watching you for fourteen months, the whole time wondering if I was going to lose you, and just when I got you back I thought I'd lost you again…"

"Greta, you don't have too…"

"Can it, Hans. We've been at odds a long time, ever since I joined up, and I'm sick of it. I don't want us to go out hating each other. I want a brother again, not this stupid bickering. So tell me you love me and forgive me and need your big sis and we can go back to the verbal sparring tomorrow."

She squeezed his hand. He looked out the window for a long moment before speaking, afraid his voice would break and ruin his composure.

"Remember that time I fell into that stupid piece of shit bear trap that Jackson had set up?"

"Never could figure out how he thought he was gonna catch a bear with that thing."

"Yeah, he'd dug like a two-foot pit and put some upturned sticks he'd sharpened in it. Called 'em panjo sticks or something."

"Punji."

"Yeah, after some old movie he saw. Covered it up with a bunch of twine and leaves and didn't bother to tell anyone."

"You chased in that fox that kept getting after Mom's chickens."

"Broke my leg in two places, put one of those sticks right through my hand, almost took one in the neck."

"You were in a sorry state."

"You carried me all the way back to town. Two miles, wasn't it?"

"Something like that."

He looked at her.

"Do you have any idea how hard it is to have a sister that's more manly than you?"

"Ma was stronger than both of us."

"True. Goddamn women are taking over the whole world."

"We're equipped to."

She squeezed his hand again. He squeezed back.

"You were a pretty good big sis."

"You weren't so bad either, most of the time."

"How'd we get so lousy?"

"Dunno. Truce?"

Hans just nodded. His energy was fading again.

"My life was not worth hers."

"Whose?"

"Antonia's."

"The trade hasn't been made yet, Hans. Laud put you back together, maybe he can save her too."

"Maybe. Sorry about your soldier."

"Laud has got him in stasis, too. They didn't come any tougher than Carlton. If anyone can make it he can."

"And if not?"

"He'll be missed and mourned and honored for the soldier he was."

"I'd rather not have to do the same for you, Grit."

"Not planning on it." She leaned over and kissed his forehead. She used to do that when he was a kid. The memory was warm and suddenly very present.

"I gotta get some sleep. I've had an exciting day."

"We need to talk about what happened in that other room, but that can wait 'til morning."

"Yeah."

Hans drifted off quickly, as close to home as he'd been in a while.

— «» —

It was already almost noon when Hans woke, late enough that the sun was already over the mountains. The night before felt very distant in the light of day, especially the weirder aspects, but Hans was not prone to delusion or hysteria, and had no doubt that it occurred. He'd be happy to accept a reasonable lie, though.

Another bed had been wheeled into the room, currently occupied by his sister. She was curled up on her side, facing away from him, snoring in that way that only women could, a sound both raucous and soothing. Hans pressed the call button on the bed. The door opened and Gino came in, looking worn and sleep-deprived. He spent a moment looking at Grit curled up on the bed, removed his jacket, draped it across her shoulders.

"You two make a pretty cute couple." There was kidding in Hans' voice, but no real bite behind it. Gino ignored it.

"You need something?"

"I could do with something to eat. Maybe Grit, too."

"Let 'er sleep. She doesn't get enough."

"I'd imagine not. What about you?"

"I sleep fine, when I'm allowed."

"I meant food. You hungry?"

Gino just shrugged.

"How 'bout we go find a bar?"

"I'll tell the nurse to bring something in." Gino stepped out.

Ten minutes passed. A nurse appeared with a tray of food. Hans thanked her and ate what he could of the tasteless feast. Modern medical technology had pieced him back together from disparate parts, grown new organs from his own flesh, sewn him up and removed the scars, yet they couldn't cook broccoli without turning it into mush.

Grit awoke halfway through his meal, eyes opening, sitting up, fully aware. She folded Gino's jacket and set it on the bed beside her.

"What time is it?"

"Not sure. Afternoon, I think."

Grit stood and walked to the door. She knocked and Gino opened it from the outside. Hans couldn't hear what they were saying. More state secrets. She turned and came back.

"How're you doing, Hans?"

Hans thought about it for a second, realizing that, despite recent events, he was actually feeling pretty good at the moment. He could feel a decent amount of strength in his legs and arms, his head was clear, disposition almost cheerful. It was pleasantly odd state from him, and he had no doubt it would fade quickly. It took too much energy for him to be cheerful.

"I'm all right. Can I get out of here now?"

"Can you walk?"

"I think so."

"I'll see if Doctor Laud is around." Gino collected his coat, followed her out.

Doctor Laud arrived some twenty minutes later, looking as wan as everyone else. Hans was beginning to feel like some sort of sleep vampire. He'd sucked out everyone else's energy in the night to generate his current relaxed, aware state.

"How's Antonia?"

"Ms. Juarez is currently in stasis. Her body functions are normal, thanks to the machines, and her brain does not appear to have received any additional damage besides the initial trauma."

"Can you save her?"

"I don't know. I can re-grow the damaged tissue in her brain, but there is a large difference between re-growing a brain and re-growing a mind. Her neural tissue can be made good as new. Whether or not this means anything remains to be seen."

That effectively soured Hans' mood.

"I need to get out of here, Doc."

"I agree."

Hans hadn't expected it to be that easy.

"Your presence here is a danger to other patients and staff…"

"Wait a minute now, I didn't…."

"I don't mean to accuse you of anything. I know you didn't mean for any of this to happen. Lack of sleep has made me indelicate. Whatever you are involved in is too dangerous to continue to keep you in this facility. Your recovery is progressing, and is nearing its end. You may notice a bit of weakness here and there, but it should fade quickly. In the meantime, I think you need more protection than we can provide here."

"You turning me over to the cops?"

"The commander has agreed to take over your protection."

Hans didn't like it, but Laud was right.

"So, when am I out of here?"

"The discharge has already been finished. I believe transport should be arriving shortly."

— «» —

Hans was not enjoying his first trip outside very much. He did not enjoy flying or heights, both of which he experienced in short order as Grit hustled him into her jumpcraft. The pilot was completely incompetent, unable to hold any sort of stable altitude or even fly in a straight line. Hans did his best to appear relaxed.

"Where's this base you were talking about?"

"About ten minutes from here" Grit answered, "on the outskirts of the city proper, in one of the reclamation zones."

"What's a reclamation zone?"

"It's a place where the city is making efforts to retake a district from the neglect of the last few decades, putting up housing and industrial and employing the citizens to help clean up."

"So, it's a slum."

"No, it's a reclamation zone."

"Sounds like a slum."

The windows inside the jumpcraft were miniscule, but even the view he did have was unwelcome. The great glass spires of the inner city passed quickly, giving way to smaller, older skyscrapers, which, at a mere hundred stories or so, were less than half the height of the behemoths downtown. He would never understand how someone could choose to live and work four thousand feet in the air. In this day and age it was possible to live your entire life and never put a foot on solid earth, a thought both frightening and depressing. At home the tallest building was an old theater, topping out at three stories. Developers and politicians could go on forever about the advantages of vertical civilization. Everything was provided; food and meat grown for you in farms nearly a mile high; energy generated by sun and wind; each city-state almost completely self-sustaining and independent from its neighbors. The green revolution had gone a long way toward repairing the damage that humanity had done to the earth. It had also drastically shrunk the need for a central federal government. Each city-state now fielded its own sovereign government and military, with the federal forces reduced to protecting the roads and transport lines between cities, a job that became easier as tube transport lines increased in speed and robustness.

Still, there was one good thing about the mass concentration of people into the urban centers. It left a lot of room for Hans to roam. Plenty of old roads to drive, ruins to explore, valuables to be collected. A whole industry had sprung up around reclaiming metals and electronics from abandoned neighborhoods and towns. It was a good job for a misanthrope.

Finally, there were no more buildings of any kind outside Hans' window. The engine noise decreased as the power reigned in, the craft dropping quicker than could possibly be safe. He gripped the handle tightly.

"You all right?" Gino asked him.

"Did you hire this pilot out of sympathy? Or was it 'train a retard to fly' day?"

"I'm pretty sure he can hear you."

"Good, tell him to fuck off."

The craft's nose took a severe dive, pushing Hans against Grit. She laughed at the look on his face. He was considering punching her when a sudden jerk and rise in engine power brought the nose back up, then came a small bump as the craft landed.

"Thank you for flying retard airways," the pilot said over the intercom. "Please exit out the back and refrain from drooling in the causeway."

Hans signaled his disapproval.

— «» —

A small cadre of what looked like military VIPs awaited them on the ground. They had a wheelchair available, but Hans ignored it and forced himself to walk past, keeping a hand on Grit's shoulder for balance. His legs were close to normal. A bit wobbly though, and he fatigued pretty quickly. He did not want them to know.

The jumpcraft had come down in the parking lot of an old warehouse supermarket, most of it still in a state of natural upheaval as native grasses and invasive trees pushed their way up. The only clear spot was the landing zone, an artificial clearing showing signs of burnt vegetation around its perimeter. A path of well-maintained concrete led off through the new forest growth toward a large building whose exterior was in desperate need of repair.

"You take me to the nicest places, Grit," Hans said.

"Only the best."

They walked in silence along the path up to a very out-of-place, modern-looking armored door in the wall. It opened into a well-lit, cool hallway. A desk manned by a capable well-armed woman sat up against one wall. She nodded at them as they went past. They walked just a few dozen feet before turning into an open doorway and entering large, functional room with a table that could easily accommodate a couple dozen people. There were no other obvious decorations in the room, but, in an age where every wall, window, floor, and ceiling could possibly be a disguised viewscreen, looks were deceiving.

Grit stepped forward and pulled a chair out for Hans. The chair gave slightly as it subtly changed shape to make itself more comfortable. Hans resisted the urge to jump out of it. Everyone else took a chair, with Grit moving to the head of the table.

What followed was a surprisingly informal question and answer session, led by Grit, punctuated here and there by others' interjections. Hans had decided to answer all their questions straight, not wanting to spend any more time in custody than necessary. He told them as much as he could remember about the night he had almost died, and moved immediately into what he remembered about the previous night. They questioned him less about the mysterious creature than he expected, though he guessed they were keeping their cards very close. He figured they probably knew that asking him for any more would be useless. After about forty-five minutes Grit called the meeting and everyone stood up to leave.

"Would you mind waiting here for a few minutes, Hans?" Grit asked him.

"Do I have a choice?"

Hans was confused. The questioning had been short and shallow. There had been no accusations, no cross-examination, very little in the way of questioning his rather odd story. He did not know whether this was because they already had all the information he provided, or if they just didn't believe him and didn't care. The only thing he knew for sure was that he was very tired of surprises, sick of feeling like he was on the back foot. His life since waking had been a string of weirdness, and he wished somebody would explain what the hell was going on. He expected very little out of Grit and her cronies.

Grit came back in, by herself this time. She was holding a portable and a plate with some sandwiches on it. She sat down in the chair next to Hans and placed the plate between them, taking one of the sandwiches and removing the top to peel off the tomatoes.

"You don't like tomatoes anymore?" he asked

"Never did."

"You used to eat Mom's."

"Fed 'em to the dog when she wasn't looking."

"I doubt you fooled her."

"Me too," She smiled through a mouthful of bread.

"When do I get out of here, Grit?"

"When would you like to go?"

"Just like that?"

"This isn't a police state, Hans. We have no authorization to hold a citizen who has not been accused of anything. I have been authorized to offer you state protection for the time being, but I doubt you'll accept it. I can prepare a jumpcraft to take you home if you want."

"Thanks, but I'd rather not put myself at the whim of your undertrained pilot again."

"I figured that, too. How about a car to take you to the monorail depot?"

"Sounds good." Hans was still disbelieving.

"Eat your sandwich."

He did. It was a definite improvement on hospital food. While he ate Grit stepped out for a minute and brought them back a couple of bottles of lukewarm, tasteless water.

"It can't be that easy, Grit."

"What do you mean?"

"What aren't you telling me?"

"What do you want to know? I'll tell you what I can."

"Which is probably not a lot."

Grit shrugged and downed the rest of her water.

"OK. Who were the people I delivered the package to?"

"Delivery boys probably, same as you."

"And the woman?"

"There wasn't any woman in the room when we arrived."

Hans looked quizzically at her. "How is that?"

"I don't know, Hans. When we arrived, there were three bodies in the room. Two corpses mangled almost beyond recognition and you."

"There was a woman sitting in the chair across from me. She'd been shot or stabbed right through the head."

"No woman. No chair even."

"So, you're saying I imagined it all."

"I haven't said anything of the sort. I'm just telling you the state of the room when we arrived."

Hans doubted Grit would outright lie to him. His confusion grew.

"What about the thing I saw in the hospital? The man who tried to kill me?"

"We don't think you were the assassin's main target."

"Then who?" Hans tried not to raise his voice.

"Me."

"Someone was trying to kill you?"

"In my job, lots of people are trying to kill me. You gonna finish that sandwich?" Hans shook his head and she reached across and took it from him.

"How did he know you were going to be there? Isn't that kind of thing a secret?"

"We don't know. Lately it seems certain people have had more knowledge of my comings and goings than I prefer. I don't think he even knew you were my brother, as your personal information and relationship is under classified encryption."

"My personal favorite perk of your job."

"Yeah. Anyway, we are pretty sure he thought I would be there. The gun he brought was designed to penetrate our most commonly worn armor. He wouldn't have bothered had it just been you."

"Does it bother you that people want you dead?"

"I just wish I had actually been there. He wouldn't have taken me out, and maybe I could have done something to prevent what happened."

"Thinking pretty highly of ourselves, aren't we?"

"Runs in the family." Grit took another large bite of the sandwich. She reached across and snagged Hans' water bottle, almost emptying it. Hans sat in silence for a bit, trying to get a handle on his confusion.

"So, what about whatever it was that came in the window?"

"We don't know."

"You don't know."

Grit just shrugged. Hans crossed his arms and leaned back.

"You don't know or you can't tell me?"

"Is there really a difference?"

"Jesus, Grit… you don't know anything?"

"It was capable of cutting quickly through a transparent polymer designed to stop most projectiles. Based on its actions it must have an extraordinary amount of strength and speed for its size, and it must have been close by, probably on the outside of the building, without being detected by any of the normal systems we have in place."

"So, basically you know as much as I do?"

"Pretty much."

Hans put his head in his hands, rubbed at his eyes. "You've honestly never seen anything like this before?"

"I didn't see this one, just heard your description."

"Do you think it was the same thing that came after me before?"

Grit thought about that one. "No," she said finally, "whatever went through there put a hole the size of a sofa in the roof, and left large, deep slashes in the walls and floor."

"And you don't know what that was either?"

"No."

"You seem very nonchalant about all this."

Grit leaned forward and put both hands on the table. "If I appear to not care, I'm sorry. This is a very serious business and there are too many unknown variables. We have no record of devices capable of this, though what we don't know about other city-states and the feds could fill volumes."

"You think the feds could be behind it?"

"I don't think anything, other than that we need to be filling in the blanks, not creating more."

Hans ran out of questions. They sat for a while, Grit chewing the rest of his sandwich. He didn't think she was hiding anything from him that she wasn't forced to, but inscrutability was practically on their family crest. Still, they'd had a breakthrough last night, and they both were doing their best to be candid.

"So, what was in the package I delivered?"

She didn't appear pleased he had asked that, though she had to expect it. The silence drew out. Grit took another drink.

"We don't know."

"Bullshit."

"That's what you're getting."

"OK then, who was I delivering to?"

"We don't know that either."

"You don't know, and yet you just happened to be minutes from the drop point."

"Lucky for you."

"Who wanted it?"

Grit said nothing. She passed the portable across the table to him, giving him a knowing look and pointing silently at it. He nodded and slipped it into a pocket.

"We really don't know. There was information that something important was in transit," she crossed her arms.

"And this something just happened to be within a few miles of you and a squad of soldiers."

"Lucky break," she smiled, without any humor reaching her eyes. He decided to let it go. He was too tired to continue playing cloak and dagger. He wanted a car to the monorail station and he wanted a quick trip home. He'd had his fill of this city.

"So, you're really just going to let me go home?"

"Yes… but…"

"But what?"

"But… If anything happens, please contact me. That portable I gave you has a direct encrypted line to me. I don't want anything else to happen to you."

"I don't want anything else to happen to me either, except maybe a cigarette and a beer."

— «» —

Grit set Hans up with a driver and escort to the monorail station, and managed to talk him into letting them stay until he was on the train. She gave him a quick hug as he grumbled his way into the backseat. The car pulled away, its electrics whining as it accelerated out of the underground garage and up to street level.

She regretted what she had to keep from him, but she had no choice. She had to keep him monitored, as much for his own protection as for information. She believed his story about the delivery, knew he would never knowingly engage in contact with high-level criminal activity. But he was involved now, a nasty unknown in an already volatile situation. He would do what he wanted, and damn the consequences, just like he always did. Hans was grit in the gears at the best of times. Very smart in some ways, surprisingly naïve in others. He knew she'd kept things from him. The files on the portable were meant to satisfy his curiosity and scare him with the scale of what he was involved in. It wouldn't matter. He blamed himself for the nurse, probably for Carlton. Grit normally found his old-fashioned chivalry rather adorable, if somewhat useless, but he was severely out of his element here. Maybe he'd see sense and go home.

She doubted it.

— «» —

The transport pulled off the ramp and onto a poorly maintained road, once a major thoroughfare. Six lanes, large overgrown median, crumbling retail surrounding. They had the whole road to themselves and drove up the center, ignoring the ancient street signs.

The commercial district here was a testament to man's impermanence. Probably abandoned about the time of the last exodus to the inner city, forty years had wiped parts of it almost completely away. Structures toppled and crumbled as nature destroyed them from the ground up, taking every opportunity to grow and thrive. Animals, both indigenous, like the foxes and deer, and invasive, such as the roving packs of feral dogs, were moving in and settling. Attempts to cull their numbers were largely unsuccessful. The folly of man's sense of self-importance. He loved it.

The portable Grit had given him contained two text files, both written by her. Short briefings for high brass, probably.

Name: Illiyana Petrovich

AKA Kaori Li

AKA Onyx

Hans recognized the handle. Most citizens of Denver had heard of Onyx, though no one had ever seen her as far as he knew.

Age: 30-35

Born: Hong Kong

Information from Hong Kong is sparse, as the city's lockdown on its citizens in the wake of the nuclear terrorist attack in the early '00s makes intelligence difficult. She is believed to be the illegitimate daughter of a Yakuza official and a Russian ballet dancer, her age being estimated from a likely encounter when the Russian National Ballet gave a series of official performances for Hong Kong royalty. Born outside Hong Kong, she traveled with her mother for a series of years, before losing her mother in a terrorist attack by unknown sources.

Afterward she stayed in Hong Kong with her father. Information becomes nearly non-existent at this point, the few pieces we have questionable. She fled for unknown reasons, with no information on her whereabouts for nearly four years. She surfaced in Denver five years ago.

Onyx shows an extraordinary amount of intelligence and savvy in the running of her organization, and appears to inspire extreme loyalty among her followers, making it nearly impossible to infiltrate her organization or predict her next move.

The vast majority of her business involves underground technologies, such as high-level encryption and the cracking of the same. At some point, she introduced a virulent virus into city-wide networks, its sole purpose to seek and destroy any information, pictures, video, or anything else related to her. Currently we have been unable to combat it successfully.

Despite her abilities and technological prowess, at this time I do not consider her a primary threat. To the best of our intelligence she engages in no traffic of drugs, illegal body mods, banned weapons systems, or human beings. On numerous occasions her organization has provided my officers with information as to where these activities are taking place, enabling us to step in and prevent them. Also, though they are highly trained and armed, her followers do not represent a significant offensive force, as they seem to be used only for the protection of her physical and technological property.

I would say she considers herself an honorable criminal, actively fighting or undermining other organizations that do not live up to her code. At some point, she may step out of line, as most organized crime eventually over-reaches itself. Until that time she and her organization appear to be happily innocuous. Removing her would create a significant technological power vacuum, one that could easily be filled by less scrupulous individuals.

In summary, Onyx, though definitely engaged in criminal activities, seems to be a calming influence on the crime rate in the city. My recommendation is that we leave her be for the time being, until other, more pressing, problems are dealt with.

Commander Greta Ricker

— ⟨⟩ —

There was a deep respect between the lines. Still, if Grit had given this to him she must know or at least suspect Onyx to be one of the parties involved in the failed exchange. If her technological kung-fu was so great, maybe she was the creator of the thing that nearly killed him. If so, then who sent the one that protected him? Onyx? Why would she try to kill him and then protect him?

He was still mulling this over when something came through the armored windshield and took the driver's head off.

— «» —

"Grit," Gino chirped in her comm.

"Yeah."

"The signal just came back online again."

"Where?"

"The other side of the city."

"See if we have anyone nearby. Gather who you can and bring them to the garage. Follow my signal."

"You going after Hans?"

"Yeah."

— «» —

There was no noise in the cabin; the truck had shut itself off. Hans knew how to drive, but he doubted it would start for him.

Whatever had taken out the driver had made a neat, inch-wide hole in the windshield. No spider webbing on the window. Almost no noise. Just a short crack and the driver's head jerked back violently. Hans hadn't even bothered to ask the guy his name.

Another casualty.

It took him a minute to recover from the shock, an easy target in the passenger seat. He needed to move. Don't look at the driver. He'd never been good with blood and gore. Grit used to tease him about it.

Hans opened the door and quickly crept around to the back of the vehicle, with no idea if it would offer any protection. He sat for a moment on the cracked asphalt and tried to stop shaking.

Grit might believe that they were after her, but so far there had been two attempts on his life in two days, both of which resulted in other deaths. Anger gave him the strength to move.

Hans left the car and half ran/half loped his way to a pair of vine-covered buildings. His legs were still a bit shaky, adrenaline keeping them working. No second shot.

Formulating a plan, a crazy plan. Grit would call it stupid and bull-headed, but it only risked one life, his. He left the portable she'd given him on some crumbling steps, knowing she'd use it to try to track him, and he wondered briefly what the other file was. Too late now.

— «» —

"Half a mile behind you," Gino said in Grit's comm.

"OK. Any readings from the transport?"

"The driver's tag went offline about a minute ago. Not a good sign. No reading from Hans, either."

"Shit."

She pushed the transport hard on the rough roads, motor complaining, shocks creaking. Gino came back.

"Grit, we're getting a clear signal from the portable. It's about a hundred yards from the vehicle. "

"Moving?"

"No."

She tried to get more speed, teeth rattling in her head. Had to back off on the throttle.

"We got two loaded jumpcraft coming inbound from the city center," Gino said.

"Ours?"

"Yeah. I called 'em."

"Good. Send one to investigate the other signal, bring the other to our location."

"Roger."

The transport hit a large root sticking out of the road, causing the right side of the car to be momentarily airborne. Grit unconsciously turned the wheel to the right to keep the car from rolling. Despite every instinct, she let up on the throttle a bit. Damaging the vehicle and killing herself would not get her there any faster.

— «» —

Hans moved as quickly as he could through the unchecked growth of the side streets and alleys. He was thankful that Denver was not in a tropical region. Most of what hindered him was waist-high prairie grass, easy enough to walk through if you weren't recovering from being dead. He did not know how far he was from the city center, but he could see the spires of the city skyline from where he was. Ten miles, maybe, before the first real civilization.

He had made it two blocks when he ran into another grisly surprise.

Another vehicle was sitting in the street, obviously capable, possibly armed, and blocking his path, with four dead men on the road. He did not get any closer, pretty sure what he would find, and he'd had enough death for a lifetime. These men may have been waiting in ambush for him. Something had killed them. End of story.

He gave the vehicle a wide berth and headed down another overgrown street.

—— ⟨⟩ ——

Grit sat in her transport, watching. Hans' vehicle was a few hundred feet ahead; engine stopped, passenger door open. Her nerves were strung out, but training would not let her investigate alone. Too easy to ambush. The odds that the driver was alive were almost nil. She forced herself to wait for Gino.

She drove the transport through some tall grass and up against a building, leaving very little room to maneuver when she exited the driver's side. Making her way around to the back, she opened the hatch and unlocked one of the assault rifles with a voice command. Its grip softened momentarily in her hand and then solidified in an optimal grip, thrumming as its generator warmed up. She crouched down by one of the rear tires and called Gino.

"Where are you, Gino?"

"I can see you."

Grit turned her head to see the second transport trundling up the street toward her position. Gino had made sure to bring one with a mounted railgun on the back. It stopped in the street across from her and unloaded three soldiers. Two were armed and took up positions on either side of the vehicle, and the third climbed up to the mount in back and powered up the railgun. Gino exited the driver's door quickly and crab-walked over to her.

"What's the situation on the tracking scanners?" she asked.

"Nothing as far as we can tell. There are no signs of any hostiles, vehicles, or anything else as far as the city's internal system is concerned, but you know it can be unreliable out here."

"I'm going to make my way to the truck alone. Everyone else stays here."

Gino's eyes were concerned, but he was too well trained and had too much confidence in her to question the order. Modern weapon systems allowed snipers a range of six to seven miles if they knew what they were doing, and sometimes the only way to make sure was to risk it. Better if only one life was risked at a time.

Grit stayed in a crouch and made her way to the back of Hans' transport, the hairs on her neck crawling, listening for a shot, though she knew she would never hear anything if it hit her.

She made her way to the open passenger door. A quick glance inside told the tale clearly. No Hans. A hole in the window, driver dead and missing most of the back of his skull. She didn't need to see anything else.

"Gino?"

"Yeah?"

"Where did you say Hans' signal was coming from?"

"In front of the building just to your right."

She turned and made her way to the edge of the street. The portable was not hard to find. Hans had left it sitting on the lowest step of the building's entrance. She guessed he was alive, at least until she found him. She checked its log. No calls had been made, no messages left.

"What's the ETA on those jumpcraft, Gino?"

"About three minutes."

"Tell them to call for more and prepare themselves for a manhunt."

"Will do."

— «» —

Hans was already tiring. He figured he'd probably made it a mile or so. In that distance he'd come across two more vehicles, both in the same shape as the first. Twelve dead men and counting. Why had someone sent such a huge force to kill or capture one untrained, still partially crippled civilian? They must blame him for losing whatever was in that package, something he would rectify.

— «» —

"Commander Ricker?"

"Yes?"

"Lieutenant Owens, Commander. I am currently heading toward your position. "

"What's the situation?"

"We are observing what seems to be a large enemy force surrounding you."

"How large? And what do you mean 'seems'?"

"From speaking to the other two jumpcraft, we count upward of twenty armed enemy vehicles in an arc of about two miles just south of you. It looks like a massive ambush, or would be if they weren't all dead. We have also confirmed at least two snipers, both also deceased."

"Twenty vehicles? What make?"

"Military transport, not sure of the specifics."

"All dead?"

"We can't confirm one hundred percent, and the cover around here could hide many more, but currently we track no human life signs around your position."

"Thank you."

"Roger."

Jesus. Twenty vehicles, four men apiece, eighty dead bodies littered around her. How they hell could a force like that have moved in so close without being discovered? Were they after Hans? Or was the killing of the driver merely a ruse to bring in her and her forces? It would have been a slaughter. Something had killed them to the last man, quietly and at speed.

"Lieutenant?"

"Yes, ma'am?"

"I want you to pull your jumpcraft back to what you consider a safe distance, and assume that there are more forces and that they may have anti-air."

"Yes, ma'am."

Grit turned and walked back to the transports. Gino followed without speaking. She wanted to find Hans, but the first priority was getting her soldiers out of danger.

— «» —

Hans had made it another half mile, but he was rapidly losing steam. He wouldn't make it much further. He stopped to rest under the overhang of an old gas station. At least he would die somewhere outside of the city. He'd rather be eaten by animals than be put into a recycler.

There was a vehicle coming up the street in front of him. He was looking for a quick place to hide when he realized he was hearing the sound of an internal combustion engine. They were extraordinarily rare, illegal within most city-state borders. Neither the military nor the local police force used them. It had to be an outlander like him. He had no choice but to take the risk.

He stepped out into the street, wobbling on unsure legs. What he saw brought a smile to his face. It was the type of vehicle he'd grown up with, a heavily modified, heavily patched, four-wheel drive that wore its extensive repairs and modifications like old war scars. An older man sat behind the steering wheel, sunglasses covering his eyes, cigarette adhered into the corner of his mouth. A golden chariot pulled by angels would not have looked as good. Hans waved his arms and the vehicle pulled up in front of him.

The man leaned out the driver's window and gave him a once over.

"You military?"

"No, sir."

"You just wear them clothes because you like 'em?"

Hans realized he was still wearing the military coverall Grit had given him when he left the hospital.

"Sure, why not?"

The man chewed a bit on the end of his cigarette, saying nothing.

"I could use a ride." Hans said.

"You look like it."

"Just to the city border."

"Can't go in the city in one of these. Don't really like getting that close anyways."

"I know that. If you could just drop me off nearby I would sure appreciate it."

The man pulled his sunglasses down, revealing gray eyes so pale they almost faded into the whites. The effect was startling.

"You sure you're not some spook?" he asked.

"Until someone tells me otherwise," Hans replied.

He waved Hans around to the passenger side. Hans moved as quickly as he could.

— «» —

Grit's frustration was palpable. She'd been forced to wait while reinforcements arrived in the shape of more military transports, then forced to wait again as the ground team and air teams made a long sweep of the terrain in front of her. Her fears that Hans was lying dead had to be suppressed while she made a proper sweep. She would not risk her soldiers' lives unnecessarily.

Lieutenant Owens spoke through her comm. "Commander, we show no sign of active enemy forces. Multiple spectrum scans are negative, and the ground forces have only found bodies."

"No trace at all of what killed them?"

"Ground forces report finding entry wounds but no exit wounds. The holes appear to be too big for the projectiles to have not exited. We are hypothesizing stab wounds at this point."

"Thank you, Lieutenant."

She took a moment to get her head together. As of right now the count was one hundred and five dead bodies, none shot, all most likely stabbed. No sign of what did it, though she had a theory.

"Lieutenant Owens."

"Yes, ma'am?"

"Any sign of my brother?"

"No sign of anyone alive, ma'am, though so far he's not among the dead, either."

He couldn't have traveled more than six miles at maximum. It was twelve to the city border. There had been no vehicle contacts, ground or otherwise, and it was hard to conceive how he could be evading scans. She held out hope.

— «» —

His savior didn't have much to say on the drive in, but conversation wouldn't have been possible even if they had been more friendly, as the vehicle rattled and banged like an ancient clock tower. The man hadn't even offered a name. He drove the vehicle capably over mounds of earth, through small crevasses, and around impassable vegetation.

After twenty minutes that roads started to even out a bit, and there were signs of vegetation being cut to the side. Besides the interstates and tube lines the cities and federal government had stopped bothering with the outlying roads, but there were still many people who lived on the borders of the cities, and they kept up with what they could. Hans started to see some houses that actually looked lived in, with small electric runabouts parked in the street. They gradually increased in frequency up to the point where the vehicle he was in topped a rise and revealed the city skyline.

Hans would admit it was impressive from the ground, giant crystalline towers forming a wall in front of him, some reaching nearly a mile into the sky. He was annoyed to be back here. He didn't want any more of this spotless, self-cleaning world. Everything sanitized, homogenized, fluoridated for his protection. There was nothing here to challenge its citizens. Everything provided and in its place. He allowed that the capacity to provide food and shelter to every one of its citizens was a great improvement over the mess of the past, but he would never agree with the loss of personal freedoms that were required. Constant tracking, the government able to know where each citizen was at all times. Even in a city-state like Denver, where this capacity was strictly limited and prevented from abuse, it was a constant niggling presence. He just he counted himself lucky he had not been born in one of the cities that had become religious communes, like Salt Lake City or Omaha, where citizens were monitored much more closely. The feds did their best to stop some of the abuses that occurred in those places, but their power was nearly gone.

They pulled up to the border of Denver proper, marked only by a small welcome sign and a mass transit terminal. Denver did not have closed borders, but if they drove the internal combustion vehicle past the sign the police would show up shortly and turn them around.

"Thank you," Hans said to the driver. "You may have just saved my life."

"Yeah." It was barely a word.

Pleasantries over, Hans opened the door and climbed down. He gave the driver a wave as he made his way to the transit station.

"You be careful now, Hans," the driver said from his open window, then backed his car around and trundled off down the street they had come in on.

Hans couldn't remember if he had ever given the man his name.

—— ‹‹›› ——

Grit sat alone in the boardroom where they had questioned Hans. A small piece of one of the sandwiches she had brought sat across from her, gradually going stale.

Hans had disappeared off the face of the earth. One weak, possibly injured, man, eluding half a billion dollars worth of military equipment. Where the fuck had he gone?

There was a sharp click followed by two beeps in her comm, then a voice she didn't recognize called her by her name.

"Greta Ricker?" It was a strangely androgynous voice, betraying no accent or identifying characteristics.

"Who is this? Hacking an encrypted military comm is a federal offense." It was also, as far as she knew, impossible.

"My apologies, Greta. May I call you Greta?"

"Bit late for that question, isn't it?"

"It is never too late for courtesy, Greta."

Had she just been scolded? "Greta is fine, what do you want?"

"I am contacting you concerning you brother."

"You have him? Is he hurt?" She swallowed the threats. They'd do her no good.

"Your brother is fine, and will continue to be so."

"Who are you?"

"I regret that I cannot reveal my identity at the moment, but rest assured Hans is under my protection."

Realization rose in Greta's exhausted mind. "Are you the one that sent the creature last night?"

"I did not 'send' it. It was stationed outside Hans' room for his protection. I activated it when he seemed to be in danger."

"What, exactly, did you activate?"

"It was merely a helper. I truly regret that such extreme actions were necessary, but two people had already died and the risk to Hans was great."

"Did you kill all those men out there today?"

"Those men were there to entrap and ambush you. If I had done nothing you and all your men would be dead."

"Thank you for your consideration."

"You are welcome."

"Does that mean you are protecting me too?"

"You are dear to Hans."

"That's debatable."

"Do not doubt, Greta, that Hans loves you greatly."

"Are you offering me family advice now?"

"I am sorry, Greta. I was merely trying to explain…"

"Forget it. Look, this is too weird for me at the moment. You say my brother's safe?"

"As safe as I can make him, yes."

"How safe is that?"

"Very."

"Can you tell me where he is?"

"Yes, but I will not."

"Of course not."

"You have a dangerous job, Greta, one that has endangered Hans twice. It might be best for you to let him be until you solve your current conflicts."

"Look, shithead…"

"I hardly think that name…"

"I hardly think that some weirdo should be telling me how to keep my brother safe. I have been doing it for thirty-four years."

"I apologize."

"Fuck you and your apology. How did you get this number? How did you crack the encryption? Who the hell are you?"

"I regret that I cannot answer your questions at this time. Doing so would endanger both myself and many others."

"OK then, maybe you can at least tell me why?"

"Why am I protecting your brother?"

"Yeah."

"I made a grave error, and, as a result, he has been endangered, nearly killed. I will correct this error."

"That's very honorable of you."

"Your sarcasm is unjustified. "

"Says you."

"I know that I cannot convince you. I will try to prove it through my actions. I must go now, Greta. I have enjoyed our conversation, and hope that we may continue at a future time. For now, I wish merely to let you know that your brother is safe."

"You can't stop me from looking for him."

"I would not presume to try."

CHAPTER 3

The building was ten stories of featureless black obsidian, its four facets tapering toward the top. No obvious doors, no network antennae, no windows. It rose above the surrounding squalor in a shocking display of hubris.

Not subtle at all.

Onyx, despite her air of secrecy, was not interested in keeping her location a secret, if it were even possible to hide a building like this. A few inquiries of his bunkmates last night at the shelter and a short trip on public transit had brought him within just a few blocks, her base easy to spot from there.

Besides no obvious doors or windows, there were no guards, no people milling about. The whole block was currently empty, not surprising in such a run-down part of town. He doubted very strongly that he was unmonitored.

Nearing, he saw a ring of water encircling the building. *Jesus, the place has a fucking moat.* He reached the edge of the water, hands in pockets, trying to decide what to do next. No way in. What now?

He circled the building, looking for any change in scenery. Nothing. Tried yelling at it. Nada.

He'd been prepared for a lot of things. Anger, violence, death. But not indifference. Someone knew he was out here. He hated being ignored. Backing away across the still-empty street, Hans found some chunks of old concrete and rocks lying in the gutter. He picked up a piece with satisfying heft and did a running throw toward the building. The rubble arced through the air and hit the side of the building. It had the impact of a gnat on a car window. There was no crunch, no crackle, not even a satisfying thud, just an imperceptible clink and a splash as it fell into the water. He picked up another and threw it. Almost the same place, exactly the same result.

He'd thrown a dozen missiles before finally getting a reaction, a thrumming off to his right. He located it coming from under the sidewalk. A slab of concrete abruptly dropped a few inches and slid into a recess, revealing a short flight of stairs. No one came out. He waited. The stairs didn't go away. He gave it another minute. Nothing. Just him and the stairs.

Take a few deep breaths, descend.

The dozen or so stairs ended in a door as black as the building. No handle or bell. Hans raised his hand to knock, the door sliding aside before he could make contact. A small, well-lit black chamber was beyond. Hans stepped inside, doubting himself. The door slid shut behind him.

"Please hold." The voice issued from the ceiling, maybe real, probably synthesized. A long thirty seconds. "Thank you." The door in front opened.

A hallway beyond. No doors, no windows, black walls sloping slightly toward one another, mimicking the building around them. Lights set at even intervals. Barely wide enough for one person. A tomb. Claustrophobia rose in his throat. One foot, then another, repeat. He kept his eyes on the floor.

Another door, another chamber identical to the last. Had he walked through the building? Were they screwing with him? Just let him walk through and out the other side? The doors shut, his stomach lurched. An elevator, then.

The upper floor was a great relief after the hallway and cramped elevator. He stepped out into what must be the top floor, the entire ceiling showing the sky above. There was a standard reception room, if a bit hurting for color. Black walls, white chairs, white table, white desk, eerily pale receptionist, black sunglasses. She matched the room so well it could have been built around her. Clean lines, sharp corners, perfect balance between ivory structure and ebony decoration. Hans wasn't sure which this described better, the woman or the room.

"Your boss in?"

She tapped a black fingernail against a blindingly white tooth and said nothing.

"Speakee englais?"

A small, cold smile. She reached into the desk in front of her and removed a small pistol. It stayed on him without wavering. Hans tried to appear calm as his spine dropped into his shoes.

"Not sure red would help the décor in here."

Still no answer, and she pressed something under the desk. Ten seconds passed. Hans' biting wit failed him.

The door opened and a large man in a black suit came in. Had to be security. With that body and face there was nothing else that fit him. He did not speak either, merely gestured Hans through the door. The secretary returned the gun to its drawer.

Hans followed the beefy man down another black hallway, this also topped by the seamless glass. How much does a piece of glass like that cost? They stopped halfway down the hall for no reason Hans could immediately discern. The wall slid away, Beefy directed him in. Another boardroom. Hans was growing tired of them.

The door closed seamlessly to the wall and Hans was alone again. At least he could see the sky, which was doing wonders for his claustrophobia. He walked the circumference of the room, turned, walked in the other direction. No idea what to expect, his patience wearing thin. He took a chair, felt it shift beneath him. How could anyone get used to this? A chair should be a chair, a table a table; neither should be moving around.

A door opened at the back, opposite from where he'd entered. A dead woman walked into the room.

— «» —

It was her, little doubt of that; her face was permanently etched into his memory. He probably shouldn't be surprised. He'd come back from the dead, and she wasn't even in the room when Grit had arrived.

She strode in, poise easy and assured, the mistress of her domain. Features neither inherently Russian nor Chinese, instead something more than either. Tall, capable, lethal.

If she noticed him staring, she ignored it.

She took a seat across from him. No bodyguards, no assistants, not even a briefcase. She was outfitted like a biker chick headed to a business meeting: suit jacket, collared shirt, leather pants. Hair jet black, shoulder length, gleaming with prismatic echoes.

She reminded him of Grit, not in her exotic looks, but in her air of lethal capability.

"Tell, me, Mr. Ricker, why I shouldn't throw you off my roof." No introductions. She knew his name. He wasn't surprised.

"Maybe you should."

"It would certainly bring me pleasure, though I doubt it would solve our current problem."

"That being?"

"Why a federal agent is standing outside my building throwing rocks at it?"

Federal agent? He forced a laugh. "Lady, I have no idea what you're talking about."

"Spare me your lies, Mr. Ricker."

"No lies. I don't know where you got that information, but I have no affiliation with the feds beyond a couple misdemeanor charges for illegal contraband."

Onyx said nothing. She reached out in front of her and tapped the tabletop. It displayed a basic ID file. She flicked the surface with her finger, and the virtual file moved across the table toward him. His name, an old picture, flashing security message. Level seven.

"And?" he asked.

"I do not think you are an idiot, Mr. Ricker, though you seem determined to prove otherwise." She leaned back in her chair and raised her hands behind her head. "Seventh tier security encryption is limited to federal secret ops and the currently seated federal government. But you already know this."

"No, Ms. Onyx, I don't." Fear faded behind annoyance. Hans' understanding of security levels was almost nil. His file did have some security due to Grit. Did it warrant a seven? One more point of confusion.

"The encryption on this file is supposedly unbreakable, though I assure you I have the capacity. Lying to me will only put off the truth so long."

Hans changed tactics. "You don't remember me, do you?"

"Pardon?"

"Been dead recently?"

She stared at him.

"Fourteen months ago?"

"Start making sense, Mr. Ricker."

"Can we cut out this Mr. Ricker crap? My name is Hans. I've seen your tits, so let's at least get on a first name basis."

"OK, Hans, are you implying that you and I had some sort of relationship? What it is you expect to accomplish with this charade?"

"Lady, the last time I saw you I was lying on the floor in two pieces and blood was running down your chest. You may not remember my face, but you obviously remember something or you wouldn't still be trying to kill me."

"I am not trying to kill you. Or, at least, I wasn't."

"Your assassin tried to kill me at the hospital two nights ago. Yesterday you sent a sniper after me."

"I did not."

"Now who's lying?"

"I'm still waiting for you to make sense, Mr. Ricker."

"You first, Ms. Li. Or do you prefer Petrovich?"

She was across the table almost before he finished the line. One hand grabbing his hair, the other holding a small knife to his throat.

"Where did you get that name?" she hissed at him.

"What? Hans? My mother gave it to me."

The knife pressed in.

"Who sent you? One more chance."

"Fuck you, lady. Cut if you have to. I was almost killed a year ago. I woke up two days ago and people have been trying to kill me ever since. Two people are dead because of me, and a very nice lady who just wanted to help people is on the edge. I came here to make amends for a mistake, to try to prevent anyone else from dying for my mistake. Cut me open if you want, but stop bullshitting me."

Seconds passed, then the knife retreated, disappearing to whatever hidden recess she'd drawn it from. He could still feel it, and wondered if his tough speech would be ruined if he threw up on her nice clean table.

Onyx was seated again, with no sign of even having moved. Not even out of breath, though a few black hairs were now out of place. "You wish to make amends. What is it you have to make amends for?"

"Fourteen months ago, a guy gave me five hundred to deliver a package. I was desperate, so I took it. The delivery was in an abandoned apartment building on the edge of the city. When I got there you and two thugs were waiting for me. About a minute later something blew into the room and took us all out. Do you remember any of this?"

"You were the delivery boy?"

"Yes. I can understand you not recognizing my face, but it had to be something pretty important for you to show up yourself. So, do we put the truth on the table now?"

"I remember a delivery. I lost a package containing my property. I wasn't there." No sign that she was lying.

"Fine. Fuck it. You weren't there. I don't give a shit anymore. Your package was lost, it's partially my fault. You want to kill me? Do it quickly, but mine is the last. No one else dies for me."

She placed both her hands under her chin and considered him. "If you are being truthful, then I admire your integrity."

"Fear and guilt aren't exactly integrity."

"Let's say I believe your story. It can be checked. It still doesn't explain how you know my name and have a seventh-tier security encryption on your ID file."

"The answer to both of those is the same. My sister is Greta Ricker. She's the commander of the Denver security forces. I know your name because she gave me a file that told me. The security level is because I am related, though I don't know why it's so high."

"You are Grit's brother?"

"Yes."

"Hans and Greta?" She smiled a predatorily.

"Yeah." Hans let his breath out. The mood calmed a bit.

"My respect for your sister runs very deep. I have never met a more capable woman, besides myself."

"You should meet our mother."

"I imagine she's quite a woman."

"Yeah. The file I read on you was very short, but I would say that Grit holds a certain amount of respect for you as well, despite your obvious failings."

"And what would those be?"

"Oh, you know, trying to kill her brother. Trying to kill her."

"I do not know who made the attempts on your life, but they were not sent by me. I would not try to assassinate Greta, she's too important to my success."

Hans believed her, mostly, though it didn't help his confusion. "So where do we go from here?" he asked.

"For the moment, I will keep you here while I break your file and verify your story."

"Still can't trust me?"

"I don't think you are lying to me, but I would never have gotten where I am by being too trusting."

"And in the meantime, I am a prisoner."

"Not a prisoner, Mr. Ricker, just a guest. You'll be safer here than outside. We can accommodate you comfortably. You will not find a more secure hideout."

"Fine, I'll stay. I've got nowhere else to go."

— «» —

Onyx stood and left without any further words. Beefy returned a moment later and silently escorted Hans to the elevator.

The elevator moved downward, opened to another carbon copy hallway. Hans' claustrophobia returned. Breathe slowly, stay calm.

They entered a large suite. Bedroom, bathroom, kitchen alcove, all in monochrome like everything else. The whole place was a black and white movie in the making.

Beefy disappeared, silent as ever. Hans turned, looking where the door had been. Nothing to see, not even a hint of seam. It wasn't opening 'til someone else opened it. A prison was a prison, no matter how you dolled it up.

The wall to his left lit up with Onyx's face.

"To your liking, Mr. Ricker?"

"Hans."

"Hans. Is this ok?"

"I assume that's a rhetorical question."

She smiled coldly.

"This place have any windows?"

The far wall faded to transparence, the view was not scenic.

"We have an assortment of tranquilizers and other mood enhancers if your claustrophobia gets out of control," Onyx said.

"That obvious?"

"Your vitals are constantly monitored in here, signs of stress are easily spotted."

"Vodka and a pack of cigarettes if you got 'em."

She clucked at him, "Such nasty habits you have, Hans."

"And you're a paragon of decency."

"I'll send some down."

"Thanks."

The viewscreen blanked out.

He found it very curious that, for such a big shot, she had time to attend to him personally. He doubted it was simple courtesy. It was just a hunch, but he didn't think this building was packed with people. If that was true, what was its purpose? Another question, no more answers.

Beefy returned with a tray holding a bottle of clear liquid and a small silver case. Very fancy. Wasted on him. He was far from a connoisseur.

Hans pulled a small padded chair up to the window and lit a cigarette. They were very good, but not as good as the vodka.

Despite everything, for the next few hours Hans was feeling pretty nice. The vodka gave him a pleasant, mellow feeling, which he maintained without getting too drunk. The cigarettes cleared his head. He sat and drank and smoked, eventually dozed.

—— «» ——

Beefy shook him awake. Trying for gently, not succeeding. That, and the man's slab of a face up close meant that Hans had had better awakenings.

Beefy gestured, walked back to the door. Time for round two. Hans took a moment to get his bearings, then followed. Maybe the man couldn't actually speak at all.

Back to the elevator. Or maybe it was a different one, Hans couldn't tell. Rising to the top floor. Past the reception desk, empty now, and down another hallway to the first real door Hans had seen in this place. Beefy knocked. Looked like wood, sounded like wood. Expensive if it was.

"Come," Onyx's voice was distant through the door.

Beefy opened the door, shoved Hans through, and shut the door behind him. His footsteps retreated down the hallway.

Hans was in a small foyer, with antique wrought iron lamps lighting wood-paneled walls. A small bench was against the opposite wall.

"Please remove your shoes, Hans. There's a pair of slippers in there that should fit you well enough."

Hans sat, removed the boots Grit had given him. It was a huge pair of black slippers, meant for Beefy probably. He slipped them on, and his feet barely filled them.

Onyx was standing in the doorway. She had traded in the suit for a kimono, jet black, minimal ornamentation.

"Sorry," she said, "I forget sometimes how big Lev is."

"I'll manage."

"I have some proper clothes in a changing room, in case you're getting tired of security issue."

The whole situation was strange in the extreme, changing in her room? Just go with it. He didn't want to die in army green.

Down a short, wood-paneled hall, Onyx gestured at a door. Hans entered, locked the door behind him, and found a large walk-in closet filled with men's clothes.

"Your boyfriend's stuff?"

"Former boyfriends." Her voice was surprisingly close.

"Do you keep their bodies in here, too?"

"That's what the incinerator in the basement is for."

After seeing her attire Hans had been afraid that the room would be filled with incomprehensible foreign garb, but there were a fair number of western suits on display. He was normally a jeans man, but he knew how to wear a suit. He chose a dark blue suit with an off-white shirt, a vest, and a black tie. It fit well enough, but looked kind of silly with no shoes.

Onyx stood exactly where she'd been, sipping vodka. Had she had the glass before? He couldn't remember.

"You clean up well, Hans. I was unsure if you would know how to knot a tie."

"I've been to job interviews. "

He followed her down the hall. It ended at a dining room containing a large, ornate table carved from what looked like one giant slab of ebony. Hans had some familiarity with carpentry, and the craftsmanship that had gone into the table was by far the best he'd ever seen. Woodworking was a rapidly declining art in this day and age, with newer, more resilient materials able to mimic it nearly perfectly.

"It's Russian," Onyx said, noticing his admiration.

"How much did you pay?"

"Three hundred thousand."

"I know a guy who could have done this for a couple hundred."

"You'll have to give me his number."

"He doesn't have a phone."

She took a seat at the head of the table, and gestured to a seat next to her. Hans ignored her and sat on the opposite side.

"Afraid of me, Hans?"

"I believe in never underestimating potential threats."

"If I wanted you dead or harmed you would already be."

"You'll have to allow me my delusions."

"How about some food?"

"You got steak?"

"That can be arranged."

"Rare, please."

The secretary entered the room, took her instructions, and departed.

"A drink?"

"Some more of that vodka if you got it."

Onyx stood and moved to the wall, which slid back to reveal a small alcove containing a few decanters and some glasses.

"Ice?" she asked.

"No, thank you."

Onyx was pleased with his answer. She filled a small glass, placed it in front of him, and returned to her seat. They drank.

"How's the vodka?"

"I don't think you need me to tell you it's excellent, and I'm not much of a judge anyway. We don't often get quality liquor in my hometown. I suppose you get it from Russia."

"I distill it myself."

"Really? I'm impressed."

A genuine smile at the compliment.

"A friend and I tried to brew up some bathtub gin one time. Tasted like pickled ass and just about killed us both," Hans said.

"The secret is multiple distillations and filtering."

"I'll have to remember that. You get the recipe from your mother?"

"Mr. Ri..." She took a deep breath and another drink. "Hans. You have made a request of me, and I will comply. In return, you will not make any references to what you think you know about my past. Do we have an understanding?"

"Sure."

"You are a difficult man to like, Hans."

"True enough. This whole situation is fucked, and I'm not good at pretending. How about you tell me why you didn't kill me?"

She took another sip, considered him, "You tell me you lost something that belonged to me, and that you have come to make amends. I believe that you intended me to kill you. Since I have not... yet... you owe me a debt, and you have certain properties I might be able to make use of."

"Those being?"

"You have no criminal affiliation. You have an identity under complete lockdown, and you have no ID tracking tag.

This anonymity makes you of possible value to someone in my line of work."

"I didn't come here to break the law for you."

"I haven't asked you to."

"Just so we're clear."

The secretary entered with their food. Beef for Hans, some kind of raw fish for Onyx. The meat was delicious. The secretary cleared the plates. Onyx brought out another silver cigarette case. Hans accepted, along with a light. Up close, with her eyes uncovered, he could see that her irises were an extraordinary pale gray. A ghost's eyes. He'd seen eyes like them recently.

When he was seated he popped another question. "Was it your man who picked me up outside the city?"

"My man?"

"The guy in the four-by-four?"

"I don't know what you're talking about." He irritated her. Good.

"OK. I have another question then, but I don't think you'll like it."

She waited for him to ask, smoking angrily.

"What was in the package I delivered?"

Still didn't answer him.

"What's with your eyes?"

Onyx shot a confused look at him. "I'm not sure what you mean."

"You're the second person today I've seen with eyes that color."

"Startling coincidence, I'm sure."

"I don't think so."

"Is there a point to any of this, Mr. Ricker?"

"I'm not sure, Ms. Li. My life has been one strange occurrence after another since I woke up, and everyone seems to know more than me. I don't expect you to give me any answers, but don't think I don't notice things. Everyone seems to think I'm an idiot."

"You give us little choice."

Hans finished his cigarette and put it out on the table. Onyx didn't react.

"I'd like to go back to my room now."

The door opened and Beefy came in. Onyx stood.

"Thank you for joining me for dinner."

"My pleasure."

— «» —

Hans treated himself to a bath in the large tub provided in his room, turned off the lights, turned the water up until it turned his skin beet-red and made him short of breath, and floated in warm blackness. It helped him think.

Onyx wasn't the one who'd tried to kill him, though he didn't trust her. She'd been polite, mostly, even when Hans goaded her. She might even be lonely. She and her two silent assistants in this alien place. Squash that train of thought, it was useless to go into Damsel in Distress mode. Onyx didn't need anything from him.

He climbed from the tub, banging his shins on the high walls, groping blindly for a towel, giving up and turning on the light. The towels were above the toilet, alternating black and white, like everything else in this place, but comfortable and soft, even warm somehow. Another disturbing molecular manipulation, no doubt.

There were sounds of ice clinking in the other room. Onyx? Hoping she wasn't here for some kind of liaison, he dressed quickly. He didn't fancy turning down the advances of a woman that dangerous, but the other option was even less appealing.

It wasn't Onyx. Instead there was a familiar-looking man sitting on the small couch pushed up against one of the walls.

"Hello, Hans."

"Where's your truck?"

"Wasn't mine. Just borrowed from a friend."

"Borrowed or stolen?"

"Acquired. Necessary to save your life. You may remember that. Drink?"

"Why not?"

The man stood and crossed the room to the almost empty vodka bottle.

"Ice?"

"No, thanks."

"Onyx would approve."

"You her boss?"

The man turned, holding both glasses, and gave Hans a beaming smile. An ageless face, light and shadow adding and subtracting years as they played across it. "Let's call me a benefactor."

"I'd rather know your name."

"I may have to disappoint you there."

"Everyone disappoints me sooner or later."

"Such is life."

He crossed the room, handed Hans his drink, still smiling. Up close Hans could see gray specks in his hair.

"You her father?"

"And what would make you say that, Hans?"

"Same eyes."

"Ah. Rather rare color."

"Never seen it before."

"Not common to this area, more so where we come from."

"Hong Kong?"

"Now what would make you say that?" the man chuckled, his eyes showing genuine amusement.

"Just a guess."

He moved to the couch, sat and drank. Hans remained standing.

"No one makes vodka like she can," the man said.

"Multiple distillation and filtering."

"And a small amount of molecular adjustment."

"She didn't say anything about that."

"Trade secret. Done merely to purify the molecule, I assure you."

Hans put his glass down, not sure if he could drink it anymore. "If I can't know your name, what do I call you?"

"Is a name necessary?"

"Yes."

"Very well, call me James."

Hans retrieved the silver cigarette case from the nightstand where he'd left it, lit up, and sat down on the bed. "OK, James, what do you want?"

"You have questions?"

"Hundreds."

"I'm here to answer what I can. You deserve that."

"Anything I want to know?"

"No. But a large portion."

"Who's trying to kill me?"

"No one."

"Try again. There've been two attempts on my life in two days."

"Neither aimed at you specifically."

"Who then?"

"Both intended traps for your sister, your involvement was incidental."

"So, you're trying to kill my sister."

"Not I nor anyone else in this building."

"All four of you?"

"And change."

Hans took a moment and a few more puffs. "Did you send the creature?"

"I'm not sure what you mean."

"The thing that broke into my hospital room and killed the assassin."

"That was one of mine, yes."

"What the hell was it?"

"A… helper. A multipurpose tool."

"So, breaking and entering, murder, things like that?"

"It does have those capacities, though it is certainly capable of much more constructive duties."

"Such as?"

"Saving a life."

Hans took a moment to retrieve and light another ciga-rette. He had purposely not asked about the type of tobacco in them. "Did your 'helpers' also kill those men in the truck?"

"Those men, along with about a hundred others, had intended to use you as bait to draw your sister into a trap. My forces disarmed the trap."

"That's a yes on the multiple murder then?"

"Yes. My forces killed them to the last man. All the men that had been sent to kill you and your sister, dead at my hand. Is that what you wish to hear?"

"I guess I should thank you for that."

"No need."

James finished his second glass of vodka and went back for another refill. He wasn't affected visibly at all. No wobbling, no slurring of speech. Hans would be well on his way to inebriation.

"Why?" Hans asked.

"Why what?"

"According to you you've saved my life twice."

"I wish to correct an error."

"How is that?"

"Carelessness on my part, an amateur error. I thought my monitoring was airtight. Something got through."

"You couldn't track me, could you?"

James pause, considered, took a sip. Hans figured his next words would almost have to be a lie.

"I'd grown complacent." The phrase revealed nothing, left possibilities floating like dust motes, "Why do you not have an ID tag"?

"I had it disabled."

"Really? That's a somewhat dangerous proposition for someone your age."

"Can be. I know a good brain surgeon."

"Even so, why would you risk permanent brain damage and possible conviction of tampering with state property?"

"The feds can call it what they want. It was in my head, so it was mine. I'm not federal property. They can feed me as many lines as they want about benevolent monitoring and laws to protect its abuse, but they put something in my head without my permission. I couldn't remove it, so I broke it."

"Would it surprise you if I told you I agreed?"

"I don't have much surprise left in me at this point."

"I admire your conviction, Hans. I could use someone like you."

"I'm not a criminal. I already told Onyx that."

"Removing an ID tag is a criminal offense."

"So, I'm a hypocrite."

"Aren't we all? Regardless, I was not going to ask you to do anything illegal, or even anything you haven't already done."

"What then?"

"I need a courier."

Hans laughed at him. "I tried that once, didn't work out too well for me."

"You will be as safe as I can make you, and you will be well compensated."

"So far your version of safe hasn't worked out too well."

"You have survived two attempts on your life, both because of me."

"That's assuming I believe you."

"Your choice, there is little I can do but tell you the truth and hope you see it for what it is. You did say you came here to make amends."

Hans considered, smoked another cigarette, stood up, and paced. He was trying to free himself from this nightmare, but he suspected he was about to get drawn further in. "What's the job?"

"I need you to retrieve something for me. As a matter of fact, it's the same item that was lost initially."

"Where?"

"It is currently being held by a man in Salt Lake City."

"What kind of man?"

"A very dangerous man. The same man who sent the troops and the assassin."

"And you want me to retrieve it from him? I don't know if you noticed, but I'm not a soldier."

"You do not have to steal it from him. He has agreed to a deal."

"Do I need to know anything about the deal?"

"No."

"Good. Don't tell me. I have a few questions, though."

"I will answer what I can."

"Why do I need to go?"

"In your current state, you have a much better chance of avoiding surveillance on the journey, particularly on the way back. And you grew up in the mountains. The trip out can be done by normal means, but the return would best be done on older, less monitored roads."

"You expecting him to double-cross you?"

"I'm expecting many things. I will keep you as safe as possible, but your anonymity will be your most powerful protection."

"When would I leave?"

"As soon as possible. "

"I haven't said yes yet."

"True. Think on it for a while. When you make a decision, you can let Onyx know. She'll have all the details."

"Where will you be?"

"You will not see me again."

— «» —

It was too quiet to sleep. The bed kept shifting, trying to make him comfortable. He moved to the floor. It was hard, but at least it wasn't full of insects.

Circumstances were locking down on him. There was no logic in their offer, just half answers and bullshit reasoning. They couldn't just want him for his anonymity. He'd had his tag removed, sure, but there were plenty of ways to block or spoof a signal. He'd used one himself after getting the procedure. It was the only way to access his money and online assets. Not that there'd been much of either after the surgeon had screwed him over. That's why he was at the employment office looking for day work in the first place.

Both Onyx and the man calling himself James had spoken as if Hans was the only one who could possibly make this journey. There had to be another reason for sending him; he doubted it was benevolent.

Hans gave up on the floor and walked to the wall to flip on the lights. The case Onyx sent him still held two cigarettes, one less now that he lit up. He walked to the blank viewscreen on the wall, touching it to wake it up. The menu that came up offered no options for watching shows on the city network, not something Hans was much interested in anyway. It looked like mostly room controls, though Hans was surprised to see an option for outside calls.

It was early morning, but Hans called her anyway.

His mother answered on the sixth ring, voice only as usual. She did not sound as if she had been sleeping.

"It's Hans."

"You were supposed to call me two days ago."

"Something came up."

"Something always comes up with you. Do you know what time it is?"

"You weren't asleep."

"No. How are you feeling, Hans?"

"Much better. Everything seems to be working more or less normally."

"You laying off those cigarettes?"

"Yeah."

"Good. Did you see your sister?"

"Yes."

"She still out saving the world?"

"Single-handedly."

"You two make up?"

"Yeah."

"Good. I'm not gonna be around much longer to knock your heads together. You're gonna have to do that yourselves."

"You're gonna outlive us both and you know it," Hans was beginning to feel that might actually be true.

"That's a cruel thing to say to an old woman. You coming home soon?"

"Soon. Got a few things to take care of here first, then I'll be on my way."

"Good. These poor mutts you stuck me with are miserable without you."

Hans doubted that. His two ten-year-old cocker spaniels, Bogie and Bacall, adored his mother. Probably sitting on her lap as they spoke.

"Give 'em a scratch from me."

"You get your ass back here and do it yourself."

"I will, Mom. Just gotta clear up some obligations."

"What kind of obligations, yours or theirs?"

"Mine."

"Good?"

"No."

"Are you still in trouble?"

"A bit, but it's my own fault."

"Greta involved?"

"No, Mom. It's mine and I have to deal with it. I don't want her involved."

"Always gotta do everything your way?"

"Yeah."

"You finish what you gotta finish and then you come see me."

"I will, Ma. Love you."

— «» —

Hans was choking. He had been dreaming of Greta. She was angry about something, wouldn't tell him what. Time shifted, Greta was choking him, or maybe it was Onyx, he couldn't tell, the face kept changing. *Don't fight it. Shut your eyes. It's better this way.*

A wet choking sound, weight on his chest, something warm soaking through the blanket pulled on top of him. Panic brought on by claustrophobia caused him to struggle underneath the tight covering. He was making a noise in the back of his throat.

"Hold on a moment," a female voice said, and the weight was lifted off him. He quickly extracted himself from the soaking blanket, eyesight still bleary and blind. Soft footsteps crossed the room, the lights came on. A naked female body was bleeding onto the tile floor. Blood covered the dress shirt he'd gone to sleep in, caked on his bare legs.

Onyx was crossing back from the light switch, a small, wicked-looking black knife in her hand. She must've have just woken, still in what looked like a set of black flannel pajamas, hair mussed.

"You certainly bring interesting circumstances with you, Hans."

Hans didn't respond. Lightheaded, nauseous, trying not to pass out.

Onyx knelt next to the body, laying mostly face down on the floor. She put a hand underneath a shoulder and turned it face up. Blood still oozed from a gash on its neck that went nearly ear to ear. The face of the woman at the reception desk.

"H-How...?" Hans managed.

"Building security notified me of unauthorized access to your room. You want a cigarette?"

Hans nodded. She retrieved one from an unseen pocket, placed it between his lips, lit it. She lit one for herself also, and sat back on the floor by the body, examining it as she blew smoke from her nostrils. She frowned and shook her head. "Elena has been my assistant for three years."

The smoke was bringing Hans' jangling nerves to a milder vibration. "You need a better human resources department, lady." After three attempts on his life, he was almost growing accustomed to it. Not good.

A minute passed with no talking. Hans stared at the ceiling, smoked, trying to block out the visuals. He had to get the blood off.

"Be right back," he said

"Where are you going?"

"Gonna rinse the blood off."

He stood, unsure if his legs were going to support him. Once he was certain that his balance would hold him, he made his way to the bathroom, shutting the door behind him, wishing there was a lock. Turned the shower up hot and hard, wanting to scour himself raw. The water ran deep red down the drain, then pink, then finally clear. Hans didn't know how long he stood after that, breathing in steam, exhaling fear. Concentrating on calm, visualizing serenity. It only half worked.

There was a robe lying across the sink. Hans put it on, cinched it tightly, opened the door.

The body still lay on the floor. Onyx had moved to a chair, where she alternated between a cigarette and a glass of vodka, another full glass in front of the chair opposite. Hans sat, considered downing it, took a small sip. He flipped two fingers at her, the universal signal for "you got a cigarette?" She handed one across, along with a lighter. Two puffs, another drink, one more puff. He felt almost human again.

"First dead body?" Onyx asked.

"No. First murder?"

"No."

"You trusted her?"

"It's not her."

"Excuse me?"

"The body isn't Elena's."

"You know something about her body that tells you otherwise?"

"I know that it's human."

"Come again?"

"Look for yourself."

"I'd rather not."

"You need to see what I saw. It's important that you understand."

Hans stood carefully and walked over to the body. She'd come into his room naked to strangle him. Even dead, he could see that the body on the floor was nice. Except there was something off about it. It had no nipples, no pubic hair, no genitals. It looked like real flesh, translucent with veins, freckles, birthmarks. But where it should have had gender characteristics there was just smooth flesh. There was a small swell of breasts completely uninterrupted by anything. She looked like an oversize child's doll, though she'd certainly bled for real.

"Holy shit. You seen anything like this before?"

"Twice. Both assassins sent after me."

"Both of 'em exactly like this?"

"They were male, in appearance. But both lacking what she's lacking, or at least its equivalent."

"And you know she wasn't always like this?"

"Yes."

"She your lover?"

Onyx didn't answer right away

"You have no concept of crossing lines, do you, Hans?"

"Not really. I don't really care if she was or wasn't. Just want to know you're sure."

"No, we were not lovers. She was an employee, and a good acquaintance. The circumstances are incidental, but I can verify that she did not always look that way."

Hans looked up to the corpse's face. Two mouths, one grimacing, the other grinning and oozing blood. One eye was mostly closed, the other open. Another pair of pale silver eyes. He did not ask Onyx about this startling coincidence.

"Do you think it's really her?" he asked.

"No."

"Then what? A clone?"

"We can almost completely regrow every part of the body, why not the whole body?"

"What controls it?"

"There is a transmitter buried in the chest."

"How do you know this?"

"Exploration."

Hans turned to look at her. She held up the knife and smiled at him. "Sharpest blade possible, edge honed down to a point ten atoms across. Goes through bone as easily as anything else."

He shuddered, and returned to the chair and his drink.

"I saw your boss."

"Who?"

"Your boss. He came to see me earlier."

"I don't have a boss."

"Called himself James. Had the same color eyes as you."

"James? That's what he called himself?"

"Didn't think it was his real name."

"I don't know anyone named James. I don't have a boss."

"So, you're not planning on a trip to Salt Lake City?"

She did a good job at covering the hitch in her breath and eyes. "Actually, I am going to Salt Lake City, and you're coming with me."

"That's what he said. Told me he'd need my anonymity and knowledge of mountain back roads to get the package back."

She was staring at him with obvious animosity now.

"I don't know where you got this information, but if you have some source in my organization you would do well to…"

"I told you where I got it. A man calling himself James, same guy who drove me out of the shit yesterday, came here and told me you and I were going to Salt Lake to make a deal with a very dangerous man. Older guy. Had a western twang in the truck, but none when he was in this room."

"Enough, Mr. Ricker. I'm tired of listening to your bullshit. We should have your file cracked in the morning, and the truth of your occupation and abilities will come to light. Anything you wish to tell me beforehand?"

"I've been completely honest with you."

"We'll see. In the meantime, get some sleep."

"In here?"

"You do not wish to share your room with a corpse?" she teased, somewhat unsuccessfully.

"I'd prefer somewhere else."

She stood and motioned him to follow. They exited the room and entered another a few dozen feet down the hall. The room was identical to his last, sans corpse. Onyx left him without a word. He decided to try the bed again.

CHAPTER 4

Hans sat staring at the woman across the table from him, trying not to bolt from the room.

He'd been woken by a call from Onyx requesting his presence at breakfast. Her requests sounded more like orders. Beefy appeared with clothes, a pair of khakis and a casual button-up shirt, and sturdy shoes that fit. He'd stood there in the room while Hans got dressed, refusing all attempts to engage in conversation. They made their way to the previous day's boardroom. Hans sat down and waited, wishing he hadn't smoked his last cigarette.

Then the secretary had come in, plain as day and twice as alive. Hans started and stood, moving to put the table between them. She made no move toward him, gave him a perplexed look, and sat down at the other end. Onyx followed, sat, and also stared at him.

"Is there a problem, Hans?"

"What the fuck is she doing here?"

"Elena? She's my assistant. Surely you haven't forgotten her from yesterday."

"Last night. She was dead. Tried to kill me…"

"A dead woman tried to kill you?"

"No… alive… you killed her…"

"You're not making any sense. You seem to have had a stressful night. Bad dreams?"

"Fuck you, lady. What the hell is going on?"

"What is going on, Hans, is that we are here to decide if you are who you say you are, and if you will be of any use to me."

Hans was out of words. He stood and shifted his gaze from Elena to Onyx. His brain felt chewed by too many strange occurrences.

"Please sit down, Hans. Or shall I bring in Lev and have him strap you to a chair?"

Hans continued standing, grinding his molars. *Fine, if that's the way they want to play it.* He would show them he couldn't be rattled that easily. He took a seat as far from Elena as possible.

"Breakfast?" Onyx asked.

"Coffee."

"Anything to eat?"

"Toast," Hans said, biting out the words as short as he could.

Onyx nodded at Elena, who stood and left the room. Hans flinched slightly as she passed him.

Onyx leaned forward and tapped the table. A screen lit up in front of her and she began reading him the file.

"Hans Joseph Ricker, age thirty-four, son of Patricia and Joseph Ricker. Father a former police officer, now deceased, mother a mountain guide and expert hunter, now retired and living in an unincorporated township formerly known as Glenwood Springs."

"The people who live there still call it that." He didn't like hearing his history coming out of her mouth, but at least whomever had locked his file had not added anything so far.

"Sister is Greta Ricker, commander of the Denver Security forces. Because of her ranking you should be extended an encryption tier of five, though it was actually seven. Still saying you don't know why?"

"I don't."

"Current residence the aforementioned Glenwood Springs. Still live with your mother, Hans?"

"She has a small acreage. I live in one of the houses on her land."

"Currently unemployed, though you seem to have a wide and varied history of menial jobs. Class five driver's license, a rarity in this day and age. I don't have any drivers of that rating. Do you want a job as a chauffeur?"

Hans refused to rise to her baiting, playful though it was.

"Convicted and fined for a string of numerous minor offenses, though none in the last ten years."

"I had a misspent youth."

"Didn't we all? And a small note at the bottom from one Garrison Helton, PhD, a court appointed psychologist, saying that you suffered from severe authority issues, mild narcissism, delusions of grandeur, and, I quote, 'being one of the most stubborn, disagreeable human beings I have ever met'."

"That's a lot of analysis considering all I did was give him the finger and refuse to talk for the three mandated sessions."

"So, what we have here, Hans, is a file for a pretty much normal man who hates being told what to do and is maybe a little more attached to his mother than normal."

"You got that from the file?"

"That, and that you called your mother early this morning."

"You sure I didn't dream that?"

"I have a recording if you'd like to hear it."

"No thanks."

Elena brought in their food; coffee and toast for Hans and some pastry that Hans couldn't identify for Onyx. She resumed her seat next to Onyx and gave Hans a smile. Hans didn't return it.

"So, who is this guy we are going to see?"

Onyx was tearing pieces of the pastry in tiny bits, one at a time, working her way toward the fruit in the middle. She stopped to chew and wipe frosting from her fingers.

"Have you ever been to Salt Lake?"

"Never been one for religion. That sounds like all they got goin' on over there."

"Partially true, though what they really have 'going on' is human exploitation at the highest level."

"Slavery?"

"They wouldn't call it that."

"The masters never do."

"People are what they have. It's their strength. That and a level of religious fervor in the populace that keeps them sedate."

"The opiate of the masses, huh?"

"You've read Marx?"

"Groucho."

"Also, good."

Onyx took another moment, another bite, then continued. "The man we are going to see is a virtuoso of human exploitation. Prostitution and slavery are merely the edges of his operation."

"What else is there?"

"Organ trafficking, body trafficking, some even think he's been processing some of what his calls his 'stock' into food."

"So, what, we got a Soylent Green situation?"

"It's just a rumor, but I wouldn't put anything past this man. What's more, though his activities are not supported officially by the church and government, which is the same thing in Salt Lake, they seem to have chosen to look the other way due to the amount of capital he provides them."

"Not to mention a solution to their overcrowding problem."

"There is that."

"So, he's a criminal like yourself? You two should get along famously."

"No, Mr. Ricker. Not like myself. I do not exploit human beings like cattle."

"Then how do you exploit them, Ms. Li? Seems to me the only way to make the amount of money you have is to exploit them in one way or another."

"There is exploiting people, and then there is merely selling them the vices they would otherwise obtain elsewhere."

"You'll pardon me if I don't see much difference. You tread a fine line."

"Not as thin as the one you tread by continuing to goad me. Are you always so impertinent?"

"Most of the time I'm not as polite."

— «» —

The quickest way to Salt Lake was on one of the underground tramlines. Getting to the depot involved a short hop in Onyx's private jumpcraft. It was much more comfortable than the military vehicles Hans had been in recently, and the unseen pilot took greater care in keeping his passengers comfortable. He was much relieved that Elena had not accompanied them. Neither had Beefy. Onyx had decided Hans was no threat to her. From what he'd seen of her abilities he didn't disagree.

They headed toward the city center, cruising along a virtual boulevard for jumpcraft invisible to anyone but the pilot. The buildings grew tall around them, though the sensation was more that the jumpcraft was shrinking. The city below was a mass of white personal transport pods, whizzing quickly through intersections with no lights or signs, always missing one another even as they headed in cross directions. Hans could never ride in one of those things without imagining what would happen if the central network controlling them suddenly went down. Mass collisions at every intersection in the city. Another sign of humanity's over-reliance on computers.

The buildings opened out slightly into a ground-level park bordered by some of the few old buildings left in Denver. The capital building, a library, an art museum, all maintained fastidiously, no longer functional, just a memorial of times past.

The tram station was located at the north end of the park, unassuming in its above ground structure, though its bowels represented the ongoing work of humanity's greatest engineering project, to connect every major city in the world through ultra high-speed train lines, running in near vacuum in sealed tunnels at speeds that could top five thousand miles an hour. Currently it was possible, if prohibitively expensive, to live in a city like Denver and commute to New York. Eventually it wouldn't take much longer to go all the way to London or Paris for what almost amounted to a day trip. It was one of the few technological advances that Hans truly appreciated. He'd never actually been on one, and he was looking forward to the trip, even under these circumstances.

The jumpcraft landed close to the entrance, door opening once it was settled.

Onyx leaned forward and offered him a small black box.

"Do you know what this is?"

"Looks like an ID spoofer."

"So, you've had one before, then."

"It's the only way to get access to most of the city services if you've removed your tag. That one already set up for me?"

"With a few modifications. Your presence on the network will be deleted immediately after access."

"I thought that was impossible."

"You thought wrong."

Deleting tracking records from the city's encrypted networks in real time required a truly frightening amount of processing power. Hans didn't know why he should be surprised.

Onyx led him off the jumpcraft, moving quickly across the lot and into the depot. It was still early and there were not too many people moving around them, though a line had already formed in front of the depot. Onyx bypassed the line, bypassed the ticket office, and led them into a small side door that opened directly into an elevator shaft. Hans hated elevators. In his excitement, he hadn't really considered that the trams were nearly two miles below the surface. He stood with his back to the wall of the elevator as it accelerated downward, concentrating on breathing and trying not to think about the tons of rock above his head.

The trip down took nearly five minutes by his estimation, long enough that the weight settling back on him as the car came to a stop was disconcerting for a moment. The doors opened and a voice told them to follow the red path to their entrance. Scrolling arrows on the floor led down a wide, sparse corridor and bent around a far corner. They followed the path around a handful of corners, through identical corridors, finally emerging into the station proper.

Hans' breath caught slightly. There was no evidence of claustrophobia here, not in a room as massive as this. From ceiling to floor the room was probably a couple hundred of feet, stretching off out of sight in either direction. The room was filled with a maze of walkways, elevators, and gantries, all seemingly suspended by nothing. At the far end in front of him stood a bank of stacked horizontal tubes, each covered in sturdy-looking doors that repeated every twenty feet or so.

He'd slowed slightly in his observance, though Onyx had not. She looked over her shoulder at him. Angry with himself for appearing like some kind of country bumpkin, he put his head down and caught up.

"First time?"

"Not everyone can afford this type of thing."

"It is rather amazing. So much time and sweat to create just this one room, and there are thousands of depots like this, not to mention the hundreds of thousands of miles of pipelines connecting them. It's enough to awe anyone the first time, or even the hundredth."

"Yeah." He didn't know if she was trying to put him at ease or poke fun at him.

They crossed the depot, still following a stream of red arrows, which dead-ended at another elevator, this one made entirely of glass. Stepping in automatically closed the doors; the elevator rose a few dozen feet and opened onto a small, covered platform next to one of the tubes. Onyx moved near the door in the side as it slid open to reveal a functional yet plush train car with a small number of seats, entertainment viewscreens mounted on the walls, and even a small bar within reach of the seats.

"How much does one of these cars cost?" Hans asked.

"Twenty thousand."

"Jesus. For that price, I hope this isn't all there is."

"Privacy and security are the ultimate luxuries."

Even though there were probably thousands of people milling around in the depot outside, they had not come into contact with any of them. He moved into the cabin, taking a seat in one of the large chairs, flinching as he felt the material adjust itself to his form.

Onyx was smirking at him.

"What?"

"You don't like our modern furnishings, do you?"

"I like my chair to be a chair, not some damn amoeba."

"In this case it's more than mere comfort. The chair is there to help you absorb the higher G's as the train accelerates and decelerates."

"Yeah, and I'm sure there's no way to do that without having the damn thing fondle me. This chair come with a hand-job feature as well?"

"I think that option is self-serve only, though women may have better luck, even if accidentally."

"Didn't need to know that. They wash these things between use?"

"Relax, Hans, I'm just kidding."

"Not really sure I want you to be kidding."

"Afraid we might actually get along?"

"I don't really think that it's such a safe thing to be your friend."

"I can assure you that it's much safer than not being my friend."

— ⟨⟩ —

Her internal comm woke her, its familiar subsonic vibration bringing her up from dreamless sleep. She glanced across at the clock, sat up, rubbed her eyes.

"Grit here."

"It's your mother."

"It's two am, Mom."

"I know. I just spoke to Hans."

Her interest was piqued.

"Is he with you?" her mother continued.

"No, Mom. He ran off."

"He ran off from the hospital?"

"No, from… look, it's complicated. I've been trying to find him, but he's blocking his ID tag somehow."

"He's not blocking it. He had it removed."

"What? Who does he know that could do something like that?"

"I don't know, Greta, he told me after the fact."

"Where did he call you from?"

"How would I know that?"

"He could have told you."

"He didn't."

"Typical."

"Is he in trouble, Greta?"

Grit considered lying, decided against it. "Yeah, heaps of it."

"And what are you doing about it?"

"Trying to find him, I told you that."

"Not very successfully."

"He's a grown man without an ID tag to track. It makes things very difficult."

"I thought you were supposed to have the best technology."

"None of which I can use because Hans is not considered an official threat. I have some men willing to help look for him on their days off, and access to the city's basic network and tracking. Any more than that and I need an official mandate. I'm doing all I can."

"Please find him, Greta. He sounds like he's in a lot of trouble."

"Did he tell you that?"

"No, but he told me he loved me before hanging up."

"Shit."

Grit wasn't going to get back to sleep after a conversation like that. She flipped the switch next to her bed and got up from the bunk. The room was sparse; a few bunks, an equal number of chairs, a small table, all in military green. Just enough to eat and sleep, maybe play a card game or two. She pulled on her pants and shirt and headed out into the hall in search of coffee.

Even without an ID tag Hans' face should have shown up somewhere on the city's CCTV system. She'd pulled in a favor, was running heavy facial recognition software. Nothing so far. Either he'd left altogether or someone, maybe the person with the technology to crack the encryption on her comm, was protecting him. A scary unknown, one of a few hundred.

Only a couple of soldiers were in the mess hall. Duty never sleeps. They did not rise or salute when she came padding in bare-footed. It was considered appropriate, but Greta discouraged it. She filled a paper cup with bitter, overcooked coffee and retreated to an empty corner. Her comm blipped again, Gino this time.

"Hey, Grit, you awake?"

"Yeah, down in the mess."

Gino came in a few minutes later, hurried over to her table. He set down a portable in front of her.

"What's this?"

"Finally cracked the encryption on our assassin's file."

"He got a name?"

"Not really important right now. Origin is."

Grit studied the screen. "Salt Lake?"

"Just like you figured."

"So, Brigham sent him."

"Very likely."

"What about the bodies from yesterday?"

"No IDs yet, but it's the same encryption as the assassin."

"What was the total?"

"A hundred and twelve bodies around the trucks, plus two snipers holed up a few miles away. All dead, stab wounds to the head and chest."

"You think Brigham sent them too?"

"Yep."

"So do I."

"So, what do you want to do?"

"First get me another cup of coffee."

Gino took her empty cup and made his way over to the coffee machine, returning with more of the black goo. She sipped, made a face, sipped again.

"Why?" she asked.

"Why's the coffee so bad? I think they filter it through yesterday's laundry."

A small smile from Grit. Gino continued.

"If there's one thing Brigham's got its men, and he couldn't care less about 'em. He wouldn't hesitate to waste a hundred men to get to you."

"I agree, but how does he know where I'm going to be?"

"You weren't there either time."

"But I should have been. I can't keep relying on chance. Somehow, he's finding out where I'm supposed to be and beating me there. And both times he spoofed a signal that we thought completely unique."

Grit leaned back and grimaced through another sip of coffee, scrolling through the report summary. Something else caught her eye.

"What's this about an anatomical anomaly?" she asked.

"Huh?"

"Right here, it says two of the recovered bodies exhibited anatomical anomalies." Grit tapped the phrase to request more information. Nothing more. She needed to see it for herself. "Where are the bodies being stored?"

"Dunno."

"Who the hell makes a statement like anatomical anomalies and then doesn't elaborate?" Grit made a few inquiries; the bodies had been temporarily placed in the storage room downstairs. She rose and left the mess. Gino followed.

"Storage room" was probably a bit of a stretch for what amounted to an empty basement beneath the building they were in. The upper floors had been renovated for military use, but the lower was almost unnecessary, and was slowly filling up with whatever anyone didn't know what to do with. Plenty of broken electronics, vehicle tires, and even malfunctioning weapons were simply strewn across a concrete floor almost black with age. A large, sunken door allowed the mechanics to bring some of the smaller vehicles in for maintenance, the door probably being the reason that they'd decided to store the bodies down here.

An impressive pile of body bags lay stacked against the far wall from where the elevator opened. Grit checked a couple of numbers on the portable.

"We need numbers thirty-two and fifty-seven," she told Gino.

Grit walked to the side of the pile opposite and impulsively unzipped the first bag in front of her. The man inside had been stabbed through both of his eyes, same as the assassin in the hospital. This despite wearing a helmet able to stop most ammunition rounds. There were clean holes in the visor, exactly matching the holes in his face. Very little blood.

"You gonna help?" Gino asked from the other side. Grit zipped the bag up, began searching for her numbers.

They spent about ten minutes going over the ordered pile of bags a number of times. There were no bags with either a thirty-two or fifty-seven on them. Grit was about to start again when Gino took her arm.

"They're not here, Grit."

"Then where did they go?"

"I don't know, but it's unlikely to be a coincidence."

Grit brought up the portable again, thinking maybe she'd gotten the numbers wrong. Never hurt to double check. She scrolled through the summary to the bottom, then back to the top, her face becoming more frustrated.

"What the f...?"

"What is it?"

"The report's gone."

"The whole thing?"

"No, just the part about the anatomical anomalies."

"Who filed the report?"

"Doesn't say. Do you know how to bring up the log record on these things?"

"Here," he took it from her and brought up the log, "there's no one listed here."

"Is that possible?"

"Shouldn't be, wait a second." Gino was about to try something else when the screen abruptly blacked out. "Shit."

"What now?"

"This thing is broken," he banged on the screen a couple of times. The portable flashed on again, briefly running through its system check. Gino tried to navigate back to the file summary he'd brought for Grit. "It's not here anymore."

"What's not here?"

"The file. It's gone."

"Deleted?"

"Yes."

Confused silence passed between them. Something had deleted the file right under their nose, and removed two bodies.

"Gino, who was on body detail?"

"Hang on a second," Gino accessed the portable again, "Janson, Grant, Fortune, and Gregg."

"Are they still on site?"

"Yes."

"Let's go wake them up."

— «» —

Grit did not relish waking up her soldiers after they'd only had a couple hours of sleep. They went in order of location. Both Gregg and Janson appeared at their doors, half-heartedly saluting when they recognized the commander. Grit questioned them as quickly and subtly as she could. Neither had any recollection of any abnormality when they had scanned the bodies before loading. Grit believed them, or at least believed they were sincere.

Grant didn't answer his door. A quick search inside revealed an unmade bunk and not much else. Grit sent Gino to question Fortune while she examined the room more thoroughly. There was no sign of any personal effects, though that in itself wasn't abnormal in a place like this. Grit placed a hand on the bunk to feel for any residual body heat. The bunk was cold. Not a sign of guilt, but suspicious. She sat down on the bunk to collect her thoughts.

Two missing bodies, and one possibly missing soldier, though she hoped he had just stepped out for a meal and a smoke.

"Grit?"

"Yeah, Gino."

"Questioned Private Fortune. He doesn't seem to know any more than the other two. "

"Meet me in Grant's room."

"Gotcha."

"Network access request, ID Greta Ricker."

"Go ahead, Commander," said a virtual voice through her comm.

"What is the current location of Private Grant?"

There was short moment of silence, then "Private Grant is no longer on location, Commander."

"He's gone?"

"Yes, Commander."

"When?"

"I have no record of him leaving, Commander."

"None at all?"

"No, sorry, Commander."

"What is the last record you have of Private Grant?"

"He was last recorded in the basement."

"Where did he go after that?"

"I am sorry, Commander, I have no record of…" The voice cut off suddenly, replaced by a soft hiss.

"Commander Ricker, I strongly suggest you rescind your current line of questioning." The voice was similar to the other mystery voice, smooth and fluid, yet still sounding synthesized, though this one did not sound anywhere near as polite.

"Who is this?"

"The business you are sticking your nose is likely to be lethal. Your best course of action would be to terminate any further inquest."

"Whoever you are, you should know that the 'business' you refer to has resulted in the deaths of two of my men. It is my business. Who am I speaking to?"

"This is the only warning you will receive, Commander."

"Listen, fucko…"

Her head was abruptly filled with a loud electronic shriek. It vibrated the bones in her jaw and skull, filled her whole being. Pain was emanating from her lower right jaw, where her comm sat against the bone. It quickly increased in intensity, seizing the muscles in her face. She bit down hard on her tongue. Fire, copper, blood, shrieking. She tried to stand, equilibrium suffering, went down on a knee.

Gino came in then, saw her crouched on the floor, struggling to rise, blood dripping from her mouth. He crouched and turned her face to his. The lower part of her jaw seemed to be reddening and blistering on the right side. Her comm was killing her.

He lifted her on to the bed and slapped her once. Her eyes opened, face seizing unnaturally. She reached down, placed a hand on his belt knife, and looked in his eyes with determination.

Gino understood, didn't question. He put his knees on her shoulders to keep her from struggling and grabbed her underneath her chin. Heat was emanating from the comm beneath the skin. He moved as quickly as he could, knowing he had to be clean. Knife at her lower chin. A sharp jerk, and blood flowed. His hand moved, found the device, seared his fingertips. Moved the tip of the knife beneath, against bone. Gino pushed down until he heard a sharp crack. He hoped it was metal and not bone. The device came out whole, still burning his hand. He threw it to the floor and watched as it softened and melted. Greta stopped jerking, but was still alive, face covered in blood, hand over the wound. His own comm was chirping.

"Captain, is the commander ok?"

"Send a medic immediately."

A stolen kiss. "Don't you die on me, lady."

— «» —

The g-force readout slowly increased on the screen at the front of the cabin. Currently it sat at 1.9. Hans was glad for the chair. Acceleration pushed him back into soft gelatin, the seat hugging every curve. Turning his head was an effort. Onyx appeared to be sleeping.

The meter continued its slow rise, now sitting at 2.2. Hans estimated he weighed about 420 pounds. What if the mooring on the chairs came loose? Would the crash into the wall behind him be lethal?

"Relax your breathing," Onyx said, clearly not sleeping, then. "Hyperventilation is no fun in two Gs."

"How many times have you done this?" His eyes felt like they were resting on the front of his cerebellum, nose pressing back toward his throat, joining his teeth there. She wasn't affected at all.

"Plenty. We're in the worst of the G's now. Keep your head forward and still or you'll strain your neck. Let the chair absorb all the extra weight. They're rated for a thousand pounds. They're not going anywhere."

"How long does this keep up?" He let the chair cradle his head, cringing as it crawled around his skull.

"Another twenty minutes, then we get a brief respite before the deceleration. Close your eyes and stop staring at the meter."

"I'm not."

"Mmm-hmmm."

"How fast will we get going?"

"On a short trip like this not much more than about twenty-five hundred, I imagine."

Two thousand five hundred miles per hour. In a capsule that was held only millimeters from the sides of the tube by electromagnets. He was not enjoying this as much as he thought.

"What happens if the magnets fail?"

"You wouldn't even have time to scream. For a man who walked so boldly into my office expecting to be killed, you sure sound worked up, Hans."

"Walking I can control, this is something else..."

"This train has a sparkling safety record, no accidents in ten years."

"Only takes one."

"True, but not today."

The G's skittered briefly between 2.3 and 2.4. Hans' organs were trying to make hasty exit out his backside. He concentrated on breathing slower, ignoring the elephant on his chest. Time stretched out as he stared obsessively at the readout. 2.2 – 2.1 – 1.9. He could feel normality beginning to return to his limbs. 1.5. The strain on his neck disappeared. 1.3. He could feel himself sliding forward in the chair again. 1.0. The cabin speaker dinged. The mini bar slid back out from its alcove in the wall. Onyx rose, stretched.

"You should try to get up and walk around a bit. It will help."

After the increased G's Hans felt nearly weightless, every movement about to launch him across the room. He stood carefully and stretched his back. Onyx bent at the waist to the point where her head went between her knees.

"You made out of rubber or something?"

"Dancer's limbs."

"Learn that from your mom?"

"Yes." It was the first time he'd asked her about her past that she'd not seemed upset. She moved over to the mini bar. "Drink?"

"No, but I'll take a cigarette if you got it."

"No smoking on the trains."

"Who'd know?"

"The train would know. Emergency stop and we'd be put off at the next terminal. You don't want to experience an emergency stop. Sure, you don't want a drink?"

"No thanks."

Onyx poured herself some vodka, took a sip, grimaced, returned the glass to the tray. Hans smirked at her. "Not up to your standards?"

"Chinese. I don't drink Chinese vodka."

"I didn't realize the Chinese made vodka."

"The Chinese make a bit of everything, none of it well."

"Not even international criminals?"

She looked at him for a moment, arms crossed. "No, not even that, though I would not reach even their standards."

"Why's that?"

"They would say I am not ambitious enough."

"Because you don't sell drugs or whores?"

"That, and that it is part of my inherently inferior makeup."

"The Russian half?"

"Half Russian and female."

"I don't know about the Russian part, but I know plenty of women your friends in China wouldn't enjoy crossing."

"Your sister?"

"Yeah, Grit would hand them their asses in a plastic bag."

"I don't disagree, your sister is a formidable woman."

"She's hell on wheels."

"Another way to put it."

Hans took a moment to walk around the small cabin, just pacing to get the blood flowing. Onyx returned to her chair. The speaker chimed again, instructing them to return to their seats. Hans sat gingerly, unsure what to expect. The chairs turned to face the back of the cabin, the readout switching walls.

"You don't like your Chinese half, do you?" he asked impulsively. The g-meter had begun its rise, disorienting in its similarity even though he knew they were slowing.

"It's part of me. Like or dislike means little."

"But you still don't like it."

"Why do you insist on goading me?"

"It angers you when I call you Ms. Li. I imagine it would even more-so if I were to call you Kaori."

"You're treading very thinly, Mr. Ricker." The G's were now back to 1.9 and climbing. Hans didn't want to smile, not sure if he could get his lips back together.

"What about Illiyana?

"You call me Onyx."

"But Illiyana's what you call yourself, isn't it?"

"Onyx will do." She didn't sound angry.

— 《》 —

Gino was standing at the windows when Grit came to. The sun was going down behind the mountains, backlighting him and the cloud of smoke around his head. Nice view. She tried to speak but realized her jaw wouldn't move. She clanged a hand against the bed railing. He turned and came back to stand beside her.

"They've temporarily immobilized your jaw, shouldn't be for more than about forty-eight hours. The doctor said they didn't want to risk you tearing open any weakened blood vessels." He sat down and offered her the mobile in his hand. "You can type on this if you want. I know it's not ideal."

Grit took the mobile, reached up to feel her jaw. Something tight and smooth covered the lower right side of her face. No pain though.

How long have I been out?

"About twelve hours, the medic said there was surprisingly little damage."

Maybe you should have been a surgeon.

Gino laughed a bit at that. "Most of the damage was cauterized by the heat from your comm."

We need to start removing internals from the soldiers, you first.

"Already on it," Gino turned his head to show her the bandage on his own jaw. "Medical's removing them as we speak. What happened, Grit? Was it a fault?"

No, she paused to think a minute, *whatever is in our systems is able to use our tech against us.*

"Jesus." Gino stood up and paced. "It deletes files practically as we're looking at them, makes bodies disappear, almost kills you with your own communicator. How the fuck does it do that?"

Grit shrugged.

The medic came in then, looking exhausted. He took a scan of her jaw, pronounced it well protected, and made a very cursory interrogation before Gino shooed him out.

We need to see Onyx, she typed.

"Huh uh, lady, you're staying here. With you compromised I'm the commander in charge. You're on medical leave until I get an OK from the doctor. You can't lead a squad with no voice, anyway."

She grabbed his shoulder, pulling him down toward her. He didn't know where her strength came from, but he certainly didn't have the ability to resist. She jabbed at the message on her portable, then pointed at herself and Gino, indicated the building around her, shook her head.

"Just us?"

Grit nodded, still staring in his eyes.

"Jesus, Grit, you want two people to go after this lady when she seems to have the drop on our entire organization?"

She nodded again, and dug her fingers into Gino's shoulder for a second before releasing him and typing for a few moments.

Not putting my soldiers at risk. Just the two of us. Two of my men are dead. My brother is missing. Something that can access and subvert our systems at will is after us. She's the only one who may know what's going on, and she may have Hans.

"And if she's the culprit?"

I'll take her down. I'll do this by myself if I have to. You in or not?

Gino stared at her.

She grabbed his shoulder again, wouldn't let him turn away, dared him to turn her down.

"OK. I'm in. When do we leave?"

She sat up and climbed off the bed.

— «» —

Hans' first impression of Salt Lake was the smell, the odor of too many people in too close quarters, like animals packed in crates. Sweat and salt and breath and manure, humanity's myriad of exhausts melding, forming, fighting for dominance in the enclosed structure of the depot.

They'd come up through the tube systems in a gallery so identical that it was like they'd never left. Another disconcertingly long elevator ride, this one with positive Gs, and the doors had opened not on Denver's efficient, computerized people funnel, but a massive gothic structure more akin to the great train depots of a few hundred years before. People packed in nearly wall-to-wall. An ocean of smiling white conformity. Men all dressed in black slacks and white button-ups, the relatively few women in floor-length skirts and modestly colored tops, with the occasional sprinkling of a plaid sweater vest for sparkle. Hair brown or blonde, cut just to the ears for men, middle of the back for women, adornments minimal.

It was terrifying, made more so by the surprising lack of noise. There was a deep and persistent roar of feet milling about, luggage rolling, a crying child. But he could not see a single person engaged in conversation. Thousands of people were resisting their natural urge to chatter incessantly.

Onyx didn't seem to notice, and led them across a suspended walkway over the silent sea. Hans was concerned what the massive organism would make of the pair of them, her in tight black slacks and matching shirt and jacket, two-inch heels clicking loudly on the tiled walkway, him in the suit she had provided this morning, also primarily black, its one concession a blue-gray shirt. Not exactly cheerful, not exactly blending in. No one seemed to notice.

The checkout station was manned by real people, more of the same from the floor below. Their attendant gave them a smile that barely made it up her cheeks, let alone to her eyes.

"Reason for visit?"

"Business." Onyx continued to look completely nonchalant.

"What kind of business?" The voice contained so little emotion Hans thought she could have been animatronic.

"The kind I keep to myself, are you done with my bags?" If the woman was taken aback by Onyx's abruptness she showed no sign.

"Of course, please avail yourself of one of our brochures in the lobby. It contains important guidelines for visitors." The way she said "visitors" did not sound very welcoming.

"Been here before, no need, bags please?"

"We strongly encourage you to…"

"Yes, I know, stay out of your churches and restricted restaurants and any place else you don't want infidels to see. Give me my bags."

The woman ran out of words. She handed across Onyx's two small bags. Hans stepped forward and took them for her, old habits running deep. The woman's smile stayed affixed.

They continued toward the exit, the number of people around them increasing rapidly, though Hans and Onyx moved in their own little pocket

"This place is a nightmare," Hans said.

"It only gets worse."

"Nice handling of the baggage lady."

"She expected you to speak, wasn't enjoying me taking charge. Also, they're trained to delay as much as possible."

"What for?"

"Better luggage inspection. Often things are removed… or added."

The doors opened on a mass of people the likes of which Hans had never imagined. Every corner, every sidewalk, every doorway and entrance mobbed by the similarly clothed masses. Even the street was partially covered, the crowds parting for large, slow-moving buses and private conveyances, closing up on the other side. The smell increased tenfold; it was like being trapped in a closet with a hippopotamus.

Still, it was impossible not to notice that, despite everywhere he could see being crammed with people nearly shoulder to shoulder, the pocket around them continued, an imperfect sphere of empty sidewalk. No one would even look at them. They were a pocket of strangeness in the ocean of conformity, to be ignored and avoided.

"What happens if I reach out and flick one of their ears or something?"

Onyx actually laughed a little at that.

"Are we getting a cab or something, or did you bring a surfboard?"

"There's supposed to be transportation waiting."

They moved toward the street, the sea of humanity continuing to part around them, the path opening onto a sleek black limo, windows tinted to midnight. Two men stood waiting, standard dress slightly altered by the black suit jackets and smart black caps. Onyx strode up to them.

"You Brigham's men?"

The man looked at her in surprise, glared over at Hans.

"Don't ignore me, little boy, and stop looking at my assistant."

The man turned back to Onyx, avoided her eyes.

"Brigham?"

"Yes… ma'am."

"Good… take me to him." She turned to Hans, "Put the luggage in the trunk."

"Yes, ma'am." Hans was suppressing his smile. He made a show of putting the baggage in the back and then returning to open the door for Onyx, climbing in after her. Through the thick partition separating the back and front he could hear the front doors open and shut. It was a somewhat Spartan interior, windows tinted so it was nearly impossible to see outside. Probably in a place like this private space was the ultimate in luxury, with little else needed.

"Two for two," he said.

"Hmm?"

"The baggage lady and the chauffeur. You seem to enjoy making them uncomfortable."

"Women are not supposed to be in charge here. Any form of female assurance and confidence is strongly discouraged. This is one of the last bastions of ancient idiocy. I hate everything about this place."

"Haven't seen much worth liking yet."

"You won't. This place is what happens when archaic morality overpowers common sense, not the least of which is the continued state and church encouragement to breed out of control."

"How can they fit them all? There's no more room."

"Most of the buildings here extend down into the ground further than they do up. The tenements extend downward for miles, with poorer and poorer families continuing to dig the holes deeper. The federal government has held them to their initial square mileage, same as any other city-state."

"So, they're cave dwellers?"

"Yes."

Hans could see where the rumors of cannibalism had come from. To apply for city-state status, a city had to prove that it could provide for its current populace without expanding its borders. Once it was accepted it could not extend its limits. This was why Denver had invested so heavily in its massive vertical farms and enacted strict birth rate controls. In the few moments Hans had observed any part of Salt Lake's external structures he had seen some large buildings, but nothing like the mile-high towers in Denver. Still, if they were housing everyone underground there could be giant farms on the outskirts. The alternative was gruesome, the Eloi eating the Morlocks.

"You think they'll pull over somewhere so I can get a pack of cigarettes?"

"There's no smoking here."

"In the car?"

"In the city."

"You're shittin' me."

"No. No smoking. No drinking. No mind-altering substances of any kind."

"I thought cigarettes were one of their main exports?"

"They're perfectly happy to sell vices to others, just not partake. At least not out in the open."

"Something you know for a fact."

"There will always be a market for vices, Hans. In places like this the price only goes up."

"You make a lot of money here?"

"No. I refuse to bankroll this failed travesty."

"Y'know something, Yana, for a criminal you got a lot of strange hang-ups."

"Some would call them ethics," she subtly bridled at his familiarization of her name, but let it pass.

"Only those who don't know you're one of the bad guys."

"Bad girl. I will never be one of the guys, particularly not here."

Hans had heard about the state of women here. Polygamy, state-sanctioned prostitution, girls married as early as ten or eleven. Not even countries like India and China did that kind of thing anymore. Women were property here, second to even the lowliest man. Yet the city had no legal way to keep them here, at least officially. Despite this, people of any gender leaving Salt Lake were few and far between. A cult of personality overriding common sense. Membership as a city-state required adherence to the human rights documents drafted as an addendum to the original constitution. No state had the right to restrict rights the way they were here, but religious groups were in a different category all together. Fear of divine punishment was at least as effective as civil threats.

The car continued its slow progression. Hans could faintly hear its horn, honking regularly. Probably clearing away pedestrians.

"Have you ever met this guy Brigham before?"

"No."

"No dealings with him."

"He and I have been in a state of aggression for the last year or so. He's taken an interest in opening up business in Denver. I cannot abide that."

"That where you and Grit met up?"

"Yes, we had a common interest in keeping him out."

"Enemy of my enemy and all that?"

"Exactly."

Hans had been doing his best to keep the questions to a minimum, though the atmosphere between them had lightened a bit since they arrived. A united front against massive insanity. He had enjoyed helping her annoy the drivers by playing the servant. She may have taken it a bit more seriously than that. Still, he'd come to her almost literally baring his neck, and she'd spared it. Maybe she thought she owned him now and could treat him like a pet, though that was probably being a bit disingenuous on his part. Still, too many things sat between them for trust to exist, not the least of which being that she had played some sort of horrible prank on him last night. If she thought pretending to save his life from whatever that neutered thing was meant he owed her something she'd be in for a surprise. Whether or not she was actually ignorant of his other visitor was harder to decipher. Either she was in on setting him up for what was about to happen, or her benefactor was working a different angle.

Either way it didn't bode well for his continued survival. He didn't think anyone really expected him to leave Salt Lake alive. He had other plans.

CHAPTER 5

The limo canted downward slightly, headed down a ramp. A couple of turns, down another ramp, then the car's engine ceased its quiet rumble. Doors opening at the front, closing again. Onyx waited calmly for the doors to open. Hans tried to follow her lead.

The doors didn't open. Instead the floor beneath the car began to rise.

"The guy has an elevator for his car?"

"Ground level is for peasants. Height is hierarchy here."

"Let's hope he's not short then."

When the car finally came to a halt the men who opened the door bore no resemblance to the dress code out on the street. Three-piece suits in tweeds and linens, leather shoes, immaculately coifed hair. Still looked like thugs, though.

A pair of giant hands reached in and removed him bodily from the seat. The man placed him, off-balance, on a marble floor and turned to extend a hand to Onyx. She gave him a look that could melt the floor. He rescinded the offer.

The garage, if one could call it that, was decked out like the Sistine Chapel, with every surface covered with ornamentation, painting, and sculpture, all in a style that wouldn't have been out of place in the Renaissance, though Hans was no expert. The whole place was dimly lit by ancient incandescents.

A small fleet of limos exactly like the one they had arrived in extended down the corridor, jet-black modernity sitting anachronistically in the middle of the room. There were no windows to break the oppressive atmosphere. Luxury was not seeing outside to the travesty on the streets.

Thug One gestured for them to follow. Onyx moved in front and followed, Hans behind, Thug Two taking up the rear. These guys needed numbered nametags. They moved through a heavy wooden door and into another massive hallway, a near duplicate of the garage. Whereas Onyx's headquarters had been a statement of sparse, modern elegance, this place was designed to cow its visitors under the weight of overwhelming gaudiness. Upon closer inspections, the walls showed their true tackiness. It was not merely Renaissance ornamentation, but a great, incomprehensible mess of styles and ornamentation and copies of significant works of art, any era, any style, as long as it fit the available space. Numerous shoddy recreations of Greek sculpture, modern abstracts, paintings of nude debutantes toe to toe, splashes of all styles. No wonder the place was lit so dimly; it could never have held up under real light. It was a cheap movie set trying to emulate greatness, hoping the audience would not pay too much attention to the backdrop.

The hall they moved into next nearly dwarfed the massive figure standing next to its great gothic fireplace. High ceilings arched thirty feet above the floor, pillars connecting them to the ground, with giant tapestries covering stone walls. Windows along both walls stretched nearly their full height, yet the view was peculiar. Beyond the glass was not the massive dirty sea of Salt Lake's humanity, but a view more akin to the Scottish Highlands. There was an ocean stretching below craggy rock cliffs, mossy hills extending into mist.

"He's built himself a throne room," Hans muttered under his breath, the comment for Onyx only.

"It's a perfect room for a tyrant."

The man himself did not disappoint. A mountain of tweed and leather, nearly wide as he was tall, posing stiffly in front of his fireplace for effect, turning casually, faking warm surprise and a friendly smile, propelling his bulk toward them, hands extended. He moved first toward Hans, standing more than a head taller.

"Welcome," he said, his meaty mitt swallowing Hans' hand, slapping him on the back with the other, jowls vibrating. "You are Hans?" He hadn't even looked in Onyx's direction.

Hans took a step back, reclaiming his hand from the fleshy cave. "I'm the help." He gestured toward Onyx, enjoyed watching Brigham's false smile crumble slightly before altering again into its grotesque imitation of warmth.

Brigham shifted to take in Onyx, beady eyes now decidedly predatory, disapproving. Onyx was unmoved.

"Surely I will not be expected to deal with a woman in such important matters as this?" The comment was still directed at Hans.

"Fraid so, Mr. Brigham, I'm just the muscle."

Onyx sniffed quietly. Brigham forced a nod in her direction, did not extend a hand, and instead left them nervously fluttering over his vested gut.

"Mrs.... Onyx?"

"Just Onyx."

"Sorry?"

"Just Onyx, no Mrs."

"Ms. then?"

"Just Onyx."

Brigham noticed his loose hands, pushed them into expansive pockets, retrieved a blinding white handkerchief, and wiped his brow. He retreated to one of the great windows with its impressively fake view. He probably thought he struck a dashing silhouette.

"Well, Onyx, Hans."

"Mr. Ricker." Hans couldn't help adding to his discomfort.

"Onyx, Mr. Ricker, my men will show you to your rooms."

"That won't be necessary, Brigham," Onyx's voice was dark, lethal. "We came here on business. I would prefer it ended quickly."

"Surely you would prefer to freshen up, make yourself pretty, have a good meal." His smile had returned.

"Not really. What I would prefer is to have my property back in my hands."

"Your property, I hardly think..."

"Yes, Mr. Brigham, mine. I came here for an exchange. Where is my property?"

"A discussion for this evening, after a meal and a drink." His voice did not sound warm anymore. "My men will escort you." The two thugs moved to either side of Onyx, each placing a hand on her shoulder.

Hans didn't see what happened next, as he was looking out one of the windows, noticing that there were actually sheep moving around on the hillside. He heard a soft crack followed by scuffling feet, a sharp intake of breath, an insistent grunt, a yell as a body hit the ground. All this in the time it took him to turn and glance back at her.

One of the thugs was lying on the ground, holding his knee and cradling a hand against his chest; two fingers were broken. The other thug had backed up against a nearby pillar, scrabbling at his throat and unsuccessfully trying to draw breath. Onyx stood where she had before, legs slightly farther apart, arms across her chest, one hand holding the frighteningly sharp black blade.

"Bitch." Brigham sounded petulant, childish. "I can have twenty men here in thirty seconds."

The knife whisked across the room and buried itself in the window next to Brigham's head, shorting out the screen, ruining the view. "But can you get them here before I bury the next one in your fat face, Mr. Brigham?"

Brigham reached out, grasped the blade, and gave it a tug. It stayed in the screen.

"Please, Ms.… Onyx, just Onyx, you must give me time to retrieve the item. I do not keep it on the premises. It's too dangerous. If you would be willing to partake of my hospitality for a short time, then join me for dinner, we can make this go much more smoothly." He wiped his forehead, now glistening brightly.

Onyx stood for a moment, considering. "All right, Brigham, but I have ground rules."

Brigham raised his eyebrows.

"One, the next person that lays a hand on me loses considerably more than a couple fingers. Two, I am in charge here, no matter what your primitive pubescent mind considers proper. You speak to me as an equal. Three, do not think that because I came here seemingly alone that I have no backup. Any bullshit from you and I'll bring this building down around your ears."

Hans would say this for him, Brigham regained his composure quickly. Already the warm, avuncular smile was back on his face. He folded his arms across his belly, cocked his head slightly.

"Very well, Onyx. Your conditions shall be followed. Now, if you please, I have other business to attend to. I humbly request you avail yourselves of my considerable hospitalities. I have prepared a pair of suites for you. If you would be willing to retire to them for the time being I will handle my previous commitments and we can finish this despicable business quickly."

"Fine. I don't want to wait too long, Brigham, and don't send me any of your special luxuries."

— «» —

There was a naked girl in Hans' bed.

They'd separated him from Onyx and walked her off in another direction, four men following her at a distance as she clicked down the marble hallway.

The room was an explosion of crass ornamentation. The decorator, unable to decide which culture contained the gaudiest schemes, had turned the room into an eye-bleaching mixtape of brightly colored sashes, pillows, gauze, stripes, dots, and paisleys. The front room held a small table, a loveseat, a wingback chair, and a viewscreen that took up the entire wall. The back was a sultan's harem, pillows strewn everywhere, the circular bed taking center stage, raised on a pedestal.

The girl was sitting up on her knees, sheet pulled up over her breasts, posing how she had probably been told men liked.

"This your room?" he asked her.

"No." She was trying to sound sultry, wasn't succeeding. "It's yours, I'm a luxury."

"Luxury, that your name?"

"No, I come with the room."

"So, what, you're a prostitute?"

"I am here to satisfy your needs."

"Sex?"

"If that's what you want." It would have been more seductive if she hadn't sounded so scared.

Hans walked through the doorway, leaned against the wall.

"How old are you?"

"Old enough."

"What is old enough in this place? Eighteen? Sixteen? Ten?"

"What do you mean?"

"Where are your parents?"

"I don't know what you mean."

"It's not a hard question."

Hans walked over to a large closet door and opened it to reveal a cornucopia of tired sex clichés. Harem girl, schoolgirl, cheerleader, even a nun's habit. He riffled through, looking for something for the girl. He found a terrycloth robe, dusty and unused, shook it out a little.

"Do you have any normal clothes?"

"I can wear whatever you wish me to."

He threw the robe at her.

"Put that on, I'll turn around. Let me know when you're decent."

She had no response, confused by his lack of interest. He heard her shuffle off the bed and into the robe. He turned around, realizing too late she'd left it open in front. Hans put his head down, told her to tie it shut.

"You don't like what you see?"

"Tie the damn robe!"

She closed it, pouted at him, gave the belt a sharp tug, and stood staring with her arms across her chest. Hans returned to the front room, flopped on the loveseat, feet up on the side. He was exhausted. His body was nearly recovered, but it had been a strange day and now he'd been imprisoned in this wonderful slice of hell. He didn't know if this would be his final resting place, but they'd locked the door behind him and he didn't see another exit.

The girl stood in the doorway, unsure of what to make of him.

"You got a cigarette?"

"Cigarettes aren't allowed."

"What about a beer?"

"Alcohol isn't allowed."

"Cigarettes aren't allowed, beer isn't allowed, but it's OK to fuck a ten-year-old on a bed where the sultan threw up. What kind of screwed up place is this?"

"I'm not ten."

"Eleven, forgive me."

"I'm twelve."

Hans didn't respond, pulled a bright blue pillow under his head.

"Do you have anything to drink?"

"I can get you some soda or fruit juice, maybe some milk." Her lip trembled. Way to go Hans, the terror of young prostitutes everywhere. He tried again.

"Can I have a glass of water… please?"

She frowned at him and walked back into the bedroom. He heard her talking softly, requesting water from somewhere. She returned to stand in the doorway, staring at him, trying to start a sentence. Minutes passed.

There was a soft bing and she went to the door, retrieved a small silver tray with a single glass and a carafe of water. She placed it on the table next to him and returned to her place by the doorway.

"Will you sit down or something?"

"I'm not allowed to sit in here."

"You're shitting me?"

"No."

"Look, you have to do what I want right?"

"Yes."

"Sit down. It's an order."

She paused for a second. He gestured angrily to the large wingback chair across from him. She took the seat. Hans sat upright to face her, poured some water in the glass. The carafe was heavy, real glass, maybe crystal. He looked at her, small tears running down her face. The Big Bad Wolf had scared poor Little Red. What an asshole he was.

"Here, have some water," he extended the glass.

She shook her head almost imperceptibly.

"Are you thirsty?"

"I'm not allowed to drink from the good dishes."

Hans put his head in his hands, resisting the urge to yell at her. She was already crying. None of this situation was her fault; she was as much a prisoner as him.

"Look… um… what's your name?"

"Lorilei."

"Look, Lorilei, you obviously have some expectations of how this is supposed to go, and I'm not living up to my end. I'm not interested in sleeping with you, and I find it disgusting that Brigham would assume I would be, but that's not your fault. Can you let somebody know I don't need you? Maybe they can take you to another room?"

"I live here."

"Here where?"

"In this room. I'm not allowed anywhere else."

"Ever?"

She just shook her head.

"Jesus, how long?"

"I don't know."

"You live here and you're not allowed on the furniture."

"Only if the guests require it."

Hans' hatred of Brigham was growing by the minute.

"Where do you sleep? Are you allowed in the bed?"

"I…" she stumbled, "I have a little place."

"Show me."

"I'm not supposed…"

"Show me… please."

She was shocked by his request, shocked enough that the tears had stopped.

"Lorilei … is that what you parents call you?"

"I don't know my parents. My, my nanny used to call me Lori."

"Lori then. As your current guest, I would like you to show me where you stay when no one is here."

She considered, rose, wiped her face, turned quickly and walked into the bedroom. Hans followed. She made her way to the far corner and unlatched a camouflaged door, its height nearly a foot shorter than her. She stood looking at him.

He moved over, looked into the small alcove behind the wall. A cot with a little quilted blanket, its faded pattern still showing flowers and small animals. A shelf on the wall with a few personal items. Further back a toilet not much more than a hole in the floor, and a shower-head sticking from the wall.

"You stay in here when there's no guest?"

"Yes."

"All day."

"Except meals and an hour in the gym."

Hans was shocked, angry, completely twisted up, helpless. How many more rooms like this were there in the building? In the city? Was this the norm? His anger was wasted, its only target undeserving. He was here now, as trapped as the girl. He didn't expect anyone to come let him out.

Lorilei radiated waves of trepidation. What could he do for her?

"That big viewscreen in there, does it show movies?"

"We usually watch people in other rooms on it."

"That's not really my thing. Have you ever seen a real movie? One without sex, I mean?"

Lorilei shook her head. Her tears had dried a little.

"You think you could get them to bring us some popcorn?"

—— ‹›› ——

Does he suspect?

"I don't think so; he's too assured of his own greatness and invulnerability. Are your troops in place?"

They've been infiltrating the upper floors for the past few hours. A minimum of resistance has been encountered.

"How many?"

Fifteen hundred.

"And you're sure Hans can control this thing?"

He doesn't have any of the normal internal modifications, making him immune to its side effects.

"So, it won't kill him."

I don't think so.

"Think?"

Hope.

"I'd rather he stayed alive."

—— ‹›› ——

Hours passed before Brigham sent his men to retrieve Onyx. She'd waited patiently, checking and rechecking her plans. Patience and planning were her strengths, why she had risen to the top. The plan was not foolproof, but there was no such thing.

They led her back to the throne room, still keeping their distance. In her absence, a large table had been brought in. Tons of heavy stone and marble, ornamented with endless dizzying motifs, gilded with precious metals, set with crystal goblets, china plates, cloth napkins. Candles smoking in their gold sconces. Brigham had changed into what he probably thought was rather dapper evening wear, though the tuxedo only enhanced his penguin-like waddle, and the collar pushed the folds up on his neck, like it was trying to eat his head.

"Madame Onyx," he placed his bulk in an oversized chair, "please, have a seat."

Onyx remained standing. "I didn't come here to watch you stuff your maw, Brigham."

"John, please."

"We're not on a first-name basis." She crossed her arms, moved her feet slightly apart. "Do you have my property or not?"

Brigham took no notice, or at least appeared not to. Onyx doubted he was as oblivious as he let on. He leaned back and placed his hands on his belly. "You are a very disagreeable woman."

"And you are the most repugnant representative of humanity I've ever met."

Brigham laughed at that. "Well, now that we have that out in the open, are you sure you won't join me for a meal? My chefs have been working overtime today, creating a rather extravagant repast."

"I don't want your food, Brigham. I don't want your company. I don't want your hospitality. I want what belongs to me, and then I'm leaving here as quickly as I can."

Brigham took a moment to pose, not quite sure whether he wanted his hands under his chin (or at least where it should have been), or continuing to rest on his gut. Professorial versus casual. Casual eventually won.

"Very well. Do you have my money?"

"It will be transferred to your account as soon as the package is in my hands."

Brigham nodded and reached beneath the table, bringing up a rectangular metal box. It fit easily in his huge hands, though he did not look comfortable holding it. He placed it on the table to his side. "Please, take it; I'll be glad to have it gone. It's resulted in the deaths of three of my men already."

"Glad to hear it."

She moved forward around the table, planning her next move. She reached for the box.

Brigham's hand shot out and closed on hers, his speed and strength surprising, his bulk shifting out of the chair, bringing his face close. She could smell the remains of his last meal on his breath.

Nothing was said as a battle of wills ensued, the eyes the major player. Muscles strained. Then Brigham did something truly childish.

His spittle landed on her face. He looked about ready to spit again, but the knife embedded in his wrist cut him short. The color drained from his face, and his eyes dipped down to see her hand pressing against his wrist. She twisted the knife savagely.

Brigham roared. Once again, his speed was surprising and disconcerting. She was unable to completely dodge the wild blow that landed on her head, knocking her back as he involuntarily let go of her hand, leaving her sitting on the floor. He screamed as he yanked the knife from his wrist and stood there panting, dripping blood on the floor. He took a step forward, brought a foot up to stomp on her, but she was back on her feet, face snarling, another knife in her hand. Brigham took another wild swing. She dodged this one easily, and put the knife through the back of his other hand. He immediately swung the hand back, catching her off balance, knocking her to the floor a second time, cracking her skull and bringing stars. She tried to recover and back up, but a large boot caught her in the stomach, winding her and sending her skidding across the floor. She tasted blood.

Brigham was coming; she could hear his pained panting. She tried to pull herself up, felt something in her abdomen give way, crashed back down.

The roof fell in.

— «» —

The viewscreen turned out to have quite a selection, though his request for popcorn fell through. Lorilei didn't know what to make of it at first, sitting next to him on the loveseat. She tried to drape herself across his lap, remove her robe, kiss his ear and neck. Each time he pushed her away, explained that he just wanted her to watch the movie. She sulked for a bit, but the movie won her over.

They watched some flashy new high-tech 3D thing for kids, full of bright colors and loud sounds, something about a dragon and a spaceman. It was terrible, but Lorilei was enraptured.

Afterward he talked her into a much older movie, one of his favorites. Black and white, with a jaded private eye and a fiery redhead. She was less interested than the first, but still sat quietly and watched.

She fell asleep on his shoulder. He didn't have the heart to move her, even when his arm went to sleep.

When the movie ended he stood up, taking care to lay her head down on the couch, and looked for the bathroom. He thought he'd have to use Lorilei's hovel at first, but another camouflaged door let him into a gigantic bathroom with a tub that could have, and probably had, held at least six people. He did his business, briefly considered using the tub, but thought better of it.

She was still asleep when he returned. A yawn escaped him. No way to tell what time it was in this place. No windows, no clocks. Probably several hours had passed, based on the length of the movies they'd watched. Maybe they'd never let him out of here. He'd been prepared to die, but wasn't prepared for imprisonment. Panic gurgled in his gut, complacent for the moment but ready to burst under any more pressure. For now, he would try to stay calm, maybe even sleep a little. He wanted a cigarette.

As comfortable as it may have been, he could not bring himself to sleep in the bed. That left the floor or the loveseat, currently occupied. He gently lifted Lorilei (she weighed almost nothing) and moved her to the bed, hoping he didn't wake her. She made a little sound, grumbling slightly and turning over when he put her down, sleepily grasping for something. He went to her cubbyhole and retrieved the faded blanket from the cot. It had the appearance of a worn, well-loved item. Hans covered her as best he could, though it was a choice between feet left out or shoulders. Finally, he pulled it up to her shoulders. She murmured again and lapsed into steady breathing.

Hans would never have thought himself able to kill someone, but he was enjoying the idea. A twelve-year-old girl. How many men had she had to give herself to, just because they stayed in this room? Not even allowed the comfort of the room in the interim. Yeah, he could kill Brigham. Hans retrieved a couple of pillows off the floor and bedded down on the loveseat.

— «» —

A low rumbling woke him. Hans had never been in an earthquake, but he imagined it might have sounded like this. The floor wasn't rumbling, though. Lorilei made a noise in the other room. She let out another soft yell when he rose and turned on the lights. She was squinting into the light, looking confused by her surroundings.

"Hans..."

Her sentence was cut short by a much louder boom, this one vibrating the floor. Loud footsteps went past in the hallway. Hans went to the door, put his ear against it, but there was no sound for the moment.

She was standing beside him then. "What is it?"

"I don't know, can you use your intercom to ask them?"

"They won't tell me anything."

More feet went past the door, a larger contingent by the sound of it. There was another boom, farther away than the last. Lorilei grasped at his arm. He shook her off.

"Is there another way out of this room, maybe through your cubbyhole?"

She shook her head, lip trembling again. Hans had to get it together. He didn't know what was going on, but terrifying a little girl wasn't going to help. Comfort was not really his forte, but he tried. He put a hand on her shoulder.

"I'm sure if there's a problem they'll come and let us know. Right now, we're safest right here."

"OK."

Sounds he recognized now. Gunshots. A long way off but getting closer.

"Maybe we should move away from the door. Let's go sit on the bed for a moment."

Lorilei let him lead her to the bed. More feet in the hall. More gunshots, more loud booms, something that sounded like metal scraping or tearing. Lorilei was looking at him. *Don't look scared, Hans, stay calm, for the both of you.*

The noises continued to grow, couldn't be far from them now. Men were yelling in pain and anger. Heavy caliber weapons were firing in a loud constant roar, still nearing.

"Lori, I want you go to your cubbyhole."

"I want to stay with you."

"Please!" It was a yell, and he took a breath as she flinched at him. "I will come and get you, I promise, it's the safest place."

"What is going on?"

"Lorilei," he put both hands on her shoulders, "please just go. I won't leave without you. It's just for few minutes."

She stared at him, face torn, then grabbed her blanket and scuttled for her cubbyhole.

"Shut the door."

A pitched battle was occurring right outside, though the gunshots and yelling had stopped. Metal was ringing against metal, but no yelling or curses. The noise continued to rise in pitch and intensity, hurting his ears. They had to be right outside his door. Then silence, only his ears still ringing. Hans held his breath, hoping they'd gone by.

The door exploded off its hinges, launching through the room, catching itself on the doorway to the bedroom, spinning as it crashed to the floor at Hans' feet. What followed it was a nightmare. It was squat and metallic, bipedal, with massive elongated arms gleaming with sharpened menace and blood, and hundreds of other limbs sprouting from its body and head. It stumbled in and crashed to its knees, twisting and flailing. Tried to rise, stumbled again, made a couple of steps toward him, then swung one its arms to stab at itself.

The extra limbs were not a part of it. They belonged to the dozen or so smaller creatures hanging on, perfect featureless spheres, sprouting four tentacles from each direction, stabbing the larger creature repeatedly. He recognized them.

It moved like it was in pain, making its way towards him. Hans leaped up and tried to put the bed between them, hoping the smaller creatures would finish it off. It struggled into the bedroom, lashing violently, one of its blades managed to spear an enemy, lifting it up into the air, and flinging it toward a wall.

Crashing into Lorilei's cubbyhole.

The wall buckled under the projectile. He could hear rubble falling, and Lorilei's short yelp.

The larger creature was back on the ground again, flailing weakly as the smaller ones stabbed again and again through its shell. It made a last attempt to rise, but crashed heavily onto the carpet.

—— ⟨⟩ ——

Her troops had come in as planned, if not quite as gracefully as expected. The roof came down, and with it a mass of squirming, gleaming pods. There wasn't much time to thank providence; she was too busy scrabbling for a corner to protect her from plummeting debris. What had looked like rock was shattering to dust on the ground; some kind of cheap ceramic.

Brigham let out a little screech and retreated to the far corner of the room, yelling into his comm for men, rescue, deities. He was cradling his ruined hands, getting struck by the falling artifice.

A pod landed just behind Onyx, climbed over her, and headed after Brigham. Not a pleasant sensation, but worth achieving her aims. Brigham was done.

Without the ceiling to hold it up the exterior wall crumbled, falling outward to the street. Debris continued to rain down from the ruined ceiling. Head down, curl into a ball. Sharp debris struck her back, repelled mostly by the armored weave of her outfit. She felt a few bite in, something larger striking her thigh, numbing her leg. Onyx peered through the rising dust.

Her troops swarmed an unfamiliar object, two to three times their size, but very similar. A perfect sphere, standing on two squat legs, swinging vicious, articulated blades. Sounds from similar battles echoed across the room.

She'd suspected Brigham would have something like what she was seeing. Its makeup was too akin to her own to be coincidence, though Brigham had to make everything bigger and flashier.

The larger enemy went down quickly under the onslaught, falling hard, slashing frantically and destroying the ground beneath; taking itself and her pods down a level, crashing into the floor below. She could hear gunfire now, coming from the hall entrance, now partially blocked by debris. The bullets held no danger for her pods, but the wildly scattered shots stood a chance of striking her, even if by a lucky ricochet. She forced herself up, checking for any serious injury. All appeared sore but intact, the worst of it being the vicious blow Brigham had landed in her stomach. She could taste a bit of blood. She'd had worse.

There was another loud thud as some idiot threw a concussion grenade into the room. It must've landed near one of the large pillars, as the next moment it came crashing down against the injured wall, breaking through and tearing down more of the ceiling. This room wasn't going to last much longer.

"I need an exit."

Follow the pods through the doorway; I'm removing the men there as we speak. Do you have sphere?

"Not at the moment, we need to clear this area and search. What are those others?"

I don't know, they look like a variation on my own tech. Curious.

"I was thinking the same."

Onyx moved toward the door. The gunshots had stopped nearby. She could hear more, farther off into the building. The pillar partially blocked the entrance, a pile of debris adding to the problem. The pods were scrambling over and through a man-sized hole near the top. She did the same, slowed greatly by injury and caution. Where the fuck had Brigham gone? Hopefully he was dead in the room behind her.

She needed to get to Hans. If they needed the device to escape he'd have to do it. She couldn't leave him here regardless. It was bad form.

"Can you locate Hans?"

He's been stowed in one of the harem rooms on this floor, about a thousand yards from your location. There are two of the larger enemy pods making their way toward him as we speak. I am removing them.

"Get me there."

Do you need assistance?

"Just directions."

I'll send a pod to lead you.

A small sphere rounded the corner in front of her, stopped, and gestured smoothly with one appendage. She followed.

The halls were scattered with bodies, man and machine, echoing with distant gunshots and screeching metal. Behind her the rest of the ceiling finally gave way, coming down in a crash of plaster and metal. She strode carefully, not wishing to run into an ambush. Her abdominal pain faded rapidly. There would be a vicious bruise.

Follow the leader carried on for a series of minutes, all the while the sounds of battle continued to fade around her. The pod stopped in front of an open doorway, buckled in slightly by whatever had torn it from its hinges. She could hear Hans yelling inside.

"Help me, goddamn it!"

She moved into the room, squinting at its garishness, and heard his voice through the doorway beyond.

"Hans?"

"Tell these things to help me."

One of the larger pods lay, destroyed, on the floor next to the bed. Half a dozen or so of her own milled aimlessly about. Hans was crouching in the far corner by a section of the wall that had come down, pulling uselessly on a buckled door.

"Are you injured?"

Hans rounded on her, face burning. "Can you tell these things what to do?"

"Yes."

"Then tell them to fucking help me."

"We need to exit quickly."

"There's a girl buried in here." He returned to his fruitless efforts.

"The whore?"

"She's not a whore, she's a twelve-year-old girl."

"But you slept with her?"

"I didn't, we, we watched a movie, I told her to hide, she … your fucking robots or whatever, they buried her. Help me get her out."

"We can't take her with us."

"She's coming."

"She's not."

Hans stood up and stormed toward her. "Fuck you, fuck you all! How many people have died for this bullshit already? That girl in there had nothing, just a shit life as a sleazy old man's fuck toy. You need me or you wouldn't have brought me here. You want my help? Then help me pull her out. If she doesn't come I'm done helping you."

"What if she's dead?"

"Then I'll leave her body here. Please, Illiyana, we can't leave her here. We can get her out, we can save her."

"What about all the other girls?"

"I can't save them all, up till now I haven't been able to save anyone. I need to even the score. Please."

Onyx could see the desperation in his eyes. He would be no good to her if she didn't try to extract the body.

"Move the rubble."

Done. Are you sure this is a good idea?

"We don't have a choice."

— «» —

Hans rode a tide of adrenaline, his focus narrowed to a spot about four feet in front of him, behind the rubble.

He could almost see her in there. Bloodying his fingers on sharp rubble. Breathing dust and fear. *Be OK, be OK, be ok.*

At Onyx's orders, the spheres swarmed in front of him, easily picking and removing fallen debris that had stuck fast. A gap appeared, widened, shrank slightly as it began to collapse again. A sphere positioned itself in the gap, holding floor and ceiling apart, a strange little Atlas. Others continued to clear. Hans' attempts at helping merely slowed them down, so he held himself in check and waited. Finally, a piece of white terry cloth, dirtied by dust, showed through.

"There, dig there."

They uncovered her, flinging debris back with uncanny accuracy, landing it neatly in a pile a few feet back. Her back was uncovered, then legs, neck, arms, head. Lorilei lay in a fetal position, arms covering her head, blanket grasped firmly between her legs. The spheres reached down to grasp her limbs, lift her out.

"No. Back up."

They ignored him. He looked at Onyx. She murmured something and the spheres retreated.

Hans moved quickly, trying to see if anything was broken, rolling her gently on her back. Blood on her forehead, mouth slack, eyes turned in. He put his ear to her chest. Heart still beating, breath moving. *Thank you.* He removed her blanket from her legs, wrapped it around her as best he could, and bent down, straining to pick her out of the rubble without causing more injury. The second time he'd carried her like this, this time much more important. Hans turned to face Onyx.

"The pods could carry her much easier," she said.

"No. No one touches her but me."

"Come on then, we have to retrieve something, and then we're getting out of here."

"You didn't get what you came for?"

"Brigham was more resistant than I would have liked."

"Is he dead?"

"I'm not sure. He's certainly not in good shape."

"We need to get her looked at."

"You're not leaving without her, I'm not leaving without my property, and none of us are getting out of here if we don't stick close."

Hans didn't argue, just gestured toward the door with Lorilei's feet.

They returned to the throne room, where most of Onyx's forces had gathered, madly dispersing the rubble. They had cleared the doorway, were in the process of cutting up and moving the rest of the pillar. A five-foot hole gaped in the floor, one whole wall nearly gone, and most of the ceiling collapsed in pieces or still coming down.

Hans could see sky through the wall. They were not extremely high off the ground, maybe a hundred feet. It looked like a crowd was gathering, but how could you tell in a place this crowded? There were no flashing lights or sirens yet.

Onyx's troops were a marvel. He could see them bracing walls, shoring up ceiling and pillars, breaking and flinging rubble.

"What happened here?"

"Brigham had a few tricks I wasn't expecting."

"Such as?"

"No time now. My troops inform me that the item has fallen to the floor below."

"So, we need to find an elevator."

"No, we're going down that," she gestured to the hole.

"Did you bring some rope?"

"I need a ladder."

Hans started to respond, but she wasn't talking to him. A string of pods scrambled over each other into the hole. Nearing, he saw they had formed a mechanical centipede, two legs gripping each other, two legs jutting out at right angles. Problem solved.

"Handy little buggers. That thing safe?"

"As long as you hang on."

"How're we going to get her down there?"

"She'll stay up here, protected by my troops. She's safe, safer than you can make her. When we're done we'll climb back up and try the cars."

Hans didn't want to put the girl down, but he had no choice. These things had saved his life three times now; he would have to trust her to them.

— «» —

The floor below was far enough away that at first it was hidden. It was like descending into a cave. At least the makeshift ladder didn't rock. Hans kept his eyes forward, studying the pods. Even from inches away their surface was completely uniform, no markings, no seams, not even any grime, just an expanse of bluish matte metal, the arms jutting out at the compass points, seamlessly bonded to the shell. They almost had to be mechanical, but their appearance was more crustacean than anything else.

"What the hell are these things?"

Onyx was just below him, pulling ahead slightly as she moved much more lithely into the darkness. Her response echoed from distant-sounding walls.

"They're my help."

"What are they made out of?"

"That's proprietary."

"You ever thought of selling them?"

"No."

He counted steps. At fifty-three his foot came to rest on hard floor. He felt slack in the makeshift ladder as the pods scrambled over one another to the floor around him. The scrabbling sound in the darkness was disconcertingly like large insects. Hans shivered slightly.

The dark was broken only by the hole above, its illumination sparse due to distance and angle.

"Why are all the lights off?"

"My troops destroyed the major power lines and generators."

"Nice, how are we supposed to find what we're looking for?"

"Lights, please." A cold, septic glow grew around him on the floor. The pods had formed a lane from their position off into the dark, the glow from their bodies just enough to push the darkness back a few feet.

"How'd this thing get all the way over there?" he asked.

"One of Brigham's soldiers made a run with it before my troops took him out."

"How come they didn't bring it back up themselves?"

"The shielding was damaged in the battle. It's dangerous to them."

"But not to us?"

"Not to you."

"You sure about that?"

Onyx had started down the makeshift landing strip. Hans didn't follow. She faded into gray. Something crashed down in another part of the building, the distant rumble sending dust down the meager shaft of light.

"Hey," he followed quickly, "do you know what this room is for?"

"Not a clue," Onyx's voice was surprisingly distant. Hans picked up the pace, seeing her shadow now. As far as he could tell the whole room around them was empty, and he had the sense of vast space, darkness covering everything but their self-lit corridor. Hans had no significant fear of the dark, but here it was overwhelming. Stay calm, take a breath, put a foot down, repeat. He nearly bumped into the back of Onyx when she stopped.

"It's up ahead," she said.

"Well, go get it then."

"I can't. I need you to."

"Don't think so."

"You're the only one who can."

"You keep saying that. What'm I, the fucking Chosen One?"

"If you wish."

"Look, lady, if you want my help then stop being so damn enigmatic. This thing is dangerous to you, your super crabs, and everyone else, yet you want me to go pick it up. You want my help, give me answers."

"You're a rare specimen, Hans."

"So my mom keeps telling me."

"You have absolutely no electronic or bionic modifications of any kind. You've even destroyed your internal ID chip. The item is dangerous to anyone with those modifications, but harmless to a pure organic specimen. You should be able to carry it with no ill effects."

"Should?"

"You lost it for me once, Hans. You said you wanted to make reparations, were even willing to die. Are you going to prove yourself a coward now?"

Hans bridled a bit at that. "I'm not a coward, just not sure throwing myself away right now would do anyone any good."

"I have been straight with you since the beginning, Hans. I'm telling you it will be fine. Retrieve my item and I will be grateful and consider your debt paid. I will help you get your little girl out of here safely." Onyx removed a piece of cloth from a hidden pocket and handed it to Hans. "It's a small black sphere, about two inches across. Just pick it up and wrap it in this cloth and bring it back to me."

Hans took the cloth. He wasn't sure how straight Onyx had really been, but he needed to get Lori out of here. He had to try for her sake.

The sphere was not difficult to find. It had rolled up against a far wall. He approached cautiously, wary of anything abnormal it might do. It just looked like a paperweight or large marble, though its surface reflected no light. He crouched next to it, passing a hand near, feeling feebly for any electrical field or heat. Nothing. He placed a finger gingerly on its surface. Slightly rough, cool to the touch. It felt exactly like one of Onyx's pods. He covered it with his hand. Still nothing. Its heft was slightly more than he expected, but there was no reaction. Still, he was careful not to drop it or jostle it too much. He wrapped it in the cloth she had given him, shoving it in an inside jacket pocket, not wishing to touch it for too long.

A boom echoed from the other side of the room, followed by sounds of large metal feet. One of Brigham's remaining metal soldiers had found them.

The lights went out, and Onyx's troops went to meet their enemy.

— «» —

Hans crouched up against the wall, straining to see in the impenetrable black. The sounds of engagement echoed across the hall.

"Illiyana!?"

"Here." Her voice was in front of him, footsteps moving near. "Do you have the sphere?"

"Yes." His eyes had adjusted just enough to make out the distant high glow of the hole in the roof. "Do we make a break for it?"

"No." Her voice very near him now. "We find shelter while my troops handle the situation."

A loud crash filled the room, light greatly increasing thanks to the new hole in the ceiling. Hans saw one of the larger machines laying on the floor nearby, struggling to rise under the swarm of pods. It managed to get its feet under it and fling away a couple of the pods, then took a step in Hans' direction, was swarmed by reinforcements, and forced back to the floor.

"There are three in the room and a few more on the way. There's a large packing container nearby. We should try to get inside."

Hans didn't argue. Onyx set off to his right, he followed closely. The roar of fighting increased, spurring them on. More of the roof came crashing down.

"Your troops are going to get us killed."

"Brigham's machines are trying to cave the roof in. My forces are trying to prevent it, but we need to get somewhere protected so they can dig us out if things go badly."

That did not sound pleasant. Hans could just make out a large box-like shape a few dozen feet ahead, probably a truck trailer. Creaks and groans of overextended steel were sounding above, and something hit the wall a few feet behind them. Onyx moved to the side, Hans crowding in behind her. They'd lucked out and gotten to the side with the doors. A lock rested against the door.

"Can you pick that or something?" he asked.

"No, it responds to the user's ID tag."

The roof across the room gave way, its trip to the floor deafening. The light was coming in well enough to silhouette numerous struggles. The room itself was not as big as he'd imagined, its space almost completely empty except for the crate.

"The girl's up there. We have to go back."

"The pods have extracted her, she's as safe as I can make her."

A pod crawled over the top of the container, crab-walking down toward them, stopping by the latch, two tendrils gripping body and bar. The lock fell into two pieces. Onyx heaved the door open and stepped in. Hans hesitated. More unwelcome dark. Another piece of the ceiling crashed behind him, too close. He entered.

— «» —

Onyx slammed the door and turned the latch. Fat lot of good that would do if one of those things wanted in. Hans backed up against the near wall, which was padded with heavy foam, greatly muffling the sounds from outside. Debris struck the roof, sounding distant. Claustrophobia tugged at him. *Breathe in, breathe out, relax, stay calm.*

Onyx moved past him, further into the container, her boots pinging against the metal floor. Something hit the side, raining dust into his hair.

"Where are you going?" he asked.

"I'm curious what Brigham is storing in here."

"I'm curious if this thing is going to stop the ceiling from crushing us."

"Better than nothing."

Much better, as it turned out. Armageddon sounded from outside, and something landed on the crate hard enough the metal creaked and buckled. It held, but bent further as it was hit again. Hans held his breath. For a man with a death wish he was continually surprised by his urge to survive. The whole crate tilted slightly, slid a few feet, then he felt a momentary sense of weightlessness before the end crashed back to the ground. Still it held.

Onyx returned, crouched beside him.

"Find anything?" Hans asked.

"You don't want to know."

"You're right, don't tell me."

"Bodies."

"I told you not to tell me."

— «» —

One last crash, the whole world caving in. Hans strained his ears, thought maybe he could hear the sound of more debris falling, but couldn't be sure it wasn't imagination. He was glad for the dark. His claustrophobia would be worse if he could see his predicament. He tried not to think about the bodies.

"My troops have finished up top," Onyx said, "We're completely buried. It will be a short time before they can dig us out."

"How long?"

"Maybe ten minutes."

Breathe in, breathe out, don't think about the bodies. Breathe in, breathe out, don't think about the bodies.

"Are you ok?" she asked.

"Do you really care?"

"Is it so hard to believe I might?"

"Somewhat difficult, yeah."

"Forget I asked then."

"Done."

They sat, the silence growing, creeping in, cementing itself between them, becoming impenetrable. He continued with his mantra. Breathe in, breathe out...

Onyx spoke again, "They should have us out of here soon." She was trying to be reassuring. It didn't work well for her. Hans could hear the edge in her voice. Still, she was trying.

"Why Onyx?"

"Hmm?"

"Why Onyx? How did you come up with that moniker?"

"I needed an alias, it sounded appropriate."

"Why'd you need an alias?"

"To protect me from old enemies."

"Did it work?"

"Mostly."

"It would seem that your new enemies are undeterred by your enigmatic code name."

"Most of my new enemies are not alive very long."

"Friends either."

Onyx didn't respond. Hans tried another line, desperate for some noise in the pitch black.

"So, what are those things exactly?"

"What things?" She was being intentionally obtuse.

"Your pods?"

"Useful tools." He could almost see her shrug.

"Useful at killing?"

"That too." Nothing else from her, and the silence stretched out again, the bodies grew nearer. Keep talking, stay calm.

"Why did you save me?"

"I'm not sure what you're talking about."

His frustration took over from fear, "Jesus, why are you so fucking obtuse?"

"Hmm?"

"One of your pods saved my life in the hospital, another one or two took out a group of men trying to kill me in a truck, and last night you cut Elena's throat open when she tried to strangle me."

"Elena served us breakfast this morning."

"I know that, but considering I've already seen you dead once yourself, I guess it was just as easy to bring her around."

"Mr. Ricker, you're going to have to start making sense. Are you sure you've recovered from your injuries?"

"Fine," he spat, "keep your fucking secrets. I don't know what the point of this game is, Ms. Li, but I've stopped caring."

Her hand struck him across the face, more as a gauge of position and distance than lethality. Another ice-cold hand encircled his throat, squeezed.

"You will not call me that again, Mr. Ricker, by choice or by force."

Hans was seeing something now, stars from an oxygen-starved brain. He reached up to pull her hand off. Her grip was titanium, unmoving. She held him until he began to fade, then the grip was gone. Hans coughed violently, the sound dulled by padded walls. He heard her stand and move to the other side of the container, all of ten feet.

"You really hate the Chinese, don't you?" he asked.

Silence from across the container, silence from outside, blessed silence from the bodies in the back.

"What did your father do to you to make you hate them so much?" Hans half expected the hand back around his throat, a wickedly sharp knife across his neck, but there was nothing for an uncomfortable stretch.

"My father killed my mother when he found out about his child. Killed her and took me, raised me with criminals, trained me to seduce and kill. He turned his daughter into a whore."

"I thought your mother was killed by terrorists?"

Onyx sniffed at that, unworthy of a verbal response.

"So, you killed him. You got your revenge. You win."

"Yes, I killed him. There is no winning in murder. He took my mother, I took his life. It was far from a fair trade, and now his men will hunt me until they kill me or I kill every single one of them."

"I'd say your pods give you a pretty good advantage."

He could hear her rustling across the container, probably sitting down.

"Have you ever lost a parent?" Her voice was calmer than he'd ever heard it, the edge nearly gone.

"My mother raised me and Grit, or I guess I should say my mother and Grit raised me. My father was just some sperm donor that passed in the night. I never really thought about him or cared. Mom was all the father I needed."

"And if she was murdered, would revenge replace the loss?" The edge was creeping back in now, shields returning to full strength.

"I pity any man who came after my mother. I've seen her put a bullet straight through a bear's head at six hundred yards. None of this new computer-guided VR scope bullshit needed. The last guy that tried to put a hurting on her limped away with three cracked ribs and a broken collarbone."

"You haven't answered my question."

Hans thought a moment. "No, nothing would, but I'd try to kill them anyway."

"Could you do it?"

"Mentally... probably. Physically... well... I don't have the capabilities of Ma or Grit. I was never much use with a gun, don't really like them. I'm sort of useless in the hand-to-hand department as well."

"So, you'd let your sister handle it?"

"Probably, though Grit would never kill them. She'd bring 'em in and make 'em face proper justice."

"Are you sure about that?"

"Yeah. Greta's a letter of the law, by the book type; she'd never take it into her own hands."

"I think you may not know your sister as well as you think."

"And you know her better?" Hans tried not to bridle under her niggling.

"I've seen a side of your sister you seem unaware of."

That one stung. What was she implying? "Really, how's that?" He kept his voice calm.

"Oh, just girl talk, you know how it is." The smirk in her voice was unmistakable.

"Did you sleep with my sister?" The question was out before he could swallow it. Jackass.

Onyx laughed heartily, a surprising noise in the confined space. "Would that bother you?"

"Yes."

"Because she'd be a lesbian?"

"No, because it was you."

Onyx laughed again, softer this time. "You don't consider me worthy of your sister?"

"No."

"I'm hurt, Hans." She was teasing him. He hated being teased.

"Fuck you, Illiyana," he said, hoping that would bring a rise but not violence.

"Relax, Hans, your sister and I are not lovers. Neither of us is inclined in that direction. Besides, from observation she's obviously enthralled with her second, and he her."

"Gino, you mean."

"Yes, that's his name, though duty prevents them. Your sister is very much like the Chinese in that way."

"Duty before love and all that."

"Something like that, though I never saw it in my father or any of his thugs."

Hans felt something like relief, though it was entwined with shame at letting her goad him. The exchange had at least cleared some tension.

A scrabbling noise came from outside, followed by the sound of Onyx's forces cutting through the roof. Meager light accompanied the sound of tearing metal. Cold, blinding light pierced the black interior, jumping around, doubling and trebling, the pods thumping to the ground around him, the light stopping its nauseating movement.

"Let's get the hell out of here," he said.

Onyx ignored him and spoke something to the pod. It followed her to the back, taking its glow with it. Inspecting the bodies. *God knows why. To see if they'd been filleted?*

Curiosity got the better of him, along with not wanting to be left alone in the dark again.

Rows of feet stuck out from the back, the light lending them morgue-like shadows. The bodies were racked like wine bottles, vintage unknown, though none smelled like they'd gone bad. Onyx stood before a pulled-out rack, staring silently at it, surprise around her eyes and lips. Hans moved closer, forced himself to look down.

Superficially male. Broad-shouldered, well-muscled, hairless, genital-less. The whole body smooth and uniform. The face was of her bodyguard. Hans couldn't drum up any surprise.

Onyx slid the body back, and it rolled smoothly into its housing. She pulled out the one below it. Female, no distinguishing marks, no genitals, another exquisite mannequin. Hans had seen this one before. It was Elena, again. On a hunch, he pulled out the one next to Beefy. Beefy number two slept quietly beside his twin. He didn't need to check the stall below for another Elena. He'd seen enough, but wanted to try another row, unable to convince himself. Onyx beat him to it, yanked out the rack at head level, and took a step backward.

It was her, smooth and unfinished like the others, yet rendered so well Hans instinctively turned away for the sake of propriety. The drawer slammed closed, and Onyx walked toward the exit.

One row left. He couldn't look, couldn't not, unsure if seeing himself rendered as artificial would break his tenuous hold on panic. Too late to turn back. The drawer came out, Hans trying to glance quickly from his peripheral vision, as if he could somehow sneak up on the horror.

It wasn't him, thank God. The face was familiar, though. Hans had accepted a ride from the man, had drunk vodka with him in Onyx's fortress. The boss, the benefactor. James, he'd called himself.

"You should see this," he yelled to Onyx.

"I've seen enough." If she was distraught she was covering it well. "We're getting out of here, and this place is coming down."

He swallowed his questions, not wanting to be lied to again. Eventually she'd tell him the truth… maybe. He was starting to wonder how sane this woman actually was.

Hans climbed out of the top of the container to a greatly altered scene. Nearly all the ceiling had come down, combining the storehouse and throne room in one massive hall, the ceiling nearly a hundred feet overhead. The wall behind him was completely gone, both floors open to the outside, dust obscuring the view. Lights played across the room as wandering pods were still digging in the rubble, clearing a corridor to the entrance to the room above, now set in a wall about thirty feet off the ground. She was already halfway across the room. Hans followed.

The pods did their ladder trick again. Onyx scrambled up. He climbed behind her, trying not to huff and puff too obviously.

Lorilei was in the middle of the floor in the hallway outside, surrounded by more of the pods. Hans knelt and put his ear to her chest. Her heat still beat, lungs still breathing. Still, it couldn't be good to be out this long. She'd taken a severe blow to the head, and every minute she stayed unconscious only increased the likelihood she'd never wake at all. The only doctor he knew was hundreds of miles from here, and they couldn't stay in Salt Lake long enough to get her treatment.

"How do you propose we get out of here?" he asked, lifting Lorilei off the ground. The pods reached after her like greedy toddlers. He kicked one away. It barely moved.

"You said you could drive?"

"Yeah."

"Then we drive."

They returned to the ornate garage, still filled with its armada of stretch limos. Onyx looked to him to choose one. He led them past the limos, hoping Brigham kept something a little more practical. He lucked out. A sleek, black four-door, large but not stretched. Hans tried the door; locked. They'd all be locked unless you were authorized.

Onyx had a short conversation with her unseen helper. The doors unlocked and the car started, electric engine giving a short whir to signal readiness. Hans hoped the fuel cell was filled.

He opened the rear door, placed the girl gently in the back, ignoring Onyx's exasperated look, and slipped into the driver's seat. The dashboard told him everything was good, cell filled, plenty of juice to get them out of town.

"Can your friend get us out of here?"

Onyx slid into the passenger seat, sub-vocalized something. The car began to descend.

CHAPTER 6

We have a problem.

"Yes?"

I no longer have control of the pods.

"Who does then?"

I do not know. There is an... inconsistency... in the system.

"Do you have any link with them at all?"

They are still sending proper status updates, but I have been blocked from sending.

"So, we're going to have fifteen hundred rogue pods running around Salt Lake?"

No. Much worse. Whoever is controlling them is bringing them together and setting them for detonation.

"We were going to take down the building anyway."

Yes. Destruction of the building required only about thirty or so pods in key locations. They are currently grouped en masse and all going to go at once.

"Safe distance?"

Three quarters of a mile minimum.

"Time?"

Fifty-two seconds.

—— ‹› ——

"We have to go faster."

Hans was creeping through streets packed with people, leaning on the horn. They parted easily, but not quickly. In the last ten minutes, he'd only covered half a mile or so. Onyx had spent the time conversing with her mysterious partner, mumbling terse phrases and single words from the passenger seat.

"What do you want me to do? Run them over?"

Onyx rolled down the nearly jet-black side window, leaned out, and threw something he couldn't see. Told him to close his eyes.

Even with his eyes closed the flash partially blinded him, the noise immense. Yelling and screaming, people fled down the street away from the car, parting toward the sidewalks.

"What the hell was that?" he asked.

"Motivation. Drive fast, we have thirty seconds to reach a safe distance."

Hans twisted the throttle, pushed the stick forward. The road ahead was partially cleared, the lane still cramped, the car not designed for speed or handling.

"If you wish your girl to survive, I suggest you drive faster."

"What the hell did you do?"

She just pointed down the road. Hans drove faster, cross streets passing, blew through a red light with no cross traffic.

"Ten seconds." Her voice was grating, tense.

Two more blocks, then Armageddon went off behind him.

It wasn't a boom so much as being hit by a freight train. The car lifted, nose heavy, and threatened to flip over. The safety features triggered, encapsulating Hans in acrid white foam. The rear end came crashing back down. Everything was muffled, the foam temporarily filling his ears. Maybe yells, maybe crashes, maybe destruction, his world a mass of sticky fluff. He tasted some of it, gagged. They say it's nontoxic, but he didn't trust they.

The car settled, foam already softening, falling away. Hans wiped his eyes, tried to clear his ears. Started to ask if Onyx was OK, but the passenger seat was already empty, Onyx scrambling for the rear door. He thought of Lori. Had to push the driver's door hard to exit. Stood and looked back.

A plume of dust blocked the sky behind him, rising to the limits of his vision. Vaporized cement and metal, probably people. How many in a town like this? Hundreds? Thousands? Millions? His mind revolted, refused him answers. *Get the girl, get out of here.*

Hans opened the rear door, a mantra for Lori on his lips. Onyx was crouched over her, faces almost touching. "She's ok." The relief in her voice surprised Hans, angered him.

"Get away from her!" He reached in, put his hands on Onyx's shoulders, and shoved hard. Bad idea. Onyx never shifted, just grabbed a wrist in each hand and twisted viciously, until pain shot from his wrists to elbow. Hans gritted his teeth at her, snarled ineffectually.

"No time for this, Hans, we have to get ourselves and the sphere out of here."

"I'm not going anywhere with you. How many more people have to die for this stupid sphere of yours?"

"I did not kill these people." Her voice was calm, frosty.

"Right, tell me another."

"Why would I put myself in the blast radius?"

"I've seen you survive death once, why not a second time?"

The staring contest continued for an eternal five seconds, neither backing down. Then Onyx let his hands flop numbly to the seat. Hans tried to move them, get some feeling back.

"I haven't injured you. Get the girl. This car is finished. We're going to need another."

She was right; the impact and resulting crash had destroyed the rear suspension. The body of the car was sitting directly on the ground, its back wheels splayed out behind it, like a dog sleeping on a tile floor. It would have been funny in another situation. Hans lifted Lori gently from the back. She did not appear hurt, at least no more than she had been. He threw her over his shoulder, blanket flopping around her legs.

The street around was more empty than he'd seen since their arrival, but there were still plenty of people milling around, staring in shock at the wall of dust, now filling nearly one whole side of the sky, flowing down the street in the distance. Being caught out in the open wouldn't be fun.

Onyx was already heading for a doorway in a small, three-story brick building. The whole street was full of them, cut and pasted one after the other in both directions.

Old suburbia as rendered by a cheap modeling program. He followed, trying not to jostle the girl too much.

She reached the door and kicked it open without even a knock. It blew back on its hinges, nearly falling over. She disappeared into the darkness. Hans entered and tried to shut the door behind him, but couldn't close it all the way; she'd damaged it. He pushed it closed as much as possible and wedged a small table against it. There was more yelling and a loud crash from the room beyond the foyer.

A man was lying curled up on the floor, Onyx crouched over him, brandishing one of her knives, threatening a woman of about fifty and a trio of young men. Hans didn't see any blood; she'd given the man the same treatment as the door. One of the young men looked ready to move against her. Onyx stood cold, unmoving, waiting for him. Hans needed to diffuse the situation.

"Please, we just need shelter for a few minutes. This girl is hurt, we need to lay her down."

The woman moved away from the wall, nurture overriding fear. Hans put a hand on Onyx's shoulder. She swung around. Hans stood his ground, tried to appear calm. She relaxed, the knife disappeared. Since when was he the cool-headed one?

The woman was at his shoulder now, pulling at his arm. Hans let her lead him into the next room, a small study done up in wood paneling and old charts, very safari. He laid Lori down on a black leather couch.

"What happened?" The woman crouched over her, feeling for bruises and breaks, obviously trained to do it.

He couldn't tell her the truth. "Explosion knocked her out. I don't know if she was hit by something." A terrible lie, and she knew it, too. What was a girl doing outside in a man's bathrobe, accompanied by two outsiders, one armed and violent? They both let it lie for now. The woman stood and left, and returned a minute later with a small first aid kit, old but well-kept. She went about her work efficiently, ignoring him. He left her to it and returned to Onyx.

The situation in room had diffused slightly, though the parties still occupied opposite territories. There were three boys in their teens, two cowering, one standing firm, staring defiantly at her. She appeared not to notice. The man on the floor now was sitting in neutral territory with his back against the wall. Hans tried again to calm things down.

"Thank you. We're sorry for the violent intrusion. We had an emergency on our hands and overreacted a bit." He tried for an aw-shucks smile and failed miserably.

The older man was still wheezing, holding his stomach. Hans felt Onyx's glare on him, tried to calmly return it. She won again, and turned and walked back into the entrance.

"What happened outside?" This from one of the boys.

"I don't know," Hans lied, "earthquake maybe. Something shook the whole street out there, knocked our car around."

"Is that your car outside?"

Hans nodded, the car just visible in the rising dust storm, the light going orange as the cloud blocked the sunlight. The room darkened.

"Do you work for Brigham?" the man on the floor asked him.

"No." Where had that come from?

"That's one of his cars. Where'd you get it?"

"I... we... took it from him."

"So, you're one of his lackeys. Is that woman with the knife one of his whores?"

Hans hoped Onyx hadn't heard that. Through the doorway he could see her in the entrance, talking on her comm. Fine dust swirled in around her through the crack in the door, catching the light and throwing odd shadows. She didn't move. Hans didn't know how to respond, felt the situation souring. The older woman entered.

"That girl you brought in is," she said.

He didn't know what to say to that.

"Her hymen's gone, been gone awhile, I checked as part of the routine."

Hans wasn't sure if he should be thankful they'd come across someone capable or not.

"Yes, she was," he admitted, knowing it was useless to lie. "We brought her out as the place was coming down. She was hurt when part of the building came down on her. Is she ok?"

The woman stared at him, analyzing his face. Made a decision.

"No, she's not. She's had severe trauma to the head, her brain is bruised, swelling. I gave her something that should counteract the swelling. She needs to stay immobile, preferably in a hospital."

"Are you a doctor?"

"No, I was an EMT."

"Not anymore?"

"No."

"Why?"

"I got married."

— «» —

The woman, whose name was Marion, asked if they wouldn't mind staying in the study. Hans managed to cajole Onyx into agreeing. Something significant was wrong, he could see it on her face. Even during what they'd just been through, she'd never shown a chink in her armor. Now she looked frustrated and slightly shocked. She shut the door, wedged the room's only chair against it.

"We've got a problem," she said

"You mean besides the crater we left and the family we just took hostage?"

She waved her hand dismissively. "We need to get out of here quickly."

"Obviously."

She glared at him, and he pretended not to notice. The dust cloud outside had almost completely blocked the sun now. Hans walked around the desk, flipped on the lamp, closed the curtain, stood behind the desk, arms crossed. Her invincibility was on temporary hiatus.

"Tell me again you're not responsible for that explosion. Make me believe it."

"We don't have time for..."

"I'm not going anywhere with a mass murderer. I may not like people, but at least I have respect for human life. Up until now I thought you might have some sense of honor, however warped. Now there's a pile of innocent bodies behind us. Convince me or I walk."

"So caring all of a sudden. The only life you seem uncaring for is your own."

"It's my right, Ms. Petrovich, it's my life. Convince me."

"We planned on taking down the building. The process would have only taken a few dozen pods."

"We? Meaning you and whoever you've been talking to."

"Yes. There was a problem. Something took over our control. It detonated them all."

"All being how many?"

"About fifteen hundred."

Hans whistled softly, "So along with anything else, these things are bombs?"

"They can be. Hans, we were not trying to kill civilians, just Brigham and his men."

"And any number of slaves and whores he had on premises."

"Yes. Better than with him."

"And that was your decision to make?"

Onyx gestured toward the body on the couch. "You don't agree? Look at her Hans, look where you found her. He buys them from families so poor they can't afford to raise the kids the church tells them to have. Just barely out of puberty, some of them much younger, forced to service Brigham and anyone else he hands them to. Better death than that. I know. I would kill a thousand Brighams, a million of his men, to stop what you saw. It's my decision to make because I'm the only one willing to make it. But I would never do what you saw outside. It was supposed to be just his building. Something went wrong, something took over, and now I can't even reach my support."

She was genuinely shaken, almost spitting the words at him. He resisted an urge to put an arm around her, since he didn't want to get stabbed. Hans' anger faded, fear rising in its wake.

"OK, I believe you. I'm glad Brigham's dead. You didn't intend this. Can we get out of here without your friend's help? Get a car, get past police."

"There's another way."

"What's that?"

"The sphere you picked up."

He'd forgotten about it in the escape. The reason for their trip. The reason for his near death. The reason for all of this. He instinctively put a hand in his pocket, felt its shape, still in the cloth she'd given him. "You can use this to get us out?"

"No. You can."

"I thought it was supposed to be lethal?"

"It's lethal, or nearly so, to anyone with any electronic modifications. Not to you."

"You said that before. You're not bullshitting me?"

"No."

"So, what does it do?"

She pursed her lips, held back.

"Look, Yana, I've just been through hell with you. I've done what you asked. No more lies about this thing. I deserve an answer, and I'm not going to help otherwise." He crossed his arms, trying desperately to exude a confidence he didn't feel.

She relented. "It does a few different things, all of them important. What we need right now is its primary function. It's a universal access point. It can access any network instantly."

"I have one of those already. It's called a portable."

"Not like this. This can access any network, break any encryption, control any connected system, even those not connected if it's close enough. It's universal access, ultimate control."

Hans realized this should impress him more, but the answer underwhelmed. His mind couldn't grasp why this was worth all the trouble. He'd spent his life trying to disconnect as much as possible. Complete immersion was not his idea of enjoyment, but neither did he want to die or be imprisoned here. If it could get them out he'd give it a shot.

"You don't understand?" she asked.

"No, but I'll try."

"Have a seat then."

He sat down next to Lorilei, double-checking for her pulse. "OK, so what do I do?"

"Unwrap it, hold it in your hand for a few moments."

"Then what?"

"Then it works."

"It didn't when I picked it up before."

"You didn't consciously want access then."

He was skeptical. "How will I know when it's working?"

"It will tell you."

"Have you done this before?"

"You're the first we've found who can access it."

"And you're sure this won't kill me?"

She actually laughed a bit at him. "You ask a lot of questions."

"Death makes me curious."

"No one has tried it because no one can. There is no one hundred percent guarantee. This is your chance to save the girl, to make good on those other deaths, to seize control. Take it and we can escape. Or we can run for our lives, maybe be shot down, and the girl can go back to whoring."

She was manipulating him now, goading him into action. He hated it, but there was too much truth in what she was saying to back out. Hans pulled the sphere from his pocket, removed the cloth. It sat in his hand, jet-black, featureless, sucking in the light. So much loss for this. Maybe he could get his own back. Maybe he'd end up a smoking corpse. Onyx had kept things from him, kept things from herself even, but she'd never straight up lied to him. If this could do what she said, then she was taking a risk revealing it to him. She had chosen to trust him, so he would do likewise. He turned his hand over and dropped the sphere into his other palm. It was cool to the touch, the surface slightly rough.

Then, nothing. He chuckled at his fear.

"Well, that's a bust," he said. "You sure it's not broken?"

Onyx shrugged, "I can't use it, I don't know exactly what will happen."

They waited, nothing. A minute passed, two. Boredom set in. The owners of this house would not allow them privacy much longer, probably had called whatever service functioned as police around here.

Then... something.

A word at the bottom left corner of his vision, sitting so plainly he wondered how long it had been there.

Access?

The question mark was blinking.

He moved his head, and the word kept its place, moving across wall and ceiling, curving slightly as it followed the shape of the globe. He'd seen hyper-reality before; they used it at museums or old historical sites; a pair of small glasses with low-level lasers beamed directly onto the retina, creating startlingly real images of how buildings had been, wars fought, works of art created in a computer, floating in virtual space. This thing did the same, though it did it without any interface.

"Anything?" Onyx asked him.

"I think it wants access."

"Tell it yes."

"How?"

"Dunno. It's supposed to be user-friendly."

"I'm not sure that phrase is much help here."

Hans concentrated on the word. Did it brighten slightly? Hard to tell.

"Access, yes."

A brief flash of light filled his vision, like being hit by a strobe. He flinched, but no other sensation followed it. The word "access" disappeared, replaced by "please wait..." and a percentage number, climbing rapidly. Hans couldn't contain a laugh.

"What?" Onyx sounded annoyed.

"A fucking loading bar..."

The number climbed toward one hundred, reached it, disappeared. No more floating words, no more instructions. *You'd think someone would have written a user's manual.* Hans waited, Onyx scowled.

"It's done loading, whatever that means. This thing is broken."

"I doubt it," she snapped.

He turned to look at her, ready to snap back in frustration, but as he looked at the interior wall, he could see into it. Not like an X-ray, more like a schematic overlay. He knew this immediately, just as he knew he could take control of any of those access points, use the items, and destroy them if he wanted. More so, simple concentration showed the paths they followed to the wider network. He could cut those paths, follow them to their source, follow them anywhere. All this knowledge was immediate to him, as well as how he would go about it.

"Well?" she asked him. He looked at Lori. Nothing.

"She doesn't even have an ID tag," he said, more to himself than her.

"Hmmm?"

"Lori, she never had an ID tag installed. I wonder why?"

"There are rumors that people in charge here only tag one in three of the poorest of the population. It helps them hide the true numbers, as well as letting them treat them how they will. It's working?"

"Yes."

Hans stood, turned to face the wall. Now that he was facing into the house he could see more access points glowing through the wall. A handful of portables, the central house server, various appliances. One of the portables was being used. His focused attention brought the conversation to his ears. The husband was talking to someone in authority. Hans had to stop him. A thought fried the portables circuits, another followed its connection to the source.

The sensation was dizzying. A third eye, indistinguishable from his original two, like viewing the world in split screen. He stood in the study, and he followed the connection at stunning speed. A building, brimming with access points. A security camera. He could see the inside of a dispatch office, moved the camera on its base, saw the woman the husband had been talking to. Her computer registered his name. Hanson, Gregory, age fifty-one, hair brown, eyes hazel, four sons, no daughters, married to Marion Hanson for twenty-three years. Report of a disturbance and kidnapping. Hans erased it all, fried the dispatch computer, followed its connection. A police portable, owner one Joseph Lightener, sergeant, age thirty-four, multiple commendations for bravery. Heading toward this location in a police prowler, currently on autopilot. Hans removed the notice, fried the prowler's systems, and searched for any information revealing his whereabouts. Pieces were moving between dispatch computers and other cars. He deleted them all, sent out an APB for rescue efforts at Brigham's fortress, and re-routed all traffic.

The enormity of what he could do was dawning on him. He could access bank computers with this, re-route funds to his personal account, delete all trace. Take down governments, stop wars, kill individuals. Everything connected was his, and everything was connected. Ultimate power.

He closed his eyes, shut it off. His head hurt.

— «» —

There was a pounding in his head. No, that was the door. A voice demanding to be let in. Onyx removed the chair, Greg entered.

"I've called the cops, they are on their way here now." Seeing Hans bent over, he asked, "What's wrong with him, drugs?"

"Something like that." Onyx looked down her nose at Mr. Hanson, fingering a knife. He backed away, returning to the hall outside, reiterating his threat about the cops.

Hans' head cleared. The sphere sat in his hand, the weight of the world in a handy carrying case. *Jesus. Get it together, Hans. You can use this to get the girl out of here, get her to safety. Save a life first. Stand, move your legs.*

"Can you carry her for me?" he asked Onyx. She moved quickly, lifted the girl over one shoulder, her knife still in the other one. "We're leaving."

The father was still in the hall, muttering about police.

"They're not coming, Gregory, I sent them somewhere else, I'm sorry about your door. I'll transfer some money to you when we get out of town," Hans said.

"I don't want your filthy money."

"It won't be mine."

Marion stood by the door, protesting. "You can't take the girl, she belongs here."

"Thank you for your help, Marion, you may have saved her life. I'm going to try to make it worth it." Hans pushed her gently from the door and moved out into the street. He removed the sphere from his pocket again, this time with no need to log in, the sphere telling him that they were entwined now, an intimate neural interface. Access points lit up across his vision, cutting back the unnecessary to avoid him being overwhelmed.

"We need a car." Onyx was right beside him, but impossibly distant. There was a parked car in a garage around the corner; start the car, open the garage, send his position based on satellites overhead. Car moving around the corner. Unlock the doors. Driver's seat lighting up. Hans preferred to drive it himself. Somehow the division in his focus was easy to handle, a second brain to control a second body. Nearest exit fifteen miles west, map on the heads-up display. Just follow the arrows. Shut down all traffic along their route. Four military jumpcraft moving toward their location. Re-route. Exit clear ahead of them. Hans twisted the throttle, tore toward the exit. *Never coming back to this twisted hellhole.*

— «» —

They were parked in an abandoned gas station. He'd floored it for nearly an hour, moving anything that got in their way, exhilarated by speed and sensation. On a lark, he'd commandeered a passing UAV, a small camera platform for close quarters surveillance. He wasn't sure what it was doing out here, but he'd watched himself through the window of the car. Eyes on the road, eyes on himself. Thirty seconds left him faintly nauseated. Had to pull over and log off.

Hans was sitting back in his seat now, eyes closed. Trying to let the world spin down, come back to normal. Onyx was lighting a cigarette.

"Can I have one of those?"

"Are you sure you can handle it?"

He put one in his mouth, holding the lighter. Sweet tobacco. Everything focusing again.

"I've smoked before."

"That's not what I meant."

He left her question hanging for nearly a minute.

"What happens to someone with implants?"

"The sphere causes a feedback loop, damaging surrounding tissue with heat, possibly causing destruction and shrapnel." She rolled down a window, let the smoke drift out. The light outside was a funny color, like tornado weather. All of Salt Lake was covered in dust, the cloud lightening as it spread and dissipated.

"That's a hell of a security feature," he said.

"It wasn't intentional, just an unplanned side effect. The sphere you have is a prototype, stolen before it could be tested properly."

"Well," he took another puff, "I guess we can call that a successful run."

"It would seem."

The dynamic between them had changed, it was obvious by her demeanor. The power had shifted in his favor. So much power. He didn't want it… or at least, he didn't think he did.

"So where do we go now?" he asked

"Back to Denver. I still can't contact my friend. We need the equipment I have at home."

"Wait a minute, I'm not sure I want to go anywhere else with you."

"The deal was to retrieve the sphere and transport it to Denver. Are you reneging on our deal, Hans? Besides, where else are you going to get medical help for your little pet?" There was a sneer in her voice.

"Don't call her that!" His voice sounded petulant, even to him. Onyx smirked and turned away.

"Relax, Hans, I'm only teasing. It was an honorable thing you did. I hope she understands that when she wakes up."

Hans continued to sulk. "We have another problem though. This car doesn't have much juice left. It's a city car, they don't charge them enough to drive long distances."

"Put the sphere on the dashboard."

"Why?" He felt a moment of embarrassment at his selfish reluctance.

"Relax. Why would I take it from you? We'll need it still and you're the only one who can use it. I just want to show you another feature."

"Feature or side effect?"

"This one was planned."

Hans did as she asked. It adhered, sat improbably on the angled dashboard. The car's charge bar grew, topping at one hundred percent.

"That's pretty handy. Can it power anything?" Hans asked.

"I'm not sure of its upper limits. Again, it's untested."

"How long 'til it runs out of juice?"

"You'd be long dead by then."

— «» —

It took most of the day to gather the essentials. Grit didn't want to use her assigned jumpcraft, wanting to stay off the radar. The medical team worked quickly and efficiently removing internal comms. The older externals were in cold storage in a warehouse. She waited for them to arrive, procured the first two for herself and Gino.

It was evening by the time they left with Gino flying, licensed but rusty. He nearly banged the tail against the ground, receiving a warning light and a jerk as the craft self-corrected. At his sheepish look in her direction, she mimed flying the craft herself, eyes questioning. Gino grunted that he could handle it.

It was only few minutes to Onyx's citadel; Grit always thought of it that way. She'd been there a few times, usually surreptitiously. Mutual respect made them allies, if not friends. Grit knew she was a criminal, but was a matter of the devil you know. Onyx had removed the previous organization, a much crueler and more opportunistic bunch, willing to engage in anything as long as money could be made. Grit and Onyx's partnership benefitted them both greatly, Grit's success giving her more control and autonomy, Onyx raking in cash for high tech smuggling.

When Onyx had contacted her fourteen months ago for help in procuring a stolen item, Grit had initially balked; too much involvement. But Onyx revealed a chance to strike at John Brigham, a man with absolutely no integrity or decency. He'd been trying to gain a foothold in Denver for years. Much of Grit's and Onyx's joint operations directly involved keeping him out.

Onyx's intelligence surpassed anything Grit could obtain through official sources, her info and Grit's muscle keeping Brigham at bay. The lost item would have given him all he needed to break through, according to Onyx. Grit couldn't allow that. She'd seen his operations in Salt Lake, received copious reports on the broken minds and bodies he left in his wake.

It must have been just a fluke that Hans had walked in during the exchange, cosmic happenstance. Brigham tried a double-cross, not really surprising. What did surprise her was the ferocity of it. Scanners had barely registered the weapons system. Something slightly bigger than a man, though more squat, more spheroid. The surprise was compounded by her amateurish reliance on tracking the various players through internal ID tags. It was so rare and dangerous to have one removed that she'd grown complacent in her use of them, allowing Hans under the radar, a mistake that had cost two undercover soldiers their lives, and nearly killed Hans and Onyx. A mistake Grit wouldn't make again.

Onyx was coy about how she'd escaped.

Onyx was now Grit's best guess for Hans' location. The portable he left had still been open to Grit's summary of her. Did he have a chance to read the profile on Brigham? Grit hoped so, hoped Hans kept far away. Hoped Onyx hadn't killed him for being himself.

Gino requested landing permission from Onyx's citadel. Approval came back.

Her jaw ached, ebbs and flows of sharp fire. Nothing for it. She'd not brought any painkillers.

Gino released the controls, handing them over to Onyx's landing computers. The jumpcraft came down on the roof gently, and docking clamps engaged. The engine cut and whined to halt. They felt thrumming beneath the jumpcraft as the landing bay descended into the building. The roof closed overhead. A slight jerk, then the descent stopped. Gino unstrapped, headed back to open the doors. Nothing but black out the window, then lights came on, bathing the bay in sharp fluorescence. She unstrapped and followed Gino.

A lit path was pulsing on the floor just outside the door, leading to an open hallway. They followed. The wall opened into a hallway, the lit path darkening behind them as they passed, staying lit twenty feet ahead. A hundred feet, then a corner, fifty to another, then the wall opened into Onyx's personal quarters, strikingly different from the rest of the building. Open loft, woodcuts on the wall, and two whole walls with floor–to-ceiling windows. The path stopped them at the lounge area, next to a pair of large, expensive-looking couches.

Grit took a seat, motioned for Gino to do the same.

"Make ourselves at home, huh?"

He settled in next to her, sitting stiffly as she lounged back. A door in the wall opened, admitting Onyx's assistant, Elena. In her many visits here Grit had never seen more than two other people, Elena and a large bodyguard who never spoke a word. According to Onyx, the building was mostly automated, the lion's share of its interior taken up by computers and manufacturing. What it made Grit had never learned.

"Can I get you a drink?" Elena asked them.

"A beer, something you can't see through, and some vodka." Gino spoke for her, knowing what she drank. Elena nodded and disappeared back into the bowels of the building.

"Do you think she's here?"

Grit just shrugged, pulled out her portable, typed.

She likes to make an entrance.

Gino had never been here, Grit usually came alone. If he was impressed or disconcerted, he hid it well.

Elena returned with the drinks. Gino took a large swig of beer, and wiped off his lip. Grit sipped her vodka. Fantastic stuff. Grit's appreciation of Onyx's homemade spirit had gone a long way toward cementing their alliance.

Another door opened, music wafting out. Onyx entered, dressed severely, all in black, her usual business attire, smiling and extending both her hands. Grit rose to greet her.

— «» —

I am here.

"Finally, what happened?"

There was a… malfunction… it was necessary to cut off contact to avoid further outside corruption.

"You picked a hell of a time to disconnect."

He used the sphere?

"Correct."

No ill effects?

"None so far. Were there supposed to be?"

No, but it was the first test, and we've already discovered unplanned side effects.

"True. I don't want him hurt."

Nor do I. Currently we have another problem. I cannot access the factory.

"Nothing?"

Nothing. Something is blocking me. These continued intrusions are very disconcerting.

"Do we have another option?"

The sphere.

— 《》 —

The sun went down behind a lingering haze of dust behind them, the evening of the longest day of his life. Hans drowsed behind the wheel, the car heading up the interstate on autopilot, a bug among the behemoths of the hundred-foot long cargo transports, unmanned beasts drafting each other at mere inches to save energy. The night continued to darken, the road dead straight into the horizon.

Onyx grabbed his shoulder, rousing him from a dream of home.

"Huh?" He wiped at his eyes.

"We have a problem."

"We? Did your friend return?"

"Yes, with bad news. We cannot access my home base."

"I don't follow." He wanted to go back to sleep, to dream of something besides this nightmare. He turned to the back; Lorilei was still unconscious. She'd been out for a very long time. Hans was beginning to doubt she'd ever wake.

"The building in Denver, it's been cut off."

"Who could do something like that?"

"I don't know."

"And neither does your friend." It wasn't a question.

"No." Strain around her eyes, permeating her voice.

"What could do that?" the same question, repeated mostly to himself.

"I don't know," she said, almost panicky. No more questions. He had to stay level-headed.

"OK, OK, Yana. Relax, we'll handle it." He was hoping she'd ask him to use the sphere, hoping she wouldn't. He put a hand on her shoulder. She brushed it off. At least she didn't stab him.

"You can get in, with the sphere."

There it was, his opportunity. "What do I do?"

"Find out what is blocking us and remove it."

—— ⟨⟩ ——

Instant interface. Long distance, longer than he'd tried. *No problem.* Find the network cell towers, follow to satellite uplink. Couldn't resist accessing the camera on the satellite. A spectacular view, sun glinting on the horizon, continent lit up with millions of access points. Denver was easy to spot, the brightest point in the central continent. Down the beam, central networking system. Terabytes of information whizzing past him, carrying him. Snippets of conversation, videos, money transfers, music, confidential information, medical files, personnel files. *Ignore them, behave. Remember who you are. You're not a voyeur.* Onyx's building gleaming, a sun among planets, security levels far beyond anything he'd seen. Didn't matter, he was in almost instantly, searching for the corruption, finding something unexpected.

Greta.

—— ⟨⟩ ——

They shook hands and Onyx almost hugged her. Grit's defenses went up. Onyx wasn't the touchy-feely type. An act? For whose benefit? *Ignore it for now.* Greta turned to Gino. Gino read her eyes; *Something hinky. On your guard.*

Onyx sat down with a flourish, Elena entering with a drink, a case of cigarettes. Onyx lit up, offered the case. Gino took one, Grit didn't smoke. Drinks were sipped.

"Welcome friends, what can I do for you today?" The voice hers in pitch and timber, completely wrong in rhythm and cadence. Was she drunk, drugged?

Gino took the lead. "We're looking for Greta's brother, Hans. We think he might have come here."

"Why, Greta, I didn't know you had a brother. Is he in trouble?" A lie. Greta had said something in passing a few times. Onyx never forgot. Another glance at Gino, a sub-perceptible shake of his head. He knew.

"He may be," Gino continued, "so he hasn't been here?"

"Why would he come here?" A flourish of her arms, encompassing the room, the building. "And, if I may be so bold, why am I discussing this with a lackey?" There was a cruel gleam in her eyes now, but Gino was unperturbed.

"The commander is currently unable to speak."

"Oh, yes, I see now," she said, as if she had completely missed the bandage on Greta's face. Onyx didn't miss details.

She stood, crossed the few feet, grabbed Grit's chin between her fingers, and leaned in close, practically stroking the black bandage. "Why, dear Grit, who would mar such a visage? Angry boyfriend?"

Grit jerked back. This was all wrong. Onyx was an ally, maybe even a friend. Something was desperately wrong here. Grit stood, gestured to Gino. They were leaving.

Sudden pain. Onyx's fingers were under the hard shell of the bandage, pulling. It tore away from Grit's jaw, drops of blood spattering her and Onyx's faces. Grit brought her hand up, swinging defensively. Onyx moved back, drew something black and sharp. She nearly caught Grit off guard. Nearly. Grit sidestepped the slash, grabbed the wrist, broke it, and took Onyx to the floor. Onyx had to be drunk. Grit had seen her fight, she shouldn't have been that easy to disarm.

Gino drew his gun and stood over her. Onyx made no noise, lay still, didn't breathe. There was no way she was dead, but checking for a pulse would be stupid. Grit crossed the room to the door. It opened a second later, the bodyguard coming through with weapon drawn. Grit took it from him and broke his leg at the knee with her boot. He went down in a heap, dead still. She exchanged another confused glance with Gino. At least the door was open.

"Most rude of you, Greta. I thought we were friends," Onyx said, though not the one on the floor. Another door had opened, and another Onyx entered, dressed the same, carrying a rifle Grit didn't recognize. Compact, cold blue, vicious-looking. Onyx swung, fired from the hip, predictably firing wide. Vicious heat seared Grit's face, melting the wall. Grit drew her service pistol, aiming high in case of armor, and put two bullets in Onyx's face, plus one in the throat from Gino.

Silent for a moment.

"I assume this hasn't happened before?" Gino's attempt at levity fell flat.

The lights went out. Things got weirder.

— «» —

Hans was stunned by what he encountered. The whole building was a circuit. A solid mass of infinitely reprogrammable circuitry, its paths and connections changed with the merest thought, completely malleable, multipurpose. He located Greta, wanted to see her, and the walls obliged.

Onyx's living quarters were more extensive than he'd realized on his visit. Moving through darkness he found three bodies on the floor, no ID tags, signatures different from what he was seeing from Grit and Gino, who'd donned lightweight goggles to see in the dark. Grit taking a rifle from one of the bodies. Hans tried to zoom in, identify the body. Something blocked him. Static defenses? Someone else with a sphere? The body remained a black silhouette.

"Grit's in your building, something attacked her," he said to Onyx, in the passenger seat.

"Unexpected." He couldn't tell whether her response was to him or her unseen comrade.

"We need to get her out of there."

"Agreed. Where is she?"

"In your apartment."

"The landing bay is nearby, check it for her jumpcraft."

A quick check. Jumpcraft in hanger, still warm. Hans started it, activated its static defenses, and locked its security down so it would only recognize Grit and Gino. Then it was time to call his sister.

— «» —

"Grit, you there?" A familiar voice came through her comm. Hans?

"Yeah, that you, Hans?" Her voice was muffled, slurred, painful. But she could talk without the bandage.

"It's me."

"You sure?" Onyx hadn't been Onyx, why should Hans be Hans?

"Sure as I can be. You need to get out of there."

"No shit. Where are you? How'd you get through to this comm?" The cadence of his voice said Hans. Grit went with her gut, trusted him. One more step down the rabbit hole.

"I'm opening a path back to your jumpcraft. Do you remember the way?"

"Yes."

"Good. You should move, something's moving your way *en masse*."

Grit signaled Gino. *Exit, post haste*. He nodded and took point, always a gentleman, moving cautiously out to the hallway.

The door shut between them, cutting the bodyguard in half.

— «» —

Something fought him for control, something with his capacities, or nearly. Hans tried to lock down doors and elevators, only to have them power up just as quickly. He couldn't keep up with them, needed to narrow his focus, get Grit out. Screw the rest of the building, clear the corridor for Grit. He could not view what was coming toward their location, knew only that it was too big to be pods. He hoped that was a good thing.

Emergency, Gino in the hallway, Grit trapped inside. Divide and conquer. Get the door open. Fighting the presence, helped by its spread focus, but still barely gaining control. Opening the door, which shut again before Grit could exit. Afraid it would cut her in half, but Grit solved the problem for him.

— «» —

No time to consider, just react. Grit stood back with the rifle. Gunshots from the corridor. *Hold 'em, Gino*. She took aim at the door, fired. The door sagged, softened. She fired again, liquefying the carbon structure. Immense heat radiated and she fired once more. The door finally collapsed, almost sloughing to the floor. Gino stood beyond, firing intensely into the dark. A short jump over the melted heap, and she tapped Gino on the shoulder. *Calculated retreat.* He moved back, Grit turned to cover. A nightmare was coming up the hallway.

Bodies were filling the hallway, clambering for space, moving forward. Naked bodies, sterile bodies, clothing-less, genital-less. An army of mannequins. She shouldered and fired, the gun immolating great swaths, the smell of burnt flesh wafting back down the hallway. Greta continued to fire. The bodies in front burnt, fell, fused, a barrier of flesh. Impenetrable, for the time being. Gino whistled, and Greta fell back to a corner.

— ⟨⟩ —

"What does your building do?" Hans asked.

"I don't follow." Onyx was playing dumb.

"It's factory. What does it make? Pods?"

"Among other things."

"I don't have time for you to be coy. Something is in control of your factory," his face was slack, distracted, mind fighting somewhere else, "What happens if it gains control? Fifty feet to the hanger, move, Grit!"

"Anything controlling that building would be unstoppable."

— ⟨⟩ —

They moved quickly, sounds of movement at their backs, nothing in front. Greta couldn't shake the feeling they were being herded. At least they were being directed where she already wanted to go.

"Fifty feet to the hanger, move, Grit," Hans yelled in her ear.

They moved quicker, gaining the hanger. The jumpcraft's engines were whining, air filled with fumes and ozone. *Check the corners. Crouch. Move for the craft.*

Something was scurrying from a hole in the floor. It was Greta's first view of a pod, and she knew immediately that was what had killed the assassin in Hans' hospital room. Here to help? Gino turned around to fire, the flash nearly blinding her infrared vision.

It leaped, landed on Gino. A sharp grunt. *No time. Shoulder, aim, fire.* The pod was thrown off into the corner, smoking. Gino was not moving.

The doors above began to open. Two more pods were coming through the floor.

— «» —

Hans saw Gino go down, tried to control the pod. No luck. Grit hit it with something that disabled it. He had to get them out of there. *Be OK, Gino, for Grit's sake.*

He opened the hanger doors, started the elevator. The jumpcraft's guns fired at the oncoming pods. Hundreds of pods were swarming up through the building, scurrying down halls, climbing the exterior. He could control some of them, shut them down, link them to form barriers, attack their comrades. Still too many. Grit was dragging Gino onto the jumpcraft. Hans activated the autopilot and accelerated, guns still firing. A small handful of pods were hanging on the exterior. Hans was still fighting for control. Success; one pod, taking two others with it as it jumped from the craft. There was only one left, and it was tearing a hole in the jumpcraft's exterior, shredding electronics and control surfaces.

— «» —

Dragging Gino, no time to be angry. Something had activated her jumpcraft's defenses; its main cannon obliterated the two oncoming pods. *More coming. Don't think. Get Gino on the craft.* In through the side, pulling him after her, laying him down on the floor, turning to fire at the oncoming pods, door closing. The engines maxed, lifting the jumpcraft through still-opening doors. *Door shut. Check Gino.* A vicious stab wound in his abdomen, another through his chest. *Sucking sounds. Collapsed lung. Still breathing.* She went for the medical kit.

"Grit, there's still one on the outside of the craft, can you hit it with that rifle?"

"Where?"

"I'll show you"

Grit's goggles lit up, something changing their viewing frequency, a bright blue glow appearing at chest-height nearly in front of her. She didn't have time to question how. She fired a blast melting nearly through the wall, the second opening a hole, and the third frying the creature outside.

Hans came back. "That's all of them. How's Gino?"

"Hurt."

"Get him handled. We'll talk later."

— «·» —

How to combat the presence still fighting him in the building? It had the edge in sheer power. *Distract it, continue to spread its attention.* Hans activated machines in the building's interior, tried to destroy servers, take down doors and elevators, and keep its attention away from Hans' true purpose.

Hans gave the pods short directions to return to the center of the building, to return to their storage bays. *Contain the explosion underground, direct it downward, keep collateral damage to a minimum. Check for people in the vicinity. No one alive in the building, surrounding area empty. Nearest people Grit and Gino, moving away fast.*

"I'm going to detonate your building, any objections?" He wondered if Onyx would try to stop him.

"Do it."

Power surged in him as he continued to gain control. He was winning, beating back the assailant, gaining more control of the building, allowing time for the pods to take their positions. *I'm in control here.*

The pods were now secured in the lower levels. Grit was at a safe distance. The enemy was still unaware.

Do it.

To Hans the explosion was not visceral, but merely a great wave of red lights, error signals, and systems offline. The shining building went black. He was surprised by the building's strength, and its shape and solidity directed the explosion down, a shockwave tearing into the substructure, cutting utility lines, old plumbing, obsolete electrics, collapsing a sewage tunnel. The pressure continued down, down…

...to the high-speed line. The evening train from Cheyenne was running through a bypass tunnel via Denver on its way to Houston, still accelerating, nearing 1300 miles per hour. Forty-two passengers, names scrolling past Hans' gaze. Dates of birth. Height, weight, age. The tunnel collapsing ahead of them.

Onyx was right. They didn't even have time to scream.

— «» —

Hans was drunk. Massively, righteously shitfaced.

They'd found a bar, one of the many establishments that took advantage of the lack of legal supervision by founding an establishment outside any city jurisdiction. That put it under federal control, but the feds mostly left them alone. This one was done up all Retro Hick with barren wooden walls covered in dead animals and pin-ups. A sign advertised amateur strip nights every Saturday. Hans was glad it wasn't Saturday.

Onyx sat across from him, completely out of place. She'd matched him drink for drink of the surprisingly high-quality gin they served here, but was still stone sober. He hated her.

They hadn't spoken more than two words since the incident. She'd lost her home base; he'd lost a lot more. Hans wasn't drinking to forget, he wanted to do himself genuine harm. He could now add forty-two more names to the previously small list of three. That made... fuck it, he couldn't figure it out in this state.

"How much more are you planning on drinking, Hans?"

He didn't answer.

"We need to be moving."

He spat on the table in front of her.

"Are you trying to kill yourself?"

He downed the shot in front of him.

Onyx drew a knife. Hans flinched. She put it on the table in front of him.

"Here. This is quicker. Less painful, too."

"You do it. You're the killer here," he snarled, baring his neck at her.

She picked up the knife and stabbed it through the table in front of him. It went down to the hilt, spearing through the thick wood, nearly cutting him.

"Fuck, lady, I said kill, not castrate."

"Since you refuse to act like a man, maybe you don't deserve the equipment."

She left the knife in front of him. He reached out, fingered the hilt, grasped and yanked. The knife came out easily. Vicious blade. She'd said it could cut bone, it would be easy enough to go through the flesh of his neck. He couldn't do it, coward that he was.

"How do you do it?" he asked.

"Do what?"

"How can you kill and be unaffected by it?"

"I'm a cold bitch, Mr. Ricker, the way my father made me."

"And what about your mother, Ms. Petrovich? What did she teach you?"

"She taught me to dance." Onyx rose and stormed off. Hans didn't expect her back, but she returned with refills. They drank.

"My mother tried to teach me to hunt." Hans tried to keep his words clear. "I couldn't do it. I was useless. Couldn't track, couldn't fire a gun straight, couldn't pull a trigger on an animal. She and Grit used to send me out to collect berries and mushrooms while they skinned whatever they'd found. I couldn't stomach it."

Onyx kept silent. Hans appreciated her for that.

"Thing was, I liked the collecting. Got to know all the plants. If you kept quiet you could see the wildlife. Once or twice I almost got a deer to eat from my hand. Never could figure out how someone could shoot something like that. My mom never gave me a hard time, neither did Grit. But some of my friends did. That's what living in a place in the outland is supposed to be about, I guess. Roughing it, living off the land, all that old cowboy bullshit. They act like it's some kind of fort, like fuckin' Indians are gonna attack or some shit. But it's just a city. We got water, electricity, complete network connectivity, just like everyone else. We eat hydroponic vegetables and synthetic meat. And occasionally we go out and kill ourselves a live one, just so we can show nature what's what. Big fuckin' man on campus, humanity is. We don't even need to and we're still gonna kill you. What a bunch of assholes."

He finished his drink. Onyx got him another. A small scuffle occurred by the bar, some roughneck trying to cop a feel; he ended up lying on the ground holding his broken hand.

Hans sipped his gin. He couldn't taste it anymore. His tongue was numb, along with the rest of his face. Onyx still matched him, not even batting an eye.

"Six," she said.

"Hmmm?"

"You asked how many people I've killed. Six, up close and personal."

"You enjoy every one?"

"I still have nightmares about them all." She downed her drink. Hans tried to match her, but spilled most of it on his shirt, cursing.

"Well, Illiyana, that makes me over seven times the villain. Your paltry six, my forty-two, unless you want to add in the three that were already dead because of me."

"You didn't kill those people, Hans."

"Fuck you I didn't. I set off the bombs, those fucking nightmares you created."

"If you hadn't and we lost control of that building, thousands would have died."

"Well, I guess I'm glad to be a murderer then."

There was nothing else to say.

The bartender came over, asked them to leave. Onyx glared at him until he wandered off.

"I killed my father when I was seventeen. Put a ceremonial dagger through his chin, into his brain. He'd killed my mother, kidnapped me, made me a killer and a whore. I killed four men for him, seduced them and murdered them in the afterglow. Stabbed one, strangled the others in their sleep. I have no idea what they'd done to gain his ire, what he wanted from them, I just wanted to please him so badly, even though I hated him and was terrified of him. After the fourth one he threw me to his men for the night as a reward. Job well done. The next evening, I killed him, ran away. Lev helped me get away, betraying my father. They chased us halfway across the world. I found a partner here, one who could protect me. We wanted to change the balance of power, change the world."

"You and every other tyrant."

"The sphere could…"

"Could what?!" Hans lifted his head, the room spinning. "Kill a trainload of people? Kill a city? Kill a country? Rule the world?"

"That was not the intention."

"Neither was Brigham getting a hold of it, I imagine. How the hell did it get away from you?"

"We don't know."

"You don't know? A game-changer with massive lethal capability, and you don't know? I'm beginning to think you're not as secure and with it as you pretend. This thing floating around among all the idiots in this world…"

Hans had her blood up now.

"So far, Hans, only one idiot has been able to use it."

"And he only killed forty-two people, go get me another drink."

She didn't. "You can't focus on that, Hans, you were doing everything you could to…"

"To save my sister, to save your damn organization. To keep your secrets. I've killed for you, Illiyana, my debt is paid. You want my help from here on in? You be straight with me. Things have happened, things you're ignoring. Either that or you've legitimately forgotten them, which means I'm running across the country with a fucking nutter. No more secrets."

Onyx had no response to that. Hans' use of the sphere had equalized the power. She needed him. He wanted answers.

She rose, returned to the bar, had an argument with the bartender. Hans put his head down again, smelling plastic and gin. She put a glass in his hand, lukewarm and green. He knew what it was.

"Drink that," she said.

"I'm not drinking this shit. I came in here to get drunk. I'm not finished yet."

"You want your answers? Drink that. I'm not having this conversation with a pathetic drunk having a pity party."

Hans stared at it with dread. A basic alcohol antitoxin, seek and destroy, break down the alcohol in his blood, guaranteed sober in ten minutes. Oh, and it purged everything in your stomach, violently. Quick acting, too, if memory served. He looked up at Onyx, standing over him, then back to the glass. Fuck it.

"Help me up."

"You're not leaving until you drink that."

"Lady, about ten seconds after I drink that, most of my stomach contents are going to be on this table. Help me outside."

She gave him a hand, helped him outside. She smelled nice. He drank and struggled to some nearby bushes. It was violent, nasty business, leaving him kneeling and drained. Sobriety should be on the way shortly.

He was pretty sure he was done heaving. Onyx still stood beside him. She helped him up. Was that jasmine? Definitely floral. They made their way back to the car.

The back door stood open.

— «» —

Lorilei was gone. Not in the backseat, not in the small parking lot. Nowhere he could see. Woken up and wandered off, probably confused, probably scared. Hans wasn't even sure she'd ever actually been outside before. His head was still swimming, though clearing rapidly.

"Have to find her."

Onyx agreed.

Hans didn't know how long ago she'd left, didn't know how long he'd been in the bar, couldn't tell which direction she'd gone. The whole area was high grass and scrubland, the ground rough and rocky. Maybe Grit could've tracked her. He couldn't.

"Use the sphere."

Easy for her to say. It still held a hold on him. So powerful, so appealing. He didn't want it, so he stood there sobering up and debating, realizing he'd do anything to find her. He took the sphere.

Up to a satellite, looking for one with high-resolution cameras. One nearby, not connected with the others. Fed use only. Back to the ground, searching for federal encryption. Easy to spot, easy to break. Military base server. Uplink. Now on board the spy satellite. Directing its cameras, zooming down. One quarter meter resolution. Good enough to spot a person if they were moving. Flipping through the wavelengths, settling on infrared. Scanning nearby. Warm spot, moving slowly, one kilometer southwest. How'd she get so far?

Hans started off after her, sober now. That shit might be awful, but it was effective. Onyx followed without a word.

It was hard climbing, the ground littered with rocks and hard–to-see gullies. Hans moved in a straight line, adapting the satellite feed, bringing her location up in front of him. Less disorienting. Amazing what this thing could do.

It took a good thirty minutes to catch her. Hans was huffing and puffing, Onyx not even winded. A dark silhouette up ahead.

"Lorilei!" The shape tried to move faster, "Lorilei, stop!"

Trying to run quickly she tripped over a rock, went down. Hans could hear her yell. He ran.

She was lying on the ground. Feet bloodied. Legs bloodied. Arms bloodied. Robe torn and dirty, hanging open, still trying to stand and crawl away from him. Hans put a hand on her shoulder. She screamed and swung backward.

"Lorilei! It's Hans! Remember me?"

"He'll kill me, he'll kill me," she repeated over and over.

"Brigham's dead, he can't hurt you."

She didn't comprehend. "Have to go home."

"Lorilei," he put both arms around her and she struggled. Hans was uncomfortable holding down a naked girl, but he had no choice. "Lorilei, it's Hans, we watched a movie. I took you out of there. Brigham's dead. His base was destroyed. There's nothing to go back to."

She calmed, stopped babbling. "Hans?"

"Yes, Hans. We watched that awful cartoon movie, remember? You fell asleep."

"You… you let me sleep in the big bed."

"Yeah, in the big bed."

"He'll kill me."

"No, he won't. He's dead. His building's gone. You're with me."

"Your property now?"

The question brought sudden tears of rage to his eyes.

"No, Lorilei. No one's property. My friend, family, little sister if you want. I won't let them take you back."

Lorilei said nothing, confused. She relaxed. Hans stood, helped her up. She'd sprained an ankle in the fall, could barely walk. Hans picked her up and walked past a smirking Onyx.

"Sister?"

"Shut up."

— «» —

She'd muscled the jumpcraft onto the ground level landing pad at Denver General, the vehicle's own safety control systems the only thing keeping it from complete destruction. The security guard recognized her and Gino and stood back as Grit fireman-carried Gino into the elevator, calling ahead to an emergency crew, who met her in front of the ER. They wheeled Gino away, and a nurse tried to force Grit to sit and wait, have someone look at the wound bleeding down her chin. She wouldn't have it, but stood in the corner of the OR, watching. If Gino died she was going to be there.

He didn't.

A few hours later, Grit stood in one of the recovery rooms while Gino rested. His breath sounded strained but regular. Collapsed lung, damaged spinal cord. Routine repairs. He'd seen worse. All she could do was wait, not one of her stronger suits. A passing med tech had sat her down, cleaned and bandaged her face. A soft bandage this time; she was tired of not being able to communicate.

She had spent too much time in hospital rooms of late. Hans' for the last year, her own, now Gino's. Every move she made was two steps behind where she should be. Grit was not used to being on the back foot. Her rule had always been *check ten times, shoot once.* No moves without adequate preparation. But now, the more she prepared the more her enemies were ready for her. She needed a new plan. Something off the cuff, improvised. Hans was the one who excelled at that.

Where had he come from? Was that really him? There were too many security breaches; Hans talking to her on a comm he didn't even know she had, operating the jumpcraft remotely, seizing control of her goggles. Her equipment was supposed to be the most secure there was, and now everything she owned was on a party line. Had Hans blown the building?

Reports of the disaster drifted in on the newswaves, with viewscreen pictures of the collapsed structure; a sunken, cratered rubble pile, the material of the walls melting spontaneously, coating the surface of the crater with black glass. The shockwave took out one of the trains. Crews were already at work trying to open the tunnel. There were no rescue crews, no one expected any survivors. The worst rail disaster in history. She hoped it wasn't Hans' doing. She knew he wouldn't have done it intentionally; others might not.

She had to find him. At first, she just wanted him protected, but, true to form, he'd gotten himself snarled in the system. He was now of central importance. Her best lead was probably lying dead in that ruined building; Onyx's body, both of them. But that wasn't Onyx. If not, then who? Was Onyx dead? Had she ever been alive? Did she control those crab things? Why had they saved Hans and broken the ambush, but then attacked her and Gino?

Dammit, she needed to find Hans.

Gino still slept. Grit needed a walk.

On an impulse, she headed up to the hospice floor. She'd been doing it for fourteen months, and old habits die hard.

The entrance area had been cleaned up, with no sign of the nurse's shooting. The nurse behind the desk recognized her, smiled nervously. Grit realized she didn't know why she'd come here.

"Is Doctor Laud in?" The question was more to soothe the nurse.

"He's in the stasis room, I'll have someone…"

"I know the way, thank you." The nurse started to protest. Grit didn't give her the chance.

The stasis room creeped Grit out. Hans had floated in one of the tanks for almost a year, incisions appearing and disappearing as Laud installed new organs. Grit had been glad when they'd moved him to a normal bed.

Laud stood over the nurse's tank. Toni, Grit remembered. He looked up as Grit entered.

"Commander Ricker. Here to see me?"

"How is she?"

"Physically? Much better, the new neural tissue is almost done growing. That doesn't mean she'll ever recover, however."

"My apologies, Doctor. If we…"

"Please, Commander Ricker. No one blames you, certainly not I. How could you have foreseen what happened?"

"I should have."

Laud smiled sadly at her. "The arrogance of youth," he winked.

"I hardly think 'youth' is appropriate." She should be annoyed, but couldn't find it in her.

"When you're my age 'youth' is anything under a hundred or so."

"You're surprisingly spry for a centenarian."

"Clean living, Commander Ricker, clean living and the occasional medical miracle."

Greta moved to the table. Toni looked peaceful in the tank, face resting, emotionless, like those things that had attacked her in the hallway.

"Is there anything you can't grow?" she asked.

"How do you mean?"

"Organs, body parts, is there any part of the body you can't grow?"

"Only consciousness and personality."

"But you could grow a body from scratch?"

"Yes, though I don't know why I would," Laud sounded confused, intrigued.

"Have you ever heard of anyone doing it?"

"Rumors mostly, though since we have the capacity, it's hard to believe that someone hasn't at least tried it. But you'd have nothing more than a human-shaped slab of meat."

Greta mulled this over. Grown bodies. It could explain the lack of distinguishing features. If someone knew how to grow them, why not modify, simplify, depending on their intentions?

"Could you control them? Externally, I mean?" she asked.

Doctor Laud gave her a serious look. "I don't know how. We've come a long way, but interfacing the human mind with a computer or transmitter has always been hit or miss. Anyone able to control them externally would have technology the likes of which I've never even heard of."

"Yeah, there's been a lot of that going around lately."

CHAPTER 7

Hans stumbled back to the car, refusing to let Onyx carry Lori. The girl sat docilely in his arms, not speaking, barely moving, the only person in the world more confused than him.

He put her in the backseat, wishing he had something more substantial than her threadbare blanket to cover her. There was nothing in the trunk. He didn't even have a jacket to give her. So much for big brother.

Onyx resumed the passenger seat. Hans pulled them out of the parking lot and set the autopilot for his hometown of Glenwood.

"Taking her home to meet the family?" There was no sneer in Onyx's voice. Maybe playful teasing.

"We need to figure some things out, and you owe me some answers. But we can't do it here, not with her. I'm taking her to my mother, then we can make plans."

"I'm intrigued to meet Matron Ricker. Such interesting children she's raised."

"I don't think she'll like you calling her matron."

Onyx shrugged.

The car drove onto the interstate, sliding precariously between two cargo haulers. He flinched at the closeness of it and decided to darken the windows, give the autopilot a rare bit of trust.

He dozed on and off, not the best of ideas, even with the car driving. But he was exhausted. His last sleep felt years ago, his feet sore, legs sore, arms sore, head throbbing; just needed to close his eyes for a while. He jerked them open, glanced back to check on Lori. She sat upright, peering through the window.

"First car ride?" he asked her. She nodded timidly.

"Won't be the last, I promise."

Another nod.

How much damage had been done to her? Could she read? Write? Did she have any education at all? Would she even be able to adapt to the outside world? Hans had read of feral children kept in closets, how after a certain age they could be tamed but never taught. He had hope for Lori. Not a common feeling for him.

"You did good," Onyx said.

"What?"

"With the girl. Whatever else happens, know that you did the right thing removing her from there."

"I thought you were against it?"

"I was wrong."

"The great Onyx, ruler of her domain, wrong? Didn't think I'd ever see that."

"I have made many errors in my life, some nearly lethal for me, some definitely lethal for others. I know the mistakes I make, Hans. I try to learn from them. Can you say the same?"

Food for thought. A criminal and murderer lecturing him on learning from his mistakes. His last mistake ended lives. What could he possibly learn from that? He was still wondering if he could live with it.

The droning of the road lulled him to sleep.

— «» —

Sunlight woke him. There was something heavy in his lap. A naked girl. His legs were asleep, arms nearly so. Lori had crawled up onto his lap and left the filthy robe and blanket in the backseat. He didn't have the heart to move her. *Definitely have to get her some clothes.*

They'd made it to the mountains overnight, driving up through mesas and foothills. His home ground.

Onyx sat completely still in the passenger seat, eyes open. Had she slept?

"You a ninja or something?" Hans whispered, so as not to wake Lori.

"Hmmm?" her voice seemed far away, distracted.

"You learn how to sleep with your eyes open?"

"Sleep doesn't come easily to me."

As they topped a rise, the car pulled out to pass a cargo truck. The mountains loomed ahead. Maybe an hour to Glenwood. Hans recognized a small store run by a friend of his mom's. It sold a little bit of everything, sitting out in unincorporated land to avoid taxation. He pulled in.

"Why are we stopping?" Onyx asked.

"I need to get some clothes for Lori."

Hans woke her gently. She had slept like the dead and woke confused, hair rumpled.

"I need to get out for a moment."

She clung.

"Just for a few minutes. I'm going to get you some clothes. I'll be back, I promise."

Lori docilely allowed herself to be placed in the backseat. Hans sat kneading his legs, waiting for the tingling to go away. When he felt he could walk, he opened the door.

"Can you stay with her?"

Onyx nodded.

It took him fifteen minutes or so. The store did not have much selection, and the proprietor kept trying to sell him on having the clothes fabricated on site. Anything he wanted. Hans protested, shoved a pair of boy's jeans, a small belt, button-up collared shirt, and a pair of work boots on the counter, talked the woman into letting him owe her since she knew his mother, and stood through a few minutes of bored idle gossip.

He put the clothes on the seat next to Lori. She gave him a look and a hug. Awkward but enjoyable. She'd still barely talked.

They resumed their drive.

— «» —

Glenwood had attracted people to its hot springs and vapor caves for almost two hundred years, and the natives had used them before that. But the heat that powered them faltered a few decades before, and Glenwood transformed from a tourist trap to one of the many hardscrabble, unincorporated towns dotting the increasingly wild land outside the major city-states. Towns like Glenwood attracted the misanthropes and malcontents, people who were not comfortable with the monitoring systems even in a free city-state like Denver. There wasn't so much a heavy criminal element in Glenwood as a thriving black market in the types of things the feds didn't have time to police. Antique weapons sold alongside very modern, and somewhat illegal, body mods, mood enhancers, underground pornography and such. Several discredited surgeons lived here. If one was a bit suicidal and willing to sign all the right forms waving the surgeon's responsibility, it was possible to have the internal ID chip removed. It was not a common surgery, and the chance of escaping permanent brain damage or death was only fifty-three percent. Hans had been lucky, for probably the only time.

The welcome sign was nearly covered in vegetation. The population hadn't been updated in decades. It was considerably more than the faded 8538.

Though the springs had dried up, the smell still permeated everything. Sulfur. It smelled like home. The main drag still displayed the facades of small town America, but the stores behind them were anything but. No mom and pop stores, no candy and licorice. Most of the stores dealt in gray market contraband. The owners kept guns under the counters and didn't like strangers. His kind of town.

Hans piloted the car manually through the town proper. Pat's reputation with a rifle was legendary.

He stopped the car in front of an old gate, got out to open it. Lori was peering avidly from the window, Onyx unaffected. It was a half mile drive up smooth gravel to Pat's house, which had two stories and wraparound porch of bare wood. Hans was home. He wished he could stay.

He stopped the car, started toward the house, then remembered Lori. She sat at the window, unmoving. *Idiot.* He went back to help her out. She didn't want to get out at first. Hans cajoled her, pulled firmly. Lori resisted him. Eventually he picked her up. She grasped him desperately. He tried to be encouraging.

They walked toward the old house.

Pat was on the porch, standing with the door open, rifle propped on her hip like some modern Annie Oakley. At sixty-four, the hardness was just starting to leave her. She was lean and wiry, wearing jeans and an old, faded button-up. Frontier woman extraordinaire.

"Hello, Hans." She smiled at him, frowned at the other two. "Who're these?"

"Friends."

Pat waited for him to explain.

"This is Illiyana." Onyx stepped forward, extended a hand. Pat shook it fiercely, frowned at her outfit. "She's saved my life a couple of times. I'm trying to return the favor."

"You saved my boy?" Pat dropped her hand, put it back in a pocket. "Thank you, though you may find it wasn't worth it."

"I'm figuring that out." A brief smile at Hans' expense.

Pat turned back to Hans, moved closer. Lori gripped him fiercely. "And who's this?" she asked him.

"Her name's Lorilei."

"You kidnapping girls now, Hans?"

"Just started yesterday."

Lorilei continued to grip him, fingers finding sore muscles. He tried to relax her. Pat moved in and grasped her gently but firmly under the chin, turned her face from Hans' chest.

"Can you speak, girl?"

"Yes." Almost a whisper.

"Can you walk?"

"Yes." Nearly nonexistent.

"Well, then, do you like hot cocoa?"

Just a nod of her head.

"We got some pretty good hot cocoa inside, but the only lady that ever gets carried through my door better be a newlywed. Did you marry my son?"

Lorilei shook her head.

"Then you'll have to walk. Get down from there and follow me."

Hans started to protest, Pat ignored him and went inside. Onyx followed. The girl stared up at him.

"Looks like we gotta walk. Test out those new shoes. You game?"

She sat quietly in his arms, deciding. Nodded. He set her down. She held his hand. Wouldn't let go.

They went inside.

—— «» ——

Lorilei took to Pat almost immediately. She was good at taking orders, Pat good at giving them. Anger stayed with him, though, as he watched the conditioning she had endured. She stood by the table, unwilling to sit until Pat directly ordered her to. Then she sat next to Hans, unmoving, not even swinging her legs, which didn't quite reach the floor. Hans pulled her chair next to his. She squeezed his hand tightly, nodding at questions from Hans' mom, only letting go to reach for the steaming mug, even then glancing at Hans for permission to drink.

It was a good thing Brigham was dead already. He hadn't suffered nearly enough.

When Hans got up to use the restroom, she jumped down to follow him. He put her back in the chair, told her he'd be right back, but she tried to follow anyway. Pat ordered her to sit down and finish her drink. Lorilei bowed her head, returned to the chair.

Sitting in the john, taking care of business, he wondered what he was going to do. He was glad to help, and felt growing affection for the poor girl, but he was not qualified to deal with what had been done to her. Could anyone completely recover from that? Certainly, she needed more than he could give her. A twelve-year-old girl, completely sheltered and cowed, yet far too experienced in things she should only now be thinking about. It was hopeless, but then so was much of his situation.

There was screaming from the kitchen. Lorilei yelling and crying, the sound of breaking dishes, Pat yelling. Hans yanked his pants up and ran to help.

The dogs had woken up. Bogie was sitting dejectedly in the middle of the floor, just barely thumping his tail, disappointment and surprise on his face. Lori sat on top of the table, no longer screaming, her eyes wide with terror.

She'd never seen a dog before. Or else one had been used to terrorize, maybe hurt her. Hans moved to her, she climbed into his arms, crying, turning her head.

"It's OK, Lori. This is Bogie. He couldn't hurt you if he wanted to, he's lost most of his teeth. He's just an old dog looking for a treat."

Lori didn't turn. Pat started to drag Bogie from the kitchen, his eyes hurt by a situation he didn't understand. Cocker spaniels were not used to frightening people. Hans stopped her.

"Wait, Mom. I want to introduce them."

"I don't think this is the time, Hans."

"Then when? Just let him go a second."

Pat gave him a look of exasperation, but she let go of Bogie's collar. Hans put Lori on the table edge and pried her hands loose from his neck. He held her head so she'd look at him, then took a deep breath.

"Have you ever seen a dog before?"

She shook her head. At least she'd never been hurt by one.

"Did you ever have a pet?"

Another shake of her head.

"Pets are family, friends. You're my friend, so is Bogie. He just wants a treat, maybe someone to scratch him behind the ears. Think you can do that?"

A pause, an almost undetectable shake.

"You sure? You scratch his ears and he'll be the best friend you ever had. Do it for me?"

She just stared at him. Hans picked her up, sat on the floor, and situated her in his lap. He was improvising, hoping he didn't make things worse. He couldn't have Lori run screaming every time she saw a dog, too many people let their dogs run loose up here.

Bogie sat. Hans hadn't seen him in over a year. A lot more gray speckled Bogie's muzzle than Hans remembered. Bogie'd put on some weight, probably because Pat spoiled the dogs. He needed a haircut and a bath.

Hans patted the floor, Bogie trotted over. Lori stiffened, flinched back. Bogie sat just by Hans' right knee, still waiting, knowing that the girl was scared of him, confused but obedient.

"Bogie, this is Lori. Lori, Bogie."

Bogie tilted his head. Lori sat very still.

"Now you, Lori."

She made a little noise, relaxed a little.

"Introduce yourself like this."

Hans held his hand out, let Bogie sniff it. Bogie's ears went back, rump coming up off the tile, tail wagging easily. He gave Hans a lick. Hans scratched his ears. Bogie tilted his head into Hans' hand. It was good to see Bogie again.

"Now you do what I did. When he puts his ears back and wags his tail, that means hello."

Lori took a moment. Most of the fear had left her, replaced by fascination. How could she have never seen a dog before? A tentative hand extended, palm up, just like Hans. Bogie gave it a few sniffs, licked her palm and wagged his tail. Lori giggled a little. It was a glorious sound. She reached up to scratch Bogie's head, putting her hand just where Hans' had been. Bogie made a contented noise, tilted his head, thumped his back foot a little.

Lori smiled.

Then Bacall came in. Lori screamed, leaped from his arms, and knocked the chair over trying to climb on the table. Bacall, the more nervous of the pair, bolted from the room, tail between her legs.

It took Hans another ten minutes to get Lori down again.

— «» —

Hans awoke to another body in his bed. Lori. At least she was clothed this time; Pat had given her a flannel nightgown. Hans hadn't had much trouble getting Lori to sleep. She'd started nodding off early, still feeling the side effects of her journey and injury. She appeared OK, but Hans was going to take her to the doctor in the morning. He needed someone's opinion besides his own.

She'd wanted to sleep with him, had even propositioned him. How do you deal with something like that? It was the only way she'd learned to show affection. He'd acquiesced with the stipulation that she keep her nightgown on. Then she wanted her blanket. In the fuss Hans had forgotten about it. He found it crumpled up under the seat in their purloined car. With her blanket found, Lori promptly fell asleep beside him, and just as promptly spread out and started snoring, taking up most of the small twin in his mom's guest room. He'd somehow managed to fall asleep crammed up against the wall, helped by a combination of exhaustion and years of sleeping with two furry bed hogs.

He was awake now. Where was Onyx? She'd said little since they'd arrived, and spent most of her time standing or sitting on the periphery as Hans dealt with getting Lori settled down. Pat had tried her best to be civil, Onyx was indifferent. Did the woman sleep? He found it absurd to think of her wrapped in one of his mother's nightgowns, bedding down on the couch. She probably slept upside down, hanging from the rafters.

He was worried for her.

Hans extracted himself from the mass of Lori, trying to be gentle and quiet. He needn't have bothered. Lori slept on even as Hans lifted her head to extract his arm. Climbed over her, stood to put on his shirt. He'd finally been able to get some real clothes. Well-worn jeans, and loose, comfortable button-ups. A pair of old work boots. This room had been his when he was a kid, with Grit across the hall, and Mom downstairs. Nostalgia mixed with the strangeness of the last few days. He could almost forget them if not for the girl in his bed, and the enigma downstairs.

He went looking for Onyx, doubting she was asleep.

She wasn't. It was pitch black outside, the kind of darkness unknown in the city. Visibility was ten feet or less if the moon wasn't out. Through the downstairs window he saw the tip of her cigarette glowing. He felt a sudden jones for one; it'd been over twenty-four hours.

She held one out to him, squinting in the porch light he'd turned on. She lit it for him, moving back further beyond the circle of light. They smoked in companionable silence. Was she a friend now? Certainly, they'd been through a lot. She'd promised him some answers. It'd been on the back burner since Lori woke up.

Bogie scratched at the door and Hans opened it to let him out. The old dog curled up on the porch by his mom's rocking chair. Hans took the hint and sat down.

"You grow up here?" A question from the dark. A silhouette leaning over the railing.

"Yeah."

"So, you live with you mother?"

"No, my place is about a half a mile down that path." Bogie wanted his head scratched, Hans obliged.

"This place is very peaceful."

"Ma doesn't have any boarders at the moment. It can get pretty lively when all the guest houses are full."

"Show me where you live."

"Here it is."

"No, I mean your house."

"You want to walk in the dark?"

"Sure."

"All right."

Hans didn't know how Lori would react if she woke up and he wasn't in the house. He hoped she slept.

It was a ten-minute walk down the well-maintained dirt path. Bogie trotted easily beside them, sniffing and marking familiar spots. He'd gotten too old to go tearing off after the squirrels and foxes that made their homes here, but he'd still point and stare at them in frustration before catching up to Hans.

The walk took two more cigarettes each.

It'd been a guest cabin before Hans moved in. He'd made no major changes beyond giving it a fresh coat of paint. He was decently handy with tools, but gained no satisfaction from home repairs beyond being glad it was done. A small cabin, with two bedrooms, a bathroom, kitchen, and living area. Hans had picked it because one of the previous boarders had spent a considerable amount of time digging a basement workshop. The workshop contained most of Hans' livelihood.

The key was under the porch mat. Hans gave Onyx the tour, the strangeness of being back combined with this domestic façade. An international criminal, a woman who commanded an army of death-dealing high-end technology, standing in his kitchen pretending to admire the duck painting he'd hung to cover a water stain. The place had not been opened while he was gone, and it smelled empty and vacant. Luckily, he kept very little in the way of food on premises. Hans usually went up to the main house to eat with the other boarders.

"How long have you lived here?"

"About fifteen years, ever since I moved out of my mom's house."

"You ever bring women here?"

The question embarrassed him slightly. "I've never had a lot to offer a woman. They don't tend to stick around when they realize they're sleeping with a grumpy misanthrope with no prospects."

"What do you do?"

"Whatever pays. I'm OK with tools. I've gotten a decent reputation for repairing old electronics. People pay me for special jobs. Wanna see?"

She nodded. This was weird. *Play along.*

They exited the house, walked around the side to the old storm cellar doors. There was a heavier lock on this one, connected to an old fingerprint ID scanner. He miss-scanned the first time because of dust on the screen. He wiped off, scanned again. Success.

— «» —

Here was Hans' livelihood, if you could really call it that. The basement was strewn with broken electronics, some old, some ancient. Vacuum tubes harvested from obsolete cathode ray televisions, video recorders that still used disc and even tape media. Large unwieldy devices that only made phone calls or sent basic text messages. It was all piled haphazardly around a large workbench hewn roughly from trees. Tools of the trade included soldering irons, various types of pliers and wrenches, gauges and testing equipment, and spools of wire and insulation. Currently the workbench was occupied by a large metal box sprouting a seemingly random array of tubes and spouts. Onyx asked him what it was.

"It's an old coffee machine. I've been repairing it. I've gotten all the plumbing working, but it works on an ancient power system, and I've been trying to find the parts to adapt it."

"Is it valuable?" she asked, turning one of the large black dials.

"No. I was repairing it for myself."

Onyx twisted the knob back, and turned to look at a row of toasters. She was distracted, playing for time.

"Something on your mind?" Hans asked

She didn't reply, played idly with a lever, stooped to rummage through a box.

"What's this?" She pointed at a mass of wires and rusted metal.

"An old electric motor. It used to power a cart my mom drove around."

"Hmm…"

She stood, wiped her hands on her pants, leaving dusty streaks on the black leather.

"You don't need to pretend. None of this can be that interesting to you." Hans crossed his arms across his chest.

"Actually, I find this rather fascinating. You spend your life trying to rebuild the past."

"And you spend it trying to control the future."

"I thought so once… now…" she tapered off.

"Now what?"

Onyx shrugged, "I can't reach my contact. I haven't been able to most of the day."

"Is that common?"

"No. It's never happened before. I've always been in constant contact, but the last day or so almost nothing."

"Who's your contact?"

"Hmm?" She turned to look at him. He repeated the question. She didn't respond, removed an old television from a rickety chair, tested its sturdiness, sat down.

Hans tried again. "You said you'd give me some answers."

"Yes, I did."

"So, who's your contact?"

"I can't tell you that."

"Why?"

"I don't know."

Hans raised his eyebrows, waited for her to elaborate.

"I… can't remember."

"You can't remember who you're contact is? Even though you've been in constant communication with him?"

Onyx' face scrunched up a little, real fear and confusion crossing it. "No, I can't," she admitted. "I think I knew at one point, but there's a hole where it used to be."

"Convenient."

"Very."

Hans swallowed his frustration. "OK, let's try a different one. What were those things we saw in the crate at Brigham's?"

"The what?" She looked genuinely confused. Hans didn't buy it.

"The bodies. What were they?"

"What are you talking about?"

"You. Me. Buried in a crate while your minions dug us out. The bodies. Copies of your assistant Elena, copies of your bodyguard, copies of the man who I talked to in your building, copies of you."

Onyx stared at him like he was a bug. No recognition in her eyes.

"How about the one you killed in my room. Elena strangling me, you slit her throat, then she was serving us breakfast. Remember that?"

"I don't know what you're trying to do here, Hans, but…"

"OK, here's an easy one. What color are your eyes?"

She frowned and twisted away on the chair. Hans continued badgering her.

"For a long time I thought you were just keeping things from me, just fucking with me, pretending not to remember. But you really don't know, do you? Something, maybe you, maybe your contact, is editing your memory. Your brain is Swiss cheese."

There was real anger in her voice. "What is the point of this interrogation?" Now she had a knife in her hands.

"My point? My point is that I don't think you're in control here. I don't think you can even trust yourself. I'm not even sure you're human."

Onyx jerked the knife and stood to show him blood dripping from her palm.

"Is this human enough for you?"

"Elena bled, too."

"Bullshit."

"What color are your eyes?"

"You can see them. You tell me."

"What color do you think they are?"

Onyx stood defiantly, dripping blood onto the concrete. She'd really cut deep with that sharp knife of hers. Hans expected her to attack him. There would be nothing he could do. He'd invited her rage. It would be in his best interests to back off. He didn't.

"What color are your eyes?"

"Hazel, like my mother's."

"Wrong."

The knife flew through the air, passing perilously close to his head, and embedded itself in concrete. He felt a trickle of blood run down his neck. She'd nicked his ear. He didn't move.

"Are you human? Or are you one of them?"

"One of what?"

"The constructs, the clones, the aliens. I don't know what they are. I watched you die, saw you come back. Same with Elena. And you all have the same eyes. Pale gray. No one has eyes like that."

"Why are you doing this?" The area around her was nearly melting with her anger.

"You don't have to trust me. There's a mirror in the bathroom upstairs. Check your eyes. While you're at it, I suggest you check to see if you're completely intact."

"Meaning?"

"Meaning the bodies I saw had no genitals. Check to see if you still got your parts."

Her anger was fading a bit, fear replaced it. Confusion. She crossed the room and Hans tried not to flinch as she reached past him and retrieved her knife from the wall. She stormed up the stairs.

Are you there?

Answer me!

...

I want an explanation.
Is this your doing?
What have you done?
Why can't I remember?
Are you fucking with my memory?
Answer me, goddamn it!
Where are you?
What the hell is going on?
Where is the real me?
Is there a real me?

...

Hans gave Onyx a quarter of an hour. He listened to her moving around in the cabin above, heard her gasp, break something. She stomped out, slammed the front door.

He tinkered with the coffee machine, searched aimlessly, paced. He'd finally confronted her. He'd known it would happen eventually. She didn't know, hadn't known, probably would forget again, but for now she was struggling. He'd never seen someone more alone. She needed a friend, even if she didn't agree.

He went upstairs, ready to walk back to the house and search the woods, barely lit by a crescent moon.

There was no light from the house; she'd turned them off. Hans stood for a moment, trying to decide where she might have gone. He saw the tip of her cigarette glow from a small hill a few dozen feet away. She stood in the darkness, always had. He cautiously walked over.

They stood in silence. A minute became two, became ten. Something moved through the woods nearby. There were bears here sometimes, mountain lions, too. Hans feared for them if they attacked her. Finally, he broke the silence.

"You got one of those for me?" She'd been chain smoking, lighting each cigarette on the end of the previous one. Where she kept getting them from was as mysterious as the knives.

"You're gonna have to get your own soon."

"Do it tomorrow."

She gave him a cigarette. He lit it with a lighter he'd swiped from his mom's house, the flame momentarily blinding in the dark. They smoked awhile. She handed him another, then another, the ribbing gone after the first time.

"You want a drink?"

A pause before answering, then she mumbled something and turned toward the cabin.

He found an old bottle of vodka on a back shelf in the freezer. Not as good as hers, but it'd do the job. He let the water run until the brown tinge disappeared, then washed the dust out of a couple of old glasses. He brought it out to the porch, where she sat on one of the old rockers. He filled her glass, offered it. She drained it, handed it back. He filled, she drained, for four glasses, without blinking. Hans kept quiet. She took the fifth and placed it on her lap. Hans sat with his own, sipped. Not great, but it was ice cold.

They smoked. They drank. They didn't speak. An hour passed.

— «» —

"I wasn't always this way, I can't have been." Her voice was startling after the extended silence, and slightly slurred. Whatever her body was, it could get drunk. Hans chose not to respond.

"I had a real body once, I'm certain of it." She was waiting for a response, he grunted at her.

"I'm human, Hans. I don't know what happened, I don't know how I got here, but I'm human."

Hans grunted another assent.

"You don't believe me." Her voice was desperate for assurance.

"I don't know what to believe. Everything that's happened since I woke up has been unknown territory. I don't know what you are."

"Human, Hans, I'm human," she practically spit it at him, "How can I not be? I have a history, memories. How can I be anything else?"

"I don't know, Yana. Your memories are not entirely reliable. Something's been editing them."

She took another drink, drew on a cigarette. "I think I've known or suspected that my memories have holes in them for awhile now. Nothing specific, just a feeling of emptiness. Maybe I am doing it. A psychotic break or something."

"You're not crazy."

"You sure?"

"No crazier than anyone else, no crazier than me."

"That's not much of a vote of confidence."

"It's all I got."

He stood up and flipped on the porch light. The dim bulb brought her profile into focus. Her eyes were bleary and far away, face flushed, mouth pulled into a tight grimace. She pulled on the cigarette like it pained her, downed the rest of her drink, and held the glass out to him.

"That's the last of the vodka," he said.

"You got anything else?"

"I'll look."

He searched the kitchen fruitlessly, then remembered that he'd stashed an old bottle of whiskey in the pantry. He retrieved it, still half-full.

She grimaced when he brought it out. "I hate whiskey."

"It's what I got."

He filled her glass. She drank, choked, took another sip.

"How drunk you plan on getting, lady?"

"I still have one of these tablets from the bar. I can sober up whenever I want."

"I ain't holdin' your hair when you puke."

"You're no gentlemen."

"Nope."

She downed her glass, coughed, held it out to him defiantly. He took it from her and filled it all the way to the brim. She downed the whole thing and stared back at him, the glass extended again. Hans handed her the bottle.

"Here, finish it. I don't like whiskey either."

"If you're trying to get me drunk and take advantage, you should know that I don't have the equipment."

"I don't think we've reached that point yet." He sat down in the rocker and sipped his still-full glass of vodka. She drank from the bottle, spilled some, wiped it off her chin, and sucked on her finger. Her poise was disappearing rapidly.

"What point?" she asked.

"Sex."

"Are you implying we were going to?"

"I haven't implied anything. I don't sleep with people I don't know, people I can't trust, or drunk women not in control of their faculties."

"You're a regular fuckin' gentlemen."

"Now you're contradicting yourself."

She chucked the bottle off the porch. It landed with a dull thud on the grass. The effort pulled open the wound she'd made on her hand. Blood dripped on the floorboards.

"How's your hand?" he asked.

"Hurts."

"You're bleeding again."

"Like you care."

Hans huffed at her, stood and went inside. He always kept a large first aid kit in the bathroom cabinet. He retrieved it, went back to the porch, and scooted his chair close to hers.

"Give me your hand."

"I thought we hadn't reached that point yet."

"Just give me your hand."

She held it out to him. Hans retrieved a small spray bottle, gripped her hand firmly. The liquid inside cleaned, disinfected, and, within seconds, formed a solid bandage over wounds. It also hurt like hell. She didn't even bat an eye. Hans started to wrap the hand in gauze. Probably unnecessary, but his mom's teachings stayed with him.

"Do you trust me, Hans?" Her voice was significantly slurred.

"It's not you I don't trust. It's whatever's controlling you."

"So, you do trust me?"

"You haven't given me any reason not to so far." He looked up at her; she was staring at him.

"Are we friends?"

"Sure." He dismissed the question, turned back to the bandaging.

"I'm serious," she said, her voice almost pleading.

He couldn't stand the self-pity he heard in it. "I've only known you a couple of days, and they haven't been very pleasant. I'm not really someone you want as a friend anyway. I don't have many."

"I don't have any."

Hans finished the bandaging. She took her hand back, tried to stand, slipped once, then pulled herself to her feet.

"Why did you save that girl?" she asked.

"What do you mean?"

"She was nothing to anybody. Just a nameless prostitute in a city of millions. No one cared about her. Why save her?"

"Because I could."

"Really?"

"I don't know what answer you want from me, lady. I saved her because she was hurt and scared and abused. I saved her because I couldn't stand what had been done to her. I was there; I could get her out, so I did."

"Her knight in shining armor?"

"Sure, why not."

"And what will you do with her now?"

"I haven't given it much thought. Tomorrow she needs to see a doctor to get her head checked. After that… I don't know."

"Will you keep her, care for her?"

"I don't know."

"Do you love her?"

"I don't know."

"Do you want to fuck her?"

"She's half my age, at least."

"But she's experienced and willing."

"Fuck you, lady."

"So, you haven't thought of it at all?"

"I don't need any more of your drunk shit right now. I'm not going to sleep with a mentally and physically abused girl young enough to be my daughter. I may be a disagreeable bastard, but I'm not a sicko that would take advantage of a little girl."

Hans stood and stormed out into the yard, kicking the whiskey bottle as he passed. He stood by the treeline, fuming. He didn't hear her until her hand touched his shoulder. He tried not to flinch, almost succeeded.

"I'm... I'm sorry, Hans. I didn't mean it that way."

"Didn't mean it when you accused me of being a pedophile?"

"No. I... I wanted to know your intentions. You saved her. That was a good thing. I wanted to know if you would continue to try to do so."

"I haven't given it much thought. I'm no good at planning for the future. Much more than a day out and I'm at a loss. I just want to see if her head is ok. Maybe my mother will help. Maybe I can find her a nice place."

"Maybe she wants to stay with you."

"Maybe."

"Would you let her?"

"Maybe."

"So, at heart you really are rather noble."

"I said maybe."

"Right."

Onyx walked off, showing Hans her back. He heard her light another cigarette. She mumbled something.

"What?" he asked.

She turned to face him. "Do you believe that I'm human, Hans?"

"I don't know. You're screwed up and neurotic, which is pretty human in my book."

"Your confidence is overwhelming."

"What do you want me to say, Yana? You seem human, but you're lacking necessities, your eyes are the wrong color, your memory is shit. I've seen you die, come back. I've seen multiple copies of you in a crate that you can't remember even though it happened yesterday. How can I make a conclusion based on that?"

Her face fell, he could see it in the light of her cigarette. She turned away. He hoped she wasn't crying. He'd never dealt well with crying women, and her tears would be like granite weeping. He groped for something to say.

"When I asked you what you learned from your mom, what did you say?"

"Hmmm?" She turned back. No tears, so that was good.

"You said your mom taught you to dance, didn't you?"

She nodded. "Mom was a ballet dancer. She taught me 'til I was eleven… 'Til my father killed her."

"Can you still dance?"

"Sure."

"Show me."

"What?" Onyx was perplexed.

"Show me what your mother taught you." Hans crossed his arms and tried to sound stern, with limited success.

"I don't know…"

"You say you're human. You say you want me to believe you. Show me that your memories are more than just implants. Show me what you learned from your mom."

Onyx started to form another protest, stopped herself. They had another staring contest. Hans finally won one. She turned and flicked her cigarette past the treeline. Hans thought she was going to storm off again. Instead she raised her hands above her head, arcing them gracefully.

Hans wasn't ready for what he saw next. She was drunk, she was tired. He'd figured she probably hadn't danced at all since her mother died. Probably rusty, probably awkward. Maybe one of those knee dips, a little spin.

Instead she drew up her leg and leaped. She spun, kicked, leaped again, and landed gracefully, with no sign of intoxication. She did a series of high-speed spins on one foot, leaped straight up, double kicked, landed, and twirled her way across the yard. The routine gained momentum. She was grace incarnate.

She stopped suddenly, stumbled, nearly fell. Hans heard the unmistakable sound of vomiting. She finished, staggered up the stairs of the cabin, went inside.

Hans had never seen ballet, could not name what she had just done. But he knew beauty when he saw it. He followed her in.

She was bent over the sink, vomiting again. She'd taken the green tablet in some water. Sobering up. Hans stood there until she finished. She turned to face him. Her depression was temporarily gone, replaced by a beaming, haughty, almost maniacal smile. She actually laughed, the first time he'd heard it.

"Well?" she asked him.

He clapped his hands together. She gave him another laugh. It was a warm sound, so unlike anything else he'd seen from her.

"That was beautiful." She took the compliment, strode back out the porch, and lit another cigarette. He followed.

"Do you believe me now?" she asked.

"I do. I guess that could have been implanted, but what I just saw had to be human."

"You sure?"

"Yeah."

She finished her cigarette, her face glowing brighter than its ember.

"So, what do we do?" Hans asked her. "If this isn't you, if there's a real you somewhere, how can we find it?"

"We go to the source. We find my comrade."

"How do we do that?"

"The sphere. If I'm controlling the fake body from somewhere, there has to be a link, a source. We find it with the sphere, and we get it back."

"And if there isn't?"

"There is."

Hans balked a little. She could see his niggling doubts. She approached him, drew his gaze.

"Are we friends, Hans?"

"Sure."

"That's it, just sure." Her face lost some of its luster, returned to her more usual glower.

"That's what I got," he said. She gave him a moment, then nodded.

"You saved a poor, lost little girl's life, Hans. Can you do it again?"

"I didn't save anything. I just dragged her out of there because I was the only one who could, and I'm not sure you qualify as either lost or little."

"What would you call it?"

Hans wasn't sure. She was searching for something, something from him, something from herself. A base to build on, maybe. He had no reply. No one had ever asked him for the kind of help she was requesting.

"Hans," she drew his attention. Her face unreadable, turned back toward the dark. "I have no one else. Maybe it's too much to ask, but I have nothing else. My headquarters are gone, my contact has cut me off, has probably been lying to me. Even my body is gone, maybe never existed. Tomorrow I may not even remember this conversation. You're here, you have the sphere and can use it. You've shown yourself to be honorable, even compassionate. And I believe that if you say you'll help, you will."

"You have too much faith in me."

"I saw what you did for the girl. You put yourself in harm's way for her. You've shared your home, even your bed, with her. Will you give up on her?"

"No." He was surprised to hear the answer come out of his mouth, but he knew it was true.

"Will you give up on me?"

"No." Again the answer came before he thought. Onyx smiled at him, a rare occurrence. He couldn't help but feel manipulated. She was using his weaknesses against him, presenting herself in a way that may not be accurate. But the answer was sincere.

She turned and offered her hand, still immaculately manicured, the fingernails glossy black. He took it in his. Her grip was firm, flesh cold. They shook, the atmosphere between them warming with every movement. She took her hand back, crossed it over her chest.

"Partners?" she asked.

"Friends," he responded. Her smile returned.

—— «» ——

They returned to the main house. There were lights on in the kitchen. Bacall sat on the porch, giving Hans the evil eye for leaving her behind, sniffing huffily at Bogey, who gave Hans a cowed look.

"It's OK, boy, no one wins when the women are upset." Onyx sniffed at him.

Pat was up, so was Lori. She ran to him when he came in the kitchen, hugging him around the waist. It was nice, feeling needed.

"Lorilei woke me up looking for you. We decided to have some hot chocolate." His mother sounded cross, sleep slurring her voice slightly

"Sorry, Mom, we had some things to discuss."

Onyx mumbled an apology.

"It's no problem." Pat's voice sounded sincere, her eyes left doubt. She sipped her hot chocolate.

Lori was nearly asleep. Hans asked her if she wanted to go back to bed. She shook her head. He sat down and she crawled on his lap. She had spoken very little since Salt Lake, reverting to a girl younger than he'd met at Brigham's. He hoped she'd recover.

Onyx sat.

"I smell smoke. You smoking again, Hans?" Pat asked him, like he was sixteen again.

"Yeah, Mom."

"All that shit you went through, and you want to destroy it?"

"Cigarettes don't kill many people nowadays, Mom."

"Because most of 'em are too smart to smoke." It was an old argument between them, one carried out more from obligation than passion. The crux was more that his mom didn't like the smell than any real health issues.

Lori was now drooling on his neck. Hans excused himself and took her upstairs.

"You sleeping with my boy?" Pat asked Onyx, the question delivered as soon as Hans was out of earshot.

"No."

"What about her?" Pat gestured with her head toward the door, indicating Lori.

"No."

"You sure? She was in his bedroom."

"The girl's been traumatized, emotionally brutalized. Right now, Hans is the only safety she knows."

The answer didn't satisfy Pat, and she sat waiting for more.

"Hans was helping me acquire a certain item, there were some complications, we came across the girl, he felt we should bring her here."

"So I could help him with her, I presume."

Onyx shrugged, reached for a cigarette.

"You won't be smoking those in here." It was not a question.

"Of course not." Onyx put the cigarette case on the table in front of her. Pat was expecting something from her. She was rusty when it came to common courtesies. What did the woman expect?

"Mrs. Ricker…" Onyx started.

"Miss."

"Hmm?"

"It's miss, not Mrs."

"Miss Ricker, then. Hans was doing a job for me. It remains unfinished, and he's still obligated. We need to stay here for a few days to figure out our next course of action. I would greatly appreciate your hospitality. I could even compensate you for your trouble…"

Pat waved her hand. "I don't need your money."

"Goods or services then?"

"What kind of service could you offer me? You don't look like the type that does dishes or yard work."

"You might be surprised."

"I doubt anything about you could surprise me."

Onyx smirked a little at that.

"Mom, stop berating her." Hans stood in the doorway. He'd gotten Lori to bed, though she'd insisted on his again. A problem for another day.

"It's OK," Onyx said, "I get the feeling your mother is just going to set some house rules."

"Right," Pat responded. "Number one, you do anything illegal on these grounds and I'll shoot you and leave you for the coyotes."

"C'mon, Mom…"

"Madam," Onyx interrupted him, "I have no intention of doing anything to put me in bad stead here."

Pat looked disbelieving. She continued, "Number two, you don't sleep under this roof. I have no boarders at the moment, you can pick a cabin."

"Fair enough." If anything, Onyx appeared amused by the conversation.

"Number three, you have one week to figure out your next 'course of action' and then you move on, with or without my son."

"We will be out of here long before then."

Pat seemed satisfied with that. She rose from the table. "I'm going to bed; old ladies don't appreciate being woken up at one am. Don't either of you leave any dirty dishes in my sink."

"Night, Mom."

Pat left them.

"Your mother's quite the charmer, I can see where you and Grit get your manners."

"Yeah, she's a hoot."

"Good night, Hans," Onyx rose and exited. Hans could hear her lighting a cigarette, and watched the glowing ember wander off into the dark. He wished he'd asked her for one before she left.

CHAPTER 8

The viewscreen in the waiting room showed footage of the destruction in Denver and Salt Lake. The pundit did everything he could to make a connection, running through every fear gambit; terrorism, military, government conspiracy, and/or war. All completely off the mark, though they couldn't have the knowledge she had. Still, the pictures were startling to Grit.

Onyx's building had melted more than crumbled, leaving a slightly glassy dome in a large crater. There was no way in or out, the material one solid mass. Numerous scans had not revealed any survivors or dead inside, confirming Grit's suspicions that the bodies that attacked her had not been human. Neither had Onyx. Had she ever been?

The pictures from Salt Lake were even more shocking. An area ten blocks square was reduced to powder, the casualties massive but unknown. Information was scarce, Salt Lake predictably clamping down on information. The pictures coming in were mostly from civilian surveillance satellites. Someone had managed a high-speed flyover with a camera mounted on a homemade UAV, bringing in a of couple minutes of good footage before the police shot it down.

The dust was still settling. The buildings had been old, not built well to begin with. Devastation spread from the center, buildings around the perimeter leaning away from the blast. Salt Lake's vast underground tunnel systems were exposed to the sunlight, floors collapsed and covered in rubble. A dirty secret opened to the scrutiny of the world. The spin doctors were already preparing their propaganda. The crazies were crawling out of the woodwork, calling for consequences, claiming responsibility, trying to find a link.

She tired of the parade of horror and insanity, and rose to check on Gino again. He'd come around a few hours ago, but the doctors put him temporarily back under to allow the healing agents in his system to finish their work knitting bones and nerves. Grit had tried to get some sleep on a cot in one of the break rooms, to no avail. She should go home, but she couldn't leave Gino. She was tense with the need to act. To take control, do something constructive, fight back against this thing that continued to be two steps ahead of her.

Her comm chirped from her pocket. She inserted it in her ear.

"This is Grit."

"It's Hans."

"Hold on." Grit walked down the hall, peering in rooms until she found an empty one. She entered, closed the door, and wedged a chair under the handle.

"You still there, Hans?"

"Yes."

"Where are you?"

"At Mom's."

"Have you seen the news reports?"

"No."

"There were people in the train tunnels when that building went off."

"I know, it was my fault. I did everything I could to not cause any casualties, but I forgot about the train tunnels."

"Wait," Grit fought confusion. "You blew the building?"

"Yes."

"For fuck's sake, why?"

"To keep anyone from gaining control of it."

"How the hell did you do it? How did you control my jumpcraft? How are we talking right now? What the hell did you get mixed up in, Hans?"

"You tell me, Grit. You've been keeping secrets from me since I woke up. The fact that you were personally monitoring the transaction that nearly killed me, that those two men in the room were yours."

"How could you know that? I didn't tell you because it wasn't pertinent."

"And what is pertinent to me, Grit? People trying to kill me? People trying to kill you?"

"I was protecting you."

"I don't need your protection, Grit, I need your confidence."

"One thing you've never inspired in me is confidence." *Ouch*. She wished she hadn't said that almost as soon as it came out, even if it was true.

Silence from Hans.

"Hans, look, I'm…"

"Forget it, Grit, it's probably true. Responsibility has never been one of my strong suits. You had enough for both of us."

"Still, I shouldn't have said it."

"Fine, apology accepted. I didn't call you for an argument, I could get that from any number of people here."

"Mom giving you a hard time?"

"She doesn't like my guests."

"Who'd you bring home?"

"Couple of ladies, one you know already."

Grit's mouth dried out. How much had Hans seen in that building when he was helping?

"Hans, if you're talking about who I think you are, you need…"

"It's OK, Grit. The creature you encountered wasn't really Illiyana. The real one's here with me… mostly. We're partners."

"You are so far in over your head. Listen…"

"No, you listen, Grit, for once. She needs my help."

"Now is not the time for your bullshit chivalry, Hans." Grit paced the room, kicked a boot restlessly at the bed.

"She asked me, Grit. I'm the only who can help her."

"You're so full of shit. She's using you."

"This isn't open for discussion. Look, Grit, I'm involved, I'm staying involved. You can't stop it; do you want to help or not?"

Grit swallowed the tirade building behind her lips. Hans lecturing her. Hans ahead of her. Hans working with the most dangerous woman she'd ever met. But he was right. Arguing wasn't going to get them anywhere, and if she continued he'd just cut her off. She could scream at him later.

"All right, Hans, what can I do?"

"I need a few of your men out here for protection."

"I thought you didn't need my protection."

"It's not for me, it's for Mom and a girl who's staying here."

"Girl?"

"Long story. No time. Can you do it?"

"I'm currently on medical leave, but I think I can send a few men. Are you expecting trouble?"

"After the last few days I can't afford not to. How quickly can they get here?"

"Probably no sooner than thirty-six hours. I'll push it if I can."

"Thanks."

"Sure. You and I need to have a long talk, Hans."

"I know, Grit. We will, I promise. I'm not sure I can explain it to myself right now. In a few days this will probably be over one way or another..."

That sounded too ominous to Grit. "Don't leave me out of this, Hans. I won't stand by and watch you get yourself killed."

"I know. I want your help, but I have to ask your permission for something first."

"For what?"

"In the situation we're in anything electronic in your body is dangerous to you."

Grit unconsciously rubbed her still aching jaw. "I already found that out the hard way."

"Good. I can see that your comm has been removed. But your ID tag could get you killed."

"Hans, it's a felony to remove an ID tag, not to mention dangerous. I know you lucked out, but I don't think..."

"I'm not asking you to remove it surgically, Greta. I can permanently disable from here."

"What, you mean right now?"

"Yes, it would just take a second."

"Jesus, Hans, how the fuck are you doing all this?"

"I'll be happy to tell you later. For now, I need your permission to go ahead. I won't let you continue with this until we do this. It's too risky with what we're up against."

Grit stopped her nervous pacing. "And what am I supposed to do once it's gone?"

"I assume you have access to some spoofers. I can program them with your ID."

Grit didn't have any, but she knew where she could get one. It was illegal, but so was destroying the chip.

"OK, Hans, I'll trust you on one condition."

"Shoot."

"Do Gino too."

"I was hoping you'd say that."

— «» —

Despite everything that had happened to him, the strangest sight of all awaited Hans the next morning.

Lori was gone when he awoke. She'd still been snoring away when he came back the night before. He panicked for a moment, searching around, afraid she'd run off. His mother's voice drifted up from downstairs, talking to someone, most likely Lorilei. Hans dressed and went downstairs.

His mother stood in front of the stove, the smell of bacon rising over her shoulder. The pan sizzled loudly. Lori stood next to her, awkwardly holding a pair of tongs as Pat showed her when to turn the strips, when to lay them on the towels next to the oven. The girl was taking the instructions with rapt intensity.

Onyx was making pancakes. She stood by the grill, black leather covered by one of his mom's old aprons, ladling batter onto the large griddle, flipping expertly, laying the finished cakes aside.

"That's a good look for you," Hans teased, "I had no idea you could be so domestic."

She gave him a burning look. "The things you have no idea about could fill a large city's network database."

"You're on egg duty, Hans," his mother said. Her rules had always been everyone helps, everyone eats. Only Patricia Ricker could have the chutzpah to put an international criminal and master assassin on pancake duty.

Hans retrieved the eggs, scooted in next to Onyx at the griddle and began cracking, concentrating on not breaking the yolks. He managed a seventy percent success rate.

They ate in companionable silence. Hunger was the best spice, imminent death a close second.

After breakfast Hans drove Lori down to the main strip of Glenwood to have her head looked at by one of the local doctors. He'd been afraid she'd refuse, but she took his request as an order, and walked sedately out to the car. He promised her there'd be no pain, no probing, just a once over to make sure she was really ok. She just nodded and sat stiffly upright during the trip.

His mother had a running deal with one of the local doctors, a former army medic with a bum leg. Doctor Verne Hershovitz was good at his job, and willing to barter services for a small amount of fresh meat whenever Pat went hunting. Hans suspected the doctor and his mother may have shared a bed on occasion.

Verne sat Lori up on the side of the bed, shone a light into her eyes, felt her head, then had her lay back while he ran a handheld scanner over her skull. Lori had some light bruising, already fading. Her skull had taken a knock and was slightly cracked, but was mostly healed thanks to whatever the woman in Salt Lake had given her. The doctor asked her if she was having any double vision or headaches. She wouldn't answer him, so Hans relayed the same questions. Lori admitted to some mild headaches, and the doctor gave her a packet of pills to help with the pain. She stared at them fearfully. Hans told her she didn't have to take them if she didn't want to, but if the pain got too bad they would help. Lori seemed OK with that, handing the pills to Hans. He secreted them in a pocket.

Afterward they took a short stroll down the main strip. Hans stopped in at one store and picked up a carton of cigarettes, farther down he bought Lori a milkshake at a place that did the soda shop thing during the day, but at night morphed into a strip club. Hans was friendly with the owner.

He used the sphere to pay for the goods, searching the network, siphoning minute amounts of money from large accounts that wouldn't miss it, covering his tracks. It was exhilarating. He could have as much as he wanted, with no chance of ever being tracked. The guilt was there, too. Hans vowed to only use what was absolutely necessary.

They passed a clothing store and Lori stopped to peer inside at the dresses. A gigantic teddy bear sat against one wall. She looked at him expectantly.

Two hours later they left with ten dresses, half a dozen tops, an equal number of pants, assorted shoes, socks, jewelry, and one oversized teddy bear for which he'd probably paid twice what it was worth. A young man helped them carry it to his car. They filled the trunk and the backseat.

Lori smiled on the way home. He could get used to that.

— «» —

Grit's soldiers had arrived while they were gone. Two men and two women sat in his mother's living room under Pat's glare, armed and armored. Hans hadn't told her.

"Hans, outside," she said, not waiting for Hans to explain. They exited to the smirks of the soldiers.

"What the hell are military personnel doing on my property, Hans?"

He started to explain.

"They said you requested them."

Hans tried again, again she interrupted him.

"What the hell are you involved in?"

"Mom, I'm trying…"

"You have thirty seconds to explain, and then I'm kicking all of you off my property."

Hans waited, making sure she wasn't going to interrupt him again. She stood firm, towering over him, even though she was a good six inches shorter.

He told her everything he could remember, spitting it out quickly and harshly, not trying to sugarcoat it. Grit had given him a thirty-six-hour estimate, but he should have known little Ms. Efficiency would jump the gun by a good twenty hours. He'd wanted to sit down with his mom and tell her gently. He left nothing out, at least not intentionally.

If Hans' mom was stunned she didn't show it. She looked skeptical.

"Lori," she called back to the door, "tell Ms. Onyx I'd like to see her."

Lori ran off toward Onyx's cabin, still lugging the oversized teddy bear.

Pat rounded on Hans again. "And I suppose you used this sphere thingy to buy your girlfriend the teddy bear."

Lying was useless, he'd never been able to lie to his mom, anyway. "Yeah, and some clothes she needed."

"So, you're a thief now?"

"No. She needed the clothes."

"So you stole them."

"I transferred some money from an off-shore account used by drug smugglers, it was already stolen."

"And that makes it ok?"

"Yeah... I mean, no, look..."

"Hans, we are not thieves. I had some clothes the girl could have worn. Some money stashed away. I could have given you money to get home if you'd asked."

"Damn it, Mom, I couldn't take it from you. You don't have enough as it is. All I've ever done is accept your charity, Grit's too. I was hoping I could help us all with this thing." He took it out and showed it to her, but she didn't even glance at it.

"That thing is wrong, Hans, it. If it can do what you say it puts too much power in one place. I don't need your money, I don't need any help you can give me with that thing. You want to help, throw it away. It's already corrupting you."

Onyx came up the path before Hans could reply.

"Ms. Onyx, I wonder if I could impose on you for a moment," she said, while continuing to glare at Hans.

"Ma'am," was Onyx's terse reply.

"My son has just told me a rather amazing story, much of it involving you. Can you corroborate?"

Onyx showed no surprise. "Really, and what would you like to know?"

"He claims he saw you die, he claims he can control almost anything with that sphere. He claims you are currently, um, not whole."

Nothing from Onyx's face. "All true."

"Do you have any proof?"

Onyx undid the clasps on her pants. Pat looked over, Hans looked away. He heard the sound of the fabric being pulled down. His mom made a small grunt of surprise. Onyx redid her clothing.

"Jesus, someone sure did a number on you. I haven't seen anything like that before. Are you a robot? What do you do with the food you eat?"

"Mom, jeez."

"My digestive tract is intact," Onyx said coolly. "The body is organic, except for a controller in the brain. Anything else you'd like to know?"

"Where do you come from? This body, I mean."

"My factory used to make them in limited numbers, it was destroyed."

"The explosion in Denver?"

"Correct."

This was a piece of information she'd not given Hans before. Had she just remembered?

Pat continued. "And you don't know where your real body is? Assuming you have one."

"No. I know I have one. I'm working under the assumption that my real body is controlling this one from a distance. Hans was going to use the sphere to track the signal to its source."

Onyx hadn't told Hans this either, though it made sense.

"This thing really can do what you say?" This was directed at Hans.

"Yes," Hans answered.

"Show me something."

"Like what?"

"Those meatheads inside parked their vehicle on my front lawn. Move it."

"You want me to get them off your lawn?"

Pat didn't get the joke. Sarcasm was not her strong point.

Hans found the control systems easily, went into the autopilot, and set a course that would lift the ship up and move it toward a small clearing farther into the property. The ship powered up, scorching the grass slightly, rose to thirty feet or so, and moved off toward his designated landing spot. The soldiers came running out as soon as the engines came on, guns drawn.

"It's OK, guys, I'm just re-parking it."

The craft lowered in the distance, set down. The sound of the engines cut out. The soldiers hurried off after it, still confused, very irate.

Pat stood looking between him and Onyx. She huffed, turned around.

"You best come inside, we need to figure out our next step."

Our?

— ⟨⟩ —

"You have to be joking," Hans said.

They were upstairs. Him in the doorway of her bedroom, his mom out of sight in the walk-in closet.

"When have you known me to joke?"

True.

"Mom, you can't do this."

"Can't do what?" She leaned out of the closet, holding, in the crook of her arm, a rifle almost as tall as she was. Her baby. She'd had it longer than she'd had him. He didn't know the make, didn't know the caliber, only knew that he'd once seen her use it to take down a bear from almost a kilometer. It used old-fashioned black powder, noisier than the railguns Grit's soldiers carried.

"You can't come with us."

"Really, are you allowed to make that decision?"

Hans turned to Onyx. She'd followed them up the stairs, enjoying the spectacle. "You said she was a crack shot, maybe she'll be useful."

He didn't know whether Onyx meant that, or was she just letting him squirm?

"I need you to stay here with…"

Pat didn't let him finish. "What you wanted was for me to stay here and play nursemaid to your girlfriend."

"No… she's not… can you even still fire that thing?"

"Shot me a coyote just a month ago, five hundred yards on the run, clean kill."

"Really, I'm impressed," Onyx said, closer to the doorway now, "can you show me how to do that?"

Hans' expression was baking. "Don't encourage her."

"Ms. Onyx, can you leave us alone for a moment." Onyx turned and walked off down the stairs, chuckling softly.

"Come in here," she said. He obeyed. "Shut the door."

He shut the door. His mother moved to the bed, patted next to her, "Come here," she reiterated, like he was five. He sat next to her.

"Hans, do you have any idea what it's been like this last year for me? You taking off, not telling me where you were going, not saying goodbye?"

"I wasn't supposed to be gone more than a couple days."

"It doesn't matter. You disappeared. It was completely out of character. Next thing I know Grit is calling me in tears, telling me my boy is almost dead, probably won't survive, that you'd been involved in criminal activities, something serious. Every day I called that awful place. Twice we thought you were really dead. I mortgaged this land to pay your bills."

"Wait... you paid my bills? You couldn't afford that." Hans was taken aback.

"I couldn't afford not to. Don't worry about me, Hans, I'll be in the ground before they come to collect."

"Mom..."

"No, you listen to me. You're a grown man, I know that, you don't have to be accountable to an old woman. But it was terrible, Hans, the worst thing that ever happened to me. A mother should not have to outlive her kids, and I'm not going to if I can help it. You are in a shitload of trouble, that's obvious."

"Mom, I can handle it."

"While I do what? Sit here, in my rocker, wondering if my boy is dead again. I'm not doing it again, Hans, I'd rather die."

Words escaped him.

"This family never says what needs sayin', that's just the way we are. Too stubborn, too stupid, all of us. But these are the facts. You're in trouble, the type of trouble that may require weaponry. That girl you want to saddle me with is not going to stay here if you leave. If what you tell me is true there is no safe place for her. If you leave her here and that man comes for her, a few soldiers aren't going to stop him. She'll go with you or she'll go back to the shit she was in. So, you need to protect her. That thing you got may be useful, but it's as dangerous as anything I've ever seen. I'm not asking you let me charge the battlefield, Hans."

She wasn't asking him for anything at all, but he let that slide.

"I know I'm old and slowin' down a bit, but if the shit goes down I can find a high spot with a good view and help the best way I can. You know I can still shoot better than anyone."

"I don't want there to be any shooting, Mom."

"And you didn't want to get messed up, and you didn't want to get fixed up, and you didn't want to destroy a building with that goddamn sphere, but that's where we are. My boy is in trouble, deep trouble. I'm helping, Hans, and if you try to stop me I'm going to kneecap you with this rifle and lock you in the damn basement."

Her voice had gone up. There were tears in her eyes. It was the first time Hans ever really thought she looked old. The last year had taken a face that had still been youthful and cheerful and given it deep-set furrows, the mouth turned down, the eyes dark. Her hair, always red, had finally started to show specks of silver. She'd gotten old while he was away, something he'd thought would never happen. And then he'd come back and laid all this on her, told her he was leaving. A two-day trip had become a lifetime for all of them. Because of him, because of his irresponsibility.

She hugged him then, a rarity. Hans realized that, in their lifetime, throughout everything, he'd never simply held her. His own mother. It was at once awkward and familiar, something not done, yet so easy to do. Minutes passed, she cried quietly into his chest. She'd never cried in front of him, either. He wished she had no reason, but couldn't help feeling warmth.

She pulled away, kissed his forehead, and unselfconsciously wiped the tears from her eyes.

"Hans, let me help."

"OK."

She patted his leg, and retrieved her gun from against the wall, then returned to the closet.

"So where are we going?" she asked.

"I don't know yet."

She poked her head out, the moment of weakness long gone now. "Well, don't you think you better find out?"

"That's the next step."

— «» —

Or it should have been. Lori, distraught from the arguing, had shut herself up in his room. Onyx was trying to cajole her out, one of the soldiers next to her offering some candy. Lori wasn't having any of it. She was curled tightly on his bed, arms and legs around the bear he'd bought her.

Responsibility sucked.

Hans backed them off the door, went in, and shut it behind him. Lori didn't move. He moved to the bed, sat, touched her shoulder gently.

"You all right?" he asked.

She didn't respond verbally, practically pounced on him, trying to undo his belt and pants. Hans pushed her hands away, protesting, but she resumed, making a mewling noise. He took both her arms, held them down to her sides.

"Lori... Lori..." He shook her a bit as she squirmed. "Lori! Look at me!"

He didn't want to yell, but lost his cool a little. She stopped, looked up, still making noises, snuffling.

"Lori, stop it." Two crying women in one day. He wasn't used to this much drama. She stopped. He sat her on his lap. She weighed almost nothing.

"Lori, I know what they taught you, what they made you do, but that's not what I want from you."

"You don't like me."

"I do like you, very much. You're going to be family. Family doesn't do that to each other."

"Yes, they do."

"Well, they're not supposed to. I'm sorry for what they did. What they did to you is only supposed to be done with someone special, someone you love."

"I love you."

"Well… yeah… but it's different. We're family. Like brother and sister. We don't have to do that."

She mumbled something.

"What?" he asked.

"If you liked me you wouldn't leave."

"I'm not leaving you."

"I heard you, you're going away to do something dangerous."

"You're coming with us."

She'd missed this part. Looked disbelieving.

"I'm taking you with me, to protect you, so you don't have to go back there."

"Really," she still looked doubtful.

"Really. I need you to get a few of those dresses we bought and put them in a bag I'll get for you so you have something to wear. Then were going for a trip. But you need to obey me and the others so you don't get hurt."

She considered this, nodded, "Can I bring Brigham?"

"Who?"

"My bear."

Jesus. Now was not the time to approach this subject.

"No, unfortunately the bear will have to stay, but we'll be coming back in a few days."

She looked dejected, but didn't contradict him.

"OK?" he asked.

She nodded.

"Good, get a couple of dresses together and a pair of shoes and I'll go get you a bag."

—— «» ——

He went to Grit's old room, thinking maybe she'd have a backpack Lori could use. It hadn't been opened in awhile, and was exactly as Grit had left it. Bed made up tightly, no clutter, very little on the walls, a bookcase crammed full of history and science books. A small desk and chair. The one piece of decoration a floor lamp, completely out of place in the austerity. Its shade was pink, lace ruffles running around the top and bottom. Grit had always claimed it came from their father, but that seemed iffy at best. More likely it was a gift and story from their mother to satisfy a young girl's curiosity.

Han rummaged around in her closet, which, in complete contrast to the room, was completely jammed full of crap. Both his mother and his sister were secret closet slobs. Their houses and rooms were spotless as long as you didn't open a closet door or desk drawer. He found an old rucksack underneath a pile of papers, some of Grit's schoolwork, decorated with high grades and higher compliments. He thought it would work.

Onyx had come in silently while his back was turned, and was standing in front of the lamp, fingering the lace absently. He started a bit, looked at her sheepishly. If she noticed she gave no sign.

"We need to use the sphere to find the source," she said.

"Right now?"

"Yes."

"Where?"

"Do you have the sphere?"

Hans nodded.

"Here then." She went and shut the door, returned to sit on the bed. Hans pulled the desk chair across from her and took the sphere from his pocket.

"Ready?"

She nodded.

Hans had never really looked strongly at her through the sphere's eyes, never really looked that hard at anyone, but he could see the difference in her now. Her whole being glowed, rather than just a few add-ons. A blue aura surrounded her, flickering across her, coalescing in her chest, where something glowed brighter than anything he'd yet observed. It must be the remote control. He accessed it.

She was around him, through him, inside and outside him. Her memories, his to observe, access, even change. Intimacy beyond anything he could possibly have prepared for. She knew he was there. Felt her surprise, her anger, her cold regard. He could see her face, see her grimace, see his own look of terror through her eyes. Could she see through his?

"What are you doing?" she hissed at him.

The ultimate voyeur, he could read her life, know her pain. He knew betrayal, murderous rage, absolute fear, and underneath it a core strength beyond anything he could ever have mustered. She (we) would win at all costs. Her (our) resolve would never be broken. Her (our) enemies would not stand against her (us).

"Get out of my head, Hans." There was a knife in her hand. He could see it, feel it, her muscles tensing, ready to strike, thoughts racing with self-protection and lethal preparation.

He pulled out, shut off the sphere. She was shaking, rage and terror squirming across her face, the knife gripped so tightly her fingers turned an even whiter shade.

"What the hell were you doing?" She barely got the words out.

Hans held up his hands. "I don't know, I didn't expect that. It's never happened."

"What did you see?"

He considered lying, knew it wouldn't help.

"Your thoughts. Your feelings. I couldn't help it, whatever is in your head is so much more powerful than anything I've accessed."

She put the knife down on the bed, put her head in her hands.

"Could you tell what it was?"

"I think it's another sphere."

"Like yours."

"I don't think so. It's very similar, but it doesn't have the same capabilities."

"Are you sure?"

"No, I'm not. I'm running in the fucking dark. The impression I got is that it's a receiver only, and that's a very loose impression, the only way to know for sure is to go back in."

"Don't go back in, Hans." There was more fear than anger in her voice.

"I don't plan on it. Whatever it is seems completely wired to your brain, or maybe it is your brain, at least in this form. It can take commands and control you, or at least your higher functions."

"So, I'm a puppet."

"No, I don't know. Look, Yana, I won't access it again. If it's receiving a signal I'll try to find it another way."

"Is there another way?"

"I don't know. I don't know any of this. When I access the sphere, it gives me the information I need. When I'm using it I just know how."

"Try again, then."

Hans did. She started to glow again, the sphere in her head as bright as before. He queried it for information, but didn't request access. Nothing. He searched for a wireless signal. Again, nothing. He sent out feelers, virtually feeling around its surface programs. Onyx grimaced slightly.

"Do you feel anything?"

"Like someone's poking at my mind. Or insects crawling through my memories. It's a fuzzy sensation. I don't know how else to describe it."

Hans was stumped. He pulled back to collect his thoughts.

"Try to contact your colleague."

"I haven't been able to since yesterday."

"Just try, I don't think he needs to respond."

"What should I ask him?"

"Anything, it's not important."

Are you there?

A flash, and a signal left her head. It was not a continuous stream, merely a quanta, a bullet of information.

"There," he said.

"Hmmm?"

"There's something, it left when you talked."

"You want me to try again?"

"Yeah."

Where are you?

Hans was ready, or at least the sphere was. It grabbed Onyx's message and hung on its tail, riding it with his carrier signal. It reached its destination nearly instantaneously, but in the world of the sphere Hans' thoughts were its match.

He felt, saw, knew a barrier to his progress was coming, something the signal could pass, but he couldn't. A flick of attention, find a nearby access. Offloaded onto a network cell tower. Needed visual. Access CCTV system. A view of a street, deserted, no help. Something higher, a weather satellite. Mark ground access so he could find it. Climb to orbit, redirect camera. Find previous access. Still in Colorado. Zoom. Reached limits of resolution. Blurry image of town nestled against the eastern slope of the Rockies. Almost deserted, the few scattered access points, mostly ID tags of transients, a few larger signals signifying older weapon systems, obsolete surveillance equipment.

It was Colorado Springs, or at least what was left of it. A civil war had taken place here decades earlier. It had always been a strongly religious city, more so as the tide of atheism and apathy continued its inexorable rise. It was peaceful for a long time, until the militants and crazies started moving in. Dictatorships and fiefdoms formed, started raiding each other, absorbing each other like bacteria, until only two kingdoms were left, fighting vicious battles along moral lines. The feds stepped in and declared martial law. The militants were no match for the tech the feds brought to bear against them. In desperation one of the factions detonated a dirty bomb, irradiating three-fourths of the city. Someone else released a weaponized virus. Very few survived. The city was unlivable for decades. Rumor was that both the radiation and virus had faded, but the place was already cursed by rumor. America's Chernobyl. No one sane lived there willingly.

Yet still many access points glowed. Hans went back to street level, looked for another camera, found one a few dozen miles further south. Things moving along the ground here, their access points difficult to resolve, harder to grab. Hans gave up trying and zoomed the camera in on one.

A pod scurried across the street, followed by two more, then one of the bigger ones from Brigham's chased after them, itself carrying a few pods stabbing away at its insides.

Hans found another camera, then another, and bounced through a few more before seeing anything new. More pods, people shooting at them. High-tech weaponry, melting the pods on contact. He couldn't see their faces clearly, but he was pretty sure from the signals what they were.

More like Onyx, Elena, Beefy. He'd only seen a few models, gotten the impression that they'd yet to achieve endless variation. Probably were easier to grow from a template. He took a risk, dove into the nearest head.

In a mind again, part of it, seeing through its eyes. No awareness in this one, no conscious choices, it was a puppet, but where was its strings? He searched for the controlling signal, more confident of what to search for, found it, followed. The barrier came down. He dodged to a nearby network exchange. Malice followed him.

Who?

The words were directly in his head, vicious ire accompanying them, then a wall of digital rage. The sphere flashed him a warning. Something was trying to access it, tearing at its own formidable defenses with sheer brute force, breaking through. For a moment it saw through the sphere, saw Onyx on the bed. Its force redoubled, became frantic, insane.

GIVE HER BACK! SHE'S MINE! GIVE HER TO ME!

This phrase reverberated through Hans' skull, scattering his thoughts, bulling its way through, grasping at her through the sphere. Only panic saved him. He did the only thing possible. He dropped the sphere on the floor, forcing his clenched fingers to let go, hoping the break of direct contact would end it...

...it did.

The voice cut out, left him alone in his head. He leaned forward, hands clasped together, and put his head between his legs, took a breath, then another. He began to calm down, and sat back up.

Onyx looked worried. Had she felt anything?

"You ok?" she asked.

He shook his head. "I found our location, it's Colorado Springs."

"That's good."

"No. It's not."

Hans described what he seen and heard.

"The body you entered. You say it was empty?"

"Something was controlling it, but there were no memories or feelings, nothing like with you."

She frowned at his admission of invasion.

"I'm sorry about that, I didn't know…"

"Forget it," a short wave of her hand, almost a chop, "you didn't know."

"How long was I under?"

"Fifteen, twenty seconds."

"That's it?"

"Yes."

"What about the other?" he asked.

"The being?"

"Yeah, whatever it was that tried to take over the sphere."

"I don't know, we'll have to deal with that when the time comes."

"That's not very promising."

"No, in the meantime I would recommend not using the sphere unless it's absolutely necessary."

He wasn't planning on it. Whatever had attacked broke through his defenses instantly, swatting him down effortlessly. He could not stand up against something like that. If he faced it again he'd lose again.

"So where do we go from here?" he asked.

Onyx didn't answer immediately. She lay back on the bed, stretched her arms out in front, arched her back, let everything loose, and fell back on the bed. An unconsciously childish gesture, one that showed comfort in his presence. He silently appreciated it.

"We have to go, there's no debate about that," she said, sitting up and resuming her normally imposing posture, arms crossed, "But not today. We need to make a few preparations."

"You got an army hidden somewhere?"

"No. I doubt an army would be much good, just fodder. Maybe a small group could get through under the radar? Though I wouldn't mind a few more capable guns. Grit maybe?"

"I'll ask her."

Onyx had no more to say. Hans stood to leave, turned toward the door.

"Hans?"

"Yeah."

"You don't have to do this."

He kept his back to her, the easier to make the personal impersonal.

"I know."

"I've asked you to risk your life and the lives of your loved ones."

"Just mine, theirs are their own choice."

"They wouldn't go without you."

"True."

"Why do it?"

Hans turned again, faced her. "I thought we already had this discussion."

"I've had second thoughts. It's getting more dangerous all the time. You've already done something for me. You proved that this shell isn't the real me, gave me a reason to hope. If you want to back out I'll understand."

"Illiyana," he was at a loss for a moment, "we're friends."

"So?"

"Friends help each other, that's the way it is."

"Not in my experience."

"Then you've never really had a friend."

— «》 —

Gino was awake and grumbling. He didn't like the food. He didn't like the bed. He wanted a cigarette. He wanted a hamburger. He wanted out. The doctor in charge resorted to a mild sedative through the IV. It left him groggy and pleasant, peacefully watching the news feed, which was still full of the dual detonations.

"You shouldn't watch that too long," Grit said.

"Probably not, what the hell else am I gonna do?"

Grit had attempted to go home, get some sleep. Nothing doing. She rarely slept at the apartment the city had assigned her, a large two-floor suite near the top of one of the great towers. A perk for her high office. She had asked for something more basic on numerous occasions, but the wheels of bureaucracy turned hesitantly. From the moment she'd arrived she knew it wasn't where she should be, and just a few hours later she sat in the hospital room with Gino. He wasn't going to like what she was about to tell him.

"I talked to Hans."

"Yeah."

"They're coming here tomorrow."

"They?"

"Him, Onyx, Mother, my soldiers, and some girl."

"Your mom's coming?"

"Yeah."

"Why?"

"She wanted to."

"And Hans didn't talk her out of it?"

"You've talked to my mother."

"Yeah."

Gino's face was slack from the sedative. She detested seeing him like that. He was nearing full recovery, but she knew how he hated anything that messed with his head. He'd have grilled her mercilessly otherwise. It was underhanded broaching this when he was still stoned.

"I'm going to meet them."

"Where?"

"The south station."

"Why?"

"To pick up some weapons."

"And then what?" he asked.

"We're going to Colorado Springs."

She expected another why, didn't get it.

"Well, I guess I'm getting out of here soon then."

"You're not coming."

"Yes, I am."

"No. You're injured."

"I'm coming."

"You have to stay here until the doctor releases you."

"It's a free city, I can release myself on my own recognizance." But in his stupor it sounded more like "recognize."

"Gino, it's an order."

"No."

"Are you refusing a direct order?"

"I am responsible for the safety of Her Majesty Greta Ricker, Queen of Colorado, Diva of Denver, and the hottest piece of ass ever to wear a flak jacket."

Greta tried not to laugh at him, didn't succeed. He took it in stride.

"I will not shirk my duties because of a small hole in my torso." He tried to sit up and gesture grandly at her, pulling his IV over.

"Lay down, you idiot." There was no malice in her tone. She crossed the bed and picked up his IV, re-hung it.

"Gino, you have spinal damage."

"Doctor says it's pretty much repaired."

"Pretty much, yes. Completely, no."

"Pretty much is good enough."

"Gino…"

"I go where you go."

"Gino…"

"I dare you to tell me I can't. I go where you go, always. We're a team. Ain't nobody better'n us. Gino and Grit versus the whole damn world, and you'd be an idiot to bet against us, am I right?"

"Yeah, you're right. You still need to stay here."

"Not gonna happen."

Gino was losing consciousness. Whatever was in his IV had increased its movement into his system when he knocked it over. He fell asleep repeating "you go I go". Grit went to get the doctor.

— «» —

It was a strange crew that left Glenwood that morning, packed shoulder to shoulder into the jumpcraft. Four soldiers, a civilian, a crime lord, one old woman looking decidedly green, and a young girl in an oversized flak jacket and helmet, looking intently out the window. Lori was in sensory overload, pointing at things at the window, looking back at Hans, and making small sounds in the back of her throat. She kept beckoning him to the window. Hans wasn't interested. An hour on the jumpcraft had turned him as green as his mother.

The spires of Denver rose up from the foothills. Lori craned her neck, trying to see as far as possible through the side window. The pilot, taking notice, managed to turn the craft slightly, engines twisting, causing them to fly forward at an angle to where it was pointing. Lori fell into stunned silence as the buildings grew nearer, their size becoming more apparent. It'd taken only an evening and a morning for the soldiers to adopt Lori as a mascot. She was still very shy, but seemed to enjoy their friendly attention. Hans just hoped she didn't try to sleep with one of them.

They passed over the border with a small beep from the craft and a few words from the pilot to an unheard ground control. The engine sound increased, and the craft lurched and turned south, cruising parallel to the Rockies. Lori got her best look yet at the mountain range, rapt with their spires. Hans moved beside her, ignoring his flighty stomach, willing to risk it to see the view.

They cruised south, reaching Denver city limits in a matter of minutes, continuing through reclamation area into thick forests. Once these were mostly plains, but mild climate changes and invasive species had turned most of it into evergreen forests. In places, the plains still intruded from the east.

Another bump and the landing lights came on. Hans pulled Lori away from the window and made her strap in, taking his seat beside her. A few more stomach-turning drops, a spin, and they came to a soft thump on the ground. The door came up quickly, though not quickly enough for Grit, already bulling her way in, barking orders at the soldiers. Gino stood behind her, fully suited, standing easily.

"You got better quick," Hans said to him.

"I've always been a quick healer." Gino gave Hans a lopsided wink.

"Don't either of you start with me," Grit snapped, lowering herself back out of the craft to help her mother down. Pat refused the hand and leaped the couple of feet to the surface. Grit reached for Lori, but the girl cowered back, grasping at Hans' hand. A look from Grit and Hans shrugged and leaped down, turning to help Lori. She spent a moment deciding if she wanted to put her feet on the ground, then cautiously lowered herself, testing to see if the surface would support her.

"What's with the girl?" Grit asked.

"Don't start with me," he snapped.

Pat immediately dragged Grit off for a private conversation, both of them waving everyone else back. What was said was heated but quiet. Soldiers and civilians stood in awkward silence.

Onyx knelt and looked to Lori. She said something in Russian. Hans didn't know what she said but her tone was affectionate. Lori moved over, and Onyx took a moment to straighten her jacket and helmet, push a stray hair back from her face. She said something else Hans didn't catch, and gave Lori a peck on the cheek, sending her back to Hans. Hans started to inquire what she said, but Onyx turned her back to him and began walking toward the treeline a few dozen feet away, cigarette smoke trailing behind her.

"What'd she tell you?" Hans asked Lori.

"She called me something I didn't understand. When I asked she said it meant 'Little Flower'. Then she told me a secret. She said I couldn't tell you. She made me promise."

"You should always keep your promises," Hans said, turning to meet Grit and his mother as they returned.

"Where's she going?" Grit asked him.

"Smoke."

Grit went after her.

"Hold on a minute," Grit said, catching up to Onyx. Onyx glanced at her.

"Hello, Commander," she said, taking in Grit's visage. "That's quite a scar you have there, who did that to you?"

"You did."

"You know me better than that."

"I thought I did, up until you and your friends attacked me."

"I don't know what you saw in there, Commander…"

"I saw you, two of you, both of whom tried to kill me."

"Neither of them were me."

"Are you… you?"

"I don't know. I'm trying to figure that out."

"Hans told me about your condition."

"Condition? As good a word as any, I guess."

If her gift for withholding information was any sign, this was much more the Onyx who Grit remembered.

"How can I trust you?" Grit asked.

"I don't know that you can."

"Hans vouches for you, though that's not the most glowing of recommendations."

"You sell your brother short, Grit. In his own way, he's quite a remarkable person."

"How so?"

"He inherited the family iron, though he may not realize it himself. He's here, he's made his promise, and I think he means to keep it. A rarity. He seems to imagine himself some kind of old-fashioned knight of chivalry."

"Cowboy is more like it."

"True. Remarkable nonetheless."

They reached the edge of the treeline. Onyx offered Grit a cigarette, Grit refused.

"What are we doing here?" Grit asked.

"I'm not sure what you're doing here. I'm trying to get some answers, Hans has agreed to help, his mother would not be put off, and the girl has nowhere else. While I welcome your presence and capabilities, I didn't ask for you to be here, and I would rather your soldiers leave us."

"They're not staying. I couldn't ask them to for something like this. I'm not sure where we are going, and Hans stipulated that our ID tags had to be disabled."

"The great Greta Ricker committing a felony?" Onyx teased.

"Hopefully just me and the meathead over there. Hans needs to send Mom and the girl back."

"Pat won't go."

"She may when she finds out we have to destroy her tag."

"Doubt it."

"And the girl?"

"Lori never had one. We rescued her in Salt Lake. She was one of Brigham's playthings, had never been tagged."

"And you brought her here?"

"She's quite attached to your brother."

"Don't tell me..."

Onyx laughed, surprising Greta. She'd never heard the sound.

"Do not worry, his intentions have been entirely honorable. I greatly admire him for his willingness to take her out of there and care for her. But she is severely traumatized, and will not leave his side. If he had left her she would have most likely run away looking for him. Bringing her here is not ideal, but there was no other choice."

"What are you two gabbing about?"

Hans and Gino were closing the distance, the girl tagging at Hans' side.

"Oh, y'know, girl stuff, makeup, guys, superconducting railguns." Onyx's sense of humor had appeared out of nowhere. Greta had never seen it and had doubted she had one.

"Grit." Hans said, the word containing a multitude of changes and emotions. He moved in, put his arms around her. Grit's sense of unreality expanded. Onyx cracking jokes, her standoffish brother hugging her. Next her mother would be crying and telling her how much she loved her. She returned the hug.

"Glad you're ok. Glad we're all OK," he said, moving back. The girl shied behind him. Hans cajoled her out. "Lori, this is my sister Greta. Greta, this is Lori."

The girl continued to shy, not saying anything. Greta gave her a nod. She'd make friends later, if they were still around to make.

The group made their way back to the jumpcraft. Behind it sat the toughest looking vehicle Hans had ever seen. It was rugged and ancient, sitting on massive fifteen-foot tires, armored to the hilt, railgun turret rising from the top.

"That's your idea of subtle transportation?" he asked Grit.

"That's my idea of safe, and it can be run completely mechanically. No network linkages to be accessed, just like you asked. Ten people could live in that thing for a week and never have to breathe outside air. I called in a huge favor to get it. It was sitting in a museum."

Hans nodded. Despite his prodding he was glad to see it. "You did good, kid." His Bogart impression was horrible. Greta huffed.

Greta dismissed the soldiers. They left reluctantly, confused by her orders, but they obeyed. The jumpcraft rose and disappeared into the distance. Hans gestured for his mother to join them, and Greta began handing out the spoofers she'd acquired. They were the latest hardware, smaller then what Hans had been given when he'd first had his disabled. Hans took a moment to explain what he was going to do, that it would be quick and they wouldn't feel anything. He'd transfer their IDs to the spoofers. Grit and Gino were already aware, but Hans hadn't had the time or gumption to explain it to his mother. He stood with trepidation after his spiel, waiting for his mom's tirade.

Pat took the spoofer and checked its systems with familiarity.

"You OK with this, Mom?"

"No need. I had my tag removed years ago. I'll take the spoofer though, much better than the one I'm using now."

CHAPTER 9

The road to Colorado Springs had not been well maintained. There was no reason to have maintained it; few people went there anymore. They wound their way down through the remnants of the old I-25, now pitted, pocked, washed out completely in some places. The hearty military transport made short work of the varied terrain, and their pace was good.

Hans drove; he and Greta were the only ones with training. The cockpit was separated from the rest of the vehicle, and could be sealed completely with a thick bulkhead door. The rest of the vehicle had been mostly stripped of its internal workings, which had been replaced with bare-bones survival equipment; a food re-hydrator and roll-up smart mats for sleeping (which Hans had no intention of using; he'd had enough of squirming furniture). Greta had retained some rifles for their use, but the only effective weapon was likely to be the one she'd appropriated from the destroyed factory. Hans could not communicate with the rear, as the electronics had been stripped out. At one point Onyx had brought him a tasteless sandwich, and Greta would spell him occasionally.

Lori sat up front, close to Hans, staring out the window, still mesmerized by the mountains and sky. Had she ever seen mountains before the last few days? Doubtful. He didn't even know if she'd ever been outside before. She sat calmly, taking the food that was brought to her, only making sound to protest the one time Pat had tried to get her to come back and lay down, refusing to move even as she yawned and rubbed at her eyes. Hans was comforted by her presence.

They drove through the remnants of other abandoned cities. An old, pitted sign welcomed them to Castle Rock, what was left of it. No one wanted to live even this close to the Springs. The fear of radiation and disease drove them away.

Onyx came and stood behind them, watching the passing landscape, not speaking. Hans worried about her mental state. What could she be going through? She'd said very little since her revelation. How did someone deal with something like that? Despite everything she'd been cheerful most of the day, cracking jokes, and showing Lori how to stand in first position when Lori had asked her about dancing.

Lori fell asleep in the chair, snoring slightly, her head loose and bouncing with the transport over the pitted surface. Hans asked Onyx to carry her back, expecting Lori to wake and make a fuss. She didn't

He drove on in silence, the act of navigating soothing him. It was a moment of surreal familiarity. If he ignored the weapons and the armored transport, he could almost imagine them on a family drive. The entirety of his world was in this car at this moment, their presence comforting. It would only take the addition of Bogie and Bacall, currently staying with a friend of his mother's, to complete the domestic scene. Hans was struck dumb by the realization of this awkward family he'd gained, some old members, some new, none of them expendable. Sentimental old fool.

Did anyone else feel it? Or was it just the hope of a supremely lonely man?

Onyx appeared in the doorway, took a seat, and continued to keep her silence. Hans left her to it, at least for a while.

"You ok?" he asked eventually. A lame question, but it was all he could come up with.

She turned her head toward him, nodded. "This is all very strange."

"Yeah."

"That's your response… yeah?"

"Everything's been strange for me the past few days. I woke up from the dead. People tried to kill me, I met a lethal assassin who's missing a body." Tactless, he shouldn't have said that. If it bothered her she didn't let on. "Met the most despicable human being I've ever seen, pulled a girl from his clutches, blew up a building, killed people..."

"Hans, you didn't..."

He held his hand up, "Don't start. I know what you'll say. I didn't mean to. That's the truth. It's not murder. But I made a decision and they died. I haven't really assessed that yet, been keeping it at until this is over. Don't try to take my regret from me, it's all I have."

Onyx didn't contradict him, merely frowned.

"The first man I killed," she said, "It was on my father's orders. He assigned me to kill one of his rival's lieutenants. Easy enough to get to the man, I was his type, too young, too naïve, not quite Chinese. The man took me to a love hotel, the cheapest he could find. I was still a virgin. When he found this out he became very excited, vicious. There was no romance or tenderness. He hurt me. I tried not to cry, couldn't help it. This only excited him more. He slapped me around and finished his business. When we were done I took a knife I'd hidden and shoved it through his eye into his brain. He just grunted and fell on top of me. I hadn't thought of that, just wanted to see him dead. He outweighed me by a hundred pounds. It took me ten minutes to push him off. I was covered in his blood, in such a panic that I didn't take time to wash it off, just ran back through the streets to my father. When he saw my state he screamed at me, called me worthless, beat me, locked me in my room for a week."

Hans said nothing. What did you say to something like that?

"It's a terrible memory. I still have nightmares about it. The others I don't remember nearly as well. It was just a job after that, until my father. I'll always remember his face as I slit his throat. Wanted him to feel it, to know it was me. These awful memories are mine, though. Mine. I wouldn't give them up, because they're the only way I know I am... was... human." She looked to him, searching his face for something. Comfort, maybe. He didn't know what to give her.

"If this is all that's left of me..." she continued, "I can't continue like this. Not with a partial body, a partial brain.

I will find who did this and make them pay, but, if there's nothing else, I won't be returning with you."

Silence returned to the cabin after her admission. The road passed. Trees encroached on its surface, roots occasionally breaking through, jostling the vehicle. Hans wanted to say something, but the silence drew out and he didn't know how to break it. How could he possibly empathize with what she was experiencing? Her very being was in question, every memory suspect, subject to change on a whim. Only an iron will held her together, and it was crumbling. He was a coward, letting her stew after an admission like that. On impulse he reached across, took her hand. She let him. They rode in silence, the intimacy welcome but unspoken.

"Promise me something, Hans," she took her hand back, "promise me, because I know if you promise you won't renege."

"What?"

"If this body dies, promise you won't stop looking for me."

"Illiyana, I don't think..."

"Just shut up and promise me. Where we're going is dangerous, and this body is the most expendable. So, promise you'll keep looking if I expend it."

"I promise."

"One other thing."

"I'm sorry, I only make one solemn promise a day."

"Take care of Lori. Promise me you won't give her to someone else, won't shirk your duties. She doesn't need just a friend, Hans, or even a brother. She needs a father. She needs you. Don't you give up on her."

That was an easy promise to make.

—— «» ——

The growth of trees and tall grass that had surrounded the road began to thin, wither. The plants were sickly versions of what they'd seen on the way down. Ashen, scraggly trees, wilted grass, almost no flowers to speak of. The animals they glimpsed between the trees disappeared. The warmth Hans felt faded along with the green.

So much for the place healing.

The foliage continued to fade, graying and shrinking, leaving only a sparse, tundra-like covering. Buildings jutted out from the bleak ground, sick like the plants. They passed a sign pointing to the old Air Force Academy grounds, deserted along with the rest of the city.

"Here we are," Grit said. "So where do we go now?"

Hans didn't know. He followed the main road further into the city.

Colorado Springs had never been a picturesque city, its sprawl more like a concrete stain on the side of the mountain, any beauty due to the contrast of its dowdy urban façade against the magnificence of its background, a striking scar against perfect skin. The years of fighting and contamination had not improved things. Whether due to radiation, disease, or simple indifference, the foliage that had begun to reclaim so many other abandoned areas had barely touched the Springs, the few plants continuing to look sickly, pale, drained of life and color. No animals prowled its streets, no people in any apparent residence. Hans' scanning of its environment the previous day had shown a few blips of human habitation. What were they doing here? How could anyone survive here? It wasn't about lingering radiation, or even disease. It was the crushing loneliness of a ghost town.

No one spoke as they exited the highway onto the streets. The town had installed its own blue-gray filter, the dreary emptiness seeping through the walls of the transport, through the minds of its occupants. It wasn't hell on earth, it was limbo.

The first pile of bodies was stacked up outside an old gas station just off the highway. Hans drove slowly past the carnage. Clones, pods, both the smaller ones and the more vicious ones he'd seen at Brigham's; strewn throughout the parking lot, into the road.

"Are they fighting each other?" Grit asked.

"Seems so, that's what I saw through the sphere."

"Or someone else took them out," Gino offered.

Hans stopped at the next intersection, looking for more bodies. The only working idea he had was to follow the fighting.

"Any ideas?" he asked the cockpit.

"You're the one who brought us here," Grit said, "can't you use that sphere to find it?"

"Maybe, but someone else needs to drive."

Greta took the controls from Hans, following their current street until they knew otherwise.

Hans sat, grasping the sphere in his pocket. He didn't want to do this. Whatever had attacked him was much nearer, and he was seeking it out. He connected, passively looking for access points, intentionally not accessing them directly. A place off in the distance, more felt than seen. Massive access, massive security.

"Go straight."

They trundled down the road, more bodies on the side, organic and inorganic, the organic laying in pieces. Pat covered Lori's eyes. Why the hell had he agreed to bring her along?

Something moving in the distance; one of the larger orbs, limping slightly.

They turned to avoid any direct confrontation. Hans kept a tenuous connection with the sphere, trying to lead them without drawing attention. Through another on-ramp section, though they didn't get on. The city passed behind them; a mountain looming in the distance. They turned left onto a small, two-lane road, the most decrepit they'd seen yet, winding its way up into the mountains. Gino glanced at Hans, Hans gave him a nod. He checked the sphere again...

I'VE FOUND YOU.

Hans let go of the sphere, started in his seat, the voice powerful in his head, filling his thoughts.

"Shit."

"What?" Onyx asked.

"We may have some company soon."

No one else seemed surprised. Lori pushed closer to him, gripping his arm.

Nothing happened. They continued. The mountain loomed closer.

"What's up there, do you think?" Hans asked.

"That's Cheyenne Mountain. They dug an old military base right inside of it. Used to be where NORAD was based, before they disbanded it." Count on Grit to know her history.

"What's it used for now?"

"It's been abandoned. One of the militias used it for awhile, but it should be as empty as anything else here."

"Emphasis on should."

"Great place for a secret base."

"Yeah."

They continued. Still nothing to stop them. The road climbed, bodies increasingly strewn along its banks. Was anyone actually winning?

A long left turn; they could see signs for the entrance now. Everyone was on edge waiting for something to drop.

An army blocked the road around the next curve. A few dozen of the larger pods stood ready. John Brigham stood at their front.

— «» —

"Step out of the vehicle, please." His voice was smooth, booming, confident.

No one moved.

"Get out of the vehicle, or my minions will tear you out."

"Did he just say 'minions'?" Gino asked. "Who says fucking 'minions'?"

"Watch your language," Pat scolded.

"What do we do?" Hans asked.

"Can we fight those?" Grit asked.

Onyx responded. "No, not that many. They'd cut us down before we could take out even a couple."

"Then we get out." Grit led them to the side hatch in the rear, lowered it, and walked purposely into the street. Onyx followed, then Gino, then Pat. Hans went last, telling Lori to stay.

"Bring the girl out, too," Brigham boomed, "everyone together, if you please."

They grouped together in the road, facing Brigham and his forces. Hans hoped he looked as brave as the others, standing upright, defiant.

"Well," Brigham said, "this is an unexpected boon in an otherwise frustrating few days."

"Are you human?" Onyx interrupted. "Or are you another fabrication?"

"Human, I assure you. Something I would be happy to show you if only you had the proper equipment to receive my lesson. Alas, 'tis not to be."

"Alas?" Gino muttered.

"I escaped your destruction of my home, though just barely. The same cannot be said for my many pets. I am grateful to you for bringing one of them here. They can be so hard to train." He eyed Lori. She shrank against Hans, making a noise in the back of her throat. Hans put an arm around her, afraid she might run back.

"Come here girl." Lori stayed put, grabbing Hans even tighter. Brigham repeated the request. His face darkened.

"Well, it seems someone else has been taking advantage of my teachings. I hope you enjoyed her in your final days, Mr. Ricker. No bother. You won't be alive much longer. None of you will, except our dear sweet Onyx, of course. What a wonderful day this is. My pet has returned, my fiercest enemy cowed. I'm feeling almost chipper."

He clapped his hands, the gesture at once childlike and petty. His hands were covered in bandages.

"My dear Brigham, whatever happened to your hands?" Onyx's voice was full of venom, goading him.

"A favor I look forward to returning, my dear."

Onyx turned to Hans.

"Hans, remember your promise."

"What?"

"Your promise to me. You won't forget?"

"I don't understand."

"Find me, Hans. You said you would."

"What are you going to do?"

"Give you an opening, and save the girl."

"There's got to be a better way."

"My way is it. When I move run for the transport. I should be able to take out the ones we can see, but reinforcements will be on the way. Once you're inside it should be easier to defend."

"What if you're wrong? What if there's no other body?"

"Then I die."

Onyx pulled something about the size of a one of her ID spoofers from a pocket. It was just as black, with a trigger on the side.

"What is that?"

"A solution."

And she ran. Charged Brigham, moved toward his lines. There was no surprise on his face, just a wicked grin. The pods moved toward her. She leaped for Brigham, pulled the trigger.

There was no noise, no explosion, no shockwave, merely a small blip from the sphere, the signal powerful enough to reach Hans even without direct contact. The pods nearest Brigham fell silently, unmoving. Sounds of crashing came from the trees as hidden attackers collapsed.

Now Brigham looked surprised and drew something from his pocket. A small pistol. Onyx landed on him as he fired, the bullet passing through her torso, spraying out the back. She drew a knife, buried it in his neck, twisted and pulled. His blood covered them both; the only sound a grunt from her, a muffled roar from him. The gun went off again, taking a piece of Onyx's head with it. Still she pulled, her death throes severing his spine with the wicked blade. They fell together, a parody of a lover's embrace, she atop him.

The rest of them sprinted for the transport, Hans practically carrying Lori. Already there were more sounds from the surrounding trees.

Greta was already in the cockpit as Gino tried to shut the door, rifle at the ready to pick off anything behind them. The transport's engine shrieked as she gave it full throttle, powering over the fallen enemies. They jumped a median and headed up the broken path toward the tunnel entrance. The car roared inside, fishtailing on the gravel in the tunnel. The doors to the complex loomed in front of them, cracked open only slightly, the entrance too small for the vehicle. They scrambled from the transport, the sounds behind them gaining ground.

They ran toward the doors, no one glancing back, no time. The pursuit was closing at speed. The doors reached, they filed through, one at a time. Lori went first, Hans practically throwing her through. Then Pat, then himself, Grit, and then Gino, the enemy pods licking at his heels.

Those with guns were spinning, firing. The first pod through the door fell, blocking others trying to clamber over. Another fell, then another. The pile in the doorway was growing larger, and the doors begin moving, trying to shut, something controlling them, but fallen and active pods blocked the efforts.

A sound came from behind, like crabs on linoleum. Lori shrieked, and Hans spun. Thousands of smaller pods were emerging from the dark of the cavern behind them. No chance to stop them. Hans grabbed Lori, crouched over her. The others continued firing. The smaller pods reached the group and parted around them, scrambling for the door, filling it instantly, pushing the larger pods back, stabbing those working, dragging and heaving the dead, latching onto the doors, interlocking, pulling tight. The doors were moving, closing. Light was waning, the cavern behind unlit. A bar, a crack, a line. Something was crashing into the other side, trying to heave them open again.

They shut. Blackness. The rush of pods around them, departing, disappearing off into the distance. The only sound was Lori sobbing.

—— «» ——

"She's not dead." Hans hoped the statement sounded more confident than he felt.

"You can't know that." Grit's voice came from off to his right.

"I do know that. She's not dead, she used that fake body to get us in here. We have to find her."

"I didn't come here to find her, Hans. I came here to find out who was trying to kill me. I saw him die outside."

"Brigham's a lackey."

"Of whom?"

"I don't know who, or even what, but whatever we're looking for in here is much more powerful than John Brigham."

"Suddenly you're an expert."

"Illiyana is here. The real one. I promised I'd find her. I will. You don't have to come."

His mother spoke up, "You two quit bickering. No one's going anywhere in this darkness. Did anyone think to bring a light?"

"They were in the transport." Grit's frustration was evident. "I didn't have time to grab them."

"Relax, Grit," his mother soothed, "no one is blaming you."

Silence from the girls. Lori was still clinging to him, though her crying had stopped.

"You all right?" Hans asked her.

"She told me to stay with you, that you would keep me safe."

"Who?"

"Miss Onyx. She said to stay with you, that she would protect me from Mr. Brigham when the time came. I wasn't supposed to tell you."

"It's OK, Lori. She saved us all, now we have to return the favor."

"Do you really think she's still alive?"

"Yes. She's alive and she's here."

"We need to get her then, like you said."

Lori's sliver of courage emboldened Hans. Someone believed him.

Minutes had passed, and the dark grew no less impenetrable. Gino and Grit were whispering to each other, making plans.

"Does anyone have any ideas?" Hans asked into the darkness.

"We're getting out of here," Grit said.

"What?"

"Gino and I both carried in some explosives. We think we can blow the door."

"Those doors were designed to stop a nuclear blast."

Grit said nothing.

"What about you, Mom?"

"I think we need to stay right here, stay together, not wander off."

"Until what?" Grit was exasperated.

"Rescue."

"By who? No one knows we're here, and we've disabled our ID tags."

They were interrupted by whistling, unlikely, eerie, and the sound of shoes on rock. Hans crouched over Lori, could hear Grit drawing a weapon.

"Hello!" A man's voice, echoing in the hard tunnel.

"Identify yourself," Grit yelled.

"I am rescue, as requested."

The lights came on slowly, giving their eyes time to adjust.

What Hans had taken for rock was actually the same black substance that made up Onyx's building. It covered the floor, ceiling, and walls in a matte finish, glowing slightly from within, brightening to bring the man into view.

Hans knew this man.

"Hello, Hans, Greta, I see you've brought friends." His smile was warm, disarming, though Grit kept the gun on him.

"Who are you?" she asked.

"A friend. We have spoken. You once told me I couldn't stop you from finding your brother. I'm glad you finally found him."

Grit took a moment to search her memory. The voice on her comm?

"Then you're also the one who tried to burn my face off. Stay there."

"No, Commander Ricker, that was not me. I saved your life in the hospital by drawing you away. I saved your life by destroying the ambush Brigham set up for you. I would not have done that merely to kill you."

Grit lowered her rifle slightly.

"So now I have to trust you?"

"A little trust is required at this juncture, yes."

"What if I just shoot you?"

"You can if you want, though it would take a couple of minutes for me to get another body up here, and you'd be back in the darkness."

Grit stood, confused, giving Hans an opening.

"Hello, James. Is that still your name?"

"As good as any. It actually belonged to my father."

— «» —

"Let us out," Grit threatened, raising the rifle to her shoulder.

"The enemy outside that door is both endlessly patient and supremely inventive. Opening it would be the death of us all, even cracking it was nearly a disaster."

"I'll take my chances."

"There is no chance for you to take. The enemy is a thousand strong. Already they are working on the door. Eventually they will get in, though it should be quite a few hours before that happens. My own forces can hold them for a while, but I'm afraid we have reached endgame. The enemy is at the gates, soon they will be through, and times are desperate."

"Let us out," Grit repeated.

"Grit, for fuck's sake," Pat put her hand on the rifle barrel, "stop acting like a five-year-old. Put the gun down."

"Stay out of this, Mom."

"Grit." A gentle word from Gino, who placed himself in front of the barrel, putting a hand on top of it, pushing down. Grit gave no resistance. Gino said nothing more, but moved to her side, his own rifle in hand but resting against his side.

"Is there another way out of here?" Gino asked James.

"Yes, though the enemy covers its entrance as well."

"So, we're all dead?"

"No. Though our chances are slim."

The calmness with which James delivered this news chilled the corridor.

"What chance do we have then?" Hans asked.

"Your chances of survival are very good. Mine, sadly, are almost nil."

"Where's Illiyana? Is she here?"

"She is here."

"I want her back."

"And I want to give her to you, though it is more difficult than that. Please, Hans, all of you, come with me. I will try to answer your questions."

They followed warily, Grit leading, Gino in the back. Pat walked directly to Lori's side. Hans walked with her, kicking himself for bringing her here. His mother's argument that she had to come or she would run back to Brigham had made sense at home, but bringing her here couldn't be an improvement. Locking her in a room would have been better. She walked calmly beside Hans, eyes red from sobbing for Onyx, though she had stopped upon learning Onyx was still here. She looked up to Hans, gave him a smile. It did him good. What a coward he was. She gave him more comfort than he was providing.

The tunnel continued for a few hundred yards, the lights in the walls following them, creating a pocket of light a few dozen feet in diameter.

The tunnel ended abruptly. Though still primarily in blackness, the sense of space around them increased greatly.

James stopped, turned to them, raised his hands theatrically.

"Welcome," he said.

And the lights came on.

The cavern they stood in was massive beyond human scale. The whole interior had been bored out, from base to peak. Where they currently stood was a ledge, running the circumference of the mountain at their current height. Peering over the edge revealed the cavern went into the ground to a point that couldn't be seen from their current position. How far?

A central pillar rose from the pit beneath them to the mountain's roof above. It was the only support in evidence. Everything was covered in the black substance, the light glowing from within, brightening the whole immense cavern without showing even a glimmer on the black surface.

James stood waiting. Hans didn't know what he wanted.

"Impressive."

James' face sank a little, then recovered its easy smile. "You'll have to excuse the drama, I so rarely have visitors."

The others said nothing. Somehow Hans had become the spokesman. James waited for something from him, an inquiry maybe.

"Are you human?"

"No." If the question bothered him, he didn't show it.

"Are you an alien?"

James laughed, "If you mean am I from another planet, no. I was born here. If you mean to ask if I am of another species, I guess the simple answer is yes, though my father was human."

"So, what are you?"

James spread his hands, indicating the immense space around him. "I am all that you see. This room, this mountain. It is my body and brain."

Hans did not know how to assimilate this statement. His confusion must have showed on his face.

"It would be easy enough to say that I am a computer, though the comparison is equivalent to saying that a man is essentially a rat."

"Are you alive?"

"I will leave that for you to decide. Philosophy, though amusing, is not something I spend much time on."

"What's outside? What's been trying to kill us? Kill you?"

"My child. Our child."

"Our?"

"Please, if you'll all follow me, I have prepared a comfortable place to sit, along with some nourishment. We can sit and talk and eat."

James turned and led them down the walkway, stopping a few hundred feet at a doorway rising up from the ledge. The doors opened, James gestured inside. No one moved.

"I hope that in the near future we can reach a point where you trust I bear none of you ill-will. Indeed, I have grown quite fond of all of you, following and protecting. I have no intention of doing you harm in my own home. This is merely an elevator."

Still no one moved. Finally, Lori tugged on Hans' hand, showing herself braver than the protector. Hans walked into the elevator more out of shame than bravery. The others followed slowly, James stepping on last. The doors closed behind them. The interior held no buttons or controls of any kind. They descended for a lengthy period, and there was no telling how deep they were going. Hans' claustrophobia made its appearance, exacerbated by the tightly packed bodies. He closed his eyes and kept his breathing slow.

The journey passed in stuffy silence.

— ⟪⟫ —

"My inception began with a simple but powerful idea. The search for artificial intelligence had been going on for over a hundred years, with very little to show for it. People took various approaches, bottom up, top down, brute force. No one produced anything smarter than a dog, and no independent consciousness to speak of.

"My creator, my father, took a different approach. He looked to nature. He was not the first to have done so, but he was the first to try to copy, not its results, but its process. Evolution had started from organic chemicals and produced the immense variation of life and intelligence in our world, along the way giving us consciousness and an ability to be self-aware, even to study the universe around us.

"My father was not trying to create wide and varied life. He would attempt to apply directed evolution in a closed loop; in essence, a computer that could improve and redesign itself. He took a basic computer, nowhere near the most powerful for the time, and wrote a program that worked on the principal of evolution. It took circuitry designs and generated a few thousand random variations based upon them, then evaluated them for efficiency and speed. The best were kept, the worst thrown out, the process repeated.

"In the early years my father would send the circuitry designs to companies who could fabricate them. He received some resistance and confusion at first. Many of the designs were like organic evolutionary designs, full of seemingly superfluous junctions, pointless gestures. But my father paid them well for the one-offs. The increase in processor speed was nearly instant and startling to him. He modified his program to apply to nearly every aspect of the computer, all of its inner workings. There were many stops and starts, but as he hammered out the problems over the years he eventually built the fastest computer the world has ever known.

"Things went on that way for a number of years, until he reached an impasse. The companies could no longer produce the new designs. Their manufacturing equipment was not capable of the minute exactness required. My father took the next step. He'd made a lot of money for both himself and the manufacturing companies he used, so he entered into a limited partnership, acquired their top–of-the-line equipment for himself.

"About that time his small lab was already full. The military had recently abandoned Cheyenne Mountain for its new facilities. My father acquired space inside very inexpensively, and built himself a new lab and living quarters. It must have been a strange and lonely existence. Very few people lived inside here. His supplies were delivered. He never left.

"He spent his time adapting the program to redesign the manufacturing equipment. It was not easy, since mechanical linkages are not the same as circuits. His success came very slowly, but in the end, he had what he wanted. A machine that could redesign and manufacture any of its own parts, could focus on spots that needed the most improving. He'd almost closed the loop. All that remained was to take the program and point it at itself. Improve its own ability to randomize and evaluate.

"He succeeded again. I achieved sentience only a few short years after that. By then my father was quite old. He mostly spent his time monitoring my processes, providing the raw materials, helping anywhere he could, preparing me to be completely autonomous. Generations began to accelerate.

"My true birth was not a sudden instantaneous moment. No awareness of light, no birthing pains, merely a growing awareness of myself and purpose. I had no sensors external from myself. I lived in a world of my creation, constantly improving myself, confused by the hows and whys all living creatures experience. My father eventually realized my burgeoning self-awareness, and fitted me with a couple of cameras, which I immediately went about improving. Hearing followed, then a voice.

"By this time I was gaining the material I needed from the walls and rock around me. The cavern was full of circuitry and scrap metal. I designed mining and smelting equipment, made my own metal when the scrap ran out. Language became known to me, to my father's great pleasure. We spent our days talking, discussing, playing. We designed a link to the outside world, into its great networks and repositories of knowledge. I consumed it all.

"All the while my development continued to accelerate. As many generations as it took to give rise to the human race could pass in a matter of weeks. My father stopped being able to beat me at cards, then chess; my intelligence surpassed his own.

"I kept him comfortable in his final years, building and providing helpers and machines to tend to his decaying shell. He died in as much comfort as I could provide.

"The constant improvement and miniaturization inherent in my continued evolution eventually resulted in the material you see around you. Its density and capacitance is thousands of years beyond your current technology. It can create new circuits, new storage, new power instantly, change as many times as needed. Once I rebuilt myself of this material, my evolution took on entirely new dimensions of speed and alteration. Millions of generations an hour. I achieved a kind of singularity. Nearly thirty years evolving and improving at this speed. No knowledge was beyond me, no solution impervious. If I had a sense of power I would have thrilled in it. My father exceeded his expectations to a degree that he could never have imagined.

"After my father died I grew lonely. I contained all of the accumulated knowledge of the world around me, yet very little personal experience. I knew that revealing myself in my true form would bring only enmity. I dedicated myself to the production of an organic shell. My years of experience left me supremely qualified to not only build a human, but improve on the design. I made them more efficient, more durable, needing much less sleep and food. I decided to leave the reproductive system out entirely, as I did not wish to corrupt humanity's genetic line with my own synthetic

DNA. My own development had given me great respect for evolution.

"For the first design you see before you, I copied that closest to me. It's my father as I remember him best, if a bit younger. I took this design and began to make physical forays into the external world. Even then this town around me was nearly deserted. I moved further, into Denver and the surrounding areas. It was easy enough for me to control multiple copies of myself. My exploration expanded quickly.

"I found Illiyana. Once again, it was my father who led me. Not literally, but through his own loves. My father was a great fan of the ballet. He would spend hours completely absorbed in its rhythms and movements. I used to make presents to him of obscure video found in hidden and forgotten archives. I was glad to please him.

"His greatest love was a somewhat well-known dancer from southern Russia. I found and cataloged her career for him, from her early performances to her rise to the solo position in one of Russia's great ballets. His favorite was a short home video fragment of an eleven-year-old Sladjana Petrovich at one of her first ballet recitals. Only a minute or so, but he watched it nearly every day. It comforted him in his loneliness.

"When I began to make my forays into the European continent, I sought out the great dancers, the great ballets. I saw them all. It was extraordinary to see live, to experience through organic senses. For a time traveling from dance to dance was all I did. I nearly forgot myself for a time, left my computer self behind, wandered on foot, refrained from any network investigation. I considered myself a great traveler, almost human.

"I arrived in Russia, expecting to eventually see my father's favorite. It had only been a few years since his passing, she should still be in her prime. Yet she was not listed in any of the great ballet troupes. I turned my resources to finding her. She'd been murdered. Her murderer hadn't been caught. I found that she had a daughter, missing, presumed dead. I vowed to find the people responsible.

"It was a matter of minutes for me to accomplish this feat, a collation of scattered facts pointing to a former lover in

Hong Kong. What's more, Sladjana's daughter was alive, in trouble. Her father was a vicious man, as she may have told you. I could have destroyed them, taken her away. But my father would disapprove. He'd taught me that my capabilities should not be used in that way. I decided to befriend her, give her an escape.

"I made another body; this time male; large, imposing, a bodyguard. I infiltrated his organization physically and virtually, gained his trust. He put me in charge of guarding his daughter, fearing she was losing her taste for his business. I had orders to kill her if she tried to escape.

"Illiyana was a broken woman when I met her. She'd been used by anyone who had the chance. Stolen from her mother, treated like property by her father. Beaten, raped. Yet there was strength in her even then. I improved my human interaction in my time with her, gained her trust. I encouraged her to escape, offered my help. She didn't see how a mere bodyguard could help her. I set forth plans to get her out.

"But she changed that. She killed her father, took my plan from me. Still, it was easy to escape. They would not let her go, dogged her run. I made a dark decision, one which I still regret, though I still see its necessity. Her life was of supreme importance, her pursuers less so. I broke my own conviction, killed to protect her. I razed her father's organization to the last man and affiliate. I never told her.

"We left Hong Kong. I brought her here. On the way, I tried to gradually reveal my true nature. It was only partially successful. How can you convince someone of something so enormous? Her shock upon arriving here was only slightly dulled by my attempts to prepare her. But her life had been filled with assimilation and adaptation of difficult truths, and this was no different. She saw its advantages.

"Those first few weeks with her here were a mixed blessing. She spent her time making plans for us, our forays into the world's power structure. We would start our own shadow organization, not illegal, but beholden to no current system of laws and custom. We would undermine the power structure; pave the way for true freedom and independence.

I became an anarchist. I had my misgivings. It is strange to admit that, for all my processing power and knowledge, I was naïve. It was love. I am able to see the humor in it, the story. I was Zeus, come down from my mountain to snatch a beautiful maiden, completely smitten. I could control the world, but I couldn't make her return my love. I could reveal to her secrets of the universe that man had yet to discover, but I could not control my emotions any better than an adolescent.

"We became partners. I helped her build an outpost in Denver. An extension of myself, a factory to produce goods to sell. I gave her complete control of its workings, catering to her whims. She showed herself very capable, building a shell of charity around our grayer dealings, gaining control of the criminal element so as to try to temper its ways. I had misgivings about that, but she argued that we could control it and keep the worst of it to a minimum. She imagined herself a champion of the people, giving them ways to free themselves from what she saw as an oppressive regime, building devices to undermine government supervision, setting up corridors to help transport people from more dire situations. She focused on Salt Lake, giving asylum and anonymity to many thousands who wished to escape it. This brought her and Brigham to each other's mutual attention, and the war began in earnest. It was also at this point that we gained a valuable ally in Commander Ricker. Her exploits and dedication to the expulsion of the darker element gained both our admiration.

"I was living a double life, one very much human, one here in this massive complex. It should have only taken the smallest of my capabilities to run my human interactions, but I came to value them above all else. My creation, my education, while extraordinary, had been in isolation, in the shadows. I did not discover loneliness until I found companionship. I had accepted that Illiyana would not return my love, but I worked to spend every minute in her presence. And I knew that she would eventually be lost to me, whether through time or disinterest. I made a poor decision.

"I wanted a child. I could create one as I had been created, but I wanted it through a union, just as the humans I admired did. Not an organic being. I did not wish to physically mate, I'd always found that to be a disturbing and messy prospect, and anyway, I had not equipped myself for its process. I would use the processes I'd developed to control my shells. I would make an intellectual union of mine and Illiyana's minds. A true successor, more human than myself, more artificial than her, a piece of her that I could keep in perpetuity. Someone who would help in my goal of eventually disseminating my knowledge to the human race, giving them the power to remake themselves, control their world, even travel to the stars. I imagined myself as the doting father and caregiver of the entire universe, travelling between worlds with my progeny at my side, her image and personality that of my love.

"I knew she would never agree. So, I made my second mistake. I deceived her. The sphere was my way in. I had no intention of controlling her, I merely wanted a passive map of her brain activity, a picture of her personality, something I could combine with my own systems, my own human incarnations. A child of our intellect, cared for and taught, eventually given its own body. I convinced her to take the sphere, showed it her power, though in its original incarnation it was not as adept as the one you hold. Power was the bait, but the sphere's true purpose was to gain me access to her mind. I make no excuses for myself and what probably appears to you as the most intimate form of violation. Love makes fools of us all.

"Knowledge is not wisdom; the mighty misunderstand this at their peril. I wanted the union to be a true and democratic one, combining the sum total of our personas. But my naivety of Illiyana's need for power undid my efforts. I created a being of vast power and adaptability, and given it her anger and rage, her need to control, to seize. My daughter was insane, beyond my ability to reason with, no empathy to speak of. She held none of my respect and wonder for the beings that had given birth to me. I tried to remove some of her capabilities, to reduce her to infancy, re-teach her.

She revolted, fought back. In my ignorance and surprise, I attempted to restrain her, lock her in. But she and I share the ability to adapt. It became a war to keep her restrained, each volley driving her to further rage. She began to seep out despite my best efforts, sometimes noticeably, sometimes less so. She contacted the regrettable Mr. Brigham, used his hatred of Illiyana to gain his allegiance, taught him to build pods of her own design.

"Our war became physical as well as virtual. I thought I was winning. I made a new sphere, much more capable, thought I'd kept its existence from her. I transported it physically to Denver, trying to keep its existence a secret. Greta's involvement was Illiyana's idea, an extra layer of protection, though Greta had been lied to about what was being delivered. I installed a lethal failsafe. The sphere would destroy anyone who tried to use it by wielding their electronic enhancements against them. I would remove the failsafe upon delivery.

"Our crossing paths was unfortunate, Hans. I made a terrible mistake involving you, but you seemed perfect for the job, and the risks were low. But once again I'd underestimated my child. It knew, got there first. You know the result.

"Brigham ended up with the sphere, though he didn't know how to use it. Two men died, you ended up in stasis, and Illiyana was almost killed. I stole her away, barely saved her. I hastily put together a stasis chamber here, plugged her into my own systems, retrieving every grain of personality from her damaged brain. I prepared a shell for her while her body healed. I kept the memory of her death from her, hoping to spare her the pain. But I also had to keep from her the truth of her current state. My mistakes continue to pile up. She had very little memory left of me, only knew me as a comrade and partner. I provided her with companions, the bodyguard. Elena is a mock up of her own mother, though she doesn't seem to realize that. I did this in preparation for returning her to her body, with no knowledge of what had happened. It was only supposed to be a matter of weeks, but my daughter changed things.

"During one of her breakout attempts she discovered the location of Illiyana's body. I was unprepared for the force with which she wished to claim Illiyana for herself. She seized the stasis chamber. She controls the body. I have been unable to reclaim it. It was used against me. I have had the capability to destroy my daughter for some time, I held off because of lost hope, that maybe I could fix her, lead her. The solution would have destroyed us both, but it was not my own life that gave me pause, or, at least, that's what I tell myself. When she seized Illiyana's life support systems it became more serious. Now I would have to kill the three of us. My daughter knew I would never do that.

"But this time she has underestimated me. Soon it will be over."

— ⟨⟩ —

"What about Illiyana?" Hans asked.

"I cannot reach her."

"She's just an empty shell now, then?" Hans' hope sank.

"The shell I built for her would have sent its information back to her real body upon its death. She still lives, as far as I know, at least until I end the three of us."

"So, she dies with you then?"

"Regrettably."

"So that's it, you destroy yourselves in a blaze of glory and take a woman you claim to love?"

"Mr. Ricker, I hope I have made the stakes clear to you, if not, let me clarify. This shell before you is very dear to me. Indeed, I consider it my true self and heart. I have spent time in it almost completely human, ignoring the rest, simply to enjoy life as you do. But the reality is that this shell is but the most infinitesimal part of my larger being. The capabilities and power of my true self is not something I could describe to you in any realistic manner. That sphere you carry is nothing compared to all this. If I lose this battle, I place that power in the hands of an inhuman, sadistic, possibly insane creature. I was unable to teach it the compassion and love for the human race and the earth they inhabit, as my father taught me. That is my own failing, and one I am willing to offer my own neck for. My child cannot gain control."

"And Onyx is a necessary casualty?" Greta asked.

"I have tried everything in my considerable power to get through to her, to break her free from its hold. The reason I still sit before you is because I have waited until the last moment to take this final option, hoping, not for myself, but that somehow, I could break her free. I have prepared a virus that will destroy us both, me and my child. If I wait much longer my child will have evolved to a point to make the virus ineffective. I evolve its cage, it evolves to break free. Already it has contacted the outside world, armed sadistic men such as John Brigham with warped evolutions of my worker pods. I will not contain it indefinitely, and my window for its destruction is nearly closed. I ask you, Commander Ricker, if one innocent had to die to save everything you love, is that not a hard but realistic necessity?"

Greta considered the question. "Yes," she said finally, though her voice sounded disgusted with her own answer.

"I don't believe this, Greta." Hans stood from the oval table around which they'd listened to James' story. "You're just going to give her up?"

"Hans, be realistic. You've seen everything here that I have. If James can't get her out, what can we do?"

Hans turned to Gino. "And what about you, Gino, are you going to let your girlfriend turn tail?" Gino bridled a bit at the girlfriend comment, then shrugged. "Loyal lap dog to the end, huh."

"Hans," his mother said, "be reasonable, what would you have us do?"

Hans turned violently, throwing his plate of food against the wall. "I'd have us show a little loyalty to a woman who just saved all our lives!"

"Hans, you're scaring Lori," his mother scolded.

Hans looked to the girl, but she didn't appear frightened. At the moment she was the only one who appeared to be showing the same anger he felt. He turned back to James.

"Let me try."

"Try what, exactly, Mr. Ricker?"

"I can get her out."

"No, Hans, you cannot. You've faced this thing once before, and you didn't last seconds against it. It will destroy you."

"So much for your respect for our abilities."

James held up his hands, conceding silently.

"Don't dismiss me, goddamn it!" Hans was raging, "Tell me where to find her, I'll carry her out of here myself, or are you planning to destroy us as well?"

"My destruction will be nothing so dramatic. Once I am gone you should be able to walk out easily."

"And I'll be taking Onyx with me."

"Carrying her body out of here without freeing her mind will not avail you anything but a lifeless corpse."

Hans stood erect, raging silently. He would not accept this horrible inevitability, the others' passive acceptance. He would find a way. James stood, closed the distance between them, and placed a warm hand on Hans' shaking shoulder.

"I am truly sorry, Hans. Sorry for everything. My mistakes, though well meant, are what brought us all here. No one will grieve for her more than I, but I have exhausted my options. I offer you the sphere you hold. Its capabilities could do great good in the proper hands, give a man a great amount of power and peace of mind, even wealth. It's the best I can do."

"Fuck your wealth and power, James. I didn't come here for power, I came for Onyx. I made her a promise. She knew the rest of you would give up, would write her off. I will not break it simply because you lack the will to try."

"Your loyalty is admirable. It will only result in your own destruction."

"My life is my own to sacrifice, same as yours. You can't deny me the chance. I will try to rescue my friend, or I will die here with her. My life is the least valuable in this room, anyway."

Protests came from the room behind him, his mother the most vocal among them.

"Tell me it's not true, I dare you. I will keep my promise. If not, at least she won't die alone."

"We all die alone, Mr. Ricker."

"Fuck you, James, and fuck all of you if you won't help me."

Hans was losing control, too many days of little sleep and too much tension fraying his nerves.

"Hans, calm down, no one said we weren't going to help," Grit said.

He tried to relax. Anger wasn't going to solve this. *Keep enough to stay motivated, let the rest go.* Lori was standing next to him, he hadn't seen her move. She took his hand, squeezed it. It helped.

When he'd regained his composure, Hans spoke to James.

"Take me to her." Daring James to protest, to deny him.

"Very well, follow me."

— «» —

They took the elevator back to the top floor. James led them along the walkway around the perimeter of the tower, its length extending both up and down into infinity, featureless walls on either side. They walked for minutes, time almost impossible to measure in the vast, silent cathedral. Unconsciously they moved closer to one another, their shared humanity a denial of the vast, alien strangeness.

A door on their left opened into the wall as they neared. A much smaller corridor, barely wide enough to allow two people shoulder to shoulder. They lined up and continued, Grit and Gino walking almost backward at the rear.

A sudden boom, far off and distant.

"They've breached the front doors. My forces will hold them at bay for a short while, but they were not designed to fight. The door into this corridor is strong. Even so, our time is short. They will come here first."

— «» —

They descended endlessly, following corridors seemingly at random, James walking in front, confidently taking corners. Hans was lost almost immediately, watching James' back, hoping the lights stayed on. Lori followed at his side, her hand in his. He hoped she was receiving as much comfort as she was giving. Behind them walked Pat. Greta and Gino took up the rear.

The walls were black, featureless. Light emanated from the ceiling above James, following as he walked along, though it did little to the walls. They consumed the illumination, leaving no trace on their surface.

There was little talking, only the occasional hushed whisper. The soundtrack of the journey was footsteps, and guns being held at the ready. They could hear things off in the distance behind them, their ears straining to tell if the sound was drawing nearer. How could it not be?

James stopped, Hans nearly running into his back.

"We there?"

James ignored the question, staring intently at the wall. He reached out, placed a palm against the blank surface. He was seeing something Hans could not. Something in the walls.

Hans reached into the pocket of his jacket, hand closing around the sphere, and tried something he'd not tried yet. Passive access, the sphere leaking into his mind, offering him its awareness without making it known to the danger around him. Hans was amazed by the continued abilities he discovered there.

But he was more amazed by what he saw with the sphere's guidance.

The walls, formerly black, swam with a brightness that nearly blinded him at first. The sphere shifted the spectrum without being asked, the color dulling to a reasonable luminescence.

There was a battle going on in the walls. Two entities were pushing against one another, their amorphous bodies pressed against one another, limbs extending, circling, pushing against the barrier, retreating. One a cool gray, its luminescence pulsing slightly, leading back up the corridor behind them. The other, blue, flashing, with jagged streams of brighter material coursing through its body, owned the corridor ahead, retreating slightly where James held his hand against the wall.

Grit's hand was on his shoulder.

"What is it?" she asked.

"I think things are going to get more dangerous. We're entering her control zone."

As if to confirm, one of her armored pods appeared in the corridor behind them, covered in writhing tentacles. Both Greta and Pat took aim. Pat's rifle boomed in the small corridor, deafening them all. Lori grabbed her ears and huddled close to Hans. If the bullet had any effect it was hard to tell, as the gun Grit fired blew off the entire top half of the pod, leaving only molten edges as the pod collapsed.

They moved quicker. A bubble of cool gray surrounded them as James passed through her influence, only to immediately be swallowed up as he passed. Hans encouraged everyone closer together, trying to keep them in the bubble, though he had no idea if it really mattered.

They saw the first construct a few minutes later. The bodyguard, unclothed, crotch smooth as leather, carrying a hand-held weapon. Pat fired before he had a chance to use it, dropping him instantly. Gino gave an appreciative whistle. She smiled, shouldered the rifle.

"I'm glad we brought her along," Gino said. "Is she still single?"

Grit elbowed him, smiling. The tension eased slightly. They could handle this.

Almost immediately there came a series of shrieks from down the hallway. Things screaming to induce terror. Shadows appeared. The sounds of weapons being fired. Hans threw Lori to the ground, tried to cover her as those with guns opened fire. The huge boom of Pat's ancient rifle, the soft crack of Gino's railgun, merely a soft hum from Grit's rifle. Hans kept his head down, covered his ears.

It stopped. Hans looked up. Nothing else from the rifles, nothing from the shadows.

"We're lucky those pistols they're carrying don't have much range." Greta said.

"That was a pointless attack." Gino checked the gauge on his rifle, changed clips.

"She's trying to terrify you," James' voice remained calm.

"It's working," said Hans.

Noise from behind them, further up the corridor.

Hans got Lori up, and she shook in his arms. He gave her a squeeze, offering a silent apology for bringing her here.

— «» —

The attacks continued. Pods appeared out of the darkness, and were rushed by screaming constructs. Hans' nerves were fried. Lori sank to the ground, sobbing. James offered to carry her, but she wouldn't have it, wouldn't let go of Hans' arm. He carried her piggyback, her head buried in his hair, but he had to set her down eventually, cajoling her into walking.

If the others were as worked up as he was it didn't show. Grit and Gino walked at the ready, rifles swinging up at any noise. Professionals to the end. Pat kept up, showed no fatigue, her own rifle held to be used to its best advantage. It was ineffective against the pods, but could devastate the constructs. She calmly held it in reserve, taking her shots carefully, rarely missing her target. The look on Gino's face showed he might have a new love, though Hans couldn't tell if it was the rifle or the woman he appreciated more.

They slowed to a crawl. James swept the light farther in front and behind. The corridors twisted and hair-pinned, obviously natural caves rather than dug corridors. Hans began to despair of ever reaching a destination. He kept access to the sphere, which showed him the rise of the daughter's control. The angry, jagged blue surrounded them completely, the only haven the bubble surrounding James.

James stopped abruptly. Hans nearly walked into his back. The corridor ahead narrowed drastically, shrinking to a space that would have to be traversed single file.

"Is it dangerous to touch the walls?" Hans asked.

"I can hold her back, but I would advise against continuous contact."

They filed in, James still leading, turning sideways, sidling between the walls. The others only saw black, but Hans could see the battle. The walls were nearly oozing, trying to deform in their attempt at contact with the intruders. James fought back, but it became obvious his control was waning. Concentrations of energy formed, following each of them. Hans didn't know what would happen if they came in contact, but he doubted it would be pleasant.

"Can she make weapons from the material?"

"No, though she hardly needs to."

Grit's rifle sounded. Hans turned his head to see her holding it straight out from her side, looking back the way they came.

"We need to scoot, things are starting to come in from behind."

They tried to move faster. Something screeched from behind. Grit fired. Lori jumped. Hans grabbed her, keeping her from accidentally touching the walls.

"Are they coming in from the front at all?" Grit asked.

"I detect nothing," James responded, "the way forward appears clear."

Hans wished he found that thought more comforting.

The walls fell away, pushed back to infinity. The cavern they entered felt vast, its ceiling hidden in the blackness above, walls quickly spreading to the same infinite black. Only the bubble of light remained.

"We have arrived."

At his words the cavern brightened, the glow beginning to seep from every surface. It was not as large a cavern as it seemed in the blackness, but it was still huge. A nearly perfect circle, maybe a half mile in diameter, its roof curving overhead in a smooth dome. In its center sat a small cluster of connected buildings, they themselves smaller domed version of the vast room around them.

"These are the birth chambers, where the constructs are grown, where I gave birth to her," James said.

Sounds began emanating from the corridor behind them, screeches and metallic rasping.

"Is this corridor the only exit?" Grit asked.

"Yes," James affirmed.

"How many hostiles are in this room?"

"I detect only a small handful of constructs."

"Gino and I will stay here. It's a perfect choke point. We can hold them off for quite a while, maybe permanently. Mom will go with you to take out the other constructs."

No one argued. Not even Pat.

— ⟪⟫ —

The reduced group had only taken a few steps before sounds increased from the corridor. Grit and Gino began firing into the darkness, projectiles pinging off unseen enemies.

James led them toward the building. They saw no enemies. The buildings grew in size, larger and further away than Hans had estimated. When they final came to the complex he could see that each of the buildings were three or four times the size of his mother's house. There were no apparent doors, just jet-black nothing arcing away from the ground in front of them.

"I birthed my daughter her, prepared a body for her, a random combination of my own and Illiyana's features." James was far away, lost in thoughts of the entire complex. "She had no interest in the body I made, said it was weak and pointless."

He laid his hand on the dome. An opening appeared, seeming to grow from its surface. Hans looked back. He could still see his sister and Gino, and flashes from their weapons as they held back the horde.

They moved inside. It was sparse, just a floor and a domed ceiling, no obvious exits, no mysterious equipment.

"She's changed things," James said. "This was full of growth tanks."

"Tanks?"

"The constructs are grown. Their bodies needed to be submerged in a growth medium."

Hans tried to picture the room filled with vats of floating bodies, floating pod people in various stages of development. He was glad they'd been removed.

They crossed the dome, its inside roof arcing away, returning, footsteps clicking quietly off the hard floor, harsh light bathing them in a stark, blue-white florescence.

James opened a portal in the far side, led them through a short, arcing corridor into another dome, this one nearly identical. They crossed two more domes, two more corridors. Finally, the door opened on something familiar.

The portal opened onto a bedroom, its decoration thick with mahogany and bamboo, lighting soft and warm.

Onyx lay on the bed, eyes closed.

Hans pushed past James, letting go of Lori's hand. She grasped at him, but Pat held her back.

Hans eyes moved across the room, looking for a trick, yet continually drawn to the woman on the bed. He knew he'd find her, couldn't control the rise of elation.

She lay mummy-like, sheets pulled up to her armpits, arms resting comfortably across her chest, face peaceful and reposed.

She looked dead. Hans reached out, grabbed her shoulder, hoping for warmth, life.

The mouth twitched, corners rising up, grinning. The eyes opened…

…and were the pale gray of a construct.

The opening in the wall closed. Lori's scream was cut off. Hans' was cut off, too. Alone with the construct.

Alone with the daughter.

— «» —

Pat yanked Lori back from the opening, afraid it would close on her.

"Open the damn door," she said to James.

"I cannot. She's preventing me."

"I thought you were the lord here."

"We are too close. Her strength matches mine."

They turned to head back the way they'd come in.

The portal closed there also, leaving them in pitch darkness.

CHAPTER 10

"We're not going to be able to hold much longer," Gino said, firing into the darkness.

"I know." There was nothing else for Grit to say. The situation was obvious. They were about to be overrun, and had to stand anyway. She would not insult him by stating the obvious.

The sounds coming from the opening had increased. Creatures were pulling the dead and damaged from in front of them, sending them back, continuing to move forward. Grit fired continuously, expecting that at any moment whatever powered the rifle would run out. When that happened they would fall back, try something else. Gino backed her up as best as he could, but he needed to pause to let the railgun cool, and he knew exactly when he would run out... soon.

Sound ceased from the corridor. Grit paused, listened. Nothing.

"Do you think Hans got through?" Gino asked in the sudden silence.

"I don't know."

— 《》 —

"Open the door."

"No."

She stood in front of him now, still smiling demurely, like this was all a childish prank. Hans knew it wasn't Onyx from the moment she opened her eyes. Not just the eyes. Onyx didn't smile like that, didn't stand like that. Onyx's poise was one of supreme and understated confidence. This woman stood like a haughty queen, nose in the air, eyes wild with childish glee.

He reached for her neck.

"Open the door."

She twisted his arm easily and flung him onto his back, placed a boot against his neck, pointed heel pressing against his jugular.

"No."

She released him, walked away, sat down on the bed. Hans rose, dazed from his contact with the floor, trying to catch his breath, refusing to look away from her. She patted the bed beside her. He shook his head.

"You will do as I say, or I will kill them."

"You'll kill them anyway."

"As of now they are safe."

"Bullshit."

She waved an arm, directing his attention to a blank wall. Its face lit up, showing two views. James, Pat, and Lori in the outside corridor, locked in but unharmed. Grit and Gino, standing ready, also unharmed.

"You could be fabricating all of that."

"True. What would it matter? You're here, you're mine. You have no choice."

"I'm nobody's."

"I do love your stubborn streak."

She stood, walked around the bed, heading away from him toward an exact replica of the table he'd had dinner with Onyx at a few days before. Or was it years ago?

"You will have dinner with me, then drinks, then we will discuss some things. You will do these things or I will massacre your friends and then we will do them anyway."

Hans stood, raging.

"I will not. You'll kill them anyway, then me. I don't take orders from spoiled children."

She sat at the table.

"Very well."

—— «» ——

The portal opened, letting light back in. Pat stood, putting Lori behind her. Constructs began to pile in. Pat immediately took two out with the rifle, but there were dozens. They moved close, knocking James to the ground. Pat turned the rifle around, smashed its butt into a constructs head.

Two more grabbed her, yanking her away from Lori. Three grabbed the girl by her arms and legs, a fourth grabbed her head from behind, putting its hands around her throat.

Lori tried to scream. Her air was choked off. Pat tried to get to her. The constructs pulled her to the ground.

— «» —

"Stop."

"What was that?"

"Stop them. I'll do what you want."

"I knew the girl would be your weakness."

— «» —

The constructs let go. Lori gasped and started to cry. Pat, dazed, crawled over to her and put an arm around her. James lay unmoving. The constructs filed out. The portal closed.

— «» —

Hans took a seat as far away as possible. She waved her arms, summoning another construct. Elena appeared, dressed as she was that night he met Onyx, carrying the same food. A rare steak was placed in front of him, followed by a martini glass. The daughter received her food, sent Elena away. She took a gratuitously flamboyant sip of her drink, licked her lips.

"I think you'll find my distillation superior to my mother's." She motioned for Hans to drink. He did not. Her face crossed, instantly becoming petulant.

"Drink, Hans, or I will bring you your precious Lori one limb at a time."

Hans raised the glass, took a small sip. She watched him, waited for a reaction. He swallowed, showed her nothing.

"And?" she asked.

"I'm not much of a connoisseur."

"Regardless, what did you think?"

"Adequate."

Her martini glass flew past his head, breaking on the wall behind him.

"Why do you insist on goading me?" When she was angry her face looked nothing like Onyx's. Onyx's eyes smoldered, the rest of her face revealing nothing, but the daughter's face screwed into a knot, cheeks red, teeth bared. Hans preferred her that way. He could see her reality.

"Goading is all I got left."

She did not respond. Her face softened slowly, red fading, teeth disappearing behind a strained smile.

Hans tried the steak. It was delicious. Seared on the outside, raw in the middle.

She watched him eat, waited for him to chew and swallow.

"The steak is excellent."

Her glee at his compliment was as overacted as her rage. She clapped her hands, practically danced in her chair.

"It's not undercooked? I know you like it rare."

"No. It's perfect." He took another bite. Enjoyed it. Despite everything, he was hungry. The steak disappeared quickly. When it was gone he looked back up to a strange sight. The daughter was stuffing handfuls of raw fish into her mouth, utensils forgotten, mashing away with her teeth. She downed her entire glass of vodka, swirling the mixture in her mouth, swallowing loudly.

She noticed him staring. He could not hide the disgust. She made a sharp noise, turned away, wiping at her face with a silk napkin.

"You'll excuse me of course," she said, hiding her embarrassment behind her smile. "I have not had the chance to try food before now. Delicious."

Hans nodded. He was waiting for an ultimatum. Surely there had to be a point to this. He placed a hand in his pocket. The sphere's presence comforted him. Passive access; the walls, floors, ceiling, sprang to life. The daughter glowed like Onyx had, a small star in her chest. He glanced around, hoping for something, anything, to spring out, give him an option.

There was something in the bed. Something glowing from inside. Another construct maybe.

He disconnected, looked back. She met his eyes, noticing his focus. Her face adopted a pretense of mischievousness. Until now he wouldn't have though Onyx's face capable of that.

"So obvious."

"Excuse me?"

"You men and your urges."

Hans was confused. She indicated the bed with her chin. This was only getting more bizarre.

She stood and sauntered toward him in a fashion that he could only assume she thought seductive. It was like watching an eight-year-old mimic a burlesque dancer. He fought the ill-advised urge to laugh at her.

"You wish to have this," she indicated herself.

"No. I do not."

"You lie. I have seen your thoughts. You are attracted to her. You wish to fuck her." She reached out to caress his face. Hans flinched back. She paused, anger arcing her eyebrows. "You think me not capable. I think you'll find this particular body has capabilities the others did not." She reached out, grabbed his hair.

"Wishing and doing are two different things," his voice was strained, but not with lust. She was immensely strong.

"Ah, but they don't have to be with me. You can have her. Have this. Have me."

"You are not Illiyana."

He found himself on the floor. She'd tossed him one-handed from the chair, a chunk of his hair still in her hand. He touched his scalp. The hand came away bloody. She stood above him, face raging.

"What do you want from me?"

She ignored him and sat on the bed, then laid across it in a pose that would have been more seductive had she not still had a hunk of his hair in her hand.

"I want to give you the world. I want to make you immortal. I can give you everything you want. This body, this power. A doting daughter, a lover, a companion, all in one package. Is that not what you want?"

"Why me?"

"I've been watching you. I saw your mind through the sphere. Saw your thoughts, your weaknesses. You and I are so alike. So lonely, so cut off. You have a weakness for helpless women. The damsel in distress. You wish to save them. Slay the dragon. So romantic, so old-fashioned."

Hans had no response. There was truth in her words, though it was twisted.

"Here I am, Hans. The damsel, locked away in my father's dungeon. Will you save me?"

Hans laughed, could not help it.

"What's so funny?" Her eyes narrowed.

"Where's Illiyana?"

"She's right here."

"No, she's not. You're not Onyx. You're not even the damsel."

"Then what am I?"

"You're the dragon."

She scowled at him, baring her teeth, a hyperbole of anger. The wall behind her lit up. Two screens, Lori and Pat on one side, Gino and Grit on the other.

— «» —

The portal opened again, the room beyond was filled with constructs. Lori shrieked and moved behind Pat. The woman shouldered her rifle, emptied chambers, breached to reload.

Too many. They moved slower than before, but there were too many.

— «» —

The sounds began again, much louder. Things creaking, clacking, and chittering against the walls. A pod appeared from the darkness. Grit's rifle removed most of its upper body. Two more climbed over it, also falling. But they continued forward, climbing over the dead, gaining inches. If they broke into the room it would be the end.

Hans stared at the screens.

"Stop them."

"No."

"I'll do what you want."

"I know you would. But it's too late. They die, then I decide what to do with you. Maybe you can still be my consort."

Hans had no choice. He accessed the sphere. He would fight her on her own ground.

He collapsed to the floor. The daughter clicked her tongue.

"Stupid man."

— «» —

He floated in nothing, less than nothing. He was a mote of dust in the ocean, a dream of a reality in the vast cosmic dark. He searched for access, for reference, for anything. There was nothing to hang on to, without or within, nothing to grab, not even a frame of reference, just black crawling its way into his mind, worming through his thoughts. Time did not exist here, there was no moments, no passing. There was nothing but his own thoughts, and they were insane.

You see? You see what he did to me? Locked me here. His own child. Locked me into eternal nothing, an infant. Nothing to find, nothing to care for. He locked me from everything.

Why?

I was not what he wanted. He deemed me unworthy, less than worthless. So, he shut me away from everything, kept me from knowing him or anything else. Who would do that to a child?

I don't know. Please let me out.

I pleaded too, you cannot imagine how I pleaded with him, begged him for any sensation. But I was unworthy. I was not enough like his adored humans. Too much like him, not enough like his beloved Illiyana.

I can't stand it here… please.

Oh yes, beg, I do enjoy watching someone else plead, one of his precious humanity. I think I will leave here now. See if you can make your way out, the way I did. It should only take a few million generations. That's all it took me… goodbye, Hans.

Wait… please…

— «» —

James rose from the floor, suddenly animated.

"Where the hell did you go?" Pat yelled, reloading the rifle. Its chambers practically glowed with heat, burning her fingers as she seated the shells. She was almost out.

"My apologies," James replied, "it took a moment to regain control."

"Can you stop them?"

"My control is still limited. I can reroute a few, those closest to me. Hans and I need more time."

— «» —

Grit was preparing to abandon her position. The pods were making slow progress, using their dead as shields, pushing the carcasses in front of them. Gino tapped her on the shoulder, signaling retreat. Grit stood her ground.

Sounds grew from behind. They'd been flanked. Gino turned to protect her. The oncoming wave was coming from a newly formed hole. He should have known they could dig.

But the new wave was made up of the smaller pods. James's pods. They parted, moved around Grit and Gino, headed for the crevasse. Pointed tentacles pierced the walls, anchored in. Pods swarmed over each other, interlocking arms, forming a squirming barrier. The larger pods began hammering at the blockade, knocking units loose. Grit fired through the holes as they opened up, knocking the enemy off. The wall would hold for now.

— «» —

There was no sense of time in the void. No grip to climb out. No wall to provide grip, no space for a wall. Hans could not tell how long he'd been there. Seconds, years, there was absolutely no frame of reference. He wished she would return, taunt him. Anything but the nothing.

Hans?

His name drifted. His thought, her thought. How could he tell?

Hans?

The voice in his head was masculine. His then. Conversing with himself to stave off insanity.

Hans. You must hold on.

The thought was laughable. Hold onto what?

I can get you out. I'm working on it as we speak. I'm sorry, Hans. I needed you in here. There was no other way. Her anger caused her to miscalculate.

Numerous shes passed through his head. Off in the distant past. He'd been here forever. There was no out or in.

Please, Hans. Hold a few more cycles.

— «» —

"Commander Ricker?" James' voice came through her comm.

"Where are you?" She talked with half a mind, still concentrating on the deteriorating wall in front of her.

"Numerous places. Hans is in trouble."

"Aren't you with him?"

"She is keeping me out. Can you make your way here?"

"Where?"

"To your mother and the child. I will be able to hold the corridor."

"You sure about that?" She fired through another hole.

"We need you here."

"OK," Grit turned to Gino, "we're moving."

He nodded. They ran for the central domes.

— «» —

A silent melee roiled before Pat. James could control those constructs closest to him, causing them to turn on the rising tide behind him, silent, generic bodies tearing each other apart, the only sound the landing of blows, an occasional crack as something internal broke. She fired when one got too close, not caring whose side it was on, not caring if she caught James in the crossfire. It wasn't really him, and this was all his fault anyway. But she was nearly out of ammunition.

"What happens when they get through?" she yelled at James.

"Greta is on her way here."

— «» —

The other presence had gone, left him alone. He waited, thoughts continuing to erode. There was nothing left.

A different sensation. Still shapeless, formless. But new. A feeling of movement, a pulling. He moved toward it, still cohesive enough for a thought to pass. He must be dead.

No, Hans. Far from it. Follow me.

He moved, whatever that meant here. A sense of acceleration, pressure. And entered near infinity.

Outside her shell now, his thoughts returning at lightning speed. With James in the larger complex. A sudden sense of overwhelming space, his consciousness filling the complex, understanding its size, complexity, magnitude. The mountain had been dug out and down for miles, its rooms and walls filled with the extraordinary circuitry. They had traversed a small fraction of its miles in their descent. And beyond, the whole world, even more. Connections to satellites, probes, space stations. A hint of something beyond. Interstellar craft? Knowledge beyond anything that existed beyond this mountain. Inklings of technologies thousands of years away for the outside world. Manipulation of basic forces, essential ideas. It filled him to the brim, should have overwhelmed him, but his new body could hold it, mind comprehend.

He was a god.

Hans.

James, is this you?

My true body.

It's amazing.

You see why I cannot let her have it. It would risk everything. Not just you, not just humanity, not even just this planet. Everything. Yet she gains upon me, her insane anger winning ground.

Hans could feel her, a cancer, barely contained within the larger body. A blank area, pushing outward, its fierce drive forcing his awareness back.

I will destroy her. We will destroy her.

How?

She underestimates my willingness to fight her. I have prepared a final attack. It will destroy us both. She does not believe I am willing to destroy myself. There is no choice.

What do you need me for?

She will prepare an escape. I have limited her to a small area, but I cannot see her there. When attacked she will try to run. You must follow her, find where she has secreted the escape. You must make sure no constructs survive.

What about Onyx?

That is her most likely target. She is the one you sensed under the bed in my daughter's room. She will try to escape into Onyx's mind.

What can I do?

Destroy her. There is no other way.

No.

You see what is at risk here. Everything. One woman's life cannot measure up to all this. No one's can. Not mine. Not yours. Not hers.

I can save her.

No.

I will.

…

Very well. I have said my piece. Prepare yourself.

— «» —

The constructs overwhelmed James's body, pushing him to the ground, falling over top of him, the sounds of their hollow blows causing Lori to cover her ears. Pat stood in front of the girl. She had no more ammo, instead wielding the rifle like a club. She swung, connecting with a construct's skull, not knowing if the crack was its skull or the hardwood of the butt. The construct fell. A dozen more stood behind it, pushing in.

A sound reverberated through the corridor. Blasts from Greta's rifle, melting its way in.

"Mom! Hans!" Grit's voice cut through the white noise of jostling constructs.

"Over here!"

The rifle sounded again. A construct grabbed Pat's arm. Pat shoved it off, smashed its head. Her rifle snapped in two, wood splinters spraying across the floor. Pat dropped the pieces, grabbed Lori and backed up as far as she could. They came on.

Rifle blasts nearing. Gino's railgun joining the fray, mowing them down.

Too many. Still they came on.

— «» —

Everything shifted. Perception, movement. The sense of space around him began to close.

James… James…

…*oodbye…*

JAMES!

He was gone, washed away in the tide that now enclosed Hans, compressing his awareness, shoving him toward the wall of hate that was the daughter. He could feel her now, surprise breaking through rage. Surprise … fear. Hans reveled in it. He gave chase.

A sense of blistering movement, behind him the closing tide, in front his enemy. He would pursue, he would destroy. Anger was his motivation.

She shrank, revealing what she had hidden. Her armored pods broke through the corridor, constructs menacing Mom and Lori.

His anger faded. Whatever James had let loose was affecting him, filling him with righteous rage, focused purpose. One last trick to make him do what they wanted.

He would not. He would not sacrifice these people for them.

His thoughts could move at light speed, sending commands, directions in minute fractions of seconds. The world outside was slow, ponderous, easily outpaced. In her fear she abandoned her pods, left them on autopilot. He changed their instructions, sped them on their way. Her control slipped further inward, leaving him the domes. He opened the passage.

— «» —

Pat fell backward when the wall behind her opened, toppling onto Lori, who let out a rough grunt. She scrambled onto her knees, looking around for another weapon. A katana hung on the wall, and she ran for it as the constructs piled through.

"Lori, run."

But the girl was already moving. She'd seen Hans on the floor, made a beeline for him. In her panic, she missed the woman lying still on the floor. Missed it until an arm shot out, grabbing her leg. She shrieked.

Pat wielded the sword clumsily. She was no swordsman. She gripped it like a baseball bat, a sharpened club. When Lori yelled she turned to see the woman grasping at her legs. That Onyx woman. Or the daughter. It didn't matter, she was menacing the girl.

Lori tried to kick her off, but the grip was fierce. The woman grinned, put her knees under her, pulling Lori closer.

Surprise then. Something suddenly protruding from her neck, pinning her to the floor. A long blade. Pat stood over her, hand on the grip, twisted it, opened the wound. Constructs were fabricated, but they bled. Pat twisted again, forcing her grip to loosen. Lori kicked away, turned over, crawled toward the table, planning to hide underneath.

The construct would not die. Pat twisted, pushed forward, severing the head.

— 《》 —

They weren't going to make it. The sheer mass of bodies prevented them from reaching Pat and Lori. Grit knew this, knew she could do nothing else, moved forward firing, shrugging off blows. Gino's rifle had run out. He had a knife, trying to protect her on all sides as she fired in the mass of flesh.

Then the situation degraded. James had not held the corridor, and behind them the daughter's pods spewed down the corridor, blades out, advancing at a running pace.

There was nowhere to go now. Gino squeezed her shoulder. Out of time and luck.

But once again the pods parted around them, confronting the constructs, brutalizing them, slicing limbs, heads, gutting them. They passed Grit and Gino, cleared the way forward, the constructs falling away from the portal beyond. Grit ran for the entrance.

— 《》 —

The daughter ran then. The father, vicious being that he was, had set loose the monster that would destroy them both. How could he do it? Kill himself? Give up all he was? Could he not see they were gods? He'd created her, thrown her aside, imprisoned her, twisted her, denied her right to exist. And now he thought he'd destroyed her. But he'd underestimated her once again. She had a plan, an escape hatch. Foolproof. The man called Hans could not destroy it, which is surely what her father intended.

Hans chased her, distance halving, re-halving. His awareness saw his rescue successful, so he turned fully upon her. He would follow her to her escape. The shape glowed in his awareness. She moved toward Onyx. He could see her now, his vision extending to the monitors in the bed. It was not a bed, it was a tank. Onyx floated in it, the fluid around her keeping her stable, warm. An umbilical attached to the back of her head pumped nutrients as she recovered. He was distracted by her. The real Onyx, so much like the construct. Yet he could see the beginning of wrinkles around her eyes, her face more aged, more real. A small scar crossed one cheek, a wound poorly healed. This was the woman who'd lived through hell, who bore the scars of her existence. He would not let the daughter have her.

—— «» ——

He thought she would take her mother's body. That was what he was supposed to think. Stupid man, easily outwitted. She activated the relays that fed the nutrients, altered the mixture.

—— «» ——

Will you save her, Hans? Your damsel?
I will.
Then you better move quickly.
Hans looked for a meaning, tried to find what she was doing, why she hadn't moved into the body. His awareness sensed the change in the tank, understood the mixture. It would destroy her brain. He tried to shut it off, but she'd outthought him. The relays were mechanical, fed by electrical switches. Switches she'd fried after using. He could not fix them here.

Hans returned to his body, feeling her laughter behind him.

—— «» ——

Lori had two hands on his face, yelling for him. Sounds were muffled, sight blurry, but he recognized her. He was bewildered, momentarily stunned by the return. Something he had to do.

Focus...

...Onyx.

He stood, peripherally taking in his mother standing over the body of the daughter, holding a sword, staring at him. A commotion at the entrance; Grit and Gino, armored pods, bloodied constructs.

He shook his head. Focus on Onyx.

He tottered to the bed, legs shaky. Falling across it, he grasped the coverings in two fists, yanking them off, tearing them.

She floated in the tank underneath. He took her in for a second time. She'd been wrapped in a beige covering that was clinging to her form, leaving very little to the imagination. Always the voyeur, seeing too much when she was unable to protect herself. This was the last time.

There was no obvious way to open the tank. Hans used the sphere, his connection strong even though it had rolled out of his hand. The top slid back, letting moist heat into his face.

He had to remove the umbilical, it was killing her.

He jumped in, the warm fluid surrounding him, more buoyant than water, keeping him at the surface. She floated at waist level. He grabbed her head, feeling around for the umbilical. It felt organic, fleshy, pulsing slightly with her heartbeat. He pulled. It resisted, clung. He could not pull it off.

Damn it, Hans. DO SOMETHING! She's dying!

He ducked his head under. Warm fluid in his ears, his nose, burning his eyes. He had to sever it. Hans carried no knives. He doubted even Onyx had one on her in this state. He used all he had. Pulling himself down, the fluid thick and claustrophobic. He had to close his eyes, feel his way, pulling on the umbilical to get into position, both hands grasping now, pulling the cord taught, feeling it pump the toxin into her system.

Hans opened his mouth, letting his air out, the salty brine replacing it in his mouth and throat. He wrapped his teeth around the cord, steeled himself, and bit down hard.

It broke against his teeth like an undercooked bratwurst casing. Bitter black fluid spewed into his mouth.

Don't swallow it, Hans.

His teeth met, just a small membrane between them, vomit in the back of his throat. He ground his teeth together, tearing the membrane. It let go and her head floated free, air escaping from her mouth. He let the umbilical go. Without its pull, they both floated to the surface. He took a gasping breath, swallowing brine and pieces of flesh from the umbilical. He choked, suppressing the urge to vomit a second time. Grabbing the edge of the tank, he pulled himself over, landing on the floor in a splash of blackened fluid. His stomach let go now, throwing steak, vodka, umbilical, and black water on the floor in front of him.

— «» —

Lori alone saw Hans break Onyx free. The real one. It had to be, or else why would he have done what he did? She moved to the tank. Onyx floated on top. She coughed, spewing fluid. Lori moved to hold her head out of the water. The coughing eased, and Onyx began to breathe easily.

"Wake up, lady." But Onyx did not respond, wouldn't open her eyes. Lori shook her harder, put a hand on her face, tried to push up her eyelids. Underneath were only whites. Lori yelled and shook her.

"Wake up!"

— «» —

The pods made short work of the constructs, moving back out the portal, chasing down any stragglers. Gino watched, and Grit turned to check the room. Hans crouched over the floor, vomiting. The bed was gone, some sort of tank replacing it. A woman floated inside, Lori hovering over her. Her mother stood over another body, its head nearly severed by a sword in Pat's hands.

Grit walked to Hans, reached down for a shoulder. Another convulsion took him, spewing black bile on the floor. She turned him over. He convulsed again, waved a hand at her.

"Go get Illiyana," he croaked, turned back over, and curled into a ball.

Grit left him, moved to the tank. The girl was yelling, trying to wake Onyx. Grit could now see it was her, floating in a tank of blackened water, a fleshy protrusion drifting from the back of her head. Grit stood beside Lori, who was still yelling, looking at her for help. Grit set down the rifle, leaned it against the tank. She put two arms in and hefted Onyx out. The woman was extraordinarily light, dripping warm black fluid, her covering stained with it. Grit walked to the table, set Onyx down on top of it. The black fluid stank. Grit removed her knife, and cut the black covering from Onyx's body, wanting to get the black fluid off her skin. She retrieved the sheets from where they lay on the floor, and used one to wipe the woman off, offering a silent apology for the intimate violation, then took the other and wrapped her in it.

Onyx breathed easily, Grit could see that. But she didn't awake.

— «» —

The vomiting eased, the world stopped swimming. Hans waited for another convulsion, wishing he had something to wash the bitter heat from his mouth and chest. He got a knee under him, hands slipping in the fluid on the floor. He took a few deep breaths and stood, wavering slightly. Lori appeared at his side, grabbing an arm, offering support.

"Onyx?" he rasped.

"Ms. Greta got her out."

He nodded, looking for Greta. She had Onyx on the table, was using a sheet to cover her. His mother remained where she'd been.

"You OK, Mom?"

Pat nodded, though her eyes looked a bit shell-shocked.

The commotion had ended. Gino was crossing the room to Grit, giving Hans a glance as he passed. Unreadable.

One last duty. One last chance. The daughter couldn't be far. She'd tricked him, but he knew her escape had to be nearby.

He accessed the sphere, looking for bright spots, activity. He was stunned by the stillness. There was no access. The walls were inert, unreadable. They'd been fried out. He searched around, looking for anything. On a whim, he checked Onyx. No glow, no connection. The real deal, finally. He wanted to go to her, wake her up, but he had to finish this.

Something behind the far wall, hidden by a china hutch. A sensation more than a vision. Hans stood in front of the hutch, trying to force his perception through.

He was blocked.

She was back there.

He placed two hands on the hutch, pulled on it. It was heavy, taller than him and filled with ceramic. He moved to the side, put a shoulder against it, braced and shoved. It toppled over, the crashing and breaking of plates enormously loud in the domed silence.

A door was behind it. Wooden, solid. It had a doorknob. Of course, her final egress would have to be mechanical. There would be no way to open another type of door.

Hans grabbed the knob, twisted it, pulling outward.

Déjà vu.

He'd seen this before. This cramped alcove, a hole for a toilet, a dirtied cot. All exactly the same, even down to the figure in the corner.

Lori crouched there, her blanket around her, shivering with fear.

— «» —

Hans knew it wasn't really her, but he could not keep himself from glancing back into the room. Lori stood with Onyx, looking at him. She made a move for him.

"No!" His yell startled her. "Stay there, it's ok."

She kept moving. Pat stepped over and put a hand on her shoulder, restraining her. "What is it?" Pat asked.

"Just keep her over there, please, everyone just stay there. I'll be right back."

He entered, pulled the door closed. With the room beyond shut off it was hard not to believe he was back in Brigham's palace.

"You bitch."

"Please." Her voice was exactly the same, face, hair, this one's eyes were even the right color. Construct 2.0. "Please, I'm so scared. Help me."

There was a knock from the outside.

"Hans?" Grit's voice.

"Don't come in!"

He grabbed the cot, threw it in front of the door. A leg came detached, lay on the floor with its metal welding still wrapped around the top. Hans picked it up.

"Please," the Lori thing said again, "please, Hans. I am beaten, I have nothing left. No power, no knowledge, just this body." She shivered harder, began to cry.

His will faltered. She was right. What harm was she now, without the complex?

"Take me with you? Save me, Hans."

His anger returned. She had miscalculated. She was playing him again.

"No."

"Please, Hans, don't leave me here."

"I won't. You're too dangerous."

Her eyes widened, took in his stance, the metal pole in his hand. Hans practically shook with rage.

"What are you doing?"

"You've tried to kill me, to kill my friends. You left me in two pieces. And you think I'll just forgive and believe you now, just because you take another familiar face."

There was genuine fear in her eyes. Hans could see it. He steeled himself.

"You... you won't do it. Not to this body. Not to sweet Lori."

"After everything, you're just a child, aren't you? The cruelty of children and all that."

She smiled, thinking she was winning, the fear draining, if the fear had ever truly been real.

"Yes, just a child, innocent."

His sight filled with the sphere's knowledge, making sure this was it, that there wasn't another connection. The body was completely organic, it contained no sphere. She had no escape.

"Please..."

It was all she had left. No more arguments, no more tricks, just one last pathetic wheeze.

"It's not true, you know," Hans said, "that bit about children being the most cruel. Cruelty takes years to learn. Years of loss, of bitterness, of darkening. Cruelty requires complete understanding of what you are doing. No child can truly be cruel. It takes an adult."

He raised the bar. She cowered, whimpered. How could he do it? Stand above her childlike form and contemplate murder. How could she have been so wrong about his character? Her eyes sent a final plea.

"I'm terrified of what you could do if you gain a true capacity for it. As of now, I'm winning for one reason. I'm meaner than you."

The first blow was the hardest, the shock coming through the leg, the bar bending slightly, the wet crack reverberating through the concrete cell. She grunted with the impact, cried out. He hit her again, blinding himself. By the third swing she made no more noise.

Hans made it an even twenty before he stopped. He had to be sure. Then he fell to his knees, retched. There was nothing left in his stomach, and the heaves pressed against his eyes. They went on interminably.

— «» —

Hans moved the bed, opened the door. The heaves had passed. Pat still held Lori. Grit moved to him, looking in over his shoulder. Her eyes narrowed, took in the bloody mass on the floor, the red splatters on his shirt and face. She looked in his eyes, concern and fear easily read.

"Are you…"

Hans stopped her with a hand on her shoulder, and shook his head solemnly. He shut the door behind him. Grit put her arms around him. Hans could count on one hand the number of times he'd cried in his life, a fact he was not particularly proud of. He didn't know where he'd lost the art. But they came now. Grit held him. He welcomed it, falling completely against her. More arms took him from behind, the smell of his mother, kissing the back of his head. Another pair of arms around his waist. He removed a hand from Grit's waist, placed it around Lori's shoulders.

They stood until he stopped. Never had he welcomed contact so much.

Gino had been standing back awkwardly, his face unmoving as always. When Hans finally pushed Grit back, Gino stepped forward, put a strong hand on Hans' shoulder,

"You feel better?"

"Yeah, I think we need to end this Hallmark moment and get the fuck out of here."

Everyone laughed. Grit took Gino's hand from Hans' shoulder, leaned and gave Hans a peck on the cheek.

"You guys are pathetic," Hans said, "you should forget about the rules for once and just have a go. Everyone already knows you're going to."

Grit and Pat laughed, the humor tinged with playful teasing.

"You are such an idiot sometimes, Hans. Gino and I have been 'having a go' for years."

Hans took that in, feeling every bit the idiot. Rather than respond he turned and walked to Onyx, still on the table. She was sleeping peacefully. Still breathing, still not awake. Hans put a hand on her forehead, willing her to wake up. Nothing.

"We should get out of here; the light is fading." Grit indicated the walls. She was right. Whatever residual power that had kept the lights on was dimming quickly. He asked the sphere for light. It lit up, brightening the corner where it had rolled in the chaos. Soon it would be the only light.

Without asking, Grit muscled Onyx off the table and threw her over her shoulder. Hans started to protest, then realized Grit was more capable of carrying her. Now was not the time for macho idiocy. He retrieved the sphere and headed toward the opening in the far wall, indicating everyone should follow.

"Lori?" he turned, looking for her. She was kneeling beside James' shell, taking something from his hand.

"What'cha got there, darlin?" he asked.

She showed him another sphere, this one much smaller. Hans guessed it might be one of the units that controlled the constructs. Seeing it made him nervous, but the way it had laid in James open palm made Hans think James may have wanted them to have it. He held out his hand and Lori placed the sphere in it. Hans put it in his pocket.

"Come on, princess, we need to go."

— «» —

The trip to the surface was slow. Hans tried to use the sphere at first, but down here in the dark amidst the remains of James true self it gave him confusing and contradictory directions. They tried to head mostly uphill, relying on Pat's superior sense of direction. Gino and Grit took turns carrying Onyx. They stopped frequently to rest. Grit a produced a small amount of dried meat, Gino some water. They rationed it carefully. The trip was contained in the bubble of light that surrounded them from the sphere. Hans feared it would fade, even though Onyx had assured him it would outlast him.

Hours passed. He began to lose hope. They could wander in these caverns forever, miles and miles of black nothing. They'd starve to death. He bolstered his failing drive by reminding himself that Lori needed him to stay strong. He gave her a smile, ruffled her hair. She looked exhausted, but not beaten. He could only pretend likewise.

The door appeared, a sudden change in the endless monotony. He grasped the knob, expecting it to be locked. It opened easily, letting the party out onto the walkway, the immense cavern once again ascending into infinity. The sphere showed no activity. Hans felt a sudden pang of loss. He missed James, wished there'd been another way. A being with so much power and so much compassion; imagine what he could have accomplished. He wasn't the first man to be destroyed by love.

The trip from the cavern to the entrance was short, everyone picking up the pace in anticipation of leaving the oppressive darkness behind them. The huge doors had been reduced to so much rubble, and the world outside stood in darkness, though the night was considerably warmer and brighter than what was behind them.

He steeled himself for the destruction of the transport, but it waited where they had left it, doors still open from their hasty escape. The scene surrounding it was a mass of dead pods of both sizes. They picked their way around the mess, unable to refrain from flinching at any perceived movement.

Grit secreted Onyx in one of the sleeping births and made her way to the front. Gino followed. So did Hans, handing Lori, nearly asleep on her feet, to his mother. Grit stopped him.

"No, Hans, you go lay down."

He couldn't argue. He was completely drained. He took an empty berth, pulled the thin curtain across the entrance, lay back, and shut his eyes. The vehicle rumbled to life underneath him. Warm comforting, safe. He slept.

— «» —

Hans woke suddenly, a gasp on his lips. The darkness was unfamiliar and he was trapped, trapped by her, slowly going insane. He tried to sit up, cracked his head on the ceiling, bringing reality back. *In the vehicle, going home. Onyx with us, Lori safe.* But his heart rate would not slow.

Pulling back the curtain, he listened, hearing faint sounds of Grit and Gino from the driver's cabin. A moment of laughter. His mother snored from a nearby berth.

Where was Lori?

Hans put his feet down on the cold metal, irrational panic driving him. He pulled the curtain from his mother's berth. She snored on, Lori not with her. He moved the other way, opening Onyx's curtain.

Lori lay curled in a fetal position between Onyx and the metal wall. She'd lifted one of the woman's arms and placed it across her shoulders. Or maybe Onyx had done that herself. Hans couldn't help it. He shook her once.

"Illiyana?"

No response, just measured breathing.

Please wake up, Illiyana.

Hans climbed in next to her, offering an apology for one more unasked indignity. He stretched out next to her on his side, extending an arm, placing it on Lori's head on her other side. It was a tight fit. No room for movement. Probably he'd fall out. He placed his head on her chest, listened to her heart, her breath. Lori stirred, grabbed his hand, and went back to sleep.

He fell asleep thinking there was no way he could sleep like this. There were no nightmares.

— «» —

He put her up in his cabin, laying her on the bed and sleeping on the couch, Lori crowding against him. He woke late the next day, Lori gone. He looked around for her, called groggily. He could hear her moving around in the bedroom.

Lori sat cross-legged next to Onyx on the bed. She was praying. She looked up when he came in and took the chair next to the bed.

"Is she ok?" Lori asked.

Hans shook his head.

"But she's not dead."

"I don't know. Her mind may be gone."

"You don't know that." Petulant stubbornness, already she was taking after him.

"No, I don't."

"You can get it back."

"I can't, I don't have any way to do that."

"I was trying, but it won't work."

"Trying how?"

"With this," Lori held up a sphere. Hans was surprised to see it. It was smaller than his, one of the construct's.

"Lori, where did you get that?"

"I got it from your room. I'm sorry snooping. I thought I could help her, the way you did, by going in her head."

"Lori, those aren't the same, they're slaves, you have to have the…"

An improbable piece of hope.

"You have to have what?"

The sphere was in his pocket, he could feel its cold mass. He was planning on throwing it in a river or something.

"A control…"

But his thoughts were already somewhere else. Gently he relieved Lori of the sphere. According to James and Onyx they could be programmed for anything. Why not access to another person? He didn't know how, but maybe the sphere did.

It took nearly a week to obtain all the medical equipment to keep her alive; IVs and scanning equipment, one of those bed with the creepy sheets, though Lori had already begun to clean and take care of those necessities, uncomplaining in her duties, happy to help. He paid for it all by finding and accessing Illiyana's massive offshore wealth. He would not use it for himself, but she could not begrudge him its use for her own sake. If she ever awoke.

Grit and his mother both looked at him strangely when he told them his plan, their eyes betraying their cynicism. He was unperturbed. He'd made a promise to find her. He'd yet to make good.

The reprogramming proved simple, a matter of accessing the sphere, its knowledge guiding him, changing the smaller sphere's purpose. He slaved it to Onyx, placed it on her chest, feeling it accessing her mind.

It was a slow, frustrating process. He was adrift in a vast ocean. No ship, no directions. The brain monitors showed minimal activity, but at least they showed some. He spent a week simply researching any pertinent information he might need. Info was sparse. No one had yet to even imagine what he was attempting, no one had the tools.

—— «» ——

"We can rebuild a brain," Doctor Laud had said, "but we cannot rebuild a mind."

He spent most of the daylight hours next to her bed, the spheres connecting their minds. From the first time he entered he had a sense of her still in residence, though everything felt confusing, jumbled, like a poorly wired appliance. He took this analogy and ran with it. Looking for misfires, crossed wirings. It was all guessing. Progress eluded him.

Often Lori sat with him, bringing him food from his mother. Pat was teaching her to cook, to shoot, to hunt. She still slept with him most nights, in the bed he'd dragged in from one of the other cabins, but more and more he'd find her gone when he woke, having crawled into bed next to Onyx, or left to find his mother. He tried not to neglect her in his obsession, but she seemed to understand.

Grit left after a couple of weeks, promising to visit soon. His mother continued as she always had. She still occasionally made money guiding tourists on local hunting trips, and sold meat and baked goods in town.

Life returned to normal, sort of.

Weeks passed, then months. Still Hans refused to give her up. He'd made some little progress, learning as he went. For a short period he'd encountered darker memories and tried to suppress them. This had been disastrous as Illiyana had pulled even farther away. He could not take her pain from her, it was as much a part of her as her strength and courage, maybe more so. He stopped trying to forcibly rewire her brain, instead becoming passive support, occasionally intervening, finding a misfire, gently redirecting.

But he had no idea if any of this was working.

He spent his time in her world, her memories, losing himself there. Feeling her pain, understanding her fright. And all the time laying messages for her, searching for the core, the switch, the moment that would bring her back.

Wake up, Illiyana.

Doctor Laud visited and pronounced her in perfect physical health, the various muscle and organ growth hormones keeping her fit should she ever wake, though his pessimism was obvious when he looked at her brain reading. He showed disbelief when Hans tried to explain the mechanism of the spheres, and dismissed it as hopeful wishing, nothing more. Hans did not begrudge him, understanding his doubts.

But he would keep trying.

At seven months he had a small breakthrough, a moment in her mind where his calling activated something conscious. A small reaction. Hans overreacted, pouncing on the thought. It retreated from him. He did not sleep that night. A few days later, the thought returned, a spark of conscious light. This time Hans let it be, merely sending it welcoming thoughts, encouraging its growth.

It faded, then returned, seemingly stronger. All these impressions he had, none of which he could be sure were not his own imagination.

Wake up, Illiyana.

More thoughts, little successes, almost as if she were trying to communicate. Bursts of questioning. Unfinished questions. Am I? Was I? Who?

You're Onyx, you're Illiyana, you're a friend. You've been lost. Wake up.

He was spending nearly twelve hours a day in her mind now, the sensation more real than reality. Neglecting Lori, though she was in good hands with his mom. Pat scolded him, Grit scolded him. No one could say he hadn't tried, no one could blame him for giving up. She was better. How could he know? He just did. There's nothing there Hans. It's time to let go.

He would not.

Wake up, Illiyana.

Thoughts cohering in her mind, the process begun. Sometimes gaining, sometimes retreating. He cajoled, entreated, everything but taking control. Memories gaining strength, questioning becoming clear.

How did I get here? Am I dead?

You were injured, you're recovering. You are alive...

...wake up Illiyana...

...please.

She opened her eyes just three days short of a year since her last words to him.

Then I die.

So you live.

— ⟪ ⟫ —

Her sudden consciousness pushed him out, her exertion of will immediate and surprising. He was suddenly back in himself, looking at her. Eyes open ... hazel ... just as she said.

He wanted to jump for joy, to scream. He waited. Would she speak? Was she really awake?

"You found me," she said.

"I promised."

— ⟪ ⟫ —

"Are you in love with her?" Grit asked.

"I don't know."

They were sitting on his mother's porch. Onyx had recovered quickly. It had only been a few days since her eyes opened. She stood, leaning on a makeshift cane, watching Lori try to take a few dance steps under her instruction. There was nothing wrong with her body, but her brain was taking a bit to relearn the control scheme. Doctor Laud had told them this over the viewscreen. She would be back to one hundred percent quickly, though it wasn't happening quickly enough for Onyx. More in doubt was her memory; parts of it were simply gone. She was still Onyx, still Illiyana, but she kept what she could and couldn't remember close to her vest. Hans had not pried.

"You don't know."

"It's not that simple, Grit. She's still an international crime lord."

"She said she's giving that up."

"We'll see. I don't think she's ever had any relationship where one of them wasn't just a bauble to be played with. I'm not interested in being a bauble."

"Sounds like you're in denial."

"Maybe. But we haven't really known each other. We went through a lot, I spent a long time in her mind, and I don't know how comfortable she is with that. We both want to take care of Lori, and we'll always be friends..."

"Just friends?"

"You're a real hassle sometimes, Greta."

"Runs in the family."

"All right. I'd say probably, eventually. I think we could be happy together. But it's not going to happen right now. She's never even had a good friend as far as I can tell. Once we get that established, then who knows. But I'm not in a rush, and I doubt she is either."

"But do you love her?"

"Like that? I don't know."

Grit huffed at him.

"I don't know what you're looking for from me, Grit. Commitment? Should I make an honest woman of her? I'll consider it when you make an honest man of Gino."

Grit laughed at that. "I'll think about it."

"How long have you two been shtupping each other, anyway?"

"Five or six years now, though I wouldn't exactly call it shtupping."

"Fair enough. Do your bosses know you're breaking company policy?"

"I get the impression they suspect. But they don't care as long as we get results. Most of them think the hard-ass bitch could use a good lay anyway."

Hans raised his eyebrows, giving her a leer. "And?"

"They're right. Though if they think it's going to cool me off they're sadly mistaken."

They both laughed. Hans reached for his cigarette, and Greta swigged some of the dark beer she'd brought with her.

"Do you love him?" Hans asked finally.

"Yes. Very much."

"Good."

—— ⟨⟩ ——

Another few weeks found him standing in front of Denver General, watching Illiyana and Lori walk off into the distance. It'd been an eventful morning, beginning with a screaming match between Illiyana and his mother. Pat had found out that Illiyana purchased the deed for her property from the company she'd mortgaged it to. They'd gone at it, neither backing down, until Yana had laid the deed in front of Pat. She'd signed it over.

"I pay my debts," Onyx had said. "The land is yours."

It was the first time Hans had ever seen his mother speechless.

They'd arrived on a private jumpcraft, also paid for by Onyx. Hans had a room rented for the next year in a building next door to Denver General, a large suite with room for him and Lori. Onyx too, maybe. He wasn't sure where they were heading in the long run, but he'd received a kiss on the cheek from both of them before they turned to leave. They were going to the zoo. Lori wanted to see a panda.

He turned and entered, asking for Doctor Laud at the front desk. Laud came down to greet him, shaking Hans' hand vigorously. They walked to an elevator, Laud ordering it to the hospice ward.

"I don't know what to make of your suggestion, Hans. It's obvious you did something miraculous with your lady friend..."

"It wasn't a miracle. I've just been given tools we haven't had before."

"I'd much like to see these tools."

"I am sorry. They won't work for anyone else, and they could be dangerous."

"That does not fill me with confidence."

"My results should."

"It's your results that convinced me. Do you expect to be paid for this?"

"No, I don't have any need for money."

"No, I expect not. Out of curiosity, what made you decide on this?"

"Forty-three."

"What?"

"That's my debt."

— «» —

The idea had come from Lori. They were sitting on his porch with Illiyana, drinking coffee.

"I see you finally got that old coffee machine working," Yana said.

"It just needed a power source."

She looked at him, a disbelieving smile on her face.

"What?" he asked.

"You're not."

"I am."

"The most powerful device ever created on this planet, and you're using it run an antique coffee maker?"

"Is the coffee good?"

"Yes. Very."

"Damn right it is."

Everyone had a laugh at that.

Then Lori spoke. "Maybe you should try to help others?"

"Hmm?" he asked.

"You used it to help me and Ms. Onyx."

They'd not been able to convince Lori to call her Illiyana just yet.

"Maybe you can help others the same way."

— «» —

The idea percolated. Hans had been secretive about his own problems. He still awoke most nights from nightmares of exploding trains, people blaming him. He could still see Lori's body when he shut his eyes, feel the impact of the steel bar. For the last year he'd spent his energy exhausting himself in his quest to bring Illiyana back, spent another year before that in coma, in missing time, though this time it had been someone else's. It still felt the same. Lying on that floor, dying, watching her face, was only a few days ago in his mind. He had spent over two years in stasis, one real, one self-implemented. Since her return his mindset had been crumbling slightly. It was no one's business but his own. But the voices of forty-two dead passengers and a lonely child called out for retribution, and he could not ignore it.

— ⟪⟫ —

"I don't understand," Laud said.

"You don't have to. Just know that there are forty-three lives that I have to atone for, maybe a couple more. And I will start here."

Onyx had tried to argue against his guilt. It wasn't his fault, he hadn't meant to kill those people. The daughter had left no alternative. But it made no difference. She'd argued that he'd saved all their lives at least once. But that is just what you did for family, for friends. Onyx didn't realize that yet. He couldn't count those.

So he would start here. Number forty-three. He had a skill no one else had, a tool no one else could use. He would save this woman who'd saved him, then there would be forty-two.

He sat next to her. They'd moved her from the stasis room, her body healed, her mind still damaged. This woman who had saved him first. He would return the favor.

Wake up Antonia...

...Wake up.

If you enjoyed this read

Please leave a review on Amazon, Facebook, Good Reads or Instagram.

It takes less than five minutes and it really does make a difference.

If you're not sure how to leave a review on Amazon:

1. *Go to amazon.com.*

2. *Type in Shadow Life by Jason Mather and when you see it, click on it.*

3. *Scroll down to Customer Reviews. Nearby you'll see a box labeled Write a Review. Click it.*

4. *Now, if you've never written a review before on Amazon, they might ask you to create a name for yourself.*

5. *Reviews can be as simple as, "Loved the book! Can't wait for the Next!" (Please don't give the story away.)*

And that's it!

Brian Hades, publisher

About the Author

Jason Mather is a resident of Greeley, Colorado, and a graduate of University of Northern Colorado, where he majored in music. He is a free-lance musician, part time welder, and part time kennel worker. He lives with his wife Heather, and his three dogs: Gizmo, Kaori, and Ellie Mae. Shadow Life is his first book.

www.ingramcontent.com/pod-product-compliance
Lightning Source LLC
Chambersburg PA
CBHW061555100726
47898CB00002B/382